Playing For Keeps

Chris Pullen

Matador
9 Priory Business Park,
Wistow Road, Kibworth Beauchamp,
Leicestershire. LE8 0RX
Tel: 0116 279 2299
Email: books@troubador.co.uk
Web: www.troubador.co.uk/matador
Twitter: @matadorbooks

ISBN 978 1800463 035

British Library Cataloguing in Publication Data.
A catalogue record for this book is available from the British Library.

Printed and bound in Great Britain by 4edge Limited
Typeset in 12pt Adobe Jenson Pro by Troubador Publishing Ltd, Leicester, UK

Matador is an imprint of Troubador Publishing Ltd

1

Footballers, by and large, are not the most romantic people by nature. Nor do we generally believe in fairy tales, with perhaps one exception. This particular fairy tale holds true for any footballer that harbours ambitions of playing professionally and at the highest level. A fairy tale that takes you from turning out on a wet and miserable Tuesday night in front of one man and his dog for £50 a week, to representing your country and playing with the best players in the world. For the modern generation, especially in the lower leagues of semi-professional football, that dream is encapsulated in the story of one man: Jamie Vardy.

"Remember Jamie Vardy?"

If I'd heard it once I must have heard it a thousand times, from friends, family and teammates. I wondered how often that phrase had been uttered in non-league dressing rooms and by hopeful footballers, agents and club chairmen up and down the country.

Vardy was the classic non-league football fairy tale. At the age of sixteen, he suffered the same heartbreak that so many youngsters suffer, when he was released by Sheffield Wednesday. His dream of playing football professionally already over, or so it seemed. From there, he joined the romantically named Stockbridge Park Steels, where he stayed for three seasons. He attracted the attention of FC Halifax Town in the Northern Premier League, and in his one and only season there, hit the net twenty-six times. His prolific goal-scoring attracted the attention of Fleetwood Town from the National League. Vardy joined them in 2011 and banged in thirty-one goals for Town that season as they won promotion to the Football League. He was already in his mid-twenties, an age that in football terms usually means that the professional football route has been and gone. But at the end of that first season at Fleetwood, Leicester City decided to take a chance on him and signed him in May 2012, for a fee of one million pounds, which was at that time a record for a non-league player. It proved to be one of the greatest bargains in football history. The rest, of course, is the fairy tale. Promotion with Leicester in 2014, winning the Premier League title in 2015/16, capped by England in 2015, selected for the Euros in 2016 and finally, the pinnacle for any footballer, selected for the World Cup in 2018. It was real *Roy of the Rovers* stuff and if you'd written it as a novel, everyone would have dismissed it as too far-fetched and said that it could never happen.

But happen it did and, although we all knew that lightning rarely strikes twice, there was that glimmer of hope for all of us playing in the non-league game that, one day, we could do the same.

On a cold, and very wet October evening in the wilds of Kent, I can't say I was thinking much about fairy tales, Jamie Vardy or, if I'm honest, much about football at all. What I should have been thinking about was the game taking place around me. Our away match at Folkestone. Although the

Isthmian Premier is not exactly the Champions League, it is a pretty good standard of football. Full of players who almost, but didn't quite make it at professional clubs. On paper, a team playing at that level was only three consecutive promotions from the Football League, although it was a lot easier said than done. But it's hardly a Sunday morning pub match with your mates. We are all paid decent money to play and to take it seriously. Normally I do, and you can't really play at this level if you don't. But on this occasion I was thinking more about a tetchy phone call with Anna, my girlfriend, who, not only didn't particularly like football, but also could not understand why I devoted two or three evenings a week to it, plus most of Saturday, for what she called 'beer money'.

This evening's game had been a row waiting to happen since the fixtures had been announced back in July. I'd kept my fingers crossed that we wouldn't be playing on the evening of October 16th, but playing we were, and to make it worse, we were away in Folkestone, which wasn't exactly close to home. October 16th was Anna's birthday. I'd had the conversation with her several times leading up to the game and of course, her birthday. She had been pretty insistent I should miss the game and spend the evening with her. I told her that I couldn't do that, as I might well lose my place and most certainly would if the manager found out it was simply to be with my girlfriend on her birthday. "So, football is more important than me?" is a question she posed on more than one occasion. That was one of those loaded questions that was impossible to answer. If you said "No, you're more important", then the answer came back along the lines of "Well, prove it then". Of course, the other answer was really not an option if I wanted to stay in a relationship with any girl!

So here I was, playing in what was, truth be told, a pretty drab encounter between two mid-table sides on the evening of my girlfriend's birthday. I hadn't had very much to do, which was probably just as well given my mind-set. As Reigate Athletics' current number one, I should have been concentrating on the game in front of me, organising my defence and making sure I was mentally and physically on my toes at all times. But I wasn't. At half-time, our skipper, John Mawembo, had pulled me to one side and asked me what was up. I hadn't realised that anyone else had even noticed.

"You alright, Matt? You're really quiet tonight. If it's cos Stevie had a pop at you, just ignore him. He does that with everyone."

Stevie B, as he was known, had given me a real mouthful during the first half. In fairness, I'd probably deserved it. I'd come out to catch a ball that Stevie was about to head clear. I'd caught the ball alright, but I'd also taken Stevie out because I hadn't called for it. At six feet four and thirteen stone, I'm not exactly lightweight, whereas Stevie is five feet six and maybe ten stone soaking wet. There was only likely to be one winner when we collided and let's just say it wasn't him. Once the physio had come on, administered the magic sponge and got him back to his feet, he let me know in no uncertain terms that he was less than pleased, sprinkling a collection of four-letter words in his tirade of abuse aimed in my direction.

Not especially inventive, but he got his message across. Now, in my day job, which this wasn't, if I'd made a mistake and annoyed a colleague, I would almost certainly have apologised, especially if I knew it was my fault. In any sport, especially football, apologies were as rare as a José Mourinho smile. The preferred method was to hurl abuse back and give as good as you got, irrespective of right or wrong. All part of the macho male thing that says you don't show weakness and don't back down. Naturally, I resorted to type and swore back, suggesting he got the hell out of my way next time, or words to that effect. Usually such exchanges are forgotten and forgiven within thirty seconds, though occasionally they fester and end up with a punch-up in training or words after the game in the sanctuary of the dressing room. I certainly had no lingering resentment for Stevie, because deep down I knew he was right. If my head had been in the game, I'd have called for the ball, and he wouldn't have been flattened by thirteen stone of teammate.

It was half-way through the second half. The wind was getting stronger and the rain heavier. Even the local seagulls had given up for the evening and found shelter. I looked around the deserted stand and terraces – it looked as though most of the population of Folkestone had decided not to come out and support their local side, which, based on the game so far, looked like a wise decision. There was probably less than 200 people in the ground, which held 4,000, and that included the small band of perhaps thirty loyal Reigate supporters, who'd made the tedious drive down the M25 and M20 during rush hour to get to the ground for the 7.45pm kick-off. As is the norm, our supporters were huddled behind the Folkestone goal in the hope of watching the ball hitting the back of the opposition's net, while the home supporters harboured similar ambitions behind my goal. Sometimes, as a goalkeeper, you become the target for a constant stream of foul-mouthed abuse. Occasionally, you might hear some witty remarks and, if the mood is right, it can generate a little bit of banter. Tonight, it was just morose behind my goal and most of them, rather like me, seemed to have lost interest in the game – and quite possibly the will to live – based on the lack of quality on view.

I knew I would have to make it up to Anna and so I'd booked a very nice restaurant for dinner the following night. But when we'd spoken just before I left for the game, there had been a distinct lack of warmth in her voice. In truth, Siberia would probably have been warmer than Anna's voice.

Typically, at that precise moment when my attention was wavering, the game suddenly decided to involve me. A long ball was hoofed clear by the Folkestone defence. We had two men back against their lone forward, so there was no real danger. That was until both our centre-backs decided to go for the same ball and ended up colliding with each other. There was quite a heated debate in the dressing room after the game as to whose fault it was, not that it mattered much. The Folkestone forward was left with a clear run on goal, with just yours truly to beat. As I came out to narrow the angle, he feinted to the left and switched the ball back to his right foot as he tried to go around me. But I had anticipated the move and dived full length and pushed the ball away with my outstretched left hand. The forward tumbled over my arm as the ball ran away for a corner. I was vaguely aware of the referee's whistle, but knew he was blowing for a corner. It wasn't until I saw my teammates surrounding him that the penny dropped. Unbelievably, he'd given a penalty! I started to protest and then watched with horror as he strode purposefully towards me and reached into his top pocket. I knew what was coming, but I was still stunned to see him brandish a red card in my direction.

It's not often I'm lost for words, but this was one of those occasions, though my teammates were making up for it, surrounding the man in black and telling him just how wrong he was. Like many referees these days he looked like he'd just left school and was having a hard time controlling my teammates. I saw him wave a yellow card in the direction of Stevie, who was pointing in animated fashion towards the assistant referee, no doubt imploring the ref to go and check. But very few would do that, as they are afraid of looking bad if they change their minds. Of course, the home supporters were loving it and their wide grins told me that they too knew it was an awful decision. We'd travelled without a back-up keeper on the bench tonight, so I took off my gloves and my soaking wet shirt and handed them to our right-back Simon Hillier, who was our designated emergency keeper. The Folkestone supporters were already waving goodbye to me and telling me to leave the pitch – well, that was the gist of their comments anyway. There was nothing left for it but to make the long, lonely walk back to the dressing room.

As I trudged off, the Folkestone manager came over and said, "Unlucky, son," and shook my hand.

A nice gesture, but totally unappreciated by me at the time. Our manager, Harry Thackery, simply glanced at me, shook his head and turned his attention back to reorganising the ten players left on the pitch. Our physio, Melissa, clambered out of the dugout, which was no mean feat, as the Folkestone ones were aptly named and presumably designed by someone who'd seen the trenches on the Somme. She didn't say anything, but just walked alongside me. Not as a show of solidarity or to offer words of sympathy, but because she had the key to the dressing room. She also knew that there is a time to chat to players and a time when silence is golden. This was one of the latter. As I walked down the players' tunnel, I heard what loosely passed for a roar from the home support as the penalty was presumably converted.

Mel unlocked the door and said quietly, "Sorry, Matt, I need to get back out there." She turned quickly and headed back up the tunnel.

That was fine by me as I really wasn't in the mood for company. I sat down heavily on one of the wooden benches where my clothes were hanging. A perfect end to a perfect evening, I thought. Not only did I have a very grumpy girlfriend to contend with, I was now also going to be suspended for the next match thanks to a straight red card. That meant our goalkeeping coach, Aaron Smith (obviously known to all as "Smithy") would have to play in the next game. Aaron was in his late thirties now, having played for Brighton & Hove Albion's U23 side when he was younger and then a whole host of clubs in non-league circles, especially in Sussex where he lived most of his life. He joined the club in the summer, at the same time as me, and we'd instantly struck up a good rapport. He was no longer interested in playing, but wanted to develop his coaching career, so he was a good fit for us. Smithy would have to cover for me in the one game.

Fifteen minutes later, I was already showered and getting dressed as the rest of the lads trooped in. I didn't have to ask if we'd lost. Their expressions said it all. Most of them said "unlucky" or "shit decision" to me as they walked past. John Mawembo and Stanislav Jokovic, our two centre-backs, both avoided making eye contact as they entered the dressing room. Stan mumbled something that sounded like, "Sorry mate."

Stan's English had come on in leaps and bounds in recent months. He'd arrived in England during the summer to work on a building site for a cousin and told people that he was looking to play football and how he'd been in the U18 team at Red Star Belgrade, one of the top clubs in Serbia. The bloke who ran the construction company knew Harry so gave him a call. More as a favour than anything else, Harry agreed to give Stan a trial in pre-season. But it was soon obvious that Stan was a good player. Typical Serbian defender: tough, uncompromising, decent on the ball, excellent in the air and was not averse to giving an opponent a quick dig in the ribs off the ball. He was a good player and a welcome addition to the team. He had that tough, east European look about him, which caused a fair few opponents to think twice about squaring up to him after a typically robust challenge. He was also quite a funny bloke and his use of the English language often had us in stitches. But no one was in the mood for any laughter or banter, especially John Mawembo.

He walked towards Stan and started to make his feelings known in typical football style by getting in his face. "That was my ball, you stupid bastard. Why the hell didn't you leave it for me to deal with?!"

Stan was soon yelling back and when he couldn't find the right word in English, he resorted to Serbo-Croat to get his feelings across. John didn't understand a word of it of course, though the words themselves were irrelevant. The meaning was pretty clear, and it didn't take a gifted linguist to know that Stan wasn't saying, "I'm sorry, John, you're right. It was my fault."

In a flash they were in each other's faces and a couple of the lads stepped in to keep them apart, as a pushing and shoving contest developed. It didn't happen often in our dressing room as we got on pretty well, but neither was it an unusual occurrence in any football dressing room after you lose a game. Into that mayhem strode Harry. Harry was unusual for a football manager. He didn't shout much and rarely swore. When he did, people tended to listen.

"Sit DOWN! All of you! NOW!"

Like guilty schoolboys, the two protagonists backed away, still glaring at one another. Everyone else found a seat and suddenly took enormous interest in staring at a cracked tile on the floor, or a piece of mud. Anything to avoid Harry's eye. Although we'd lost thanks to a diabolical refereeing decision, we all knew that we'd played poorly. Not one of us could say, hand on heart, "But I had a good game, boss."

"Shocking. Pathetic. No imagination. No passion. No commitment. No EFFORT!"

Harry gave enough of a pause between each word to let them sink in. He was right. We were an odd side. Put us up against a team flying high in the league, or even in a league higher, as we'd demonstrated in the FA Cup, and we'd probably beat them. Yet we kept losing or drawing with teams around us, or beneath us, in the table. It was as if we didn't really take them seriously enough. Or maybe we thought that simply turning up was enough. We knew we were a better footballing team, so sometimes a few of us were probably guilty of thinking that all we had to do was walk out onto the park and we'd pick up the three points. But football doesn't work like that. You have to earn it. I know it was frustrating the hell out of Harry, as well as quite a few of us. But we just didn't seem to be able to raise our game to beat mediocre sides. A good sports psychologist could probably have had a field day with us, but, at our level, the manager or assistant manager needed to fulfil that role.

Our assistant manager, Jez Morley, was leaning against the dressing room wall, arms folded, just shaking his head and looking as though he'd just sucked on a lemon. Football dressing rooms are great places to be when you've won, but feel like a horribly small, cramped and oppressive broom cupboard when you've lost. There's no hiding place and you just have to sit and take it as the manager gives vent to his feelings. On this occasion, however, Harry just turned and walked out after the words, "No effort." Jez followed him out, closing the door behind him. You could have heard a pin drop for the next minute or so. Players sitting with their heads down, water dripping from saturated shirts, shorts and hair.

It was then that our skipper, John Mawembo, spoke up.

"He's right, lads. That was nowhere near good enough. We should have beaten that lot tonight. Beaten them easily.

Yeah, we can blame the ref. Diabolical pen. But we can't blame him for putting in a poor shift. We're better than that. We all know it. We've got to stop thinking we can just turn up and win. All of us. The league is our bread and butter and we've got to start putting some performances in. None of us are guaranteed a place for the cup game and right now, none of us could complain too much if the boss decides to make some changes. It's up to us."

There was silence for a few moments as the words sunk in and the lads reflected individually on their performances. Then Stan got up and walked across towards where Bo was sitting. A couple of the lads started to get up, fearing a repeat of what had happened when they walked in earlier. But Stan just thrust out his hand towards John and said, "Sorry, skipper."

Bo looked up, smiled and took Stan's hand. "Next time I'll just knock you out of the bloody way you big Serbian lump!" But it was said with a grin.

It was as though someone had popped a balloon; one that was full of frustration, adrenaline and tension. The dressing room slowly came back to life, as people started to get changed. Although there were several comments about the ref, the conversation was generally about other things, as few of us wanted to remember the previous ninety minutes. Most footballers develop a very short memory and intentionally so. It's all about the next game. If you've had a good match then that's great, but it counts for very little the next time you step out onto the turf. Equally, if you made a mistake or just had a stinker, then the last thing you want to do is talk about it or remember it. Stan wasn't quite ready to let the game go though.

"How did ref think was a pen?!" Stan asked me as I finished dressing. "He maybe forty metres away. Vanker!"

Stan was still getting to grips with English and I wasn't sure that the English he was picking up – and in some cases, being 'taught' by some of the lads – was going to add much to his overall vocabulary and command of the language, though it was certainly helping him integrate into the team.

I just shook my head and said, "It's done, mate. Can't change it. What pisses me off is that I'll get a ban now and, even if we appeal, I bet they don't overturn it."

As in the pro game, there was an appeals process, but that only worked if the game was being videoed (it wasn't) or there was a League official in the crowd (there wasn't). Basically, I was stuffed. It was going to be a long ride home in the coach.

An hour later, we pulled up at the BP garage on the M25 for a toilet and drinks break. Although it was obligatory that the away team were fed by the home team after a game, the quality of the food was variable. The reality was that you didn't always feel that hungry straight after a game, plus no one wanted to hang around long when we'd lost and still had a ninety-minute coach ride back to the ground. So, although Folkestone had laid on some chilli and rice, a lot of us didn't eat much. We often stopped off at a service station to get a burger or some drinks on the way back. I took advantage of a moment of relative solitude to hop off the coach and call Anna. No way was I going to do that on the coach surrounded by my teammates. They would have loved to have listened in and offered their helpful suggestions once they'd worked out I was talking to a girl.

"Hello? Anna? It's Matt..."

"Yes, Matt. What?"

That told me all I needed to know. I was still firmly in the dog-house. I was already beginning to regret the call.

"I was wondering if I could drop round on my way home to give you your present. I can be there in about forty minutes."

"It's already late and I've got work in the morning. It will be nearly midnight before you get here." Otherwise known as bed-time, I thought. I'd even had the foresight and meticulous attention to detail to put my work clothes on a hanger in the back of my car, just in case I was allowed to stay. It was starting to look as though I'd been hopelessly optimistic.

"Anna, it's your birthday and I really want to see you." Insert foot in mouth I thought, as soon as the words had tumbled out of my mouth.

"I know it's my birthday," came the icy reply. "I've been sitting here on my own while all my friends have been messaging me and asking me what I was doing tonight." Oh crap. If there was a thermometer attached to this call, it had just gone way past zero.

"I'm sorry. But we're going out tomorrow night. It'll be great." I was trying desperately to recover the lost ground, but I already knew that the battle was lost.

"Tomorrow is *not* my birthday, is it though?" Her words just hung there for a second. There was not a lot to say at this point and I was getting the feeling that whatever I said was going to make it worse rather than better, if that was possible. "I'll see you tomorrow night, Matt. Bye."

I was still holding the phone to my ear before it fully registered with me that she'd hung up. *Well, that went well,* I thought. A perfect end to a perfect evening. I toyed for a moment with the idea of just driving round to her place anyway, but swiftly dismissed it on the grounds of health and safety. Anna had a fiery temper and I was more likely to get a pair of heels slung at me rather than being welcomed with open arms if I showed up there tonight.

I put the phone away in case any of the lads saw me and asked who I was calling this late and slunk back onto the coach. I just hoped I'd be forgiven by tomorrow night.

The coach dropped us off at the club house car park around 11pm. I unlocked the car door and saw my work suit mocking me on its hanger in the back. I sighed and put some music on as I pulled out of the car park. It was dark, cold and miserable outside, quite fitting for the mood I was in.

2

As I shut my eyes on the train journey to work the next morning, I reflected on just how much life can change within a few days. The previous Saturday had been probably the highlight of my footballing career to date. We'd made it through to the fourth qualifying round of the FA Cup and been given a home draw against local rivals Woking, who were in the National League and effectively two divisions higher than us. I'd had to explain to Anna why it was such a big deal and why she simply had to come along to watch the game. That took all my persuasive powers. She'd only ever been to a football match once in her life, and that was as a guest in a hospitality box at Chelsea, with pre-match dining and padded seats to sit in. I don't think she really appreciated the "compare and contrast" opportunity that seeing us play gave her! That said, even Anna had heard of the FA Cup, and she was mildly interested when I explained it to her.

We'd already played and won three matches in the qualifying rounds to get this far. But they had been against clubs in leagues either on a par with us or beneath us in the football pyramid, so we'd been favourites to win – although in any cup competition, being favourite doesn't count for very much, especially in the FA Cup. But against Woking, even though we were at home, they were clearly the favourites and had been having a good season thus far. What did get Anna interested was when I told her that if we did manage to beat Woking, then we'd go into the First Round proper of the FA Cup, with a chance of drawing a Football League side. "You mean like Chelsea?" she asked. That led to me trying to explain how the big teams in the Premier League and the Championship only came in at the Third Round stage. In the end, I'd resorted to showing her all five divisions on my laptop, including the National League and showing her how the whole promotion and relegation concept worked, though that may have confused her even more. But the main thing was that she understood that it was a huge game, both for me and the club. She jokingly promised she'd come to the match and be a WAG for the day. I'd queried whether that meant she'd dress like one too and suggested high heels, a short skirt and a low, plunging neckline. I honestly had my tongue firmly in cheek when I suggested it.

"So, you'd really like me to come dressed like that then?"

I quickly decided that discretion was the better part of valour, opting for a more diplomatic response, rather than the one that I wanted to give.

"If you did, I know you'd look absolutely fabulous," I said, still with a degree of cautious optimism that she hadn't just said no, or words to that effect!

"You'll just have to wait and see..." she said, giving me a look which would make the Pope blink and swallow.

In the end, she turned up in jeans, knee-high boots and a top that was the polar opposite of plunging and revealing, although she still looked incredible and attracted a lot of looks from my teammates, who'd only seen Anna very briefly when she picked me up after a pre-season game.

The game itself was a cracker. It was played in front of our biggest crowd of the season by far, which added to the atmosphere. For a league game, we're lucky to get around 200 people, but Woking had brought a good number of supporters which meant a crowd of 796 according to our secretary after the game. The game started off like a typical cup tie, as there was a lot riding on it. For the players, there was the glory of winning in the world's oldest cup competition, plus the prize on offer of a game against a Football League side in the next round. For the club itself, the prize money in the cup was a gift from heaven. Most non-league clubs operate on a shoestring and rely on volunteers and sponsorship from local businesses to get through each season. The prize money in the FA Cup was a lifeline. Apparently, we'd made over £20,000 just getting to this round and we'd heard that there was another £19,000 for the winners of the fourth qualifying round. Not that any of the players cared about the money going into the game. This was all about the glamour and prestige of a cup run.

The pace of the game was frenetic right from the start, and tackles flew in. There wasn't a great deal of good football, but it was exciting to watch, or so I was told afterwards. When you're playing, it's sometimes hard to appreciate the overall quality of the game. The match certainly didn't get off to the best possible start for us though.

Woking got a debateable corner after ten minutes and swung it into the box. As a goalkeeper, you get a split second to make a decision when it comes to crosses. Do I stay or do I come and get it? If you elect to come for the ball and don't make it, there's a fairly good chance that the ball will end up in the net. I thought about coming for it, but there was a mass of bodies in my way, so I elected to stay on my line. My next act was to pick the ball out of the net after the big Woking centre-back arrived unmarked, to plant a bullet header into the top corner. The ball was past me before I could even move. As he wheeled away to celebrate with the Woking supporters massed behind my goal, the inquest into the goal was already beginning around me. Fingers were being pointed and questions asked, but it didn't really matter at that stage. We were one down and needed to respond. And respond we did. Only five minutes later, Stevie B hit a screamer from all of thirty yards, but the ball smacked against the Woking crossbar and was scrambled away to safety. We were in the game and gradually getting our passing game going.

But after twenty-two minutes, disaster struck. We'd been playing the ball around the back nicely, when Stan was closed down by one of the Woking forwards. He elected to play it back to me, but badly underhit the back pass. The Woking forward latched onto it and bore down on our goal, pursued by Stan. Rather than try and take it round me, he tried to place it past me as I came out to narrow the angle. I had guessed what he was going to do and was already moving that way. The shot hit my foot but rebounded straight into the path of the onrushing Stan, hit him on the knee and flew back past me into the net. He had his head in his hands as the Woking supporters cheered and laughed at the same time. It wasn't his fault. Just one of those things that happen in football sometimes. No one said a word to him. We were two–nothing down and seemingly on our way out of the cup.

But 2–0 is a funny lead in football. I always think it's a dangerous lead. When you're two up, you always relax a little, far more than you do when it's only a single goal. It's great if you go on and score a third, but if the opposition pull one back, it's amazing how often the momentum shifts towards the team that have scored, even though they're still one goal down.

If you get one back, it gives you confidence and there's that feeling that you can get another. So, when our left midfielder Jake Bennett curled a stunning free kick into the top corner of the Woking goal a few minutes before half-time, we were the team who had the momentum going into the half-time interval, even though we were 2–1 down.

Harry got us settled down quickly and totally ignored the two goals we'd conceded. I like that about him. He leaves all of that until after the game, when the adrenaline has left our systems and we can look at it more objectively, instead of it becoming a shouting match as people get blamed or blame someone else, which is rarely productive. Instead, he focused on what we needed to do. We normally play a 4-2-3-1 formation and had done all season long. But Harry had seen that we were getting some joy out wide against the Woking full-backs, so he elected to capitalise on that. He took off Jake and brought on our young, but speedy, left-winger, Addi Rivas-Thomas. Addi had been in our U18 team last season. He was good on the ball, but his real attribute was electric pace. Sometimes he was too quick for his own good, and he beat himself without any assistance from a defender, but on his day, he was capable of being a real handful for any full-back. It was a brave move by Harry, taking off a player who'd just scored a cracking goal. To say that Jake wasn't pleased was something of an understatement, as you'd expect, but, credit to him, he wished Addi luck as we went back out.

Sometimes substitutions fail dismally, leaving supporters scratching their heads and wondering whether the manager had lost his last grip on sanity. On other occasions, they can look inspired. Luckily for us, this was one of the latter, as it took Addi about two minutes to have an impact. John Mawembo clipped a ball into the channel for Addi to chase. Addi gave the Woking full-back at least a five-yard start, but he ate up that distance in a flash and got to the ball first. He whipped in a dangerous cross that Charlie Rose ("Rosey") was only inches away from reaching. Five minutes later, and another ball out to the left flank found our speedy wide man, and once again Addi left his man for dead. I could see some frantic signalling from the Woking bench, and it was soon clear that the right-sided centre-back was being told to move further across to cover his hapless teammate. It also sucked in their right-sided midfield player too, as he was being told by the slightly panicked right-back to give him more cover. As a result, Woking were now looking a little unbalanced and space had been created in the middle. It didn't take us long to take advantage of that extra room. With all the attention on our left side, we worked the ball to the right, where there was now loads of space. A quick one-two between Rosey and midfielder Tommy Richardson put the striker clean through on goal and he drilled a right-footed shot low into the bottom corner to make it 2–2. Suddenly, we were the team on top and looking the more likely to go on and win it.

Their keeper made a couple of good stops as we began to dominate possession. With ten minutes left, it started to look as though they'd weathered the storm and we'd have to settle for a replay at their place. But we were still on the front foot, looking for the winner. A deflected shot from Rosey gave us a corner. We score very few goals from corners because we're not a particularly tall side, and I think we'd only scored once from a set piece all season. But cometh the hour cometh the man; the man being Stan. Stevie put in a great in-swinging corner, head height with pace and Stan was first to the ball. His glancing header beat the Woking keeper and although the defender on the far post got his head to the ball, he couldn't stop it flying into the roof of the net. Absolute bedlam ensued! Stan whipped off his shirt and, waving it wildly, went sprinting around the pitch, yelling loudly in Serbo-Croat. No one else in our team had got near him until he ran into me and we hugged one another, before the rest of the lads piled on top of us. Even Anna admitted afterwards that she was jumping up and down in the stands, screaming with the rest of the players' wives and girlfriends and hugging girls she hadn't even met before. I'm not sure that I would have believed it if her story hadn't been corroborated by John Mawembo's wife, Simi, when we were chatting in the bar after the match. Her first introduction to Anna had been a wild embrace at almost exactly the same time that Stan and I were locked together. I just wish someone had captured that on video!

But there was still eight minutes left, plus stoppage time. Now, you can tell a team all you like *not* to defend too deeply when the clock is running down, and they are hanging on to a lead. Harry was telling us exactly that from the dugout as we lined up for the restart. The players themselves *knew* they shouldn't do it, because all it does is surrender both territory and possession. Even when you clear the ball, it keeps coming back as there's no one higher up the pitch to hang on to it. We all knew it. Every football supporter knows it. Harry began screaming at us to get out. Jez was screaming at us to get out. Our home supporters were yelling at us to get up the pitch. Not that we heard any of it. But safety in numbers was in our heads and so we gradually sank deeper and deeper, until it felt like our formation was something like 8-1-1. Anna said she could barely watch the final eight plus minutes; she was so nervous.

It was almost inevitable that Woking were going to create something. Either a good chance or a half chance. The question was, could they take it? A groan went up from the home supporters when the digital board went up to show there was a full five minutes of added time. My defenders were throwing their bodies in the way to block shots, head crosses clear or make desperate tackles. But deep into added time, one shot from the edge of the box did find its way through the crowd. I flung myself to my right, just managing to get my fingertips to the ball and deflecting it slightly. The ball cannoned off the post and away for a corner. Several Woking players had their hands on their heads, as did a lot of their supporters, as I briefly turned to face them. My teammates were mobbing me, but I pushed them away, imploring them to concentrate on the corner. In it came. Up went John, Stan and two of their players. The ball dropped almost on the six-yard box. Woking's right-back, who'd had such a torrid second half, was perfectly placed and met it on the half volley as it dropped. I just made myself as big as I could, but he couldn't really miss from that range. The next thing I knew was Stan hauling me to my feet and yelling something. Three or four of the Woking players were on their knees, unable to believe they hadn't scored. The ball had hit me full in the face and ballooned over the bar. The local paper described it as a miraculous save in their match report. In truth, I knew nothing about it, but I was happy to take the plaudits. A minute later, the referee blew for full time. My mouth was bleeding, which I didn't notice until I saw some photos after the game, but I didn't care. We went absolutely nuts!

We spent the next ten or fifteen minutes hugging each other, hugging the boss, the coaches, supporters, and in fact anyone who came near us. I ran over to the stand where the wives and girlfriends were sitting and picked out Anna and gave her a big grin as I punched the air. She gave me a big smile and had her hands above her head, clapping us as we walked off. We certainly milked the moment and it must have been a good twenty minutes before we finally headed for the dressing room. Our supporters were gathered around the tunnel, cheering and yelling and clapping as we went in. Anna was standing with the other girls and all of them were waving and yelling at us too. Simi, John's wife, had their two-year-old son on her shoulders and was crying with the emotion of it all. John climbed over the pitch-side advertising hoardings and shouldered his way through the crowd to embrace her. It was very touching, although Simi later confided to Anna that the big man had covered her cream coat in mud and sweat and to please remind her next time not to let him get close until *after* he'd changed and showered! Anna was grinning ear to ear and blew me a big kiss. I couldn't get close to her but waved back as people patted me on the back and said things like "Brilliant save, Matt", or just "Well played".

The dressing room was just mad. We were jumping around and still embracing one another. Drinks were being thrown around and the music box in the corner was playing Neil Diamond's "Sweet Caroline". We collectively belted that one out more than once! People were coming in and out of the dressing room, offering their congratulations. It would probably seem odd to other people, but no one was especially worried that we were in various stages of undress as they popped in. Muddy and sweaty kit was being thrown around and all our normal rules of respecting our dressing room were put on hold for around forty minutes.

We were through to the First Round proper for the first time in the club's history, so it was not only a great win to put out a National League side, we were also breaking new ground. The chairman was even more pleased. Not only from the footballing point of view, but because of the prize money from the FA. For the bigger clubs, it meant very little, but for clubs like us, it could sometimes mean the difference between staying afloat financially or going out of business. It also meant we were potentially able to attract better players, because we could afford to pay them more. I remember Anna being initially surprised when I told her we were getting paid to play. It certainly wasn't a fortune, and none of us could live off it, but it was nice bonus. I knew a couple of the lads like our skipper were on £250 a week. I was getting £150 a week, in part because I was young and relatively inexperienced, as well as being new to the club, but also because I had a decent job, so the money wasn't a big deal for me. Playing was more important than the money, although at least it covered my petrol bill.

We'd all heard stories that other clubs in our league were paying players somewhere in the region of £400/500 a week. That was certainly the exception, but some clubs were better off than others and that is always the way in football at any level. The bigger the budget, the better the players and the more chance of success. It doesn't always guarantee success, but it certainly gives you a much better chance to make it happen.

I finally got to the bar and spotted Anna. She came over and gave me a big hug and kissed me on the lips – or at least tried to. Now that the adrenaline in my system was draining away, my mouth was quite sore. I winced and pulled away quickly. She looked surprised and then her eyes widened.

"Oohh! Your mouth's all swollen, luv! Does it hurt?"

"Yep! That's what happens when you stop a football with your face!"

Or at least that's what I was trying to say. Anna said it sounded as though I was talking with a mouth full of food. She smirked at me and said, "I may not know that much about football, but aren't you supposed to use your hands as a goalie?!"

I just rolled my eyes. "Very funny." Though even to me it sounded more like "vewy furry".

"Oh, well, I'll have to make sure I keep away from your

mouth tonight in that case," said Anna coyly. But before I could think of something suitably witty by way of a response, Anna was on to the next topic.

"That was soooo exciting! I was jumping up and down, especially when we" – I did notice the use of the collective noun and inwardly smiled – "got that go-ahead goal. I was cheering and hugging everyone at the end! I was hugging all the other girls, even though we'd just met! They were just so nice and explained things to me. I guess I probably sounded like a real schmuck asking them so many questions. I never thought you'd win after the other team scored those goals. Everyone around me was saying how amazing your saves were. I don't know how you dived so fast and got your hand to that one that hit the goal" – I didn't try and correct her – "but when you saved that kick right at the end, everyone around me just had their mouths open. Miriam, the girl next to me, had her hand to her mouth and turned to me and just said, 'Oh. My. God.' It was so funny, and I was so proud of you! My hero!" Finally, she paused for breath. I was grinning at how enthusiastic about "soccer" she'd suddenly become.

"Aww, you'll make me blush! I'd love to say it was my brilliance but honestly it was pure luck. It hit me rather than me saving it. I just tried to get something in the way of it, although I'd have preferred it not to have been my face," I added ruefully. "I think we need to brush up on your football vocabulary if we're really going to make a true WAG out of you. Talking of which, what happened to the heels and skirt?!"

Before Anna could answer, a very striking brunette appeared in my line of sight and was heading our way. I recognised her straight away as the football reporter from the local *Surrey Herald* newspaper. We'd spoken at the start of the season, on the day that I'd signed. I liked her, as she not only knew her stuff but was tough enough not to be intimidated by brusque managers or randy footballers. I'd heard a couple of great one-liners she'd used to put a couple of my teammates back in their place, which of course soon became legendary around the rest of the team. I'd made the mistake of talking about her to Anna and saying how good she was. I'd simply meant as a reporter and a writer, but in hindsight, that had been a mistake.

"Hi Matt. Congratulations. Brilliant stop at the end."

"Hey Jess. How are you doing? Oh, this is my girlfriend, Anna. Anna, this is Jess Gallaway who's the football reporter on the local paper."

"Hi Jess. Yes, Matt told me *all* about you. It must be so difficult being a girl in a man's world like football."

Uh-oh. It was delivered sweetly enough, but even I noticed there was a little bit of an edge to the comment. The two girls were now completely ignoring me and looking at one another.

"Oh, not really, Anna. It's very easy if you actually understand the game."

Ouch! That made it fifteen-all I reckoned. But I didn't really fancy playing referee between them. I opened my mouth to try and rescue things, but Jess beat me to it.

"Matt, I just wanted to get a quote from you about that superb last-minute save, and any thoughts about the next round," said Jess.

"Matt said it was pure luck," offered Anna, helpfully.

Jess just arched an eyebrow quizzically and looked at me, waiting for a response

"Umm, yeah, it was lucky. I just made myself as big as possible and I was lucky enough to get in the way, as my face proves! Any keeper needs some luck too and I had a share of that today."

"Typically modest, Matt. But if you keep on making top-class saves like that, you'll start attracting attention. Do you have aspirations to play at a higher level?" probed Jess.

"Of course. We all do. But I'm very happy here. It's a great club and we have an outstanding manager and a good young team. It's fun playing here and who knows how far we can go in the cup."

"Can I use that as a quote?" asked Jess.

"Sure. Why not."

"Great. Any thoughts on the next round?"

"I really don't think it matters, though obviously we're all hoping for a home draw. It would be great for me if we drew AFC Wimbledon as I was in the academy there, which I think you know, so it would be fun playing them and seeing some old teammates."

"Perfect. Thanks, Matt. Oh, and nice to meet you, Anna."

Anna nodded and watched Jess walk away. I made certain I did not allow my eyes to linger on Jess or follow her hip-swaying walk across the room to seek out Harry. Most of my teammates had less inhibitions though, which was certainly noted by Anna.

"She's very cute, isn't she?" Anna was watching her as she walked away.

I was trying to work out if it was a statement or a question. I was also doing my best to work out what was a good answer, rather than one that could get me into very hot water.

"I guess so. But she's good at her job and certainly knows her stuff."

"Hmmm. I bet it's kind of nice for her being the focus of all this testosterone on a Saturday. Still, it's sort of an odd job for a girl to do," said Anna, rather disdainfully.

The conversation wasn't going anywhere good so I tactfully changed the subject.

"The draw for the First Round is taking place on Monday

evening. A lot of us are planning to come down here and watch it on TV. Would you like to come?"

"The draw is on TV?" Anna looked very surprised.

"Yep, live on BBC2 at 7pm. All the teams in the First Round get put into a bag with a numbered ball to see who plays who. Usually some retired footballers do the draw."

"Hmmm…it doesn't sound that thrilling."

"Oh, but it will be!" said a voice behind us. "The most exciting evening in our club's history and we've been going 107 years now. It will be a great night."

It was our chairman, looking unusually smart in his white shirt and club tie. Normally, he looked as though he was part of some scheme to try and convince middle-aged men that they looked good wearing stuff from Sports Direct, even though it was designed for youngsters or athletes. Brian was neither. But he was a great bloke. He'd played football in his younger days and had made a fair bit of money as an insurance broker by all accounts, which he used to buy the majority shareholding in the club five years earlier. You didn't buy football clubs to make money. If anything, the reverse was true and Brian had certainly ploughed a fair bit of money in over the past two seasons, according to those that knew. New floodlights and a new playing surface were two of the more obvious benefits we saw as players. But he was always ready to have a chat with the players and had a great relationship with Harry, our manager, which is important in any football club or it leads to all sorts of issues.

I did the introductions. Brian is a very engaging character and pretty soon, he was making it sound as though Anna would be attending the Oscars. But he did a good job of selling it, because after ten minutes, Anna was laughing and promising she'd be down at the club on Monday night. By now the post-match party was just getting going and it promised to be a long night. As Brian walked away, Anna saw Jess looking our way and kissed me full on the lips. It was very nice, if a little painful, but I couldn't help but think it was intended more as a message for Jess.

3

With an effort, I opened my eyes, remembering where I was. Anna was still asleep beside me, her long hair splayed out across her pillow and over my arm, which was still wrapped around her. We'd stayed in the bar longer and both drank more than we'd intended, as the celebrations had continued long into the night. So much so that we both abandoned our cars in the club car park and got an Uber back to Anna's flat. I looked at my phone on the bedside table. It was almost 10 am on Sunday morning. I looked blearily around the bedroom. Our clothes were scattered everywhere. I think I'd started undressing her even before we'd made it through the front door, and it had been an ungainly, but very erotic, shuffle, as we gradually removed items of clothing along the way, before finally arriving at her bedroom.

Anna had tried to keep her promise about avoiding my damaged mouth, though it was hard for both of us to remember. At the time, a combination of alcohol and lust had helped me to forget the pain, but this morning both my lips and also my nose hurt like hell. The nose had also helped stop that last-minute shot. I just hoped Anna had some paracetamol handy.

We'd wrecked her bed and pretty much exhausted one another, which is why we'd both slept so late. Mind you, judging by the rain lashing against the windows, staying in bed that morning felt like a pretty good option. It was to become an even better one. Anna stirred, stretched luxuriously and then rolled over to face me.

"Hey there, handsome," she said, pushing her hair from her eyes.

"Hey there, beautiful. Want some coffee? Or breakfast in bed?"

She looked at me for a long minute, then smiled mischievously and said, "Dumb question, pal."

Breakfast would have to wait awhile.

An hour later, we were still in bed, arms and legs wrapped around one another, as we lay quietly and half asleep in the afterglow of some more energetic lovemaking. Though by now I was getting desperate for a coffee and for something to eat. There had been the usual pasta dish for the players after the game, but that was about fifteen hours ago and I was famished.

"I don't have much food in the fridge for a decent breakfast. Shall we go out and get brunch somewhere? My treat for the conquering hero." Anna was smirking.

There was really only one response to that. I flicked her shapely naked backside with my finger hard enough to make her jump.

"Owww! Boy, that's it. No more sex. For at least twelve hours!" she said, pushing me away. "I'm getting myself some orange juice." She was smiling naughtily. "Want some?"

"That's fine. Twelve hours is perfect as I need to regain my energy anyway. Yes please to the juice. Then I'm heading for the shower, but, as there's a sex ban, you'd better not join me," I said, grinning at her.

Anna returned a couple of minutes later, with two tall and very full glasses of orange juice and handed one to me as I sat up in bed. I took it and promptly spilled a little down my chest. I looked at my hand and it was trembling slightly, no doubt from all the exertions in the previous ten hours.

She laughed. "And I thought you were good with your hands, Mr Goalie!"

"You know I am. But this is your fault. You've drained me, girl. I bet I can hardly stand up. You're an insatiable harlot!"

Anna sat naked on the bed next to me, looking as sexy as hell, and rather pleased with herself.

I drained the juice that I hadn't spilt and hauled myself out of bed. I then discovered it wasn't only my hands that were shaky. My legs also felt like jelly from the combination of a nerve-racking football match and a couple of high-energy workouts that Anna had given me over the previous ten hours. Not that I was complaining, as Anna's workouts were a lot more fun than the normal workouts in training, that was for sure. I headed to the bathroom and turned the shower on. I was betting I wouldn't be alone for long. Sure enough, I'd barely got the water hot and stepped under the powerful jets before the shower door opened and Anna stepped in.

"Room for one more?" she asked, as the water cascaded down her body, plastering her long hair down her back.

"Not really, but I think I can make an exception for you this once," I said gallantly.

The shower took rather a long time and we used copious amounts of shower gel and water on each other before we decided we were sufficiently clean to be allowed out.

Brunch had become lunch by the time we were dressed and presentable. It was only as we were about to head out we remembered that we were both car-less, so the first order of business was to get a cab to take us back to the club to pick up our respective vehicles. By the time the taxi arrived and had dropped us in the club car park, it was already midday, so I volunteered to drive and we set off for The Well House, a favourite local pub of mine which served excellent Sunday roasts. It was one of those country pubs that, unless you know it's there, you'll never find it, hidden away down a narrow country lane.

A couple of months earlier, I'd been driving down that same lane, on my way back from meeting a couple of mates for a lunchtime beer at the Well, and, to my shock, I nearly drove straight into a large black-and-white cow! It must have somehow escaped through the fence in a neighbouring field and was happily munching on the roadside grass! With no way past the large animal that was taking up most of the narrow lane, and no obvious way of getting the cow back into the field, I opted to reverse back up the lane to the pub to see if they might happen to know the owner of the cow, who would no doubt be much more adept at cow-herding than I was. I thought it was an inspired bit of detective work but judging by the slightly bored response I got from the barman back at the Well, it was a relatively routine occurrence. He phoned the farmer and was told he was on his way to deal with the escapee. But, being a bit of an animal lover, I decided it was my public duty to try and warn other road users venturing down that lane that there was a large mammal waiting for them around the next corner and caution might be in order. I went outside and stood in the road, feeling very public-spirited. That feeling didn't last very long. A rather ancient-looking Ford Mondeo driven by an elderly gentleman, whose head only just appeared above the steering wheel, completely ignored me as I waved him down and if I hadn't jumped backwards at the last minute, I may well have ended up in A&E. I can only assume that the Mondeo managed to manoeuvre around the cow, as I didn't hear any squeal of brakes, or cow for that matter. I was relieved that the next car belonged to the farmer and he took over from me, thanking me for my help.

Happily, this time the only beef that I saw was the roasted variety on my plate, albeit not for very long as I was ravenous by that point. Anna opted for the same and seemed to be equally hungry, as the conversation became almost non-existent for fifteen minutes. Highly unusual for us, as we always found plenty to talk about.

"So, are you happy to come down and watch the draw on TV tomorrow night then?" I asked, once the plates were empty.

"Um, to be honest, I just said that to keep your chairman happy and I didn't want to embarrass you. It's not really my scene, Matt. I still don't really get why everyone's so worked up about it."

"It's a bit of history for us. We've never got to this stage before and we could draw someone big. It'll be fun watching our name come out."

"But it's not like you going to be playing Chelsea or West Hampstead, is it?"

Stifling a grin, I thought momentarily of correcting her, but decided to let that one go. "No, but for us, getting any league club would be huge, whoever it might be. It's our moment in the spotlight, hopefully."

"I promise I'll come to the game, Matt. But you go on your own tomorrow. All your pals will be there anyway. You don't need me hanging around too."

I could see her point, though I was disappointed because I wanted her to be part of the occasion. We'd had a pretty special night and a good morning, so I decided it wasn't worth pushing it. She had, after all, said she'd come to the game. I wondered if she'd still come if we happened to draw Carlisle or Doncaster Rovers away. I'd know soon enough. At least the FA Cup had given us a little bit of common ground when it came to football. Up until the game against Woking, Anna had never shown any interest at all. She liked sport, which was a plus in my book, but it was tennis and swimming that were her passion, not association football. But over the past few months, we'd discovered we had a lot in common.

We'd met on a Wednesday evening in early May, at a bar in Canary Wharf where we both worked, albeit for different companies. It was a balmy night and warm enough to sit outside. I was at a leaving drinks for one of the girls from our marketing team and Anna was with a group celebrating a colleague's birthday. Our respective groups just happened to be next to one another and, as the evening wore on, we sort of mingled. I'd spotted Anna right from the get-go. A 5-feet-9 brunette in heels and a figure-hugging dress is always likely to make an impression on me. Being six-four, I did have a thing for tall girls, so I'd been checking her out for much of the evening, subtly of course, or so I thought. Try as I might, and to my frustration, I hadn't been able to get close enough to engineer a chance to speak to her. It was my turn to get the drinks, so I had gone inside and shouldered my way to the bar. I had just managed to attract the attention of the busy bartender when someone tapped me on the shoulder. It was the tall brunette. In her heels, she wasn't far short of being at my eye level, which was an unusual experience for me.

"Hi there! As you've managed to get to the bar, would you mind ordering a few drinks for my crew too? I'll give you the money!"

"No problem." I tried to come up with the devastatingly witty one-liner that would have her in fits of laughter. But instead I came up with another devastatingly original line.

"Can I buy you a drink?"

She did laugh, though I thought more out of sympathy. I did notice she had a great smile though.

"No points for originality."

"OK. So, let's just say I was momentarily tongue-tied by the sudden appearance of a gorgeous brunette at my shoulder and was desperately searching for a clever line to keep her talking to me."

"Ooh much better! You've moved up the leader board. That was worth maybe seven out of ten." She was still smiling, but now looking at me. "I was wondering if you were ever going to come and talk to me or just keep staring at me all evening!"

So much for me being subtle looking at her, I thought.

"I imagine a girl like you gets rather bored with guys constantly hitting on her, so I thought I'd just bide my time and pick my moment."

"Oh, I see. And when was that moment going to be exactly, as we've already been here two hours? Next week? Next month?" She was still smiling and looking quizzically at me.

"I didn't think there was any real hurry. I knew you'd hang around and wait until I came over, or you came over to me," I said, grinning. Actually, I knew nothing of the sort, but it sounded good.

"Oohh! I see that you don't suffer from a lack of self-confidence, mister! My name's Anna, by the way."

"Hi Anna. I'm Matt. I heard you talking to some of the others a little earlier. I've been trying to work out where you're from. I'm guessing somewhere from the east coast of the States, but I'm not sure."

"Pretty good guess. I was actually born and raised in Boston, but I spent a year at university over here."

"Why?"

"Well, my mom's English and she wanted me to experience some of her country and also the Brit way of learning. She said it would be good for me to have a bit of culture in my life! So, I ended up going to Durham on one of those year-long exchange courses."

"And how did that work out – the cultural bit, I mean?"

"I have to admit it was a little tough at first. Especially getting used to the accent up there! For the first couple of weeks I had no clue what people were saying to me! It was like a foreign language when we went into the local town or bars. But she was right, and I think I now feel as comfortable here as I do in the US. My folks come over and visit every so often and I still get back to Boston a couple of times a year. OK. That's enough about me. How about you?"

"So, how far back do you want me to go? I could stand here and bore you for hours talking about me, when I'm much more interested in learning more about you."

Anna smiled and rolled her eyes at that. But she began talking and I kept asking her loads of questions. In fact, it wasn't until representatives from both my group and hers came to find out what had happened to their drinks that we realised that we had completely forgotten the rest of the world even existed. We ended up exchanging numbers and I knew I was besotted. She was entertaining, funny and quite stunning in a very natural way.

The next day, I wondered how many hours I could/should wait, before I called. On one hand, I didn't want to seem too desperate, but on the other, I wanted her to know how much I wanted to see her again. I settled on 11am, which seemed to be a sensible compromise. Naturally, I got her voicemail. As I did when I called an hour later. And two hours after that. I was just beginning to think that maybe I had misinterpreted the signs the previous evening, or she'd changed her mind. Or maybe she already had a boyfriend, which the more I thought about it seemed highly likely. Gorgeous girls like that would have a queue waiting around the block. Maybe she was ignoring my calls. As the afternoon wore on, I became more and more convinced she wasn't going to call. Then my phone rang.

"Hey, it's Anna…"

"Who?" I said jokingly.

"Anna. Umm, we met at the bar yesterday evening…" She sounded a bit hesitant now.

"Oh yes. That fabulous-looking Yank that I've being trying to get hold of all day!"

She laughed. She had a very nice voice and quite a sexy laugh.

"I did see a few missed calls. Sorry. I'm actually in an all-day meeting and so I snuck out to return your call in case you figured I was ghosting you!"

"Never thought that for a second," I said lying though my teeth. "Sounds like I'd better be quick. So, when do I get to see you again?"

"How about tomorrow evening?" she said.

"Umm…I can't tomorrow as I've got training. How about Friday?"

"Training? For what? Can't make Friday, as I'm seeing some pals."

"Football training. Every Thursday night. OK, how about Saturday evening? But it won't be until about 9pm as we're away to Margate."

I think that was Anna's first inkling that, although I didn't have anyone else in my life, she was already in competition with my first love – soccer, as she insisted on calling the beautiful game. Eventually, we settled for lunch on Sunday. Lunch lasted all afternoon and the date ran well into the evening. We got on like a house of fire. The only pauses in the lively conversation were caused by trying to eat the food we'd ordered, which had got cold as we'd largely ignored it. We ended up going from lunch to dinner, although neither of us were especially hungry. When we compared notes later on, we both just wanted an excuse to keep the evening going. We were both oblivious to our surroundings and indeed everyone else. It wasn't until the waiter politely asked us if we wanted our bill at the end of the evening that we suddenly realised we were the only ones left in the restaurant. I had been so focused on listening and talking to this wonderful girl that I'd completely lost track of time and pretty much everything else.

It turned out that we didn't live that far apart. I drove her back to her flat and walked her to the front door. Although I desperately wanted to go inside with her, I also knew I didn't want to rush things, so I simply asked if I could see her again. She admitted later that it had crossed her mind to invite me in, but she was also impressed that I hadn't made a move on her and behaved like a perfect gentleman. She gave me a quick peck on the cheek and told me to message her and we'd fix something up. It was a rather quick goodbye and it made us both laugh later when we compared notes. She said she had to do it fast before she weakened and invited me inside. But as I walked away that night, I was already looking forward to seeing her again. Now all I needed to do was convince her that I was the man of her dreams.

4

The bar at the club was jam-packed. I arrived at little after 6.30pm and I was amazed that it was full already. As I eased my way through the mass, I was greeted by a number of our regular supporters, although there were a lot of faces I didn't recognise. It felt like most of Reigate was crammed into the place to watch a little bit of history being made. I spotted a few of the lads who had found a spot for themselves close to the bar, but with a good view of the TV too. I started to edge towards them, although everyone wanted to talk to me, so progress was measured by one foot at a time.

"Hey Matt, what are you drinking?" John was closest to the bar and tall enough to manage to attract the attention of the hard-pressed bar staff, who were being rushed off their feet.

"Diet Coke please, mate!" I had to shout to make myself heard properly. I'd driven down to the club so there was no point in having anything stronger – yet. We might have cause to celebrate if the draw was kind to us, so I wanted to save my one drink for that.

The progress I had made came to a halt when I quite literally bumped into Jess, who was turning away from the bar with a couple of drinks in her hand. The one in her right hand made contact with my left arm and probably about half of it ended up on my arm and my jacket. As I'd come straight from work, I was still suited and booted. Unfortunately, it was a light grey suit, so the results of the spillage were immediately obvious.

"Oh, Matt! I am so sorry. Look at your suit!" Jess really didn't need to tell me to look.

"Don't worry. It wasn't your fault. It was me that bumped into your arm."

"Oh shit. I will pay to have it dry cleaned."

"Jess, honestly forget it. It's no big deal. It needed a clean anyway! Can I get you a drink to replace that one?"

"Good luck with that! It took me fifteen minutes standing at the bar to get these. Besides, the drink that ended up on your suit was for your chairman. I'm sure he'll have others on the way."

She smiled at me, which, when I thought about it, was a little unusual. Normally Jess had her "game face" on when talking to me and others and was very serious about her job. A couple of the other lads had dubbed her the "Ice Maiden". But I must admit I always found her very professional. A woman just trying to do her job. Yes, she could be a little serious sometimes and rarely smiled, but I think they called her that because she had rebuffed more than a few advances from amorous players. So it was nice to see her smile and seem a little more relaxed.

"I'm sure he will. But shouldn't he be buying you drinks so you write nice things about us?"

"I *always* write nice things, Matt." Jess adopted a wide-eyed, innocent look which made me laugh. "You don't believe me?" She now pretended to look hurt.

"Jess, you're a journalist! I don't think anyone ever uses the word 'nice' and 'journalist' in the same sentence! Don't tell anyone, but I do enjoy your articles. Even the one that took the piss out of me!"

A few months earlier, at the start of the season, Jess had referred to me specifically in her analysis of the current squad and the prospects for the season. She had called me "Unknown, unproven and unusual". The latter was a reference to the fact that I had a university education and worked in the City, which was not the usual background for a non-league footballer.

"I didn't take the piss! It was just a play on words. But hang on. You said you enjoy reading my articles?! No one here has ever said that to me. Can I quote you?!" She laughed as she said it and I realised I was seeing a different and more interesting side to the Ice Maiden.

"Did I say that? Gosh, I really don't remember. I may have been misquoted."

"Really? When I'm one of the star reporters on Sky Sports or writing for a national newspaper, you'll be begging for a word with me, not the other way round! Besides I'm off duty tonight, so you're safe!"

"Is that your game plan, Jess? All joking aside, from what I've read, you're wasted writing for a local rag. I wouldn't be at all surprised to see you writing for a proper newspaper one day – or on Sky Sports. You certainly know your stuff."

"Awww…that's nice of you to say that. A girl can always use a compliment." She had a nice smile. "So, what about you? Are the dizzy heights of Reigate Athletic the limit of your footballing ambition? My sources tell me that a pro club had a look at you a few weeks ago." She raised a now familiar quizzical eyebrow as she said it.

"I have no idea who your sources are, but I very much doubt that somehow. I'm 'unknown' and 'unproven' don't forget!"

"OK, OK! I might never live that one down. But seriously, is your work career more important, or would you really like to play football at a higher level?"

Although the bar was still heaving, I'd shut all of that out and I was just enjoying the conversation with Jess. We'd never chatted before and she was very easy to talk to, probably because she was off duty for once and didn't need to ask me questions for the sake of writing something. I was conscious that John was waving in my direction to indicate my drink was waiting for me, but I was in no hurry. If nothing else, it would enhance my reputation with the rest of the team that I was chatting to Jess!

"To be honest, I've never thought that much about it. After AFC Wimbledon released me when I was fifteen, in my head, my dream of playing pro football was over. Getting my exams and going to uni seemed a much better option than trying to make a go of it in football. Now, I've probably missed my opportunity so it's more about just going out and enjoying it, rather than having any sort of dream about playing pro."

"Yeah, I get that, especially when you're earning shed-loads of money in the City. But if it happened, and someone did come along and wanted you to sign for them, then what?" Jess wasn't taking no for an answer.

"A bridge to cross, if and when it happens. I'll worry about that some other time." I smiled. "So, are you going to stop being a journo and asking me lots of questions now?"

"Occupational hazard." She smiled too. "But I was right about you. You are unusual for a footballer. Usually when I talk to a player, his eyes move towards my chest at some point and it's not uncommon to get asked for my phone number. You're different. But then you also have a very attractive girlfriend, so you don't need my number." The smile was still there. I assumed she was teasing me, but I couldn't quite work it out. Was she inviting me to try and get it? As I was thinking that through, she was asking another question.

"I don't see her here yet. I assume she's coming?"

"Nah. It's not her scene. She's not really into football. The game against Woking was her first game, well apart from the VIP seats at Chelsea, but I'm not sure she saw much of the football when she went there!"

"Really? Wow. I'm very surprised she doesn't want to be part of this chaos and have drinks spilt all over her by clumsy journalists!"

"I very much doubt you are clumsy. I just assumed it was some clever ploy to get chatting to me and lower my guard enough to get me to reveal my career plans and all the dressing-room gossip that will propel your career to new heights!"

"Damn! You saw through my cunning plan. So Matt, what is the gossip from the dressing room and the career aspirations of the league's best keeper?" She was smiling again, and I had to agree with Anna. Jess was very pretty. She was not quite as tall as Anna and her brunette hair was shoulder length, although tonight it was tied back in a ponytail. She also had large brown eyes which I was noticing for the first time as I was looking into them.

"If I told you I'd have to kill you, and that would deprive *The Times* of their next great football writer."

"Fair point. I'll settle for getting an intelligent quote from you after the draw is made. Deal?"

"Deal. I'll come and find you."

"I hope you do." She smiled and turned away, leaving me wondering just how to react to that last remark. I decided I was in danger of reading way too much into it and smiled to myself at the normal male arrogance lurking just beneath the surface, thinking that every woman finds you irresistible. I fought my way over to where John and some of the other lads had established base camp, and my drink.

"I was thinking of bringing your drink over to you, bro, but I didn't want to interrupt! I didn't think she was gonna let you go!" Stevie was smirking and so were Stan and John behind him. "The Ice Maiden melts! What did you say to her? I even saw her smiling!" Stevie was his normal subtle self.

"It was no big deal. She just wanted some dressing-room gossip, so I told her that it wasn't true that some short guys make up for their lack of height by being bigger elsewhere. Well, not in your case at least!"

The rest of the boys cracked up laughing. Stevie was grinning too. Dressing-room banter usually follows a tried-and-tested formula of jokes or boasts about penis size and sexual prowess, which are invariably at or near the top of the list. Shrinking violets aren't normally found in football changing rooms. Luckily, I was saved from further interrogation about my conversation with Jess, by a shout of, "Oi! Turn it up!"

The draw was about to begin. As usual, the BBC had trotted out a couple of ex-pros to manage the difficult task of pulling wooden balls out of a velvet sack in hopefully the right order, to produce a set of fixtures for the First Round of the FA Cup. Although it was hard to hear anything above all the hubbub, we could all see the graphic which showed the numbers of some of the "giant killers". Smaller clubs like us that had made it through to this stage. Our ball was number twenty-nine. As the balls were emptied into the sack, the noise subsided considerably and there was a real feeling of tension and excitement in the air. I glanced around the bar and most people were transfixed to the screen. But as I looked round, I noticed Jess, who was glancing in my direction. We held eye contact for a few seconds longer than was necessary before she went back to looking at the screen.

The first dozen fixtures came and went and each time a ball came out, there was a quick buzz of conversation before it died again in anticipation of the next ball emerging. We were hoping we wouldn't get another non-league side. We all wanted to draw a league side. Ideally at home, although there were some huge clubs like Sunderland and Portsmouth that none of us would have minded visiting.

"Number twenty-nine, Reigate Athletic will play..." A pause as the hand delved into the sack. A home draw, I thought. That was good for us. You could cut the air with a knife as the hand on TV pulled out a numbered ball.

"Number forty-two, Bromley."

A huge groan of disappointment went around the bar. Another National League side, just like Woking, except they were currently lying second in the table and were being tipped for promotion to the Football League this season. We were all a little disappointed, though as Stevie pointed out at least we were at home. Playing someone like Dover away would have been even less exciting.

People were already starting to drift away from the bar. The balloon had been well and truly pricked and all the excitement from earlier in the evening had been replaced with a rather disappointed air. We all had plenty of respect for Bromley, who were doing well near the top of the league, but it just wasn't the same as drawing a Football League side. I had a quick chat with Stevie, drained my Coke and was thinking of making tracks. Then I remembered my promise of speaking to Jess. I started to weave my way through the thinning crowd in the bar, but I noticed that Jess was already making a beeline towards me.

"Hey! What do you think of the draw?"

She looked at me mischievously, knowing that I might struggle to say something she could use. But I'd already thought of something to say. I truth, I wanted to impress her with something thoughtful to cement my reputation of being a little different. The best thing was that it was pretty much true too.

"OK, Ms Reporter, if you promise not to hurl any more drinks at me, you can quote me as saying: 'While I think a lot of people associated with the club would have wanted to draw a Football League side, I take a slightly different view. We're not happy just to be in the First Round. Our goal is to get to the Third Round. We're at home. We've already beaten a National League side in Woking. Bromley are obviously a good side. But they will be looking at the draw and not relishing coming to us. It gives us a chance of making the next round and then we're only one game away from the Third Round and playing one of the big boys.' That's it."

"Wow! That's pretty good! I can certainly use that. But is that what you really think? You must be a little disappointed?"

"Maybe a little, but my initial reaction is that it does give us a chance of making it through to the Second Round and then we're only a game away from playing Man City or Chelsea! The main thing is we're at home and I fancy our chances at home."

"I love that optimism! Right, armed with that inspiring quote, I'm going to tackle the chairman and see what he thinks of it. It was fun chatting to you, Matt. I hope we get the chance to do that again one of these days." With that, and before I could think of a suitable response, Jess turned on her heel and headed over to where the chairman was holding court with the press officer and a couple of the other directors. They didn't look that thrilled. I was watching Jess walk away when my mobile rang, and I saw it was Anna.

"Hey babe."

"Hey gorgeous. I was watching the draw on my cell as I'm

still at work. I couldn't believe that a lot of the guys here were watching it and really excited about the fact that you guys were in it. Maybe I should have come after all. So, was it good or bad? I have no clue."

"We were just debating that ourselves! I think it's good, but not as good as we hoped for. Well, not as exciting as it might have been. But it gives us a chance of going through to the next round, so it's interesting, if not exciting. If that makes sense?!"

"OK, well I guess that's good then! So, am I gonna see you later? Or are you drinking with your buddies and pretending you're talking tactics?"

"Oh, I think I can just about squeeze you in this evening."

"Wanker!"

I burst out laughing. I had made the mistake of telling Anna about some of the more popular English swear words used in most football dressing rooms. She had obviously heard them all before, but it became a bit of a joke between us. She had latched on to this one in particular and seemed to get a kick out of using it when talking to me. Bad mistake on my part. Though hearing it come out with a slight American twang always made me laugh.

"I love you too, darling. What time will you be back?"

"As long as the fricking trains work, then it should be around eight-thirty, so if you drop round about nine that should work. Bring an Indian with you. I'm starving."

"Yes, ma'am! You want the usual?"

"Yes, hon. But don't forget about the food too!"

She hung up, leaving me speechless and laughing at the same time. She had a wicked sense of humour, which is one of the reasons why we got on so well. I looked around and it was only the die-hard supporters and some of the players left. Jess seemed to have gone and I was conscious of feeling a little disappointed. Then again, that was a complication I definitely didn't need with things going so well with Anna. If only Anna understood my football world a little better. More like Jess did. She would have understood the situation with me having to play a game on her birthday. She would probably have come to the game with me and we'd have had a meal after the game. I shook my head. This really wasn't a good line of thought. A ten-minute chat with Jess was hardly anything to go on anyway. She probably had a boyfriend, and, besides, not every girl is going to fall head over heels for me, even during my five minutes of fame! Laughing at myself, I went back to finish chatting to the lads and kill a bit of time before getting the food and heading over to Anna's. I also needed to pick up a different suit and some clothes for the next day as I had no intention of sleeping at my flat that night.

5

I had served my one-match ban for getting sent off at Folkestone and was ready to play again. There was no danger I wouldn't get back into the side. Like a lot of clubs, we didn't have a reserve team, so very few goalkeepers of any ability wanted to be the reserve keeper – the bloke who went to training every week, turned up for games, home and away, sat on the bench but never got to play. The chances of a keeper getting injured during a game were quite small, so unlike the other substitutes who probably had a 50:50 chance of getting on, the sub keeper had almost none. So, it was quite common to have a goalkeeping coach who could also fill in for a game or two. Of course, if your goalkeeper picked up a longer-term injury, you went out and signed a replacement. But for my one-game ban, it was a no-brainer that Smithy played and then I would be back the following week. As it happened, we were playing Chertsey, who were rooted to the foot of the table and we won comfortably, 3–0 with Smithy pretty much a spectator.

But I was back for Dulwich Hamlet away. Dulwich are

something of a non-league phenomenon in that they regularly draw home crowds of between 1,500 and 2,000 paying customers, and for a top of the table clash, you might get nearer to 2,500. They had been up in the National League South for a few years but were relegated last season. However, all the talk during the close season was about them bouncing back and they had made several big-name signings in the summer. They had the money and they had the fan base and probably deserved to be in the National League. They were the bookies' favourites for promotion before a ball had been kicked and were currently flying high at the top of the league. They were unbeaten and had only dropped four points all season with two away draws. It was going to be a tough afternoon and a few sides had left Champion Hill in recent weeks with their tails tucked between their legs after a real hiding. We all were determined that wasn't going to happen to us.

As I turned to pick the ball out of my net for the third time, I bitterly remembered how determined we'd been in training not to become another of Dulwich's easy home wins. Yet here we were, 3–0 down and the worst bit was that we'd only played around twenty minutes. The blue and pink army behind my goal were ecstatic and cries of "Can we play you every week?" were starting to become more frequent. Sometimes in football, you have to accept that the other side is just the better team, and, for the opening twenty minutes, Dulwich had quite simply ripped us apart.

Their opening goal after twelve minutes was a culmination of some flick passing in our box and then the forward chipped it over me as I came out. The second, three minutes later, was what footballers call a "worldie". A shot from around thirty yards that quite simply flew into the top corner. I dived, but knew I wasn't going to get anywhere near it. It was a bullet and I don't think any goalkeeper in the world would have got near it. The third goal, after nineteen minutes, was from the penalty spot after our left-back, Jamie Redmond, had been a fraction late with a challenge. It was a stone-wall penalty and we barely bothered to dispute it with the ref – it was that clear. I went the wrong way from the spot kick, and we were three down. This could get embarrassing, I was thinking. Not ideal preparation for our cup tie in two weeks if we went down by five or six. Funnily enough, we weren't playing that badly, even though we were losing. The first two goals were just quality goals and the third, well, that was just one of those things that happen. Dulwich were swarming all over us, but I pulled off a couple of good saves and we made it through to half-time without conceding any further goals.

I think we all expected to get a rocket from the boss at the interval. We got the opposite. Harry came in and very calmly said that Dulwich had played exceptionally well in that first half. There wasn't much we could have done about the first two goals and he admired the way we had dug in after the third goal went in. Lesser teams would have thrown in the towel he said. He also asked us a question: how many times, he asked, have you watched a team play a great first half and go in three or even four up, but in the second half come out as flat as a pancake? He was right. We'd all seen it happen, even at the highest level. They think the game's already over, he said. They won't be at 100% in the second half, no matter what their manager tells them now. It's human nature. They'll relax and start coasting. The next goal is huge, Harry said. If they get it, it's game over for sure. But, if we get it, it will put just a seed of doubt in their minds. If we get a second, it's game on and they will be the team under pressure. Make sure you get that goal, he said and then he walked out. We sat there in silence for a moment just letting it sink in and then we all started talking at once, geeing each other up. As the buzzer went and we stood to go back out, Harry came back in.

"Lads, we're going to play 3-5-2 second half. Jamie, as you're on a yellow already, I'm taking you off. Antonio, get stripped as you're coming on to play with Rosey up front. We need to have a real go at them," he said.

Wow. Gutsy call, I thought. We'd only played this formation in pre-season a couple of times. Fair enough taking Jamie off as he'd been carded for the penalty and we didn't need him getting a second yellow. Bringing on Antonio was a big call though. We'd signed him on loan from Sutton United the previous week. Big and strong, he looked like a centre-forward. He'd also looked good in training, but then again, a lot of people look good in training without the pressure of a game situation and defenders kicking lumps out of you.

It was do or die. We could just as easily ship five or six if this didn't work. But Harry had pumped the lads up and there was a belief as we walked out. I passed a couple of the Dulwich lads in the tunnel and overheard one asking the other how many goals he'd got this season. The implication was that there were more for the taking. The first ten minutes of the second half were fairly forgettable, as we adjusted to our new shape and Dulwich were content just to pass sideways. Then we scored. The proverbial goal out of nothing. Rosey was out wide on the right and knocked a pretty innocuous ball into the Dulwich box. There were four defenders and Antonio in the area. It was one of those classic moments. The defenders all left it, thinking their keeper would come and claim it, while the keeper was expecting his defenders to deal with it. In the end, they all left it to each other, and the ball ran through to Antonio at the far post, who could scarcely believe his luck and finished from six yards. A lack of concentration, just like Harry had predicted. Now it was 3–1. I tipped a shot from twenty-five yards over the bar, but we were having the better of things. Our five in midfield outnumbered their four and having two up front meant they couldn't play out from the back as easily as they had been doing in the first half.

With a little over fifteen minutes left, we had a corner on the right. We piled bodies into the box and sent both John and Stan forward. The corner came in and John did just enough to stop the Dulwich defenders clearing the danger. The ball dropped to Stan's feet at the far post, but he had his back to goal and had a defender tight up against him and was being forced away from goal. But Stan was cute and, instead of playing the ball out to one of our players, he stopped dead. It caught their defender by surprise, and he put both hands in Stan's back to stop himself colliding with our big defender. As soon as Stan felt the contact, he went down as though a sniper from the main stand had picked him out. To say it was a tad theatrical was an understatement. But the ref blew his whistle and pointed to the spot! Cue mayhem. The Dulwich players surrounded Mr Damian Rickett from Hertfordshire, with stunned disbelief all over their faces. The Dulwich fans were booing loudly. A Dulwich player angrily grabbed Stan by the arm to pull him up and no doubt give an opinion about how easily the six-feet defender went down. Stan didn't take kindly to the helping hand, nor, no doubt, to the abusive comments being offered and pushed the Dulwich man away. Inevitably, other players from both sides got involved in the melee, with the referee doing his best to restore order. Eventually, calmer heads prevailed, and Mr Rickett booked both Stan and the Dulwich lad. After several minutes delay, our skipper placed the ball on the spot and walked back his customary six paces. With the Dulwich keeper doing his best to distract him and around 2,000 people booing loudly, John calmly jogged up and side-footed the ball down the middle as their keeper went left. We'd pegged it back to 3–2. Game on!

Suddenly it was Dulwich who were looking unsure. No doubt they were thinking, do we defend or keep trying to play our football? Their coaching staff were sending out a barrage of instructions, and made a couple of quick substitutions, but we had the momentum. I just knew we'd get at least one opportunity in the last ten minutes. Funnily enough, it was Dulwich who had a great chance to clinch it when they played a ball over the top and our back three stood with their arms in the air, convinced the lone Dulwich striker was well offside. But the assistant kept her flag down and suddenly it was a one v. one. I did almost exactly the same as I had done at Folkestone; showing the forward one way and then the other. I dived full length as he went to go past me to try and push the ball away. I didn't make any contact with either the ball or their forward, but he went down in a heap and 2,000 voices all screamed "Penalty!" at the same time. I heard the ref's whistle and had my heart in my mouth as I saw him running towards us and reaching for his pocket. He pulled out a yellow card. My heart sank – until I realised he was showing it to the Dulwich man for simulation! Brave man, I thought, as the home crowd reacted angrily. In fairness, I think a lot of them knew it wasn't a foul, so the anger was muted. Conscious time was slipping away, I grabbed the ball for our goal kick and hoofed it upfield. No time for niceties now. Antonio leapt highest and flicked the ball on. Charlie Rose had anticipated that Antonio would win it and was already on the move. As the ball dropped, around twenty-five yards from goal, Charlie caught it sweetly on the volley and the ball dipped over the Dulwich keeper and into the net to make it 3–3! I must have sprinted seventy yards to join the lads mobbing Rosey. What a strike! Harry was yelling at us from the touchline to get back into position and concentrate. We didn't want to give it away now. Dulwich and their fans were stunned. The whole stadium was quiet except for a small band of Athletic fans singing, "We're going to win 4–3!"

Straight from the kick-off, we won the ball back and we played another long ball towards Antonio, who again won his aerial duel. This time Rosey played it wide to Addi, who fired in a low, hard cross around the penalty spot. Jake Bennett had timed his run superbly and, without breaking stride, fired home though a crowded box to make it 4–3! But as he wheeled away to celebrate, I noticed the assistant with his flag raised. The rest of the lads were chasing Beno who had gone to celebrate with our fans, but I was more interested in the ref running towards his assistant. After a brief conversation, the ref pointed for a free kick for offside and disallowed the goal. This time it was our lads who were chasing the man in black and demanding to know how it could be disallowed as Beno had several players in front of him, so he couldn't have been offside. This time it was the home supporters who were cheering the officiating crew. Talk about drama! There was barely time for the free kick before the ref blew for full time. It had been a cracker of a game and players from both sides recognised it and warmly embraced after the final whistle. I did go and shake hands with the ref and his two assistants. I congratulated him on a good game, in part because he hadn't been conned by the forward pretending I'd fouled him! I politely asked him why the goal had been chalked off and he explained that Stevie had been in an offside position right in front of their keeper and in his view, unsighting him. I said fair enough and walked away. As it turns out, when I saw the video later, he was absolutely right to disallow it. The female assistant had also been spot on not to give offside when I had the one v. one. Funny how often the officials get things right, I mused later.

Half an hour later, I wandered into the Dulwich bar to get some food and a drink. To my surprise, there was Jess talking to Harry. She nodded to me as I walked past. No smile. All business. The Ice Maiden is back, I thought, inwardly chuckling to myself at how my own ego had made more of our last meeting on the night of the cup draw. I got a bowl of pasta and sat with some of the lads to unwind and chat about the game. There was plenty to discuss. We were all nominating Stan for an Oscar for "Best dramatic fall in the box" this season, much to his amusement, though he was still maintaining that he had been pushed. Beno summed it up best when he said, "My four-year-old pushes me harder than that lad pushed you, Stan!" But we'd take it. Decisions often even themselves out over the course of a season. We'd had a bad pen given against us at Folkestone and now we'd got a soft one against Dulwich a few weeks later. Poetic justice? None of us had seen the video of the disallowed goal, so we were still debating that one. I needed another soft drink, so headed back to the bar for an orange juice and lemonade. As I was handed the drink, I turned to go back to my seat and bumped right into – Jess! This time she was the recipient of a quantity of drink over her coat.

"Oh shit! I'm sorry, Jess! I didn't see you behind me!"

"So much for keepers having peripheral vision! We can't go on meeting like this, Matt!" She was smiling, despite the patch on the front of her coat.

"I'm surprised you're here. I thought you had other clubs you had to write about?"

"We chose this as our 'Game of the Day'. Top of the league against the FA Cup giant killers. Makes for a good story and it was a brilliant game of football to watch."

"Glad you enjoyed it. It was fun to play in too."

"I just spoke to Harry and he said the players deserve all the plaudits for turning that around."

"He would say that." It was typical of Harry not to take any credit. "He was the one who changed our formation and brought on another forward when we were three nothing down. Not many managers would have the balls to do that! Plus the brilliant psychology he used on us at half-time."

"Whoa, hang on a sec! The formation change I noted down and it certainly was gutsy, but what's this about psychology?!"

I repeated what Harry had said at half-time and told her how much he made us think as players. I said it made a nice change to have a manager who challenged you intellectually and emotionally, rather than all the macho bullshit you normally hear.

"That's brilliant! Can I use this in the report? It gives such a great insight into the team, and into how Harry is bringing out the best in you."

"Umm…I'm not sure he'd want me to be giving away too many of his secrets…"

"How about I ask Harry if I can use what you said?"

"I'd rather you didn't, Jess, to be honest. I don't want him thinking I tell you everything that goes on in the sanctity of our dressing room."

Jess's smile vanished from her face.

"I've never asked you to do that, Matt, and I never would. But if that's how you feel about it, that's fine. I'll respect that you told me it off the record. See you around."

She turned and walked out of the bar. How did that happen I wondered? One minute we're getting along great, and the next she's storming off. I appreciated that she wanted to get some good copy for her paper, but I assumed she'd understand that I can't tell her everything that goes on behind closed doors. At least it puts everything into context, I thought. She wasn't interested in me as such, simply as a good source of quotes and news. But I still felt a little disappointed at how the conversation had ended.

"Hey Matt. What's up? The Ice Maiden looked a bit pissed as she walked away from you. You turn her down, or did she turn you down?" Stevie was winking and smiling at a few of the other lads. But I had an ace to play.

"No, mate. I just wouldn't tell her what we discussed at half-time. But you'd know about being turned down by the Ice Maiden, wouldn't you?!" I knew for a fact that Stevie had asked Jess out but had been rebuffed in no uncertain terms. The reason I knew was because Stevie had made the cardinal error of telling a few of us and had then come up with the "Ice Maiden" nickname for Jess. The rest of the lads burst out laughing. Stevie blustered and tried to make a comeback, but he was toast. The banter resumed, but I was only half-listening. I was still thinking about the exchange with Jess and whether I could have handled it better. Oh well, I decided, the damage was done.

Later that evening, I was at Anna's with my feet up and getting ready to watch *Match of the Day*. Anna was in the bath having a long soak. My mobile rang. I didn't recognise the number, but decided to take the call, just in case it was one of the lads needing a lift to training or something. Several of the lads didn't drive, so I was often their go-to for lifts to and from the local train station.

"Hello, is that Matt?" It was a girl's voice and sounded familiar.

"Yes, who's this?"

"Matt, it's Jess. I got your number from Harry. I told him I needed to ring and apologise for being such a bitch to you earlier. I explained that you told me something off the record and I got in a huff because you said I couldn't use it. He just laughed and said a journalist apologising was such a rare occurrence, he just had to give me your number!" She was talking quite quickly, and I suspected she'd had a glass or two before she'd made the call. "Anyway, I just wanted to say I'm sorry and I hope you will still talk to me. I promise it won't happen again and I won't do my best Ice Maiden impression on you!"

"Hey Jess, no big deal," I said, lying through my teeth. "I probably should have just let you ask Harry and let him decide. And I understood you were disappointed. You're a professional doing your job. I get that."

"Phew! Thanks for being so understanding, Matt. I thought you'd be annoyed with me."

"Nah, I'll still talk to the Ice Maiden! I didn't know you knew your nickname though."

"Oh, I've heard it in passing a few times, shall we say. Anyway, I don't want to disturb your evening and I'm sure you've got better things to do than talk to me. Thanks, Matt. Bye."

"No worries, Jess. Bye."

As I put the phone down, Anna walked into the room, wrapped in a bath towel.

"Who were you talking to, luv?"

"Oh, just the journalist from the *Surrey Herald*. She rang to apologise for her behaviour earlier."

"The pretty one, you mean? How did she have your number?"

Uh, oh. This had the potential to quickly spiral in a downward trajectory. It had all the hallmarks of a crash and burn conversation. I explained in more detail what had transpired earlier and how she'd got my number and how it was a quick call to apologise. Anna was standing looking at me. Her arms were folded across her chest and she looked less than pleased. I didn't need to be an expert in body language to read the signs.

"So, this girl rings you at 10pm on a Saturday evening to say sorry? It couldn't have waited until Monday?"

"Hey Anna. I just took the call. She got my number from Harry, not from me. It was a short call and all she did was say sorry. End of story."

"Hmmm. I think she has the hots for you, Matt. I don't want to sound like some jealous, possessive bitch myself, but I hope you can see it from my point of view. If she looked like the rear end of a bus, maybe I'd feel different. Stay away from her, hon. She's trouble."

I wasn't too thrilled at being told what to do, I have to admit. I could understand Anna's perspective, but I also thought she was overreacting a bit. I saw Jess because our lines of work interacted. End of. I also didn't think Jess was "trouble", plus I might have a little difficulty staying away from her as she was always welcome at our games and at the other grounds we visited. But rather than say any of that, which would no doubt have gone down like a lead balloon, I opted for that tactic known as "deflection".

"I only have eyes for one woman," I said, in my best bedroom voice, "and she's standing right in front of me. The most beautiful girl I've ever seen." I stood up and pulled her towards me. She didn't resist. I pulled the front of her bath towel that she'd tucked in. It fell in a pile at her feet and I ran my hands over her smooth, naked body, kissing her behind her ears, which was one of her weak spots.

"Looks like I got all clean for nothing," she whispered huskily in my ear, sighing gently.

"Looks like," I agreed. She pushed me down on the sofa. Oddly enough, I was no longer thinking about watching *Match of the Day*.

6

After the game against Dulwich we had two more league games to fit in before our First-Round tie against Bromley. We had a comfortable home win against Bognor Regis Town and then we had a horrible trip to Margate on a Tuesday evening.

To begin with, it's about a two-hour journey down there, assuming the M2 is behaving itself. It wasn't. There was an accident which added forty-five minutes to our journey time. I heard the club secretary on his phone to Margate trying to give them a rough ETA and then speaking to the match referee about delaying the kick-off. We eventually arrived at 7.20pm for a nominal 7.45pm kick-off. Harry wanted the game to be delayed to 8.15pm but the ref said that was too late and we'd kick off at 8pm. We were all stiff and cramped from being on a coach for the best part of three hours. To make things worse, it was blowing a gale. Margate's ground is only about a mile from the sea front and the wind was whipping in off the sea. They also have a 3G surface, which, personally, I'm not overly fond of. I can see the financial benefits to a club but give me grass any day. On an evening like that, a 3G surface makes things even worse. To call the game a football match would have been rightly challenged under the Trade Descriptions Act. My goal kicks were reaching the half-way line and then being blown back twenty to thirty yards. My kicks from hand were even worse. One I kicked blew all the way back and I ended up catching it on the bounce! It was a lottery. We ended up losing 1–0 to a goal that owed everything to the conditions rather than anything that the opposition did. We couldn't wait to leave.

The only thing that made us smile was when we heard Margate's top scorer had arrived at the ground ninety minutes before kick-off and couldn't work out why the ground was locked, and the lights were off. He phoned his manager to ask him if the game was off. His manager asked him what he was talking about, because he was at the ground himself and it was open, with the crowd streaming in. It then dawned on the manager to ask the player where he was. He said he was at Reigate's ground. He had thought it was an away game! I can only imagine what was said at that point between player and manager when he realised where the player was! They say that footballers aren't the brightest, but turning up at the wrong ground is taking the biscuit. If that had been me, I'd seriously have thought about leaving the club because you'd never, ever, live that one down. The abuse you'd get before every match and the constant reminders of this is a *home* game, or this is an *away* game, would have driven me mad. It was the one bright spot on a pretty torrid evening.

I called Anna on the way home, bemoaning the evening generally. I shouldn't really have expected any sympathy and I didn't get any. She simply reminded me that I chose to do this, and not so subtly reminded me that we'd both been invited to dinner at a top West End restaurant to celebrate one of

her girlfriend's birthdays and that she'd had to go on her own
and explain that her boyfriend was playing his soccer again.
The enthusiasm she'd shown at our game against Woking
hadn't lasted too long. Perhaps the game against Bromley
would rekindle it. Perhaps. I wasn't banking on it somehow.
I did point out that a footballer's career is a relatively short
one. A few days later, and somewhat out of the blue, she came
back with the retort that goalies play until they are much older
than outfield players. I was sort of impressed, and she was also
right. I asked her how she'd found that out. She just looked at
me. "You're not the only one with friends of the opposite sex."
Ouch! I got the less than subtle message.

But we'd settled into something of a routine together. She
had accepted, albeit a little grudgingly, that I was committed
to my football career and Tuesday and Thursday evenings
and pretty much all-day Saturday were write-offs. She began
to take note of where we were on a Saturday in particular. A
home game meant that we could still socialise in the evening.
An away game most likely meant it was an evening in front of
the TV, as I often wasn't back at my place or hers until 7.30 or
8pm, dependent upon how far we had to travel. We sometimes
met up for a drink and dinner after work on Mondays and
Wednesdays, but that was often a little last minute, as we had
to adjust to each other's work commitments. But Fridays and
Sundays were always ours. Fridays were usually socialising
with friends, or just dinner for two. I had to be a little careful
socialising, as I didn't want to drink and didn't want a late night
either, so I usually drove, and we were normally home before
midnight. I think Sunday was our favourite day. Really lazy
Sunday mornings, getting up late and maybe heading out for a
pub lunch. There were so many good pubs in and around the
area, we were spoilt for choice. Very occasionally, the routine
was interrupted by a trip to the physio on Sunday, usually to

deal with something that had happened on Saturday, but Mel, our physio, lived in Epsom, so it was only a twenty-minute drive. Anna sometimes worked out at the gym or in the pool on Sundays, but usually tried to do that more on Saturdays when I was AWOL. We were pretty comfortable with each other, and, despite her lack of interest in my favourite pastime, we never ran short of things to talk about.

As the game against Bromley grew closer, so the media interest grew too. Sky Sports interviewed both the chairman and Harry. It made the rest of us feel a little more like full-time professionals when you turn on the TV and watch your manager being interviewed. I read a few bits that Jess had written about the upcoming game. I hadn't seen her since the phone call. She was no doubt off covering other games. As luck would have it, we didn't have a midweek fixture the week before the Bromley game, so we had two full training sessions to prepare. In the early season, we used to train on our pitch, but come October, we generally used an all-weather surface at a local school in order not to damage our own playing surface once it started to get wet with the onset of winter. But the weather leading up to the game was good, so Harry agreed with the groundsman that we'd train on our pitch, which we all preferred. The training facility at the school was OK, but we couldn't use the showers there as it was all locked up. That meant we had to drive home in sweaty gear, or, even worse, soaking wet, sweaty gear if it was raining.

Tuesday night's session was devoted to setting the side up to play against Bromley's formation. Even at our level, we had people we could ask to go and scout the opposition. I actually saw the report – it ran to four pages. There was an analysis of every player in terms of strengths and any weaknesses; the formation they played; attacking and defending set pieces, especially corners; anything unusual, such as people who had long throws etc. It was very thorough. Bromley normally played a 4-1-4-1 formation, so Harry asked our U23 side down to train with us and set up as Bromley did. As they were only playing with one striker, Harry felt we could play out from the back quite comfortably. We also practised playing our preferred 4-2-3-1 and the 3-5-2 that had served us well at Dulwich. As long as everyone knew their jobs, it gave us some tactical flexibility to switch during a game. In one of her rare moments of interest in football, Anna asked me what all those numbers meant when pundits talked about formations. As we were out for dinner, I asked the waiter (who luckily knew me and was a football fan) for eleven salt and pepper shakers. I then laid them out on the table in front of us and explained the pros and cons of different systems and the weaknesses that could be exploited. To my surprise, she watched closely and asked some really good questions about our planning. When I expressed that surprise, she reminded me that part of her job was advising on strategy, so this stuff was much more up her alley. We certainly got some amused looks from fellow diners that night.

Training often involved a degree of standing around, as we walked through some of the ways we were going to combat the Bromley formation, and then exploit it when we could. The training on Thursday evening only lasted an hour. At this stage of the season, we didn't need to do a lot of cardio work as we already had twenty plus games under our belts. I did a pretty intensive workout with Smithy before we all went into the dressing room to watch some video of Bromley's last few games. Harry had set up a TV, and we watched some of their set pieces and some of the goals they'd scored and conceded in recent games. Like a lot of National League sides, they were big and strong, and, because they were able to train full-time, they would certainly be fit. I paid particular attention to their corners and free kicks. I was looking to see if they had anyone in front of the goalkeeper at corners (they did). That always makes it difficult as you have to try and go around or sometimes through some big lump if you want to catch or punch the ball. In and around the box, they seemed to like to have a strike at goal, rather than trying intricate passes. I noticed two or three of their lads tried curling shots rather than relying upon pure power. Something else to watch for. Somebody had also put together a short clip just for me – their penalties. They'd been awarded three to date and their number eight took all three. Two went to the right of the keeper and one down the middle, though I think he just mis-hit the one down the middle as the pitch was wet and a bit muddy. All the penalties were high, rather than on the floor. I tucked that bit of knowledge away in case I needed to use it.

After the video session, we went to the bar for a quick drink. The chairman was in there, with a couple of fellow directors. When he saw me, he waved me over.

"Hi Matt. How's it going?"

"Fine, Brian, thanks."

"Listen, Matt, *Back of the Net* want to do a short interview with myself and one of our players. Apparently, they spoke to that girl at the *Surrey Herald* and she recommended you. Are you up for it? We'll do it tomorrow night in the boardroom at around 7.30."

Back of the Net was a non-league radio and internet show that had thousands of followers on Twitter and on YouTube. I'd listened to some of their shows and found them to be both entertaining and quite controversial, which of course made them interesting. It was nice of Jess to recommend me. I had done a little bit of media training at work and I knew that it was the sort of stuff that Anna did at her agency too, though given I only had twenty-four hours' notice, I doubt they could work miracles! But, if Jess thought I'd be good, then I probably ought to give it a go.

"Sure. Sounds like fun. I'll see you tomorrow night, Brian."

As it was a Friday night, I told Anna what was planned. I said it wouldn't take long and I should be done by 8pm. She asked why they'd chosen me. For a split second I almost told her what the chairman had told me, but I decided that discretion was the better part of valour. Mentioning Jess as the source would probably be a bad move currently, so I told her the chairman had asked me, which of course was true. Anna was quite interested and said she'd be happy to give me a few tips. I asked her if she wanted to come over to my place and give me those tips in person, but she declined with a laugh and said it was already 10pm, and we both had early starts the next day. I hadn't expected her to say yes, but it was always worth a try! She did email me over an "Idiot's guide to press interviews", which actually was quite useful. I think the most useful tip was to speak slowly, take your time and think before you speak!

The following evening, I walked into the boardroom five minutes ahead of schedule. Brian was already there, chatting to the two *Back of the Net* guys, who were fiddling with microphones and cables connected to laptops. Introductions were made and I sat with Brian while we waited to start. He looked nervous. It suddenly occurred to me that he probably hadn't done anything like this before. We both put our headsets on and Mickey, who was the one who would be asking the questions, counted us down.

Armed with my new-found skills, I enjoyed the interview. Most of the questions that I had to field were pretty straightforward – what we hoped would happen and a little bit about the previous round against Woking. It was all going well until Mickey said to me:

"So, Matt, rumour has it that some pro club scouts have been watching you in recent weeks. I understand you've already got a career in the City, but is professional football something you'd consider?"

Brian looked surprised and obviously hadn't heard those rumours. I decided to give a similar answer to the one I'd given Jess when she'd asked me the same question.

"Well, Mick, I think the first thing to say is that, as far as I'm concerned, they are just rumours. It's not unusual to hear those rumours during a season, especially if the team is doing well or is in the spotlight like we are. If it proves to be real, then I'll cross that bridge when the time comes."

"So, you wouldn't rule it out then?"

"Like I said, Mick, it's all pretty hypothetical and the league is full of stories about professional clubs looking at certain players."

"But if it was true, Matt, what then?" Mick certainly wasn't letting me off the hook.

"Of course, it's flattering if it is true, but right now my focus is on playing for Reigate and the big match we have tomorrow."

"OK, Matt, that's fair enough. And that's a nice way to wrap up tonight's interview, as Reigate Athletic prepare for the biggest game in their ninety-seven-year history. Thank you, Brian, and thank you, Matt. Good luck tomorrow."

We shook hands with Mick and the technician and strolled out of the boardroom. Brian looked thoughtful.

"So, had you heard those rumours then, Matt?"

"Only last week, Brian, to be honest, but, like I said in there, there are always loads of rumours around. I take it all with a pinch of salt."

"Very sensible, Matt. The only reason I ask is that you're not on contract. If a professional club came in for you, it would mean we would lose you for nothing. Would you consider going on contract? I mean, it just means you get a guaranteed wage and it gives both you and us a little security for the season."

"I don't see why not, Brian, but that's Harry's domain, isn't it?"

"Oh yes. I'd need to talk to Harry of course, but I just wanted to sound you out first. Thanks, Matt. I'll chat to Harry this evening and we'll get back to you in due course.

We shook hands and I headed to my car. I was meeting Anna at some new Indian restaurant in town. As I switched on the ignition, there were a lot of thoughts swirling around in my head. The chat with the chairman about being on contract was nice, although clearly they were looking after themselves rather than me. But I understood why. A few seasons earlier, I knew they had lost their Player of the Season in exactly that way. Brentford had come in for him, and, because he wasn't on contract, they didn't pay anything at all when they signed him. Some clubs will do "the right thing" and make a token payment, but if there's no contract in place, they don't have to do anything, and the player is free to sign. If there is a contract, then the club has the right to demand a fee for the player, which then becomes a negotiation. The other thought that had occurred to me since the interview, was just where had Mick got that information from? Maybe he had got his own sources, but it sounded a lot like the same things that Jess had asked. Had she fed him those questions? It began to feel a little like a set-up. We had talked about all that pro scout interest off the record. But she had been the one to suggest my name to Brian. I started to feel a little pissed off. I didn't like being played like that. I pulled over and got my phone out. I found Jess's number and dialled it.

"Hello?"

"Jess. It's Matt."

"Oh hi, Matt. How did the interview—"

"Jess, did you give Mick those questions about the pro scouts looking at me?"

"What? No! Of course not."

"It just seems quite a coincidence that you suggested my name and then I got those same questions that you asked me."

"You sound annoyed. Just for the record, all Mick did was ask me to suggest a player I thought would make for a good interview. I gave him your name. Which I'm beginning to regret now. That's all. Is there anything else, Matt?" Jess's voice had got quite icy.

"Look, I'm sorry if I jumped to any conclusions, Jess—"

"Bye Matt."

I sat there with the phone still in my hand. The feeling of being pissed off had completely disappeared. Instead I felt a little stupid and very much regretted the call I had just made. I sat there thinking for a few seconds. On one hand, I could just let it go. After all, she'd been a little grumpy with me only recently – although she did have the good grace to call and apologise. Or I could call back and apologise. If I did it now, there was probably a good chance she'd ignore the call. Maybe I'd do it tomorrow after she'd calmed down a little. I put the phone down, started the car and pulled away. A hundred yards down the road, I pulled over again, much to the irritation of an Audi driver behind me, who was way too close anyway. I stopped the car, picked up the phone from the front seat and dialled Jess's number. It rang four or five times. Just when I was about to end the call, she picked up. I didn't give her a chance to say anything.

"I'm a complete tosser sometimes. That was very unfair of me to accuse you. I'm really sorry. Shall we call it even?!" I waited for her to say something. There was a slight pause, which seemed to last quite a long time, before she responded.

"I agree. You are a complete tosser." At least she didn't sound quite as angry as before.

"OK, OK! Fair enough. Look, I am really sorry, Jess. I just got caught on the hop a bit and put two and two together and came up with five. Truce?" I asked hopefully.

"Truce. We're even!" That was better. She sounded more relaxed again. "Thanks for calling back. I was steaming. You've either brave or stupid, or maybe you just haven't seen me ready to kill!" She sounded like she was smiling now.

"Well, they say goalkeepers are mad, so maybe I just reinforced the stereotype. Anyway, I'm glad you no longer want to kill me at least."

"I don't think I actually said that!"

"I'll sort out some bodyguards for next time you want to interview me." This time she actually laughed.

"You really think that would make you safe from me?! Dream on, mister!" I laughed at that. Part of me was thinking I should end the call, as I'd done what I set out to do. But I didn't.

"Fair dos. Maybe I should just agree to phone interviews in future. Anyway, I'm glad we're friends again." She didn't agree or disagree with that one, so I pressed on." So, what are you doing in on a Friday evening? I thought you'd be out on the town having fun."

"I was going to the cinema but got blown out. You interviewed very well, especially when Mick was pressing you on that whole scout business." Interesting change of direction, I thought. I guess she doesn't want me prying into her private life. "Anyone would think you'd had media training!"

"Thanks. I will admit to a small amount of coaching, but I'm just getting prepared for when one of those pro team scouts sign me up and I'm being interviewed by you on Sky Sports after a game!"

"Very funny. I'll probably have to wait in line while all the other outrageously attractive presenters, who know bugger all about football, get their questions in first," she said with a sigh.

"How can you say that, Jess?! You know I'd give you that exclusive interview as long as you promised not to throw a drink over my Armani suit!" That made her laugh out loud. I liked hearing her laugh.

"I'm never going to live that one down, am I? OK, you have my word. The only thing is that you need to get that pro contract first. Just a small detail."

"And you need to get picked up by Sky Sports to work with all the other pretty airheads!" I said with a chuckle.

"MATT! Actually, I'm trying to decide if I'm insulted because you likened me to an airhead or flattered because you put me in the same 'pretty' bracket as the other airheads!" I knew she was teasing me now, but it was all good fun.

"Jess, all I can say is…NO COMMENT!"

"Oohh! You complete…TOSSER!" We were both laughing now and it felt pretty good.

"So, am I back in your good books now?" I said in a mock pleading voice.

"You're assuming you were ever in my good books, mister! Let's just say I don't dislike you as much as I did ten minutes ago!"

"I'm hurt. How could you dislike a nice guy like me? No, don't answer that!" I said quickly. "I'd rather not know." She was giggling as I said it. "Good job I called back in that case."

"I did consider just letting the phone ring, but I really wanted to give you a piece of my mind as I thought I'd let you off lightly the first time!"

"Lightly? The ice was about a foot deep by the time you hung up!"

"I didn't get my nickname for nothing. You're lucky you

don't have frostbite!" The conversation went back and forth so fast, I was having to keep on my toes to keep up with her. She was a lot of fun. Just then, I heard an incoming text. Anna! Whoops. She was probably wondering where I was. Much as I wanted to keep our exchange going, I knew I'd better wrap it up or I'd be in trouble with a woman for the second time this evening.

"Well, I'm sitting in my car which is parked on double yellow lines"– which was true – "and I'm getting more than the occasional helpful suggestion from fellow motorists that I move it, so maybe I'd better. It's been a lot of fun chatting to you, Jess." It really had been.

"Likewise, Matt. I hope you thaw out in time to see your girlfriend! See you soon."

"Bye Jess." I was left wondering about her last comment. Was it my imagination, or was there just a little bit of extra emphasis upon the word "girlfriend"? I had the distinct feeling that Anna and Jess would not be sending each other Christmas cards this year. I hoped I didn't get caught in the middle of their next meeting. I might need a tin helmet. I quickly sent a text to Anna saying I'd be there in ten minutes, started the engine and pulled away from my illegal parking spot, hoping that our dinner conversation would be just as much fun.

7

It wasn't often you saw a queue at the gate waiting to get into the ground. I was on the pitch warming up with Smithy about thirty minutes before kick-off and I could see a line of people patiently waiting to get in through our rather antiquated turnstiles, which, rumour had it, were cast-offs from Millwall's old ground in Cold Blow Lane before they moved to Bermondsey. One of the club's sponsors had ties with Millwall, so it wouldn't surprise me. In that case, the turnstiles were probably at least fifty years old! We were expecting a decent crowd. Bromley normally averaged around 1,500 for their home games, and, as the two grounds were only fifteen miles apart, we were expecting a fair few of their supporters at the match. The Bromley supporters were coming in via the other entrance at the Church End, and there looked to be a few hundred already there, comfortably outnumbering our own supporters. That said, most non-league supporters thought they could turn up ten minutes before a game and stroll in. That was certainly the case at Reigate normally. But we were expecting in excess of a thousand today as Bromley had requested 500 tickets for the game. We were hoping the locals would turn out in force to support us. It's not often a club like ours reaches the dizzy heights of the First Round of the FA Cup.

I saw Jess was interviewing Chris Kavanagh, the Bromley boss, near the dressing room. If she saw me, she gave no indication of it. I'd already seen Anna, who'd taken my advice and got to the ground early so she could park easily and not have to queue up outside. She had been chatting to John's wife and the two seemed to be getting along well. I wasn't too sure where she was now, but more likely in the bar, rather than standing around in the light drizzle that was falling on a chilly, gloomy and very typical November afternoon.

I always went through the same warm-up routine with Smithy and by now we both had it down pat. We started with some passing, as the gaffer liked us to play out from the back when we could. That meant my ball control and passing had to be pretty good, so it was important to get plenty of touches now and get the weight of pass right on the slick surface. We then moved onto close-range reflex stuff from a few yards, and then shots from ten to fifteen yards that required me to dive full length. Next it was crosses from both sides, and, finally, some goal kicks with me aiming for Smithy, who was standing just inside their half. Usually we were called in about fifteen minutes before kick-off. That gave me a chance to change out of my muddy warm-up gear and do my last-minute stretches and little rituals. We were all settled and ready when Harry came in ten minutes before the start to give his final talk. It was usually short and to the point. If we hadn't taken things on board tactically by then, it was probably too late. I had learned from own training in the workplace that most people struggled to retain more than three or four points, and Harry had obviously worked that out for himself years ago.

"Right, lads. I don't need to tell you what a big game this is. I don't need to tell you there will be a big crowd out there today. And I don't need to tell you that they are a good side. You know that." He paused and made eye contact with each player as he looked around the dressing room. "What I will tell you is that if you all do your jobs, play the way I know we can and play the game and not the occasion, then we will give them one hell of a game. If we do that and play to our potential, I don't care whether we win, lose or draw. What matters is we play for each other and for the club. We do that and we'll enjoy the afternoon. Don't be afraid to play our football. We know we can match anyone on our day."

The referee's buzzer sounded to tell us it was time to line up in the tunnel. "Good luck, lads!" With that, everyone got up and started shouting, geeing each other up. We were shaking hands, bumping fists and generally wishing each other good luck. I got behind John and we filed out of the door. The tunnel was very narrow, and the Bromley players were lining up next to us. We were almost shoulder to shoulder, but we were completely ignoring them, and they were doing the same. It makes me laugh when I see Premiership players being all matey with the opposition and giving them hugs. Very different in non-league football. The ref and his two assistants squeezed past us to the front of the queue of players. You could cut the atmosphere with a knife, but that might have been due to the strong smell of embrocation, mixed with sweat. Moments later, we began to walk out. Bob, on the PA system, was playing the "Eye of the Tiger" theme from *Rocky III* as usual. An oldie but a goodie, as he liked to say.

"Ladies and gentlemen, please welcome the teams from Bromley and your very own REIGATE ATHLETIC!" There was applause and some shouts of encouragement for us. We had some of the youth team players as mascots. I think they were U10s and had no idea what was going on. I took my little lad by the hand and walked onto the pitch. I looked down and he was wide-eyed as the chants from the Bromley supporters began. Compared to the normal smattering of applause that greeted our entrance, this was seriously noisy. We lined up in front of the main stand and then did the obligatory handshakes. I still don't really see the point of these. Both teams do it in a very perfunctory way, without any eye contact or words exchanged. The exception is sometimes that the goalkeepers will wish each other luck, as our brotherhood know that every keeper needs his share of that. Not today though. The Bromley keeper, kitted out in a natty all-purple kit, totally ignored me. Fair enough, I thought.

Handshakes over, John called us in, and we gathered in a huddle near the centre circle. Bob was reading out the teams and the Bromley fans were making quite a racket, so it wasn't easy to hear what he was saying. Not that it mattered. He pretty much said the same thing before every game; start well, give everything, total commitment, nothing else will do. Or words to that effect with a few adjectives thrown in for good measure. We broke the huddle and John went to do the coin toss. I pulled on my gloves. I'd bought myself a new pair. At £50 quid a time I couldn't afford to do that too often, but I felt that the game deserved it. Bromley had won the toss and elected to attack the goal where their supporters were massed behind. That meant I had to jog the length of the pitch to change ends. I did what I normally do when facing visiting supporters – I clapped them as I got close. I think it always took them a little by surprise and sometimes they even clapped back. It just avoids the usual abuse and vitriol that invariably comes the way of most keepers. It is often only a short-term reprieve and the first perceived injustice of any sort opens the floodgates. It's a strange thing. If people on the street called me the sort of things that the average opposition supporter called me during a match, the police would probably get involved. But in a football stadium, it seems that almost anything goes. As long as it's not racist, everyone turns a blind eye to it.

Occasionally, you get some good-humoured banter going with supporters behind the goal, but that is the exception rather than the rule. I remember playing in an FA Vase game away to a club near Southampton a couple of seasons ago, before I joined Reigate. I made a save early in the game and I started getting this abuse from behind the goal. I ignored it and wandered out to the edge of my box, but I could still hear it. It was one voice and he was effing and blinding and generally calling me every name under the sun. At half-time, as I was about to walk off, he was still going, so I looked at the culprit for the first time. To my surprise, he was a white-haired old man, supporting himself with a stick! I assumed it was some youngster. I was genuinely shocked. But it shows that they can be any age and from all walks of life.

After all the hype leading up to the game, it was something of a relief when the ref blew his whistle to start the match. We kicked off and used our normal routine of playing it back to Stevie, who knocked a long ball towards Antonio and Charlie, who had sprinted down the left touchline. The idea was to get into the opposition final third quickly. It wasn't often we won the ball, but sometimes it was headed out for a throw and it gives you a chance to build early pressure. This time it worked. Bromley had obviously watched our kick-offs and one of the centre-backs had lined up on that side, but Antonio challenged for the ball and stopped the defender getting a clean header and it went for a throw. For the next ten minutes, Bromley barely got out of their own half. We were closing them down quickly and giving them no time on the ball, picking off passes and winning a lot of tackles. If they had any notion that we might have an inferiority complex, it was quickly dispelled. Then, as so often happens, Bromley sprang a counter-attack.

Simo, our right-back, gave the ball away cheaply near the half-way line. With most of the team committed forward, suddenly we were left three v. two and we were the two! The Bromley left-winger slid a great through ball between John and Stan. I'd seen the pass coming and was already sprinting out of my area to clear it. But the Bromley centre-forward was quick. I consider myself no slouch, but what started off as 60:40 in my favour, was quickly becoming a 50:50. I was ten yards outside of the penalty area and, if he got there first, he'd touch it past me and have the simple task of slotting it into an empty net. I had to get there so I launched myself and slid the last couple of yards on the wet surface. So did their player. I just got there first and hacked the ball into touch. Their player got there a fraction after me. Instead of making contact with the ball, he made contact with my right ankle. There was no intent, but the speed of the collision made it a bone-juddering impact. According to Anna afterwards, I screamed as I got hit. I didn't like hearing that, but it certainly hurt. There is no protection down there and his studs had caught my ankle bone. I spoke to Melissa later, and she said she was out of the dugout and already running out onto the pitch towards me before the ref had even waved her on. She was worried there might have been a break.

I stayed still. Most players will tell you that the ones that roll around after going down aren't seriously hurt. It's the ones that stay still you worry about. The body effectively goes into a protective mode and is starting to run its own internal diagnostics. The first instruction to the body always seems to be, "Don't move while I figure out how bad the damage is." At this stage, all I could feel was extreme pain. I was aware of voices and then I heard Mel's voice.

"Go away. Let me have a look." The natural inclination for concerned teammates is to gather around. By all accounts the Bromley forward was also apologising to me and my teammates. But no one was blaming him. If anyone thinks there has been any malicious intent, that will often start a twenty-player pushing and shoving match. But it was just one of those things that happen in a contact sport. Not that was any consolation to me. The initial shock was wearing off and my ankle was radiating pain.

"Where did he catch you, Matt?"

"Left ankle," I managed to say through gritted teeth. Melissa gently pulled my hands away as I was clutching my leg just above the ankle.

"Oh my!" she said. That didn't sound good. I opened my eyes and looked. My sock had a great big hole in it and the ankle was lacerated with a couple of deep gouges caused by the studs sliding across the ankle upon impact. She made me lie on my back while she assessed the damage. She wiped off the blood and signalled to the bench for a substitution. As soon as she did that, the Bromley physio came out to help her. That's when everyone knew it was serious. As soon as Mel did that, Harry immediately told Smithy, who for once was on the bench as a substitute, to start warming up in case I couldn't continue. The Bromley physio was examining my ankle too now.

"Looks like he needs stitches at the very least. Can you move it? Can you wiggle your toes?" I could move my toes and confirmed I could. "I'm going to move your ankle now. Tell me how much it hurts on a scale of one to ten." Melissa was still wiping blood away while the Bromley physio, who was also a slightly older woman, gave me the instructions. She rotated my ankle to the left.

"Oww! Shit that hurts. Eight!" She rotated it the other

way and got pretty much the same response, although slightly more colourful this time. My eyes were shut tight, trying to deal with the pain, so I didn't see the two physios exchange looks and the Bromley physio mime for the stretcher. Mel nodded and the Bromley lady stood up and made the sign for a stretcher. Naturally, I was unaware of any of this. However, Anna, sitting in the stand, was watching in horror. She was sitting next to Simi again and Anna was clutching her hand. When the ground staff started to carry the stretcher on, she told me later she felt like throwing up and wanted to cry.

I was still lying on my back with my arms across my eyes as the physios worked on my ankle and had no idea that a stretcher was coming out until I heard Jeff, one of our groundsmen say, "Let's get him on the stretcher." That was when I opened my eyes and saw the orange stretcher next to me.

"No way! I'm not coming off!" Which sounds very macho and probably sounded very stupid to those around me. "It's not broken, is it?!" I didn't think so, but needed confirmation. It was the Bromley physio that responded.

"No, it's not broken, but there may be a fracture and there are a couple of nasty cuts that need stitches just above your ankle. There may be some bone bruising too, but we can't tell."

"Get me on my feet."

"Matt, you can't—" began Mel.

"Mel, HELP ME UP!" I needed to see if I could stand on it. The two physios helped me to my feet. That brought a generous round of applause from most of the crowd, including the Bromley supporters behind me. I think everyone was relieved I didn't need a stretcher. Simi told me later that all Anna could say was, "Thank God. Thank God he's OK. Thank God..."

I put weight on my left foot. Waves of pain shot through it as I did. But the pain was a little less acute than it had been when the Bromley physio was moving the ankle initially. Gingerly, I took a few steps on it unaided. It still hurt like hell, but I could walk, after a fashion anyway.

"Sit down. Take these while I strap your ankle." The Bromley physio didn't have what you might call a "bedside manner", but she was in charge and Mel was deferring to her. I assumed the tablets were paracetamol. She gave me four, which is probably not recommended normally, but with the aid of a water bottle, I swallowed them down. She then proceeded to strap my ankle, without taking the boot off, in a figure of eight.

"If I take the boot off to strap the ankle, it might balloon up. We'll take a look after the game, but this will hopefully get you through it."

It wasn't until later, when I had a chance to think about it, that I thought about the generosity of the act. She was their physio, helping a key opposition player. She could have told Mel I must come off. She could probably have convinced me. But while she was treating me, she was not Bromley's physio. She was simply a medical professional trying to help someone. It was a superb example of sport, and indeed non-league football at its best. So many people from our club went up and thanked her after the game and I know Brian sent her some flowers on behalf of the club, which I thought was a nice touch. Of course, at the time, all I cared about was playing. She finished the strapping and the two women hauled me to my feet. The initial extreme pain had subsided a bit. It didn't feel great, but OK. There was more applause as the two physios gathered up their gear and I limped back to my goal. Harry was looking at me with his arms spread wide in a sort of "Are you OK?" gesture. I gave him a thumbs up. Not that I was feeling "thumbs up", but I didn't want the opposition to see that I was any worse than I looked! Simi later said she had to almost physically restrain Anna from going down to the pitch at one point! When I got up to carry on playing, Anna was shocked.

"Is he nuts? He can't carry on. Someone tell him! He's crazy!" Several people were looking around and Simi said she had to enlist help from Charlie and Stevie's girlfriends just to calm her down and try and reassure her.

"Of course," Simi confided in me later, "we all thought you were nuts too!"

The play restarted with a throw-in. Harry's instructions to the team were to try and protect me as much as possible. I was still struggling and the first time I was forced to run on it, five minutes or so later, it hurt like hell. But now the shock had worn off, it was getting a little less sore. But I wasn't too sure how I was going to get through another sixty plus minutes. We were defending brilliantly though. A solid yellow and blue wall in front of Bromley. Our back four were immense. They knew I was unlikely to come to collect much, especially crosses, so they took responsibility to head or kick everything clear. But sooner or later, Bromley were going to find a way to test me. It came in the twenty-fourth minute. For once, we didn't close down their player quickly enough. I assumed their players had been told to shoot on sight to test me. Their central midfielder unleashed one from fully thirty yards. He caught it perfectly. Luckily for me, it was above me and only about a yard to my left, so I didn't have to move laterally too much. I jumped backwards and flicked it over the bar. Luckily, I could land on my back and not on my dodgy ankle. It was one of those saves that looked good rather than being especially difficult, but I was pleased to have made it. It seemed to lift my teammates too, who saw that I could still make saves and I wasn't a total passenger. We even started mounting a few attacks of our own as we got closer to half-time. We hadn't really carved out a chance worthy of the name, but then nor had they.

I was relieved when the whistle went for half-time. Smithy immediately rushed onto the pitch to help me, but I pushed him away and made a show of walking off unaided to let everyone, especially Bromley, know that I wasn't too bad. I made sure I didn't look for Anna in the stands as I walked past. Seeing her looking worried or upset wouldn't help. Selfish? Yes. But I had to be for the next forty-five minutes.

Mel re-did the strapping around the ankle and asked how it was feeling. I replied rather testily, as it seemed like a pretty daft question to ask. But she told me later that she had to make sure the strapping wasn't too tight in case it cut off the circulation to the foot. She then strapped a bag of ice to the ankle with cling film, which I could only just feel though the sock and the bandages.

Harry was encouraging us and talking through a few tactical changes, though to tell the truth I wasn't really listening. I was mentally getting myself ready to the second half. I knew it would hurt and I knew I wasn't going to be able to move like I normally could. But I had to find a way.

In all honesty, the second half was a pretty dour affair. We nullified most of Bromley's attacking intent. Harry had brought on an extra holding midfielder, Yannick Lemare, who had been plying his trade in the French third division last season. He was big and strong and well-suited to playing the role, though, like most French players, he had a nice touch too. The ankle was actually getting slightly easier as the game went on. I assumed the paracetamol were kicking in. I even came to gather a cross, much to the surprise of Stan, who heard me call for it and to his credit, left it for me rather than take matters into his own hands. Beno wasn't too far away with a curling free kick that shaved the left-hand upright, while a Bromley header from a corner went narrowly wide. I collected a couple of shots from distance that were pretty much straight at me.

I did have to dive to save an effort from just outside the box, but it was at a comfortable height and on my right side, so I was pushing off to jump with my right foot rather than the damaged left one. Harry had bravely brought on Addi for the last ten minutes, to see if his electric pace would unsettle the visitors.

With just over five minutes left, Bromley had probably their best chance to win it. It came from a free kick that was floated in from near the half-way line – too far out for me to come and claim. For once, neither John nor Stan could get to it. The Bromley centre-half and skipper met the ball beautifully and I could only watch as it flew towards the top corner, smacked against the bar, and bounced down before Jamie hooked it away. We were now hanging on a little, happy to take a draw and live to fight another day. In added time, Stan hoofed the ball clear. The Bromley right-back, just inside his own half, went to trap the ball, but made a complete mess of it. It bounced and went under his foot. Addi was in pursuit and although the full-back had a yard start, his was a standing start while Addi was eating up the ground. He got to the ball first and sprinted clear. He had just got into the box when the right-back made a desperate lunge from behind. He was never going to get the ball and instead clipped Addi's right leg. Down went our winger. No hesitation from the ref. He pointed to the spot. The Bromley players surrounded the ref telling him that Addi had dived. He hadn't, but footballers always complain when a pen is given. Hard to explain why, as refs rarely ever change their minds. Up walked John to take the kick. The Bromley fans behind the goal were booing loudly and doing everything they could to put him off. John was calmness itself. He strolled up to the ball as normal and hit it hard down the middle. The Bromley keeper had dived left but not far and had trailed his legs as he did. The ball struck a leg and ballooned over the bar. Pandemonium among the Bromley supporters. Their players were leaping all over their keeper, who was trying to remind everyone there was still a corner to face. John was on his knees by the penalty spot, with his head on the ground. Stevie hauled him to his feet and went to take the corner. The corner was headed clear and seconds later, the ref blew for full time. 0–0. That meant a replay.

We weren't sure if we were pleased or disappointed. Disappointed because we had a chance to win it, but pleased because we were still in it. Bromley looked happier, probably because they had been given a lifeline and the replay would be at their place. We shook hands with each other and the opposition and applauded our supporters, while the Bromley lads went and applauded their noisy fans at the Church End. My main priority was to get into the dressing room so Mel could assess the damage to my ankle. I saw Anna, who'd pushed her way to near the front. She looked worried. I waved and smiled to let her know I was OK. I'm not sure she believed me. It was a bit chaotic, so I didn't try to go and talk to her. The last thing I needed was getting trodden on by someone. I pushed through the crowd of people by the tunnel and finally made it to the relative sanctuary of the dressing room. John was already in there, sitting quietly with his head bowed. I was about to go over to talk to him, but in came Mel, all business. She started to unwrap the strapping around my ankle, asking me how it was feeling. It actually felt OK. Sore, but not as bad as when it first happened. I said that to Mel.

"Yep, adrenaline will do that, Matt. It's when all that wears off a little later that we'll get a real idea of the damage," she replied. She took off the last of the strapping. My sock had quite a lot of blood on it, as did the bandage around the wound.

"OK, Matt, let's get the sock and boot off." I gingerly unlaced the muddy boot and pulled it off. That did hurt. Finally, I pulled the tape off the sock and gently rolled it down and off my foot. Mel got to work with some antiseptic wipes, cleaning away the dried blood and bits of mud and grass that had stuck to the wound. I could see two deep gashes. One just above the ankle bone and one on it. The one on the bone was still bleeding.

"Looks like one or both might need a couple of stitches, Matt. I'm going to put these butterfly stitches on now, but I suggest you get down to the hospital and have it looked at properly." That wasn't what I wanted to hear. That meant going to Casualty on a Saturday evening and for something like this, that was certainly not critical, I could end up there for three or four hours. "The good news is that I don't see too much swelling. This will hurt, but I've got this bucket of water and thrown a load of ice cubes in there. If you can put your foot in there and leave it for ten minutes, that will help reduce any swelling." Never argue with a physio. I slowly lowered my foot into the freezing water. It was excruciating! To say it took my breath away was an understatement. Absolute agony for the first minute or two until the cold does its work and numbs the foot. I sat back with my eyes shut, gritting my teeth and just waiting for the pain to subside. Slowly, very slowly, it did, and I gradually let my breath out. Most of the lads were now in the dressing room and a few were asking how I was. I gave largely neutral answers. I knew they all wanted to know if I was going to be fit for the replay.

Just then the Bromley physio popped her head around the door.

"Hi, just thought I'd check in to see how he is?"

"Please come on in," said Mel, smiling, "Matt, this is Vanessa. She really helped me out on the pitch today."

"Hi Vanessa and thank you for all your help. It was really good of you," I said, half-hoping she'd offer to take a look.

Not that I didn't have confidence in Mel, but clearly Vanessa had many years more experience and it wouldn't hurt to get a second opinion. She was clearly a mind reader too.

"No problem, guys, glad I could help. Melissa, I don't want to interfere, and you've done a great job, but do you want me to take a quick look?"

"Yes, please," Mel replied quickly. Luckily, she was no prima donna and was more than happy to get advice, as she was still learning her trade. Vanessa smiled and walked into the room, ignoring our half-naked players. She gently lifted my foot out of the bucket and started to move it gently.

"Let me know if any of this really hurts. It will hurt a bit, but I just want to make sure there's nothing more serious like a fracture or ligament damage." I nodded and held my breath, hoping that she wouldn't find anything worse. She rotated the ankle and then moved it up and down and side to side. It was sore, but nothing she did triggered any dramatic surge in pain. She kept nodding to herself as I reported largely negative results to her manipulation.

"OK, I don't think there's any significant damage. Mainly bruising and of course those two stud marks," she said, peering more closely at the lacerations.

"Mel thought that they might need stitches…" I left the unanswered question hanging there. Was Mel right?

"Yep, she's right. I think it would probably be a good idea to close them up a little. But you only need a few in each. No big deal," Vanessa said with a wink at me. "Unfortunately, though, for the replay…" Uh, oh, I thought, she's going to rule me out. "I think you'll be OK to play. Unfortunate for us that is!"

"Phew! You had me going there for a moment! But seriously, thank you for all your help. You've been really great. Just need to get ready for a fun evening at the local hospital waiting to be stitched up, instead of going out to dinner with my girlfriend." I made a face. I could imagine Anna making even more of a face, as we were due to have dinner with another couple that evening. Vanessa looked at me, as if weighing up what she was going to say.

"OK. So, here's the thing. I am a qualified nurse. I'm training to get my physio qualifications as I fancy setting up on my own, I'm doing Bromley this season to get some practical experience and because their previous guy got poached last summer." She paused. "I can put stitches in for you. I'm obviously not able to give you any anaesthetic, but once your foot has been in the ice bucket for fifteen minutes, you probably won't feel a thing. I can't guarantee it won't hurt, but I can do it here and now. May not be quite as neat as a hospital might do it, but down on your ankle, I doubt anyone will notice anyway. Up to you," she said, shrugging.

"Wow! That would be brilliant! Thank you so much! It will save me from the even bigger risk to my health if I had to cancel dinner!" Mel rolled her eyes at that and Vanessa smiled. Even if it did hurt a bit, it would be less painful than four hours at East Surrey Hospital.

"Right. Get your foot back in that bucket. Mel, chuck some more ice in. I'll pop back in ten minutes with my sewing kit." She walked out, chuckling.

"No way that you are going to have that done in here," Beno said, wincing. "I hate needles."

Antonio chipped in. "Yeah, man. I do too."

"Hey, it's me that's having it done, not you," I pointed out. "Bunch of wimps."

Harry, media duties finished for now, finally made it into the dressing room. The first thing he did was to come over and check on me. I gave him the relatively good news that I should be fit for the replay. He looked relieved. I also told him how much Vanessa had helped me and Mel.

"I'll speak to Brian, and we'll get some flowers sent from the club on Monday. Least we can do." With that, he went to John to console him and tell him to get his head up. A lot of the lads had hit the showers already as Harry had been so long doing interviews.

"I'm not going to say anything to the lads now," he told Jez. "I'll ask them to come in on Tuesday night, so we can discuss the game today and prepare for Saturday and the replay. Let 'em know, will you?" Sometimes, we came to the club, looked at videos and chatted about the performance with the boss and the coaches. I doubted we'd do any training at all on Tuesday and assumed the replay would be on the following Tuesday night at their place. The foot was completely numb by now and the dressing room was the normal chaotic scene of muddy and sweaty kit being thrown into a pile, with tape, discarded energy drinks and strapping all over the floor. We all took it in turns to clean up before we left any dressing room, home or away. Harry was a stickler for showing respect for 'our home', but also showing the same respect when we were on the road. There was plenty of banter now and several of my teammates were suggesting I should have got an Oscar for my dramatic yell when I got hurt. Footballers are not renowned for being sympathetic. It was already being suggested that I'd "milked it".

"I go down and I get Mel. Matt goes down and *he* has to have TWO physios! One's not enough for our star keeper!" Stevie was leading the abuse. Even Mel was grinning away. I was largely ignoring them. Trying to defend myself would have been like a red flag to a bull. Even John was now getting good-natured stick for his penalty miss. The lads knew they had to get him to forget it, and taking the mickey was one way of showing him we were all relaxed about it.

"John lives near Bromley, doesn't he?" Charlie asked.

"He was probably scared he'd get lynched and missed it on purpose!"

John wasn't having any of that. "Least I hit the target with my pens, bro!" That brought howls of laughter. Charlie took one in pre-season and it went about ten feet over the bar. Arguably one of the worst pens I'd ever seen. It was all good. We were a tight bunch. You can't have that sort of exchange if there are factions or people who don't get on in a team. Not everyone will be best mates. That's impossible. But it soon becomes poisonous if a couple of players dislike each other. People invariably take sides and that is a killer for team spirit. When that happens, someone needs to leave the club. The banter was still flowing when Vanessa came back in.

"Ready, Matt?" I smiled and nodded, trying to look nonchalant. In reality, the idea of having stitches put in without any anaesthetic seemed far less appealing now than it had done fifteen minutes earlier. But the reaction of a few of the lads was priceless and made me feel like a real hero!

"Whoa! I'm out of here!" Beno quickly stuffed his gear into his bag and headed for the door, closely followed by Antonio, who was barefoot as he hurried out, carrying his shoes and socks. Some of the other lads had been in the showers when Vanessa had been offering her services. Jamie and Stevie were equally adamant that they needed to be out of the door before the stitches were put in. Vanessa sighed heavily.

"Mel, help me get this young man into your physio room. We'll do it there, as there are so many big babies in here!" She was smiling as she said it. They helped me hop out of the room into the tiny room which had a physio's table in it. If you had more than two people in there, it was crowded. I got myself onto the table and lay back. I decided to stare at a damp patch on the ceiling that looked a little like a map of Italy. Although I wasn't especially squeamish, I could do without watching the needle going into my skin. My foot was very numb and that was some consolation. The procedure took about twenty minutes in total, largely because Vanessa was talking Mel through it. The numbness was wearing off by the time the second lot of stitches were done. I felt the sensation of the flesh being pulled for the first set, but they didn't really hurt. The second lot did. Quite a lot. I tried to think about something else. Finally, Vanessa announced she was done. I sat up and took a look. There was a lot of black thread.

"You'll need to have these removed in about 10 days. Your GP should be able to do that for you. Wear an ankle support if you have one. That will help keep any swelling contained as it will probably swell, especially overnight. I'll show Mel how to strap it up and protect it as much as possible. Of course, I can't guarantee it won't get kicked by someone. If it does, make sure Mel knows so she can check the stitches. It will hurt. That's for sure. But hopefully you'll be OK." She started to pack up her gear. "Just one thing. Don't tell my lot I did this for you. They'll be mad at me for getting one of the opposition fit!"

I promised that her secret was safe with us. I hobbled back to the dressing room. I was going to be the last to get showered and changed, except for John and Simon, who were on cleaning duty and were taking their time. Mel put a plastic bag over the foot taped at the top to keep the stitches dry. The hot water felt good as I relaxed for the first time in a few hours.

8

I had only just got through the door of the bar when Anna came rushing up.

"Oh my God, Matt! Are you OK? The guys said you have loads of stitches in your foot!" The words were tumbling out as she hugged me. "You shouldn't be standing on it. You need to sit down. I was so worried when—"

"Hey Anna! Slow down! I'm OK. Really." I held her face with both hands and looked into her eyes, smiling. "I'll live!"

She looked a little relieved and smiled tentatively. "You... wanker! You had me SO scared for a while. I thought you were hurt bad. That must have been the longest five minutes of my life. When they brought the stretcher on, I thought you had bust your leg or something awful. And I could not *believe* that you carried on playing. Are you crazy?!"

"Well, I am dating you, so probably yes!"

She laughed at last. "Yeah, my mom would probably agree that you need to be crazy to date me! Let's go find a table and get a drink. I need one!"

Jamie and his girlfriend Louise had a table, but when

Louise spotted the two of us approaching, she jumped up, hauled Jamie out of his seat and offered us the table and the seats. Jamie went off grumbling about "wounded heroes". We sat down and Anna was about to get us drinks when I spotted Vanessa with the Bromley lads. I explained to Anna exactly what she had done. Anna immediately got up and went over to her. I saw her give Vanessa a big hug and the two of them were talking animatedly for several minutes. Harry then wandered over and shook Vanessa's hand. I doubted her request to keep things under wraps was going to work. Just then I felt someone tap me on the shoulder. I looked around. It was Jess.

"You do know how to make yourself the centre of attention, Matt. You're a journalist's dream!"

"Yeah, I just do it, so you have stuff to write about. Just doing my bit to help the local press." I smiled, though I was also a tad nervous as Anna was not far away. Possibly a bit guilty too, because I did enjoy Jess's company.

"So, how is the ankle? I heard you had stitches. Will you be fit for the replay?" She had quickly switched into journalist mode. "I have to say a lot of us were worried when we saw them call for the stretcher."

"Not as worried as me!" I laughed. "But our physio and the Bromley physio were just brilliant. It says everything you need to know about football at this level, that she came to help me like she did, even though she was helping an opponent." I gave Jess a bit more detail about how she came into our dressing room and all that she had done.

"Wow. I mean, I saw her helping on the pitch and, to be honest, I've seen that before. They are all medical professionals and they wouldn't hesitate to help one another. But all that stuff after the game too. That's pretty amazing. It would make a great extra piece. Putting rivalry aside for the greater good. I think I'll go and chat to them both. Thanks, Matt. Another nice story you've handed me! You're a star!" She turned to go. "Oh hi!" She had almost bumped into Anna.

"Hey there," said Anna, without a great deal of warmth. "Pick up anything good from my boyfriend for your rag?" Ouch. I certainly didn't miss either the words "my boyfriend" or "rag" in the sentence. Nor did Jess. She smiled sweetly.

"Your boyfriend has been really helpful as usual. I'm just off to interview the two ladies that patched Matt up. It will make a nice story for my 'rag." Without waiting for a response, Jess spun on her heels and sauntered off, leaving Anna silently seething.

"So, what time are we meeting your friends?" I know exactly what time we were meeting, but I was trying to redirect the conversation and take Anna's attention away from Jess for a moment.

"Why the hell is she always talking to you, Matt?!" Anna's voice was steely. "There are ten other players in the goddamn team." She was still looking in Jess's direction, who was on the far side of the bar chatting to Vanessa, while a couple of the Bromley lads were hovering hopefully nearby.

"Anna," I sighed, a little theatrically so she knew the topic was not of any interest to me. "She's just doing her job. She said she talks to me because I'm a little different from the average footballer, so she gets some different things to write about. That's all it is. Nothing else." I reached for Anna's hand as I finished. At my touch she yanked her hand away as if she'd been stung by a bee.

"Jeez! Men can be so goddamn blind sometimes." She marched off towards the ladies' room, leaving me perplexed and slightly annoyed. I didn't really get how it was my fault. In fact, I didn't really get what I'd done except respond to questions asked by a journalist. I could hardly refuse to talk to her. I'd even had my ankle stitched up, without any anaesthetic just so that we could still go out this evening. I sat there with my Diet Coke thinking that life was pretty unfair sometimes.

Just then, Harry came over and sat down next to me. He wanted to know how my ankle was and whether I'd be fit for the replay on Tuesday week. Normally the replay would have been a few days after the first game, but Bromley's ground was having some repairs done to a floodlight, so it had been agreed with the FA and the two clubs that if a replay was needed, it would be Tuesday week. As things had turned out, that was a stroke of luck for me. Harry suggested that I go and see the AFC Wimbledon club doctor. He had been a coach there for a couple of seasons, and we had first met when we were both at the Dons. There was still a link between the clubs and Harry would sometimes ask for the occasional favour. In return, we sometimes hosted their development team games at our ground, and, on a few occasions, we'd had one of their players on loan, usually a player who needed some game time after an injury. Harry gave me the doctor's mobile and said he'd already spoken to him. An appointment had been arranged for the next morning at 9.30am. I inwardly groaned. That was the part of the week that was reserved for Anna and me to spend a little bit of quality time together. But I appreciated the effort that Harry had gone to and I also knew that I really did need to get it checked. Tomorrow morning would be a sensible time to have a look at it and decide what to do. Mission accomplished, Harry moved on to his next conversation, leaving me wondering whether to mention the appointment to Anna now and risk making her mood worse or wait until later tonight, when hopefully her mood would have improved.

I looked up and saw Anna walking back towards me with Mel, the two of them chatting and, much to my relief, laughing. Anna was smiling as she sat down, and Mel headed to the bar.

"OK, pal, I guess I owe you an apology," I must have looked

surprised. "Yeah, yeah. So, I got a little bit annoyed by your lady friend, I admit."

"But I—" I tried to interrupt, but Anna just held up her hand.

"When a girl tries to say sorry, you need to hear her out." I closed my mouth and did what she suggested.

"I bumped into Mel in the restroom and she said to me how lucky I was to have a fella who was prepared to have stitches without any pain killer just so that he wouldn't let his girlfriend down on a night out. I felt like a real jerk when she was telling me, and really moved that you would do something like that for me." She was looking into my eyes, smiling as she did so. "You are really something, Matt. Maybe I can make it up to you later," she said with a wicked smile.

"Maybe," I replied, grinning. I did think of mentioning my appointment with the doctor the next morning, but something told me it could wait.

9

The alarm on my phone sounded and I quickly reached to switch it off. Anna stirred, mumbled something and turned over, snuggling into my body. The evening had been fun, but at a certain point, both of us wanted to be alone. Anna had made that clear, both by telling her mates how I needed some rest after the nasty injury earlier, coupled with her hand high up on my thigh on two or three occasions under the table. I thought it rude not to reciprocate and made her gasp at one point, which she covered up with a quick fit of coughing. But by the end of the evening, we were both acting like a pair of horny teenagers, and there was a trail of discarded clothing that led from the hallway in Anna's flat all the way to the bed. I smiled as I recalled the rest of the night.

But the smile gave way to a grimace a few moments later as I swung my legs out of bed and put a little weight on my injured ankle. I should really have spent time icing it last night, but I had other things on my mind! Right now, the ankle was reminding me that perhaps that hadn't been the smartest thing to do. I hobbled to the bathroom and turned on the light. The ankle was a bit of a mess. I was pleased to see some of the bruising had already come out, but less pleased to see the area around the stitches had bled a little, mainly because Anna would be suitably unimpressed if I'd ruined another set of bed linen. I flexed the ankle. Understandably, it felt stiff and sore. It was a good job I didn't have to play for a week and the replay was still ten days away.

Finishing in the bathroom, I limped into the hallway to try and track down yesterday's clothes. For once, I had actually thought to pack some clean clothes, but they were in a bag in my car and, for some reason, they hadn't crossed my mind the previous evening, once Anna had started whispering some very creative ideas for the night ahead in my ear as we parked up. So, I had to recover last night's clothes before I could go and bring in the clean ones. My shoes, shirt and black jeans were easy to find, but there was no sign of my socks and boxer shorts. I shuffled slowly into the bedroom, my eyes growing accustomed to the half-light and picking out Anna's bra and one of my socks. I assumed my boxers were probably somewhere in the wrecked bed. I decided not to disturb Anna, who was asleep again. At least I had located enough clothing to allow me to go down to the car without alarming the other residents.

Luckily, there was a lift in the block, otherwise it would be four flights of stairs to negotiate, which wouldn't have been much fun. Moving slowly and carefully, as the pavement was wet from all the overnight rain, I made my way to the car. I grabbed my bag from the boot and headed back into the flat to change. Once fully dressed, I scribbled a quick note to Anna and left it on the kitchen table. It was already 8.45am so I needed to get moving.

The only good thing about an appointment early on a Sunday morning is that the roads are likely to be quiet, and so it proved. I made it to the address in Southfields by 9.20. As I pulled up, I saw the front door open and a young bloke wearing an AFC Wimbledon jacket walked out. At least I had the right address. The door was still open and a tall, silver-haired man stood in the doorway.

"Good morning," he said. "Harry's goalkeeper, I assume?"

"Morning. Yes, that's me." I locked the car and walked up the path to the house. "Thank you for seeing me."

"Not at all. Come on in. I'm Alan, by the way." He held out his hand.

"Matt," I replied, shaking the doctor's hand.

The doctor walked into the first room on the right. It had been converted into something that looked like a GP's surgery, only a lot smarter and newer.

"Right, shoes, socks and trousers off and then lay on the couch so I can take a look."

The physio couch looked brand new and was certainly a step or two up from the battered one at the club Mel was forced to use. The couch's back was set in an upright position which enabled me to see what was going on. The doctor first peered closely at the wound and the stitches. Then he gently moved my ankle from side to side and up and down. One movement brought a sharp intake a breath.

"Hmm. That's sore, is it?" He looked quizzically at me. Part of me was thinking I should just say no and man up, but I also realised that if I wanted to play in the replay, I'd better be honest.

"Yeah, a bit, mainly around the ankle bone."

"That's to be expected, as I imagine the bone took a fair bit of the impact." He prodded around the area with finger and thumb. My entire body was tensed up as each bit of pressure from the doctor's fingers sent waves of pain of varying degrees through my body. After a few minutes he stopped probing.

"Well, the good news is that I don't think there's any break or fracture there, nor does there appear to be any ligament damage. But as there's still a fair bit of swelling so we won't know for sure for a few days. There's the outside chance of a hairline fracture or a piece chipped off the bone, but I don't think that's the case. The stitches look fine, and the wound itself looks clean, so the main thing is to get the swelling down. Lots of icing and elevation for the next forty-eight hours."

"So, what do you think my chances of playing on Saturday are?" I had a feeling I knew what the answer would be.

"Well, Harry said he wants you back playing as soon as possible, but without risking further injury. If you play Saturday, I'd say you run a real risk of not being fit for the FA Cup replay. One knock on there on Saturday and it's likely to swell up again, not to mention the chance of the stitches getting torn. If I were you, I wouldn't. And I'm happy to tell Harry that's my recommendation." He smiled as he said it. "Anyway, that's it, so if you want to get your things back on while I wash my hands."

"Thank you, Alan. Really appreciate you fitting me on a Sunday morning."

"It wasn't a problem. I've got a couple of other players coming over this morning, so I was glad to help Harry out." He showed me to the door. "Give me a ring on Wednesday and let me know how it feels then."

"Will do. Thanks again."

A range of conflicting thoughts went through my mind. On one hand I was relieved that it didn't sound like it was anything more serious than bruising. I didn't like the idea of missing the game next Saturday, but it was probably the sensible thing to do if I wanted to guarantee playing in the replay. I knew I should probably let Harry know. But then again, why spoil his Sunday morning? If he was that desperate to know, he'd no doubt call me, or more likely the doctor direct. I put my phone back in my jacket. First things first. Get myself back to Anna and figure out what we were going to do with the day.

I made good time back to Anna's flat. I rang on her doorbell. She hadn't given me a key to her place and I hadn't asked for one – I thought that was her decision, if and when she wanted to. Anna opened the door in a big fleecy dressing gown. She looked as though she'd just got up, but still managed to look drop-dead gorgeous.

"Hey luvvie. I saw your note. How did you get on?"

I ignored the question and took her in my arms and gave her a long, passionate kiss as we stood in the doorway.

"Wow! You sure know how to greet a girl! But maybe we'd better get inside before we do that again!" She closed the door and took my hand, leading me towards the bedroom. I didn't resist too much.

By the time we'd both showered and dressed, I was starving. I could never get over how little Anna ate, especially for breakfast. She was having some coffee, while I was wading through a big bowl of bananas, grapes and natural yoghurt, which would be followed by toast and a couple of cups of coffee. We sat at her breakfast bar, just enjoying that feeling of not having to do anything in particular. I gave Anna a quick run-down on my visit to the Wimbledon doctor, including his recommendation.

"You ARE going to listen to him and give next Saturday a miss. Right?" It sounded more like a statement than a question.

"Well, he said to call him Wednesday and tell him how it's feeling. I think I'll probably wait until Thursday to make a final decision."

Anna rolled her eyes and sighed heavily.

"You are just plain nuts. You know that, right? You carry

on like this, pal, and you won't be able to walk by the time you're fifty!"

"You planning on being around still?" I asked, smiling and changing the subject. Or so I thought.

"Nice try. I'm trying to figure out whether to be mad with you, or just give up on you ever seeing sense when it comes to that game and your body!"

We were both looking into each other's eyes and smiling. She was making an effort to sound exasperated, but it really wasn't working. We ended up deciding that a lazy morning of reading the papers and drinking coffee was a perfect way to spend a damp and dreary Sunday. In deference to my injured status, Anna popped out to get the papers and a few bits and pieces. I raided her freezer for the ice-cube tray and found a plastic bag to put them in. I spent twenty minutes with the makeshift ice pack on my foot. Just as I was removing it, my phone pinged, and I saw I had a message from Harry. It was short and to the point:

Spoke to Alan. Resting you Saturday. Want you back for Tuesday. See you at training on Thursday. H

Well, Anna would be pleased, I thought, and at least the decision was now out of my hands. I admit I had been toying with playing on Saturday. I usually healed pretty quickly. But the decision was no longer mine.

Anna arrived back about half an hour later, with a couple of Caffè Nero coffees and fresh croissants. We sat on the sofa and chatted while we drank the coffee and munched on the croissants. She suggested we spent the day at home, which surprised me, as Anna loved exploring the shops and surrounding area. She surprised me even more when she suggested we go over to my place so I could watch the football on TV. It was Liverpool v. Chelsea and Anna knew I was a big Chelsea fan. I had Sky Sports installed at home, but Anna didn't for some odd reason. I must have looked surprised, so Anna explained her thinking:

"Hey, you've got a bad ankle and need to rest it. I've got a bit of work to do to prepare for a meeting first thing Monday and I know you're desperate to see the match. So, we can pretend we're an old married couple this afternoon. You relax and watch sport on TV, and I work!"

It sounded good to me. I didn't enquire whether she was going to stay the night or not. I'd be able to work that one out based upon whether she took a bag and spare clothes with her. I doubted she would, as she liked to be organised on a Monday morning and staying at mine wasn't ideal in terms of logistics. In the end she didn't stay, but that didn't stop it being a really lovely, chilled day, where we just enjoyed being with each other. It didn't hurt that Chelsea managed to salvage a draw with a last-gasp equaliser too. With the rest and the icing, the ankle was feeling a bit easier by the end of the day. I'd already emailed my boss and told her that I'd hurt my ankle and was planning to work from home on Monday and maybe Tuesday. She was fine about it. I usually managed to get more done from home anyway, as there was no wasted time commuting, or with the chat that goes on in an open-plan office.

But although I enjoyed the day, my ankle and the FA Cup replay were never far from my mind. I knew it was going to be a long week ahead and that I had to be patient. It wasn't miraculously going to get better in forty-eight hours. I was already mentally adjusting to the idea I was going to have to miss the league game on the Saturday. Even before I'd got his text, I'd have put money on Harry telephoning the Wimbledon doctor for an update within an hour or so of my visit there. Harry would always go with medical advice. I knew from chatting to the lads that there were other managers that just expected you to play through the pain, often at the risk of making it worse or creating a long-term issue. They were more concerned about the results rather than the player. Harry wasn't like that. He listened to medical advice, as well as to the player. There were always players who wanted to play in spite of carrying an injury. Sometimes it was because they didn't want to let their teammates down, but other times it was because they were worried about losing their place in the side. Selfless or selfish? The manager had to decide. But Harry had made the decision already about Saturday, which at least meant I didn't have to.

Anna left around 9pm. She had cooked dinner for both of us before leaving, but warned me as she walked out of the door that I'd better not get used to being spoiled, as it wasn't going to last. She got a slap on her toned backside for that. In return, I got an extended middle finger as she walked slowly and very provocatively to the lift. I was still grinning when I closed the front door.

10

The draw for the Second Round always takes place on the Monday after the First Round matches. We were in the draw, even though we still had the replay against Bromley to get through. I decided my ankle wasn't best suited to watching the draw standing in the crowded bar at the club, just waiting for someone to accidently kick me or tread on me. I consoled myself with a beer while Anna and I watched it live on the BBC.

It was very much the same formula as it was before. Ex-pros, two bags of balls and a lot of excited footballers and fans the length and breadth of the country waiting to see who their team would face. It wasn't quite as much fun as being with everyone in the clubhouse, but I knew I'd made the right decision.

I didn't feel quite the same excitement as I had for the draw for the previous round, mainly because we hadn't yet secured our place in the next round. Mind you, there were a lot of big clubs in the Second Round and all of us were hoping for one of those big teams. Home or away, I don't think any of us cared. The draw was still in its early stages when the presenter read out:

"Number fifty-five, Grimsby Town."

"Will play...number forty-seven, Bromley or Reigate Athletic."

I sighed. Not the glamour tie we'd been hoping for. Grimsby were near the bottom of League Two and were having a poor season.

"I guess that's not what you wanted, right?" asked Anna, looking at the expression on my face. "I guess you'll just have to beat those guys too then before you match up against Chelsea!" She always made me smile.

The tie was due to be played in the second week of December, which was one bit of good news as far as I was concerned.

The week dragged as I thought it would. Although the ankle improved a little, I was really glad I didn't have to walk on it much and in the end worked from home for the whole week. I ended up popping down to the ground on Tuesday night to see Mel. She couldn't do much except gently massage the area to try and help disperse some of the fluid gathered around the ankle. She was gentle, but that didn't stop me tensing up every time she touched it and sweat breaking out on my body as her fingers did their work. Harry popped his head around the door to check how I was doing, but only for a minute. It's a funny thing. When you're injured and not playing, you get a strange feeling of dislocation. You're no longer part of the group anymore. Most injured players don't go into the dressing room before or after a game. It's not that they're made to feel unwelcome, it's simply that feeling of being of no value to the team. A spare part. I felt that way already.

By Wednesday I was feeling a little stir-crazy. I'd rung the Wimbledon doctor and we'd arranged for me to go and see him on the Saturday morning at AFC Wimbledon's ground in Plough Lane. I hadn't been to their new ground, so it would be interesting to see it. I hadn't seen Anna since Monday as she'd had to go to Paris for a few days for some new client pitch, so I had to content myself with The Champions League group stage on TV. As usual, Chelsea were making life hard for themselves, with two draws from their opening couple of games in their group and a scrappy 2–1 home win against a poor Lyon side didn't auger well for the latter stages. I did manage to speak to Anna for a short while, but she was out to dinner somewhere in the centre of Paris and it was noisy, so the call was brief. I will admit to a little pang of jealousy that she was out in Paris with some male colleagues, which surprised me a little. I knew she wasn't the sort to mess around and I knew she would be honest with me if she ever wanted to change our relationship. I shook my head sadly at my own insecurity, putting it down to having too much time on my hands.

By Thursday, I needed to go food shopping so went to the local Asda. I spent much of the shop desperately trying to avoid every other shopper, most of whom seemed to be on a mission to either step on my foot or run over it with a trolley. One or two got the glare I normally reserve for match officials. That evening I went back to the ground to see Mel, who was much more positive about the progress I'd made. She said the swelling had gone down quite a bit and there was better movement in the joint. It did feel a bit better, but it was good to hear Mel sounding positive too. It didn't stop me feeling like a spare part again though, in spite of a few of the lads poking their heads around the door to give me some good-natured abuse for missing training.

Anna returned on Thursday afternoon, but as I had to spend the evening at the ground being treated by Mel, we agreed to wait until the next night.

By Friday evening, I found I was really looking forward to seeing her. It had only been a few days, but I had missed her. I stopped off at a supermarket to pick up a bunch of flowers for her.

She seemed just as pleased to see me as I was to see her. She opened her door and I didn't even make it inside before she threw herself into my arms and we spent a minute or two just holding each other. Once I made it across the threshold, she picked up a gift-wrapped box off the coffee table.

"Just a little something I picked up while I was in Paris. I hope you like them," she said, looking just a little nervous. I undid the wrapping and opened a small black box. Inside was a pair of expensive-looking cufflinks for my work shirts.

"Wow! I wasn't expecting anything at all. These are really lovely." I looked up at Anna, slightly stunned.

"Well, as the saying goes, I saw them and thought of you," she said, smiling. "But I do hope you like them."

"Like them?! They're awesome, to use one of your favourite words! Just perfect." I paused for a second then looked up smiling. "Thinking of me while you were away then?"

"Oh, every now and again, in between trying to deal with all the hot French guys who kept trying to get me in the sack." The smile was more of a smirk now.

"Yeah, I guess it must be hard for you, being such a guy magnet," I said with mock sympathy.

"It is tough, let me tell you. But I kinda have this thing for one guy right now."

"Oh really?" I asked, pulling her to me.

"Yep. He's OK. Bit of a jerk sometimes, but sort of cute too." Anna was snuggling into me.

"Umm…you said you'd arranged for us to meet some of your pals?" my voice tailed off as Anna kissed me.

"They can wait. I think we ought to test your fitness levels hon," she said, taking me by the hand and leading me into her bedroom.

An hour later, we'd managed to make ourselves presentable for a night out. We ended up in a local restaurant in the middle of Reigate and stayed there until the owner practically threw us out close to midnight. Normally, I would have been reluctant to stay out eating and drinking on a Friday night, but with no game the following day, I decided to let my hair down a little, especially as neither of us were driving. One of the other couples had volunteered to give us a lift back.

The next morning wasn't pretty. We both had hangovers, although Anna was suffering more and decided to return to bed after we'd both got up around 9am. I didn't have that luxury as I had to be at Wimbledon's ground by 10.30. Saturday morning traffic around Reigate was always a little busy, as the "yummy mummies", as Anna called them, were out and about. I knew from painful experience that the Wimbledon area could be busy too, although the ground itself was really Southfields and not in the town itself. Nonetheless, Saturday morning traffic was always a bit unpredictable and delays a strong possibility, so I wanted to give myself enough time. Having gulped down some toast and coffee, together with a couple of paracetamols, I said goodbye to Anna and told her I'd see her later. There was a muffled grunt from under the duvet which I assumed was goodbye.

In the end I made pretty good time, and an open window combined with the paracetamol meant my head was soon feeling better. I pulled up at the gate at Plough Lane and I had to admit I was impressed when the security man looked down on his list and said I was expected. The car park was almost empty, though that would probably change soon as the Dons were at home that afternoon. I parked in a visitor bay just inside the main entrance. Alan had told me where to go and I made my way to the players' entrance. There was a security guard on duty at a desk just inside the door and, having given my name, it only took a quick check of the list and I was waved through.

I found the medical centre just opposite the dressing rooms. I knocked on the door and heard Alan's voice telling me to come in.

Alan was standing with a man dressed in a Wimbledon tracksuit. They were both looking down at what I assumed was one of the Dons' players, who was lying face down on one of the treatment tables.

"Hi Matt. Pop yourself down on that table over there and I'll be with you in a moment."

I'd dressed in tracksuit bottoms with shorts underneath to make things easier to dress and undress. I took off my trainers, socks and tracksuit bottoms and sat on the table.

"I think Morten will be ready to play next Saturday, but I wouldn't risk him today or Tuesday," Alan was saying to the tracksuited figure.

He'd had his back to me when I'd come in, but now I recognised him. It was the Dons manager, Jimmy Doyle. I assumed the player was Morten Lundqvist, the Danish striker who'd already scored eleven times this season.

"Shit. I was hoping he might be ready for Tuesday." Doyle sounded exasperated.

"I know, Jimmy. But bring him back too quickly and that hamstring will go again. I pretty much guarantee it. And it's a strong possibility he'd do more damage to it and be out for much longer."

Doyle sighed.

"Sorry Alan. I know it's not your fault, but with Pierso and Macca out too, we're short up front. But that's my problem not yours!" He slapped the doctor on the shoulder and turned to face me.

"Harry's keeper? Am I right?"

"Yes, that's right," I said, surprised that Doyle knew who I was. "And I just wanted to say I'm really grateful for the help that the club's given me."

"No problem at all. I've known Harry for years. We both played in the academy here and have stayed in touch ever since. I even tried to get him here as my assistant a while back, but he liked where he was. My loss, but we keep in touch. Anyway, I've got a fair bit to do so I'd better crack on. Good to meet you and I hope you're fit for the replay."

"Cheers. Best of luck today and for the rest of the season," I offered, as Doyle smiled and turned to leave.

"Thanks, son. Alan, see you soon. Morten, once you're finished here, drop by my office and we'll finish off that conversation."

Doyle walked out and, a few minutes later, the doctor told Lindqvist that he was done and free to go too. The Danish striker gingerly got off the treatment table and headed towards the door, nodding in my direction as he left. Alan walked over to me. "Sorry to keep you waiting, Matt. How's it feeling?"

"It's OK. Much less painful to walk on, but I haven't tried anything other than walking."

The Dons doctor didn't say anything. He looked at the ankle and prodded it a couple of times to test my reaction.

"That hurt?" He asked, peering over the top of his glasses.

"A bit, but not too bad," I replied.

He repeated the prodding on a few more parts of the ankle and then picked my leg up and started to rotate the ankle, gently at first but then with a little more gusto.

"How's that? Any sharp pain anywhere?"

"No, more of a dull ache than sharp pain."

"That's good. OK. Try and push against my hand. Good. How's that feeling?"

"OK. A bit sore, but nothing too bad."

"That's good. The wounds have healed nicely, and stitches look fine too. Although it's probably a day or so too soon, I think taking them out now gives them more time to heal naturally rather than do it tomorrow or Monday. I'll just grab my scissors." He went over to a small medical bag on a table.

"So, how am I looking for Tuesday?"

Alan returned with a small pair of scissors and began to cut through the thread, pulling it out as he did.

"If you were a professional footballer, I'd say yes, you're fit to play. But you're playing for fun at the end of the day. You have other priorities, such as your day job, to consider. If you get another knock on the ankle it might put you out for two to three weeks. Equally, if you get an impact right on that wound, as the skin is only just healing, it will probably open up again. That's all I can really say. It's up to you, Matt."

I was silent for a moment as I digested what I'd just heard. I was a little disappointed I had to admit. I'd fully expected to be told I'd be fine for the game on Tuesday. Now I was being told it was basically my decision.

"Understood. Thanks, Alan. What will you say to Harry?"

"Exactly the same. Basically, it's down to you and, of course, him."

I thanked Alan, got dressed again, and walked out, not entirely sure what my decision should be. I knew what I wanted to do, but the doctor had made a good point. This was a hobby for me after all, not my livelihood and maybe I ought to think about that more carefully. As I drove back to Anna's, I did think about talking it through with her, but I pretty much dismissed that idea, as I knew Anna would take the pragmatic view and tell me to be sensible and sit it out. I decided to wait until Monday and then go down to the club with Smithy and have a proper fitness test. That way I would know for sure if I could play. The last thing I wanted to do was tell Harry I was fit if I really wasn't and ended up letting everyone down.

I buzzed on the intercom and Anna let me up through the main door without asking who it was. I made a note to tell her off about that, but probably not today, as Anna with a hangover really was a bear with a sore head.

She opened the door for me, still in her PJs and slippers.

"Hey lover," she said, with an attempt at a smile.

"Hey beautiful. How's the head?"

"You are such a bullshitter. I look like crap and we both know it."

"You always look beautiful to me," I replied gallantly. But it got a smile.

I had picked up some coffees and Danish on the drive home, so we sat at the kitchen table while Anna slowly came back to life. In her own typically direct style, she didn't wait long to ask the question I knew she'd ask.

"So, Mr Macho, are you gonna play Tuesday?"

On the drive over, I had pretty much decided to bluff my way through this conversation and tell her that I'd been cleared to play. In my mind, it was almost the truth, as the doc hadn't actually said don't do it. So, worst case, maybe it was a little white lie to tell her I was fit. Oddly enough though, sitting at the table facing this girl I'd only known for a few months, I found I couldn't do it.

"You know, I was going to just say yes. But what I really want to do is to get your advice and your perspective, even though I have a feeling I know what you'll say," I said smiling.

"Wow! OK, hit me with it."

"So, I was told by the doc that there's some risk attached to playing. Another smack on the same spot could open up the gash or do some more damage to the ankle. He said it was really my decision. It is, but I wanted to get your thoughts too."

The look on Anna's face was priceless. For weeks afterwards I kept talking about that moment and saying if only I'd taken a picture of her expression!

"Jeez! I am just blown away that you are asking me! Wow. Give me a second to get my fuddled head in gear," she said, taking a long sip of coffee while I waited expectantly.

"OK. The sensible thing to do is to sit it out. If the doc said you could do more damage, you have to think about the future. You also need to think about your job. I know they're pretty relaxed there, but if you end up on crutches and not able to go to work for the next few weeks, they might be less than impressed. So, if you're asking for my advice, I'd say you really shouldn't play."

I opened my mouth to respond, as it was pretty much what I expected her to say, and I was about to launch into a counter argument. But Anna held up her hand in a "stop" gesture.

"Hang on, pal. I'm not done!" She paused before continuing.

"I may not be mad about soccer and think you are completely insane playing as a goalie, which has to be the most dangerous position on the field. But one of the things I love about you, and there are a few, is the passion you have for that game and what it means to you."

I was tempted to say something, but I knew she was just warming up and staying silent was by far the best option for now.

"I may not get soccer, but I do get how big a deal this game is to you, and to everyone else at your club. I also get that while this is not exactly a 'once in a lifetime' game, it's not far short of that. Bottom line. I think you should play if you think you can. That's my advice."

Now it was Anna's turn to wish she could have taken a

photo. She said later that I looked totally stunned. In truth I was. I had been so sure she would tell me to be sensible. That my health was more important. That it was only a game. How wrong I was. And I thought I knew this girl!

"Bloody hell! You're pretty amazing. Do you know that?!"

"Yep. Been telling you that for months," she said, laughing.

"Modest too. One of the things I love about you," I said, reaching for her hand and interlocking my fingers with hers.

"Seems like we love a few things about each other then."

"Yeah. Strange that," I said, squeezing her hand. "And you always look beautiful. Even now!"

"Such a liar!"

We were both laughing, but also intuitively knowing it was quite a significant moment in our relationship. Days later, Anna told me how moved she was that I had asked for her advice, despite knowing that it would probably be advice I didn't want to hear. It meant so much to her that I had involved her in my decision. In return, I told Anna that I'd thought about just telling her I was going to play, but it had felt wrong not being open and honest with her, and in the end that meant more to me. We both understood that my simple decision to make Anna part of my decision-making had been a big step.

We ended up talking some more about my decision, and in the end we both agreed that my plan to do a fitness test with Smithy on Monday was the most sensible thing to do. We probably talked for a good hour just around my decision and once we'd talked it all through, I felt really good about it. I phoned Harry and told him. Naturally, he'd already been on the phone to Alan and got his take on my fitness. He agreed that a fitness test on Monday was the best option and made it perfectly clear to me that he would support me whatever decision I made. It felt great to have so much support, though in the end I knew that the final choice would be down to me.

I arranged to meet Smithy at the ground at 7.30pm. There was a 3G training area, which had been built the previous season, which would be a good test for me as it was the same surface that Bromley had at their ground. Much to my surprise, Anna told me that she was coming with me. I told her she didn't need to, especially as it was cold and there was some light drizzle. She insisted and reminded me it was a whole lot colder on the east coast of the US for most of the winter than it was in Surrey. I surrendered.

The groundsman had put the lights on for us at the training pitch. Anna stood behind the goal with an umbrella and wearing several waterproof layers. She gave me a thumbs up as Smithy and I walked out of the changing rooms, both in waterproof tracksuits. We'd had a chat about how the test should run while we got changed. I started off just doing a gentle jog to get myself warmed up and the ankle loose. It would be a supreme irony if I ended up pulling a muscle because I hadn't stretched properly! I was jogging across the pitch and then turning and coming back again. After ten of those at a very gentle pace, Smithy told me to speed up a bit and go to half pace. He asked me how it felt. I gave him a thumbs up. After a few more, he told me to go to three-quarter pace. I could feel the impact of foot on ground going up the ankle and in the stitched area. It was uncomfortable, but it wasn't especially painful. Certainly manageable. I stopped, breathing heavily after the running, but feeling relatively good. But I knew the next few tests would be more revealing.

Smithy had brought out some cones and set them down at intervals of about eight to ten feet. I'd be sprinting to one, turning and going back to the start. Then to the second cone and back and so on. In football, everyone refers to them as "doggies" for reasons I was never too sure about. When I played basketball, we used to call them "suicides" which seemed far more appropriate. The short, sharp runs and quick turns would be much more like the sort of runs I'd typically do in a game and would put a lot more pressure on the ankle. I didn't start at full pace for the first few, but gradually built up speed until I was almost flat out. I did three sets of doggies and was bent over, hands on knees at the end. But the crowd of one broke into applause and gave me a thumbs up. So far, so good. The ankle was holding up.

Time to do some goalkeeping. I stood on the goal line as Smithy stood a yard away, throwing footballs for me to catch as I shuffled a few feet to either my left or right. After a few minutes, he moved back a few yards and started volleying the ball at me with far more pace and at varying heights. It was part of my normal pre-match routine and got the handling and reflexes going. I felt pretty good and turned to give Anna a wink to let her know I was OK. She was busy looking at her phone. Oh well. It probably wasn't the most exciting thing she'd ever watched. Smithy moved further back and started firing "proper" shots at me from the edge of the box. I now had to dive around properly. Taking off was fine, although it hurt a little going to my left as I was pushing off on the damaged ankle. But again, it was manageable. After five to ten minutes, we both agreed I was moving OK.

Smithy then went out to the touchline so he could loft some crosses into the area for me to collect. I'd known all along that this was going to be a real test, as when I jumped, I always took off on my damaged left foot. You do gain more height taking a few steps and jumping off one foot, as the momentum and bringing the other leg up helps generate more lift. Plus, as a keeper, by bringing the right knee up, it offers you some protection from opposition players intent on smashing into you. The first cross came in and I caught it OK. But it hurt. I suppose because it was fully stretching all the muscles, tendons and ligaments. Anna was looking at me and saw my grimace.

"You OK?" she asked from behind the goal.

"Yeah. It's a little tender, but I'll live!" I smiled to show I was fine.

Smithy was holding his arms wide, questioning if I wanted to continue. I gave him a thumbs up. Another ball was floated in. I caught it comfortably. It hurt. The process continued. Jump. Catch. Pain. But although each jump hurt, it wasn't enough to make me unable to jump. It was just bloody sore. We called a halt. The odds were I'd only be called upon to catch a few in the game, and with luck my defenders could deal with the majority if they knew I was less likely to come and get them.

One last test remained. Kicking the ball. First of all, Smithy played balls along the ground to me, so I could pass them back to him, simulating the sort of short passes I might give to my defenders in a game. That was all fine, as I was using my good right foot. Then he played passes back and told me I had to hoof the ball as far as I could. Slightly trickier, as the left foot was now taking most of my weight. I was getting less distance than usual as I wasn't that fluid in my movement. But again, it was OK. Finally, I tried a few kicks from my hand. I found my normal style caused me to pivot a bit on my injured ankle and that really did hurt. I adjusted my method and pivoted less. The kicks weren't going quite as far, but it was a reasonable compromise. Last but not least, I tried a few goal kicks. They were by far the most difficult because it was striking a stationary ball and I had to generate the power with all my body weight on my left foot as I struck the ball. After half a dozen crap kicks and a fair amount of discomfort, I gave in. The best option would probably be for one of my defenders to take any goal kicks. Not ideal, but not a disaster.

"So, what's the verdict, Matt?" asked Smithy.

Good question. I was certainly not 100%. My lateral movement seemed to be OK and I could run and turn. Crosses were going to be difficult. Dead ball kicking was a problem too, but Bromley hadn't really stopped us playing short goal kicks in the first game, so we could probably get around it.

"Hang on, Smithy," I said, and went to the barriers behind the goal where Anna was still standing patiently. I leant over and give her a quick kiss. She felt cold.

"So, Mr Goalie, what's the verdict?" She looked at me quizzically.

"Well, I think I'm OK to play. Not 100% but probably good enough."

"Your call, luv. I'll back you. That was kinda interesting watching that though."

"Really? I thought you were looking at your phone?"

"Only to get the photo setting right. I took a bunch so I can send to a few of my girlfriends back in the States," she said, smirking.

"But I had my back to you most of the time..." my voice trailed off as her grin grew wider. "You bad girl!"

"Cute buns, mister. Especially in those tight pants!"

I just shook my head sadly. But I had to admit it was funny and I was also a little flattered deep down. I wondered if I'd get away with doing the same one day. I had my doubts.

"OK, I'm going to take these buns back to the changing room now. Do you want to wait for me in car? I'll be as quick as I can."

"Sure thing, luvvie. I can start editing my photos while I wait," she said with a teasing smile.

Luckily Smithy had been far enough away not to hear any of the exchange. If he had, I might have had to kill him. The thought of that getting back to the dressing room made my blood run cold. I'd not live it down for weeks. Maybe the whole season. The woman was dangerous! But a lot of fun too, I had to admit. Plus, I couldn't imagine many, or rather any, of the WAGS turning out in this weather to watch a fitness test!

"So, mate, what are you going to do?" Smithy had picked up the cones and was waiting for an answer.

I realised I hadn't answered the question from either Smithy or Anna. But I knew the answer.

"I'm going to play, mate. I'm good enough. I'll give H a call once I get to the car."

"I think you're good enough too, son. Never any easy decision to take when you're not quite right, but yeah, good enough," he said, raising his gloved fist for a fist bump.

I duly obliged and started to thank him. It was odd in some ways, because by declaring myself fit, I was stopping Smithy playing and said as much.

"Forget it, mate. I'm pleased you're fit. I'm nowhere near match fit and though I played on Saturday and did alright, the rust is still there."

He was right. I'd watched the game on Saturday after I'd left Anna to return to bed to cure her hangover. He did OK. But the understanding between him and the back four wasn't quite there, and we'd conceded a goal when Stan thought Smithy was coming to collect a through ball, but Smithy thought Stan was dealing with it. In the end, they left it to each other, and a grateful Tonbridge forward had nipped in and poked the ball into the net. In the end it didn't matter too much as we won 2–1. But that sort of understanding takes a little bit of time to gel.

I showered quickly and headed for the car. I realised I was limping a little, though that wasn't hugely surprising. It would need more ice on it tonight when I got home. I opened the passenger door and said in my best upper-class English voice:

"Home James."

"You're gonna be walking if you're not careful, pal! I'm wet and cold. I deserve a medal!"

"Hey, I really do appreciate this, you know. Thank you."

I glanced across at Anna. She did look a bit bedraggled and was shivering despite the car heater blasting out warm air.

"But you still look stunning. How do you do it?"

"You're full of shit sometimes. I look like crap," replied Anna, though she was smiling as she said it.

I leant across and gave her a kiss on the cheek. Even her cheek was cold. I put my hand on her leg.

"I owe you. I hope you weren't too bored and cold. Let's get you home so I can warm you up!"

Anna rolled her eyes and removed my hand from her leg. The demister had cleared the windscreen enough for her to see out, so she started the engine.

"You have a one-track mind sometimes," she said, shaking her head sadly. "But I actually found the whole thing kinda interesting. I've seen you play in games but never seen some of the stuff you have to do to get yourself ready to play."

"That sort of session usually lasts for maybe an hour in total on Tuesdays or Thursdays. I've always said to the rest of the lads that I'm probably fitter than they are. I do the same fitness work they do for the first half hour and then while they're standing around working on their team shape or doing little passing drills, I'm flogging my guts out with Smithy, who's a real bastard when it comes to hard work!"

"I gotta admit, I thought goalies just sort of stood around and caught the ball sometimes before I watched you work out. No wonder you're so fit," she said, pausing for effect before adding, "I'm *such* a lucky girl!"

"I'm glad you realise that," I replied, ignoring the sarcasm.

I dug out my phone and hit the button to call Harry. He

answered on the second ring. If I didn't know better, I might have thought he was sitting there waiting for my call.

"Hi Matt. Just spoke to Smithy. He said you did well except for the kicking?"

I should have known! I wondered if Smithy had been instructed to ring Harry as soon as we'd finished. Probably. Harry always liked to get more than one opinion.

"Yeah, the ankle felt OK, gaffer. Not sure about taking goal kicks, but that'll only be a problem if I have to kick long. Let's hope they let us play short."

"And Smithy said you were struggling a bit with your jumping for crosses?"

Obviously, I wasn't going to be allowed to gloss over anything. But Smithy had just given Harry a warts-and-all assessment, so I couldn't really complain.

"Yeah, not 100% but I can manage. I'll be fine, Harry. I'm fit to play."

Anna glanced at me as I said it. There was a pause on the end of the line. Suddenly I realised that Harry was making his decision. I'd rather stupidly thought that it was my decision to make. But Harry had listened to the AFC Wimbledon doctor and Smithy, as well as me. It was clearly a gamble to play me. The pause was probably only for a few seconds, but it seemed to last longer.

"OK, son. You're in. At least in the cup I can name an extra sub, so we'll have Smithy on the bench, just in case."

"Thanks, boss. I won't let you down."

"I know. Bye, Matt."

I let out a sigh of relief as I hung up. For a moment I thought he was going to tell me I wasn't fit enough to risk playing. It was a gamble, but during the course of a season, every manager took risks with players who were carrying an injury. It always irritated me to hear spectators having a go at a player. Quite often that player was playing in pain and was only out on the pitch because he'd been patched up and was doing it for the team. I've seen players who should have been at home lying in bed ill, somehow get through ninety minutes on adrenaline only. It was pretty rare to put out a team during the course of a nine-month season where all eleven starting players were 100%.

"I'm pleased for you," Anna said quietly. "Pleased, because I know how badly you want to play. Though that won't stop me worrying about you."

"Thanks, babe. I appreciate all your support. I'll be fine."

"I hope so. I don't intend to become a full-time nurse and chauffeur."

"So, no nurse's uniform then?" I teased, to lighten the mood.

"Oh my God! You don't give up, do you?" But she was laughing as she said it.

We moved on to chatting about other things for the rest of the drive home. If I was completely truthful though, I was only half-listening as Anna started telling me about a new project at work. I was already thinking about the game the next day. Now the decision had been made, I could finally focus on it and start to get my head right. The main thing was to get the injury out of my mind. If I started to think about whether I could or couldn't do things as well as normal, it would put doubts in my head and that would affect my decision-making.

As any sportsperson will tell you, once you start having doubts about your ability to perform, the chances are you'll perform badly. A lot of people think sportspeople are self-confident to the point of arrogant. Of course, some are. But for the majority, it's about having a mind-set that doesn't allow for self-doubt. If you don't believe in yourself, how can you expect others to believe in you? It's a fine line. If you do become arrogant, you're setting yourself up for a big fall at some point. Sport has a way of bringing you down to earth in a hurry. For every high, there's a corresponding low around the corner. The trick is not to believe all the hype if things are going well and not listen to all the criticism when things go south. That's why maintaining a healthy amount of self-confidence is important, especially for a goalkeeper. Every time the ball hits the net behind you, someone, somewhere, will think you might have done better. Aside from the occasional "worldie", where everyone understands that the best keeper in the world would probably not have stopped it, every other goal is a question mark. Could he have done better? Of course, I always ask myself that, and sometimes the answer is yes and hopefully you learn from that. But unless you've actually played in goal, it's hard for others to give an accurate assessment.

"Matt?" We'd stopped at the lights and Anna was looking across at me.

I realised that I had stopped half-listening and had zoned out completely.

"I asked you if you're going to miss me?"

I knew I was in trouble as I had absolutely no clue what Anna was talking about. I considered telling the truth and admitting that I hadn't been listening. I put that idea on a par with getting into the ring with the heavyweight champ of the world. The second option was dangerous but slightly more palatable.

"Of course I'll miss you. I miss you every minute of the day we don't spend together."

At least that part was true. The trouble was that I didn't know why or when I might be missing her. I hoped that my bluff wouldn't be uncovered.

"You know, ever so often you say something that just makes me feel like I'm floating in the air. You can be quite the charmer," Anna said softly. "I'll miss you too, but it'll only be for those ten days. I'm not expecting it to take any longer."

Now I was really puzzled. Ten days? What the hell was this about? I assumed it was something to do with her job, as that's what she'd been talking about when I allowed my mind and concentration to wander. Luckily, Anna's attention was on the road ahead, as it had started raining more heavily. She wasn't able to see the confusion written all over my face. Anna must have taken my silence for apprehension or sadness.

"Hey, we'll be fine. I promise I'll call you every day. We'll just have to figure out a good time to call with the time difference. I guess you probably don't want me waking you up in the middle of the night!" She laughed as she said it.

I laughed too, but mainly because it seemed the right thing to do. OK. Time difference. That was a clue and obviously overseas travel. She sometimes went over to New York as her company was based there.

"Yeah, I need my beauty sleep!"

"We'll figure something out. It'll be easier when I'm with my folks as I'll be able to call at any old time."

Ah, the mist was thinning! Anna's parents lived just outside of Boston, in a place called Belmont, which was funny as there was a village by the same name about twenty minutes from Reigate. But it meant she was almost certainly going to the east coast of the USA. I decided to try a question.

"Sorry, but how long did you say you were going to spend with your folks again?"

"Probably three or four days. I haven't seen them for the best part of six months, so it'll be great to catch up with them and my sisters too if they're in town. I wish you could come too, but I realise it's all too short notice with your job and the other love of your life that I have to compete with!"

I didn't know whether to be miffed that she hadn't asked me

or relieved. It would have been great to spend time out there, although if she was working for a chunk of that time, I'd have had to entertain myself. That probably wouldn't have been too hard in the Big Apple though. But it would have been difficult to have missed another game or possibly two depending upon when Anna was going. Which I still didn't know!

"Let's plan on doing that some other time in that case. I'd love to meet your folks."

"You would?" Anna sounded pleased. "Oh, they would love you. My dad's a big sports fan. I'm sure you'd get along great."

Anna started talking about her parents, her sisters and home. This time I did listen more carefully and asked questions at the right time. By letting Anna talk, I eventually got to find out that she'd be flying out on Sunday week and staying for ten days. The Monday to Friday would be working in the company's NY office and then she'd go to see her parents and spend a long weekend with them, before travelling back the following Wednesday. I was pleased for Anna. Even though it was fun for her being in a new country and meeting different people, including me I hoped, she was still away from home and her family. She was very close to her folks and her sisters, as you'd expect from an Irish family. When we were getting to know each other, I'd learned that her parents were originally from Dublin, but had moved the family to Boston before Anna was born. She still thought of herself as Irish, despite the Boston accent. Of course, Boston was an Irish town, and one of America's most famous sports teams, the NBA's Boston Celtics, even had a leprechaun as their mascot. I'd never been, but Anna said the place was packed with Irish bars and Irish flags. I hoped I'd get a chance to go one day, with Anna as my tour guide.

Anna pulled up outside my flat. We exchanged a brief kiss and I headed indoors. Anna was going back to her place as she tended to do during the week. I was left to ice my ankle and watch a little TV before getting an early night, ready for the big game the following evening.

11

The good thing about having a full-time job is that it puts football, especially non-league football, into perspective. If you have a bad game, or the team is playing poorly then only a relatively small number of people will know or care. Life goes on around you as normal, which isn't the same in the pro game of course. The bad thing about having a full-time job is that it also puts non-league football into perspective! Doing the daily commute with thousands of others who all look as though they'd rather be somewhere/anywhere else than on that train or Tube, is not what you would call motivating. The thought of having football as your main job, starting work at 10am, doing something you love and being outdoors in the fresh air, is a lot more appealing.

The day of the game, which was a Tuesday, was just another ordinary working day for me. I got up, commuted into London Bridge and then squeezed onto a crowded Jubilee Line train out to Canary Wharf. Not a great deal of fun, although on some mornings I stopped off at a Caffè Nero as a reward for surviving another commute. I tended to read the free copy of the *Metro*, starting, naturally enough, at the back with the sports section. It's not exactly a heavy-duty read, so I usually have a book with me for the rest of the commute. I tended to read sports biographies or crime thrillers. But on that Tuesday morning, I found that I was reading pages without taking anything in. My mind kept drifting away, thinking about the replay that night. Even the national press was giving the game a mention. The romance of the FA Cup is still very much alive, but really lives off one or two non-league sides getting through the early rounds to come up against a big name. Everyone loves those stories of bricklayers and postmen coming up against millionaire footballers. It really doesn't happen anywhere else in the world. That said, us against another non-league side wasn't quite setting pulses racing yet, although the winners of our replay would be going into the hat with all the big boys and that alone guaranteed a degree of interest.

It was on occasions like this that I realised how lucky I was to be playing football at a decent level. But it also made me want more. I enjoyed my job. It was interesting, challenging and well paid. However, it wasn't the same as playing football full-time. I envied the lads playing for Bromley. Although they weren't in the Football League, they were actually full-time professional footballers. That's what they did for a living. Of course, the wages they were on couldn't compare to the outlandish wages that clubs in the Premier League paid. The wages in every football club in the land vary enormously, not just between clubs, but also within clubs. That, of course, can lead to friction and even a degree of animosity within a team if certain players are getting paid more and others think that they are worth as much. Football clubs have to run as a business, trying to balance wages and income. Those that don't and try and spend their way to success in the short-term usually come unstuck. Every league in every country in the world has horror stories of how once famous and revered names have tumbled down leagues and sometimes out of existence altogether, thanks to financial stupidity on the part of the owners. Most of the lads in National League sides get paid on a weekly basis and that usually didn't include the close season – May through to July, when pre-season began again. The figures that I'd heard varied anywhere from £15,000 to £50,000 a year. The top end is certainly a decent salary, but, at the lower end, £15,000 wouldn't get you much when it comes to a place to live and money to pay the bills.

The upside of football not being your livelihood was brought home when I'd been injured ten days earlier. Of course, it wasn't a serious injury. But we all knew good players that had ruined knees and could no longer play. That's sad at non-league level, but obviously life-changing if you're a professional. Many players have no other skills to fall back upon, as all they've really done since they'd been at school was play football. Every footballer, and probably every sportsman or sportswoman, thinks, "It won't happen to me." We all think we're invincible. Even if it's not due to injury, at a certain time or age, every athlete goes past their "sell-by date". There are younger, fitter, better or cheaper players coming through on the conveyor belt and eventually the older players face the chop. It's amazing how few prepare for that day. Even if you've done well financially out of the game, most players have the next thirty to forty years ahead of them, and faced with the daunting task of starting a new career. There are only so many coaching or media jobs available. So, I knew on one hand I was lucky, playing football and having a well-paid career in place. Yet, on the other hand, the dream of every footballer – and I was no different – was to play professionally.

Most of my colleagues at work knew of my "other job". A few who loved their football would always ask me on a Monday how the game on the Saturday had gone. But there were plenty of others who really didn't care and equated it to park football. That had changed since the FA Cup had catapulted Reigate Athletic and me into the limelight. I found myself even being asked for tickets for the replay (which I didn't have). Three or four were planning on coming to the game, especially since the capacity at Bromley is over 5,000, so getting tickets was far easier than for the first match at our limited capacity ground. I had thought that being in work would be a good distraction, but people kept dropping by my desk to ask about the game or just show some interest. Whatever the reason, I got very little done. So, it was something of a relief when I left work. As we had to report at Bromley's ground ninety minutes before the 7.45pm kick-off, I actually left work at 4pm. Luckily, Sarah, my boss, was very understanding. She had a daughter who played for Chelsea ladies in one of their youth teams, so she was very familiar with the demands of football clubs. She had suggested I drop the firm's name into my next interview on Sky or the BBC. I assumed she was joking, but just in case she wasn't I made a mental note to see if I could.

The journey home was uneventful and, having collected my kit and changed into the club's tracksuit, which we all had to wear on match days, I set out for Bromley's ground. It was a typical November evening. Dark, cold and with the threat of rain in the air. The forecast was one that gave a possibility of heavy showers during the evening. As we were playing on 3G, it wouldn't make much difference, except that the ball would probably zip off the wet surface that much quicker.

Bromley had spent a fair bit of money on their stadium in recent years, with the ultimate aim of getting promotion into the Football League. What they hadn't spent money on was their car park and I did my best to avoid pot-holes full of water as I drove slowly in. It wasn't terribly well-lit, and I made a quick mental note to watch where I was walking. The last thing I needed was to put my injured foot in a pot-hole!

I walked through the players' gate and nodded to their steward. I strolled around the pitch to the main stand and down the tunnel to the dressing rooms. As usual, I was one of the first there and got the choice of where to change, which was one good reason for arriving early. I could never understand players who arrived late and blamed traffic, trains and everyone else. Way too much stress for me. The rest of the lads arrived in dribs and drabs, offering the usual mix of greetings and abuse. I got a little more abuse than usual, with an underlying theme that I only bothered to play in the big games now and playing in ordinary league games was a bit beneath me. By 6.45pm, an hour before kick-off, everyone was there and getting changed into their warm-up gear. We always went out on the pitch to warm up around 7pm for an evening game, which gave us about thirty minutes to get loose. The stadium, which had a capacity of 5,000, was largely empty. But that didn't mean much. Spectators arrive quite late for non-league games and you really didn't get an idea of the size of a crowd until ten minutes before kick-off, and even then people were usually still streaming in.

I went through my normal pre-match routine with Smithy, except we avoided the normal crossing practice. We didn't want anyone from the opposition noticing that I was jumping awkwardly. We wanted them to believe I was fully fit. I felt OK, though the occasional twinge served to remind me that I wasn't a hundred per cent.

At 7.30pm, we were called back into the dressing room. We all sat around doing our own last-minute bits and pieces. We all had odd and quirky habits; John didn't put his shirt on until we were lining up ready to go out; Stan always kissed the crucifix he wore on a chain under his shirt; Jamie wore two pairs of socks; Stevie and Rosey always sat next to each other; Simo always had his knee strapped by Mel, even though there was nothing wrong with it. We all knew it was a little ridiculous, but woe betide anyone who messed with our own little rituals. Me? I always put my kit on in exactly the same order. Shorts first, then undershirt, then left sock, right sock. Shin pads next. Strapping on each wrist before finally putting on my goalkeeper shirt. The gloves I never put on until I was running out onto the pitch.

Harry never says that much just before a game. He's usually gone over the opposition and individual assignments both at training and in the fifteen to twenty minutes after we arrive in the dressing room, before we warm-up. In the ten minutes or so before we line up to go out for the game, he usually just goes around to individual players and reminds them of one or two things. He came and sat next to me and just asked me if I was OK. Naturally, I said I was fine. He punched me lightly on the shoulder and wished me luck.

It was usually Jez Morley, our assistant manager, who got us fired up by yelling and shouting. The theme tonight was that Bromley believed they'd done the hard work and were thinking all they had to do was walk out on the pitch to win it. That might even have been true. If it was, it would work in our favour. There is something psychologically challenging about playing a team from a lower league. You know the players aren't as good, man for man. You know that you should beat them, and eight or nine times out of ten you probably would. You also know they will be up for it and you must not take them lightly. And yet, you do. That's why there were always cup upsets. The root cause is usually that the team from the higher league have gone into the game with the thought that 80% would probably be enough. Once you start a game in that mind-set, you're in trouble. It doesn't even need to be the whole team who are thinking that way. It just takes three or four players and, before you know it, the opposition scent blood and raise their game to 110%. Sport is a lot about momentum. If you allow your opponents to gain momentum, invariably you're in deep trouble.

The buzzer went, which was the referee calling us out. We stood up, shaking each other's hands, wishing one another good luck, as we normally did. As we walked out onto the pitch and lined up to do the pre-match ritual of the handshake with our opponents, I noticed that the ground had filled up a lot since we had finished our warm-up. There was probably well over a thousand now, including a small band of Reigate Athletic fans in a group behind the goal to the left, which is where I headed after the handshakes. As I ran towards the goal, the Athletic fans began to applaud, and I did the same in return. There was probably a couple of hundred of them, with their yellow and blue scarves and banners tied around necks and the pitch hoardings. There was a clash of colours tonight though, and as the away side we had to change. We were in all red, which several of the boys thought were our "lucky" colours. Every bit helps. I was wearing all green as I normally did.

We kicked off and quickly got our passing game going. The 3G surface suited us as we liked to play short passes and retain possession, so having a flat, rain-slicked surface certainly helped us. For the first ten minutes, we probably had at least 60% possession and were camped in the Bromley half as we knocked it around. Eventually, one of the Bromley midfielders decided that enough was enough and clattered into Stevie. It was late, but not enough to warrant a yellow card. Just letting our players know that they could expect a few tackles to come flying in. But, for all our possession, we didn't really threaten their goal.

As so often happens, Bromley then scored with their first attack after eighteen minutes. It was a classic sucker-punch too. It came from our own corner. Both of our centre-backs had gone up. We always left at least two or three players back to mark whatever men the opposition left up-field, always making sure we had one extra man. Bromley had left two men up, so we had Simo, Jamie and Stevie G back to mark them. But just as the corner was about to be taken, I noticed one of the Bromley players drift out from his own area to make it three v. three. It was obviously a planned move. I yelled at Simo to pull someone else back, but it was too late as the corner was already on its way. Bromley cleared the ball up-field and suddenly it was three against three. No, it was four against three as another Bromley player had sprinted out of their box ahead of any of our players. We were in trouble. One of their forwards got to the clearance ahead of Stevie and turned, weighing up his options. Stevie was in front of him, but that meant Simo and Jamie had three players running and couldn't mark them all. Simo opted to track the player nearest to him, but that left Jamie with two to mark. The lad with the ball chose the right option and played it wide left, where Bromley had the overload. There wasn't much Jamie could do as the two Bromley players exchanged a couple of quick passes, which left Jamie on his backside, and with just me to beat. I advanced to narrow the angle, but as I closed the player with the ball down, he played it square to his unmarked mate, who had the simple task of tapping it into an empty net.

There was already quite an inquest going on, but although a few fingers were being pointed, I knew it was more down to a well-worked move on their part, rather than poor defending by us.

Credit to the lads though. We could have crumbled a bit, having been arguably the better side in the opening quarter of an hour. But we didn't. We quickly got our composure back and began playing our football again. Bromley though had their tails up and were closing us down quickly. We did carve out a great chance for Antonio, when a clever through ball from Beno put him through. But Antonio's effort was straight at their keeper who blocked it comfortably. We were very much in the match, but it was a tight game, with few chances at either end. Ten minutes before the break, one of their midfielders had the ball some thirty yards out. Too far out to have a shot, I thought. Wrong. He decided to try his luck. He caught it well enough, but as I started to move to my right, it got a wicked deflection off Beno and went the opposite way. I readjusted, pushing off my injured left ankle, but with some of my weight still on the opposite foot. I managed to twist and throw myself to my left, getting my left hand to the ball and turned it behind for a corner. My ankle objected loudly.

There was rapturous applause from the Reigate faithful behind the goal. But I didn't really notice. I was in a fair bit of pain and so I stayed down, hoping the pain would ease. My ankle was on fire. I just lay there as Mel rushed to my side.

"Is it your ankle, Matt?" she asked, kneeling beside me.

"Yes," I said through gritted teeth. "But pretend to check my arm. I don't want them knowing it's my ankle."

"What? But I need to check your ankle!"

"Just do it, Mel!" I practically yelled at her.

She looked at me as if I were mad but did as I asked and started checking my left arm. All I wanted was to buy a little time for the pain to subside, as I hoped it would. And it did. I gingerly got to my feet and continued my Oscar-winning performance by flexing my arm.

"You OK, Matt?"

"Yeah, we can take a look at half-time, Mel," I said quietly.

Mel jogged off and I started to organise everyone for the

corner. Bromley put both centre-backs in the six-yard box just in front of me. The corner was whipped in, right into the six-yard box. I called for it and attempted to punch the ball clear. But instead I ran into one of the two Bromley players. I must admit, I made a bit of a meal of the contact, but luckily the ref saw it my way and gave a free kick against Bromley, much to the irritation of their players and supporters. Not that it worried me.

I took my time with the goal kick, knowing that I had to get through to half-time. Luckily, Bromley were letting us play it out from the back and then pressing us when we started to advance the ball. That suited my ankle, as all I had to do was side-foot it to Stan or one of the full-backs. There was always an element of risk playing this way, but that's what Harry wanted us to do, and most of the time we did it pretty well. But on the stroke of half-time, we didn't. Stan tried an ambitious pass into Beno. It got to Beno's feet, but two Bromley players and the ball arrived at almost the same time. Beno had nowhere to go. He tried to hold it and buy a free kick by going down theatrically, but the ref was having none of it. Suddenly, Bromley had the ball deep in our half and with both our full-backs out wide, it was a two v. two with our centre-backs. Stan and John used their experience by not committing and trying to buy time until reinforcements arrived. But in doing so, it gave the lad with the ball a bit of space. It was the same player who smacked one from thirty yards earlier. This time I was ready for the shot. But he caught it beautifully from twenty-five yards and it was arrowing towards the top corner. As I started to dive, I knew it was just for show, because I wasn't going to get anywhere near it. I didn't. The ball cannoned against the underside of the bar and came straight down. As the ball bounced, Stan was on hand to hook the ball away for a throw-in.

The Bromley lad was wheeling away as if he'd scored. I

had no idea because it had happened behind me. I looked across to the assistant and she wasn't running back to the half-way line to indicate a goal had been scored. She had her flag up for a throw. The Bromley players surrounded the ref, imploring him to award the goal. He waved them away at first but belatedly decided to go and speak to his assistant. Refs outside the pro game didn't have goal-line technology to help them. Their conversation seemed to last forever, but twice I saw the assistant shake her head. We held our breath. The ref turned and walked away from his assistant and indicated a throw-in. The Bromley crowd and players erupted in fury. A couple went over to the assistant and began yelling at her. Stan went over and started to push them away. One of the Bromley players shoved Stan hard in the chest and Stan squared up to him, snarling back. Before it got out of hand, the ref sprinted over and issued a yellow card to each player, which aggrieved Stan as he'd been trying to protect the official.

The game restarted with a throw, although there was a chorus of boos from around the ground. Someone once said football's a funny game. It certainly can be, because less than sixty seconds later, we equalised. It was a bizarre goal. Their keeper had rolled it out to their centre-back just outside the box. Antonio shut the centre-back down quickly. His speed surprised the Bromley player and he had to hurry to play it back to his keeper. But he didn't look. He hadn't noticed the keeper had moved wide of his goal to try and make the pass easier. The ball went past the keeper towards the goal. Normally, it wouldn't have been a problem for the keeper but as he turned to chase the ball, he slipped on the wet surface. The ball rolled slowly towards the goal with both Antonio and the Bromley centre-back in hot pursuit. From my angle it was impossible to tell if it was going in or not. The ball won the race, but hit the inside of the post at almost the same time as

Antonio and the Bromley player arrived, both sliding in. All three ended up in the back of the net. We were level!

There was a stunned silence around the ground, except for our 200-odd supporters behind me and a small number of wives and girlfriends in the stand, who were all going mad! Several of the Bromley lads had their hands on their heads, unable to believe what had just happened. Talk about rubbing salt in the wound! One minute they thought they'd scored to go two up and the next minute it was 1–1. We played another minute before the ref blew for half-time. I noticed a couple of stewards rush out onto the pitch to escort the officials off. One of the Bromley coaching staff was walking in determined style towards the three officials. I couldn't hear what was said, but in very short order, the ref reached into his back pocket and brandished a red card. A couple of the Bromley lads also wanted to have their say as the officials neared the tunnel and another yellow was shown to the Bromley skipper. Harry was ushering us away and into the dressing room.

As we grabbed drinks and sat down, I called Mel over and started taking my boot and sock off. As I had strapping on the ankle to support it, we didn't have time to take that off and have a proper look at it.

"The only thing I can really do is to put more strapping on and make it a bit tighter. Do you want that?"

"Do it, Mel."

In truth neither of us knew if it would help much, but that was about all we could do. I reached into her first-aid bag for the bottle of paracetamol. I'd already had two before the game. I tipped four into the palm of my hand.

"That's too many, Matt," said Mel, looking up from the bandage she was winding around my ankle in a figure of eight.

"I'll be fine. I just need to get through the next forty-five minutes."

She shook her head, but didn't say anything else. The ankle was still throbbing, but the strapping felt nice and tight. I just hoped it didn't cut off the blood supply.

Harry's half-time team talk was short and to the point. He said we had been the better side up until they'd scored. He told us that the equaliser had rattled them and a few of their lads had lost the plot. We all knew the psychological effect an equaliser can have in first half added time, let alone conceding a goal like that. He told us to be brave and attack, because if we scored again, he said the game would be over.

As we walked out for the second half, I heard a few of their players still moaning about "the goal" that wasn't given. I knew Harry was probably right. We had a great chance to win this game. I ran towards the big stand which had Glyn Beverly in big letters at the top and where most of the Bromley supporters were gathered. I think it's fair to say I didn't receive a warm welcome. My birth right and parentage were certainly questioned, as well as my sexual preferences. But I was also hearing the word "cheat" more than once, usually with an adjective or two to accompany it. It was a bit harsh calling us cheats. In truth, I had no idea if it was a goal or not. But I could understand their frustration.

Their frustration doubled eight minutes into the second half. For once, Stan launched a long ball from the back, rather than play to feet. Antonio beat his man in the air and flicked the ball on. Rosey had timed his run to perfection and the ball fell perfectly for him. It was bouncing and as the keeper came to meet him, Rosey lobbed it over his head and watched as it bounced into the vacant net. He carried on running straight towards the mass of Reigate fans and threw himself at the cheering mass, joined moments later by the rest of the team. Well, except me. No way was I going to run ninety plus yards on a bad ankle if I didn't need to.

Harry was right. The second goal so soon after half-time had Bromley reeling. For the next twenty minutes it was all us, as we dominated possession and had a string of chances. But their keeper pulled off a couple of great stops, while Antonio missed a sitter. I had nothing much to do. But while it was still 2–1, the game certainly wasn't over. The Bromley lads knew it was now or never and began to throw caution to the wind. They piled men forward. But we were looking solid and the few shots they had failed to hit the target. But with ten minutes left, Bromley put together arguably the move of the game. One of their midfielders played a quick one-two. Then another. Then a third interchange with his centre-forward on the edge of our box and suddenly he was through on goal. His touch was slightly heavy though and gave me a chance. I sprinted off my line and threw myself at his feet. He touched the ball to the left as I did, but I'd anticipated that and got both hands on the ball and pushed it away for a corner. But for some reason the referee gave a goal kick, thinking their player had got the final touch. The Bromley players surrounded the ref again and the Bromley skipper, who was a big lad and towered over the ref, was particularly vociferous. It wasn't the best thing to do when you'd already been booked. The referee had reached his breaking point and reached for his pocket. A second yellow card was shown to their skipper, immediately followed by a red. Booing echoed around the ground, interspersed with the old, familiar chant of "You don't know what you're doing".

I saw that Harry wanted to make a sub and assumed that he'd bring on another defender to keep it tight at the back. But much to my surprise, I saw he was bringing on Addi and taking Beno off. It was a bold move, replacing a midfielder with a winger. I saw him indicate to Stevie that we were to go to a 4-3-3. Stevie nodded and barked instructions to the rest of the lads as Addi came on. I understood Harry's plan when

I saw that Bromley, having lost one centre-back, were going to play the rest of the game 3-4-2. It was a gamble. The Bromley lads, to their credit, despite being a man down, really went for it. Roared on by the home support, they poured forward and began to put us under pressure. High balls were being pumped into our box. Normally, I would probably have come and caught a couple, but with my jumping limited, I decided it was better to leave it to my defenders. But as the game went into its dying moments, another high ball came in. This time I had to come for it. I jumped and tried to catch it, but I got very little height. The Bromley centre-forward jumped higher. His flailing arm caught me right in the face. It was not intentional, but it was a clear foul and stopped me gathering the ball. But the whistle never came, and the ball dropped to a Bromley player who lashed it towards the vacant goal. But Simo had covered me and was back on the line. He stuck out a leg and, purely by luck, the ball cannoned off his knee and away to safety. The collective groan from the Bromley supporters was music to my ears.

This time it was our turn to have a go at the ref, led by yours truly. I was furious. To me it was such an obvious foul and I couldn't believe it hadn't been given. My name was the next to go into the ref's notebook, which in hindsight was probably fair enough, as I went on too long and too loudly.

Bromley had everyone up for the corner, including their keeper. We left Addi up-field and they kept one defender back. Everyone else was in our penalty area. The ball was fired into the near post and it was met by Stan's forehead, who got there ahead of a crowd of players. His powerful header cleared the box easily. I yelled for everyone to get out. But I was watching a footrace between Addi and their last defender to get to the loose ball first. It was no contest – Addi is like a greyhound. He latched onto the ball and, with the last defender trailing in his wake, he ran from inside our half towards their unguarded net, with their keeper forlornly trying to get back. As soon as Addi got the ball, we knew no one would catch him. He was just too quick. We were already celebrating as he entered the penalty area, before nonchalantly rolling the ball into the net. This time, there was no stopping me. At something between a sprint and a hobble I went to join in the celebrations, and we all leapt on top of Addi, who disappeared under a pile of red shirts. At 3–1, everyone knew it was over, and the Bromley fans were already heading for the exit.

Both teams played out the remaining few minutes and as soon as the final whistle blew, we went to celebrate with our fans. Although they were gutted, all the Bromley players shook hands and wished us well in the next round, as did the Bromley manager, which I thought was a great gesture. That didn't stop the officials being booed off though, and there were still words being exchanged as they marched off, surrounded by stewards. Not that we cared as we stood right in front of a cheering mass of yellow and blue, clapping our hands and pumping our fists in the air. I suddenly noticed Anna, leaning over the advertising hoardings, a big beaming smile on her face and cheering with everyone else. I later found out that she'd left her seat in the stand and spent the whole of the second half standing with all the other Reigate fans. She said it was much more fun and it helped to share the nerves and tension with others. I broke ranks and walked to her. She flung her arms around my neck and said something, but it was hard to hear. The rest of the lads followed my example and were soon shaking hands and embracing our fans. I noticed Anna got hugs from most of the lads. Funny that! It was a great feeling and none of us wanted it to end. Anna gave me a big kiss which got another cheer from the Reigate faithful. Slowly, we started to drift away and head for the dressing room.

By the time we reached the relative calm of the dressing room, we'd done most of our celebrating and we just sat there feeling a sense of quiet satisfaction. Mel was there almost as soon as I walked through the door, ordering me to take my boot and sock off. She later told me that she'd spent the whole of the second half worrying that she'd strapped my ankle too tightly. She quickly went to work with a pair of scissors and cut through the tape holding the strapping in place. It felt good to get it off at last.

"How does it feel? I can see it's swollen again," she asked.

"Pretty good actually. No worse than it did before the game."

"Yeah, though that's probably adrenaline. Give me a call tomorrow. I may need to see it before Thursday."

I thanked Mel and gave her a big hug, which I think surprised her. I got changed in record time. Usually, I tend to take a while. But today, I wanted to get to the bar and celebrate with Anna and everyone else, especially as people probably wouldn't stay too long with work the next day.

When I walked into the bar, everyone was watching a TV screen. Bromley had filmed the game and they were showing some of the key moments. I recognised my girlfriend, even though she was still wearing her big coat and hat. Even Anna was watching the TV. I saw the reason why. They were showing the shot that hit the bar. There were some "oohhs" and "aaahhhs" as they replayed it in slow motion. Because there was only one camera, which was on the roof of the main stand, it was almost impossible to tell if the ball had crossed the line or not. It was certainly close, but I can understand why it wasn't given. Hard for the assistant too, as she was level with Stan, our last defender, and he was on the edge of the box, so she was at least eighteen yards away from the goal line. Of course, the Bromley supporters in the bar were arguing that it had crossed the line and our spectators were arguing back. But it was largely good-natured and with a bit of banter thrown in.

I put my arms around Anna's waist. She jumped a little in surprise.

"Oh, it's you," she exclaimed. "I thought I was being manhandled by some strange man." She laughed.

"No such luck I'm afraid, sexy. It's just me."

"You'll do. Oh my God! What a game! I swear I have never been so damn nervous. Especially the last quarter."

I let the reference to American Football slide. The fact she was here and so excited by one of my matches was more than enough. If you'd said this would happen when we first started seeing each other, I think we'd both have laughed hysterically at the absurdity of such an idea.

"Can you please stop getting hurt though!?" She rushed on with barely a pause for breath. "I think I've aged maybe ten years in the last month or so, watching you. How's your shoulder?" She touched my arm.

I explained that there was nothing wrong with it and it was a little gamesmanship on my part. I got a whack on that same shoulder for my troubles.

"Oww! What was that for?"

"Worrying me, you…wanker!"

We both started laughing. I asked Anna to get a drink for me so I could go and get a plate of food. I was starving. I could never eat before a game, so apart from a banana, I hadn't eaten anything since lunch. It was chilli and rice, which suited me perfectly. I grabbed two bowls: one for me and one for Anna. A bit naughty, but I doubted whether many of the Bromley lads would be coming in. If I'd been in their shoes, I'd just want to get home. Anna had got our drinks and I shouldered my way through a number of our supporters, who offered their congratulations and patted me on the back as I squeezed past. She was standing with Simi and Kat, who was Simo's lady.

Just then I spotted the Bromley physio. I quickly handed Anna's bowl of chilli to her and told her I'd be back in minute.

"Hey Vanessa!" I called to her.

"Don't you dare speak to me! I'm in big trouble for getting you fit to play this evening!" She was grinning as she said it, so I assumed she was joking. "Congratulations, by the way."

"Thank you. I just wanted to come and say thanks again for looking after me after that first game. It was really nice of you."

"Felt like the right thing to do, even if I did get a fair bit of stick for it from our lads."

"Well, I didn't do much tonight, so they can't really blame you," I offered.

"Really?" She laughed. "I think that save when you twisted in mid-air wasn't too shabby. Oh, and nice acting job, by the way!"

"Was it that obvious?" I said, smiling.

"Probably just to me. It was when I saw Mel do a double-take and look so surprised that I worked it out. How is it, by the way?"

"It's sore, but I guess that's to be expected."

"Yep, will be for a couple of weeks. Anyway, I'd better go pack all my gear up and get home. Best of luck in the next round. I hope you get a big draw!"

"Thanks, Vanessa. All the best."

We shook hands and I returned to Anna and the girls. John and Simo had joined the group and Anna was chatting happily with them. It was great to see how quickly she'd become part of the group and actually seemed to be enjoying it. It was then that I spotted Jess standing with Harry, holding her phone out in front, obviously interviewing him. I turned my back quickly to avoid any eye contact. I really didn't want Jess and Anna getting into a catfight tonight.

"That was really sweet of you, Matt, going to speak to Vanessa," Anna said quietly to me.

"Least I could do. She didn't need to help me at all. Nice lady."

"She is, and talking of nice ladies, I see your favourite journalist is over there," she said, nodding her head in Jess's direction.

"What?" I turned to look. "Oh, Jess you mean? Looks like she's busy with the gaffer."

"I've heard that word a few times now. What the heck does it mean?"

I was relieved to change the subject and decided to take the chance to move the conversation on.

"You know what? I have absolutely no idea at all. It's just like saying 'boss'. Just a word that's used in football for a manager for some reason. Hey fellas," I said to my teammates, "any idea what the word 'gaffer' means?"

Both John and Simo gave me a blank look.

I got my phone out, in part to keep the conversation in relatively safe waters and in part because I was a little curious. It's funny how everyone picks up and uses a word, without knowing what it means.

"I'll google it," I offered. I scrolled through a couple of entries. "It says that it started getting used in football in the 1970s and was originally used on construction sites to refer to the boss or foreman."

"Cheers, Matt. I feel so much better for knowing that mate," said Simo, with his normal deadpan delivery.

"Piss off, Simo," I replied, and the group dissolved into laughter.

I risked a glance over to where I'd seen Jess. She was now

talking to the Bromley manager, which I imagined would have been a colourful interview. But she had her back to me and there was no danger of any eye contact. I felt a little guilty, trying to avoid her, as she was just doing her job. But Anna and Jess didn't seem to like each other much and I really didn't want to get caught in the crossfire.

We finished our food and drinks. Gradually the place was starting to empty out. It was almost entirely our lot that remained, but even our supporters and some of the lads were starting to drift away.

"Guess it's time to go, good-lookin'. Some of us have gotta work tomorrow," said Anna, stifling a yawn.

"Sorry if I'm boring you," I teased.

"It's OK. I'm used to it." That got a giggle from Kat as I rolled my eyes.

We'd come to the game separately, as Anna had made it clear she wasn't getting to any match ninety minutes ahead of time. We walked out together. Much to my surprise, she was parked in the players and officials' car park. I asked her how she'd managed that, but she just winked, and I laughed, knowing how charming she could be. I was disappointed we were having to say goodnight, as I was still wired and I knew it would take me ages to get to sleep. But this was our weekday routine now and it worked, most of the time anyway. I watched her drive away, before getting into my car a little gingerly, and feeling grateful I'd bought myself an automatic, which meant I could rest my left ankle. Although it was cold and wet, I was feeling on top of the world.

12

Anna's trip had been brought forward a few days and she was flying out on Thursday morning. She'd be gone pretty much the same length of time, but it now looked like a period where I wouldn't be playing or training to keep my mind occupied. Harry had told me he was resting me for the league game on the Saturday and then for the Surrey Senior Cup tie on the following Tuesday, which would give my ankle a chance to heal. It wasn't much of a conversation about it. He just told me. End of discussion.

We'd talked about her trip and Anna had promised to call whenever she could and certainly when she was with her folks. She had banned me from coming to the airport to see her off though, claiming it would make her too emotional. She did, however, want me to meet her when she flew back. That seemed like a long time away.

As it was our last night together for a while, we were going to break the rules and I was staying at Anna's. Bless her, she'd even bought some champagne to celebrate our cup replay win, but we decided to save it for another occasion, as her departure didn't seem cause for a celebration. But she soon cheered me up and reminded me how lucky I was on a lot of fronts. To still be in the Cup at this stage was a very rare privilege for anyone outside of the pro game, and secondly, I still had her! She was right, on both counts. We cuddled up, chatted and opened a bottle of wine instead. She needed to pack and get organised, but she wanted to get my opinion on some of her work outfits she was thinking of taking with her. We ended up having quite a lot of fun, as Anna paraded up and down like a catwalk model in several outfits. In truth, the girl looked good in anything and I told her that. She pointed out I was supposed to be helping her choose outfits, not flatter her. I did focus and helped her choose four outfits to take. I thought we'd finished, but she said she needed help with just one more outfit. She walked out a few minutes later, in a black and very sheer negligee.

"Gee. I dunno if this will look good on me or not. What do you think, luv?"

I think I was probably sitting there with my mouth open. I certainly found it a challenge to string together anything coherent.

"Very, um, eye-catching!" I mumbled.

"I'm glad you approve. Because this is what I'm wearing tonight."

Suddenly the evening was a whole lot better. I did, however, ban her from taking the negligee with her!

The next morning, we said our goodbyes and headed to our respective jobs. Anna was light and breezy and said the time would fly past and she'd be back before I knew it. I adopted the same attitude and told her to enjoy her time with her folks and not feel under any pressure to call me. She just laughed and told me that she'd call every day. Although I was pretending it was all cool, I knew I would miss her. A lot. But no way was I going to come across like a clingy boyfriend. I knew that wasn't her style either.

Obviously, a few people from work had kept an eye on the result of our replay against Bromley. I walked into the open-plan office and headed for my desk to find a big map of the UK spread across my desk. Someone had helpfully circled Grimsby with a red marker pen, and, just to make sure, there were a number of arrows drawn on the map, all pointing to the town. I looked around suspiciously, but everyone was studiously staring at monitors and avoiding any eye contact with me.

"Very funny guys. I did know where Grimsby was."

That broke the spell and a dozen or so people started grinning and laughing. Much to my surprise, it was Sarah, my boss, who owned up.

"Sorry, Matt. When I originally watched the draw with Hannah, my daughter, we were both really hoping you'd get one of the plum draws. But when you ended up getting Grimsby, we just had to laugh. After you won last night, it was Hannah's idea to do the map, so you can blame her!"

I had to admit it was quite funny, at least in an ironic sort of way. A lot of my friends and colleagues had admitted to watching the draw too and there was a lot of sympathy that we didn't draw one of the big guns. But it was nice to hear how interested everyone was, and to me it just underlined the magic of the FA Cup. There was little doubt that it had lost some of its glamour and prestige, with everything now geared around qualification for the Champions League. But there was no other cup competition in the world that could rival the history and the litany of upsets and shocks that was woven through the hundred plus years of the competition.

The day went quickly, and I was soon on the train home. As always, I read the free *Evening Standard* newspaper before

I picked up a book. I opened the sports pages first as I always did. Much to my surprise, there was a big article on Reigate Athletic. The *Standard* always covered the London clubs, and we just about qualified as Greater London. The story was about our rapid rise through the leagues in recent seasons and there were quotes from our chairman and Harry throughout the piece. Both were putting a very positive spin on our match against Grimsby, with the chairman saying he thought we had a real chance. Harry was more sanguine and pointed out they were at least sixty-three places above us in the league tables, taking the two leagues above us into account. But he did say it was a one-off game and, as everyone knew, the FA Cup threw up shocks every season. He was also at pains to point out that we had important league games before the cup tie in early December and he needed his players focusing on the next few games. I tucked the paper into my rucksack and also picked up a few spare copies that people had left behind them as I got off the train. I made sure to scan a copy and email it to the new American branch of our supporters club, as Anna was now calling herself.

The next few days passed slowly. Anna and I spoke every day on the phone as she'd promised, and it was usually the highlight of my day. I went down to the club for more treatment on the ankle, but in some ways I was quite happy not to be playing at Enfield on the Saturday. It was one of those injuries that was just going to take a little time and rest. Truth be told, it had swelled up a lot on the day after the Bromley game. I could only just get a shoe on. Naturally, when I went for treatment, Harry had checked in on me and no doubt spoke to Mel too. He made it clear that I would be selected when I was fit to play and he wasn't going to rush me back.

I decided to travel to Enfield to watch the boys and cheer them on. By 5pm, I'd rather wished I hadn't. It was a desperately poor game. We ended up losing 2–1 to a goal five minutes from the end. We'd certainly deserved a draw, but it was clear that the effort the boys had put in on Tuesday night was taking a toll, especially in the second half. Smithy, who was deputising for me again, had no real chance with either goal, which I was pleased about. There's nothing worse than coming into the team and then feeling like you've let them down by making a mistake.

Sunday was a much better day. One of my mates from school was a Chelsea season-ticket holder and had managed to get me a ticket for the local derby against Arsenal. It was very rare that I got the chance to go to Stamford Bridge, so that in itself was a real treat. To then watch us thump Arsenal 4–1 made it a very enjoyable day out and we had a few beers after the game to toast our heroes.

By Tuesday, I had to admit I was getting frustrated. The ankle wasn't healing as quickly as I'd hoped. Even if I had been fit, I wouldn't have been playing in the Surrey Senior Cup tie. Harry was giving most of the first team the night off, after a hectic schedule, and was using the competition to try out some of the U23 lads, mixed with some of the first team squad that had spent most of the time on the bench in recent weeks. I decided to go down to the club to watch. Partly because I thought it was the right thing to do to support the lads who were playing, and partly because it was just something to do to take my mind off Anna and dodgy ankles.

These local league cup games usually attract one man and his dog by way of spectators, but when I arrived at the ground about ten minutes before kick-off, even the dog was missing. It was almost deserted. We were playing Chipstead, who were only a few miles down the road from us and a division lower. I could only assume both sets of supporters were in the bar staying warm until the game started. Not a bad decision,

I thought, as it was certainly a chilly November night. Just then I heard someone calling my name. I turned and saw Jess walking towards me.

"Hey Jess. I'm surprised you're here tonight. Not exactly a glamour tie for a top sports reporter!"

"To be honest, Matt, I'm not here because of the game. We're doing a big feature on you guys which we're going to run just before the Grimsby game. So, I was planning to talk to a mix of people from the club. You know, the die-hard supporters, tea lady and everyone in between," she said, smiling.

"I'll look forward to reading it. You write really well."

Jess did a mock curtsey. "Why thank you, kind sir! High praise indeed," she said, with more than a tinge of sarcasm.

I rolled my eyes but couldn't help laughing. I could have put it a little bit better, so I probably deserved the sarcasm.

"As you're not playing tonight, how about I start with you?"

"Sure. But aren't you tired of getting quotes from me?"

"Nah. You'll do. Let's go sit in the press seats in the stand and I can put the recorder on."

We strolled into the stand and up the six flights of steps to the press seats. They had the words "press" on them, plus a couple of wooden fold-out tables. No expense spared for our friends in the press I'd thought, more than a few times.

We sat down and Jess switched on the recorder on her phone and set it down on the table between us. It was a snug fit as the seats were close together. Jess took out a sheet of paper which had a few hand-written questions scribbled out in rough.

"So, Matt, how do you feel about going to Grimsby?"

I had learned that you need to think when you answer a question from a journalist. Not that I expected that Jess would use anything I said out of context, but seeing words in black and white doesn't always capture *how* you said them or indeed meant them. And that could make all the difference. I was very well aware that we'd been fired up before by something the opposition had said about us before a game, and I didn't want to give the Grimsby lads any extra motivation.

"It will be a tough game. Although they're not having the best of seasons, Grimsby are a Football League side, have a tremendous history and we certainly respect the club. In some ways, it doesn't matter who we're up against. We're playing against an EFL side in the Second Round of the FA Cup. That's a dream come true."

"Very diplomatic, Matt. OK, so how about you? Will you be fully fit for that game as I understand you're likely to be out for a week or two?"

I looked at her and wondered where she'd got that from. Not many people knew that and no one, as far as I knew anyway, had said it was going to be for a few weeks.

"Oh yeah. I'll be fit and raring to go. I should be back for Saturday's game."

"Oh, OK. I thought you might be out longer. But you've had a bit of stop-start season, haven't you? Suspended, then injured."

"Yeah, I guess that's true. But it happens and you just have to deal with it. No one is irreplaceable."

"Everyone says you're a very modest bloke, but what do you make of the rumours that you've got a pro club or two watching you?"

"Don't believe everything you hear is what I'd say. We all hear a ton of rumours about people being watched, but it's usually bullshit," I said, smiling. "Umm…maybe I'd better say 'rubbish', not bullshit!"

"Too late! It's on tape," she said, smiling. "OK, Mr Modest, one last question. Tell me one thing that you think is better about the non-league game compared to the professional game?"

"Hmmm…that's a good question," I said, buying time to think of something. "Maybe it's the fact that we all do this because we really enjoy playing the game. I mean, most of us have full-time jobs, so getting to training or matches mid-week can be quite stressful, especially if like me you're relying on public transport. It sounds a cliché, but we do it for the love of the game and not for the money."

"So, you don't think professionals enjoy the game as much?"

"I don't know. It's their livelihood. They're under a lot of pressure, especially if things aren't going well, so I do wonder how many of them really enjoy it. From a fan's perspective, I think it's that you can still get so close to the action and you can talk to players after the game. There's more of a bond between the players and supporters at non-league, because we get to know each other."

"Two answers for the price of one. Thanks, Matt."

Jess leant forward and switched off the recorder. The teams were just coming out onto the pitch and the crowd had trebled in size; from ten people to around thirty. Jess got up to go. She bent to pick up her phone from the table just as I started to carefully manoeuvre to get out of my seat. Suddenly, our faces were a few inches apart. For a moment, although it seemed longer, time stopped, and we were looking into each other's eyes. Then someone called my name. The spell was broken. As I turned to see who was calling me, Jess moved quickly away.

I saw it was Graham, one of our supporters who came to nearly every home game, rain or shine. He wanted to know why I wasn't playing, so we had a chat for a few minutes. But I was a little distracted. Had something just happened between Jess and me? I couldn't quite work it out. I was feeling strangely guilty too, with Anna gone less than a week. Jess had called me modest, but here I was thinking that another girl was interested in me! I swiftly convinced myself that, first of all, I had imagined it, and, secondly, I was turning into a stereotypical footballer, thinking women would throw themselves at me! I laughed to myself at that thought and turned my attention back to Graham's questions.

Two hours later, after we had struggled to an uninspiring 1–0 victory, I was in the bar having a drink with Stan, who had also been rested for the game. It turned out that Jess had also spent time talking to Stan earlier, mainly about his time in Serbia and playing at Red Star. I had already checked the bar when I'd walked in. There was no sign of Jess. I wasn't sure whether I was disappointed or relieved. Maybe a bit of both.

"That reporter," said Stan, "she very beautiful. I think I ask her out."

Stan was many things: tough, loyal and built like the proverbial brick shit-house, but I doubt even his mum would call him good-looking. With his shaven head and broken nose, he looked more like a cage fighter than a footballer.

"I think she already has a boyfriend, Stan, so prepare to be disappointed."

I slapped him on the shoulder as I said it. I had just lied to my teammate and I had no idea why. I was pretty sure Jess didn't have a boyfriend from what another football reporter had said a few weeks ago, when we'd been talking about reporters who asked tough questions. I'd laughed and said that Jess Gallaway fell into that bracket.

"Ah, yes. She can be a real ball-breaker when she gets rubbed up the wrong way. No wonder she's single!"

What the hell was I doing? Jess could take care of herself and it wasn't for me to start screening prospective dates for her. Was I being protective? Or just plain jealous? The last thought really stopped me in my tracks. It was a stupid thought. I was in love with Anna. Jess was pretty and she was fun, and we could probably become good mates. But that was it. I told Stan I had to make a call and I went out to my car, got in the passenger seat and dialled Anna's number. She picked up almost immediately.

"Missing me?" She asked, with a laugh in her voice.

"Nah. I just got bored hearing about a six-feet Serbian's romantic interests, so you were my excuse to leave him at the bar."

"Wow, you are all charm sometimes, mister! I thought English guys were supposed to be gallant like knights of old?"

"The armour was too heavy and gets rusty in all this wet weather."

"Well, they did warn me that English men were the most unromantic in the world."

"Yet you let one into your life?"

"Just a social experiment. To see if they were right."

"How's the experiment going?"

"Early days still. Gotta do way more research."

"Weeks? Months?"

"Hard to say. But I wouldn't rule out years."

"That's so dedicated of you."

"Yep, but a girl has to make sure. I can't do this research half-assed and expect people to buy into my findings."

"Fair point. And how do the initial findings look?"

"No way José. This will be a Harvard research paper one day. You'll just have to wait."

The conversation went back and forth like that for another fifteen minutes. It was a lot of fun and it had been the same from the day we met. We were always taking the mickey out of each other, but it was always playful and never mean-spirited. Both of us were laughing and Anna was complaining her ribs were aching as a result by the time we ended the call. After we'd hung up, I sat in my car grinning. That girl was just hilarious. My odd thoughts about Jess had been blown away. Now all I had to do was survive the next few days without my girlfriend.

13

"You think THAT was acceptable? Well, let me tell you that it's NOT!"

It was pretty rare to see Harry lose his temper, but he had every right to do so. This was my first game back and we'd been thumped 4–1 at East Thurrock. At Enfield we'd been a little unlucky, but that certainly hadn't been the case tonight. Arguably, we'd been lucky. It could have been six or seven. I'd had a good game and had helped keep the score down with several decent saves, but that didn't make me feel any better.

"You're all thinking about the bloody game against Grimsby. That's what your problem is. Well, let me tell you this, gentlemen; if you play like that again, there's a number of you who won't even make the squad for Grimsby, never mind the bloody TEAM!"

With that, Harry stormed out and slammed the door behind him. What made it worse was that he was almost certainly right. We'd played the game tonight as though it didn't matter, and we really didn't give a toss whether we won or lost. I knew that we hadn't done that consciously. But, maybe subconsciously, that's where our heads were at the moment. It was a busy time of year football-wise. We had a few extra league games to fit in because of our cup run. The cups always take priority over league games, and we'd played four qualifying rounds and the first round proper, plus a replay. So, six games to make it to the Second Round. But that meant several league fixtures that had to be postponed. As a result, we were well behind the number of games played by most of the other clubs in our league. If we won those games in hand, we'd be in the top five in the table. But we had to win them, and we'd just lost two on the trot.

We needed to get our heads right and start picking up points again, or we were going to go to the FA Cup game in a bad run of form. Form tends to go hand in hand with confidence; if you're playing well, confidence is high and that helps keep the run going. But the reverse is also true. Get into a poor run and it eats away at your confidence, and, if you're not careful, it results in a downward spiral. Right now, we'd lost two away league games, against decent opposition, so it was nothing to panic about. But lose another couple and suddenly we'd be in a poor run of form at precisely the wrong time.

To make matters worse, I'd been kicked on my injured ankle. Right now, it was very sore, and I'd been limping heavily for the last twenty minutes of the game. After watching the Surrey Senior Cup game, I'd decided to phone the AFC Wimbledon doc and get his take on why the ankle was taking time to heal and whether I should be playing again. He had said there was likely to be bruising to the bone and that can take several weeks to disappear, assuming there was no further trauma to the area. I guess getting kicked right on the ankle would be classed as further trauma. For the first time, I was beginning to have genuine doubts that I would be fit for the cup game.

It was a quiet coach journey back to the club. No one was in the mood to do much more than listen to music on their headphones or try and sleep for the hour and a half it took us to get back. Close to midnight, I limped off the coach and eased myself into my car. At least Anna was due back the day after tomorrow and I had her call to look forward to. I plugged my phone in to recharge as it had died on the way home. The first thing that popped up was a WhatsApp message from Anna, saying she wouldn't be calling this evening as she was out with her pals. But the real bummer was that she was also staying a couple of days longer to spend more time with her folks. She'd explain when we next spoke, the message said. Perfect, I thought. A crap way to end a really crap evening. I knew I was being a bit unfair, because Anna had called every day as she'd promised to do, and we'd had a couple of really lovely calls, where she told me how much she was missing me. But this was one occasion where I could have done with her lifting my spirits.

I wandered off to the kitchen, feeling a bit sorry for myself. I grabbed a large yoghurt and a banana, as I'd eaten some pasta after the game. I also pulled my bag of frozen peas out of the freezer, which served as my ice pack. I plonked myself down in my armchair and switched on Sky Sports to catch up with the football results.

I went to bed soon after as I was knackered, but had trouble getting to sleep. Around 3am, I was half awake when my phone pinged. Another message from Anna. Actually, it was a picture of her and her pals out at a restaurant. I assumed that's why she wasn't calling as it wouldn't be private. She looked like she was having fun. There were a couple of good-looking guys either side of her, grinning away too. A pang of jealousy shot through me. Quite ridiculous I knew, but I couldn't deny it. I knew she hadn't sent me the photo to make me jealous and would have laughed at me and called me ridiculous for even thinking that. And she'd be right to do so. The phone pinged and another photo appeared. This one was of Anna on her own, presumably a selfie, smiling and blowing a kiss at the camera. The text underneath just had four letters:

TOUL.

It was our shorthand for "Thinking Of You Loads". I quickly typed back:

TOUL2.

I got a smile back and *sleep tite XXX.* I did sleep tight that night.

Anna actually called me the next morning when she woke up, which was around midday my time. She explained that the restaurant was noisy, and it had been chucking it down with rain outside, which meant she hadn't been able to nip out to call me. I told her that I was surprised that a little thing like a thunderstorm could stop her calling me. She called me a name and the banter began. It was a fun call until she made the mistake of asking me how the game had gone. I told her the result and tried to move the conversation on, but she then asked how my ankle was. I made some glib comment about it still being attached to my leg. She called me another rude name and persisted with the question, almost as though she sensed I was holding something back. I eventually told her the truth, but insisted it was nothing to worry about. It didn't sound like she was convinced. I told her not to worry and just enjoy her last few days there.

What I hadn't told her about was my conversation with Harry earlier that morning. He'd noticed me limping and asked if it was the ankle again. I told him it was, but I'd be fine for Saturday. Harry ignored me and told me he'd rung the Wimbledon manager again, and I had an appointment with their physio at 4pm that afternoon. I tried to protest, but Harry was having none of it. In truth, I was quite pleased to be going, if only to get some piece of mind, and that the latest setback wasn't anything serious.

I got to Wimbledon's ground in good time. Once again, everyone knew I was expected, and my name was checked off against the requisite lists. I strolled into the physio's area at five to four. I was seeing the physio rather than the doctor, though I didn't actually know his name. There were two guys there working on injured players when I walked in.

One of them looked up and said, "You Harry's keeper?"

"Yep, that's me."

"OK, grab a seat. I'll be about ten more minutes with this lump."

The "lump" in question I recognised as the AFC Wimbledon keeper, Rhys Davies, who was also Wales' number one. He looked across to me and grinned.

"I hope you're not seriously injured, 'cos this boyo couldn't treat a broken fingernail," Davies said in a lyrical Welsh voice.

"Lucky for you, I'm not the sort to hold grudges, you lanky git," the physio fired back.

I smiled. Football banter was the same in every club. Davies turned out to be a really nice bloke and started chatting away to me. People often talk about a "Goalkeeper's Union". There certainly is a bond between those wearing the gloves. I always make a point of going to shake hands with the opposition keeper after a game and will always compliment him if he's made a good save during the game. It's more often than not reciprocated too. We were still chatting away when we exchanged places on the treatment table.

Derek, which I eventually discovered was the physio's name, started by asking me what had happened and the cause of the original injury. I told him about the stitches and being seen by the club doctor. With the background out of the way, he moved the ankle around. Davies said he had to get home to the missus, so we shook hands and wished each other luck for the rest of the season.

I certainly got a thorough exam and Derek made me do several exercises to check the mobility of the ankle. A couple of the exercises caused me to wince in pain. Derek didn't say much. He put some pads on my ankle, which was wired to an electrical impulse machine that fired small charges of electricity, which in theory helps improve blood flow and aid the healing process.

"I think you need to rest this for at least seven to ten days and ideally a couple of weeks."

I had a strange feeling of déjà vu. Sitting on a treatment table and getting unexpectedly bad news.

"You can probably carry on playing, but I think you've got some deep bone bruising," Derek said. "It's not going to go away overnight and will probably take weeks, if not a couple of months to go completely. The problem is when people hear 'bone bruise', sometimes they think it's a less severe injury than it actually is. Bone bruises cause damage to the inner layer of bone, which is not as strong as the outer layer of bone."

I must have looked sceptical, or maybe just confused, because he carried on talking.

"If you carry on playing, there's a risk that another blow there will cause a fracture or a break. Or worse still, a bit of bone breaks off and then you'll need surgery to remove it. Even without another trauma to that same spot, there's a good chance you'll end up injuring something else, because your body is naturally trying to compensate for the injury. I often see a player with an injury that's caused by some other problem elsewhere. You'll probably end up with a hamstring, knee or calf injury in the other leg, which is having to cope with an imbalance to the weight you're placing on your injured leg."

"So, if I do rest it for a couple of weeks, I should be OK to start playing?" I asked with a degree of nervousness.

"The main thing is that the rest gives the injury and the swelling a chance to settle down again. If we can get you running normally, then the risk of an associated injury to another joint or muscle is greatly reduced. But it still means there is a risk to the bone if you get another whack on the same spot." He turned off the machine and wiped remains of the blue sticky gel off my ankle.

"Understood. Thanks, Derek. Really appreciate your time." I got up off the treatment table.

"Before you go, I'm going to give you a rehab programme, which includes a number of exercises to get blood flowing into the area and improve the mobility. But you'll need to do your part by following the RICE protocol. OK?"

RICE was something every sportsperson knew very well: rest, ice, compression, elevation. Often uncomfortable, but it always worked.

"Yep, thanks, Derek."

I walked to my car ten minutes later, wondering what to do. I hadn't been told to definitely stop playing. It was more of a suggestion, or a precaution. It left the onus very much on me to take a decision. Last time the decision was pretty much made for me by Harry. Plus, it was only one game. If I rested for a couple of weeks, it would mean missing three or four games, which wouldn't be good. As I was about to start the engine, my phone rang. It was Harry. I sighed. I still wasn't sure what to say.

Harry got right to the point and asked me what the physio

had said. I told him the truth. I imagined that Harry might also speak to the physio himself and I didn't want to get caught out. Harry listened and didn't say much. I paused and waited to hear his verdict.

"Listen, Matt, the last thing I want is for you to play hurt and just end up making it worse. But Smithy is away with his work next Saturday, and, as you know, we're playing Leatherhead who are top. I don't want to put the U23 lad in because he's just too inexperienced. If you play this Saturday, I will then rest you on the Tuesday and then the Worthing game the following Saturday, so you'll get ten days off. Plus, I need you to do a job for me."

"A job?" I was intrigued.

"Yep, on the Saturday of the Worthing game, I want you to go to Grimsby, to watch them play and do a report for me."

"A scouting mission? But couldn't someone else do it?"

"Like who? Jez and the rest of my staff will be at our game against Worthing. I don't think any of our directors know enough about the game to do a scouting report. None of my mates will do it as it's just too far and they'd want to be paid for it. The club will pay for your petrol or rail ticket. Grimsby will give us a ticket to the game and put you in the press box. It's already sorted. Fancy it?"

The more I thought about it, the more I thought it could be quite interesting. Anna would be back by then. I wondered if I could sell her on the idea of a weekend in Grimsby! Might take a little bit of persuasion.

"OK, if that's what you want, boss, you can count on me."

We ended the call and I drove home, deep in thought. I had wanted to play on Saturday against Leatherhead. We'd played them in the opening game of the season and we'd been on the wrong end of a 4–3 score line, but it had been a hell of a game. We'd been 3–2 up with about ten minutes left, but we'd got overexcited and tried to score a fourth instead of digging in and holding what we had. Leatherhead had broken away and equalised with five minutes left, and, while we were feeling sorry for ourselves, had grabbed a winner in stoppage time, which was a real sickener. But we'd felt we were the better side for most of the game and we wanted revenge. Although we'd lost two matches back to back, we were only eleven points behind them and had three games in hand. So, if we beat them on Saturday, and of course won our games in hand, we'd be right back in the title race.

When I got home, I googled trains to Grimsby. It wasn't exactly a straightforward journey and it meant changing a couple of times, going from Kings Cross. It said it would take about five and a half hours. I then looked at how long it would take me to drive it. Best part of four hours, traffic dependent of course, but at least I'd be able to come and go as I pleased and not have to hang around waiting for trains.

I was still contemplating the journey when Anna WhatsApped me to tell me she was booked to fly back to Heathrow on Thursday night. I messaged her back:

Thanks for letting me know babe. You going to call later?

Planning to, but I don't want to wake you up

I don't care. I'd rather talk to you than sleep

Aww. Maybe you can be romantic after all!

Maybe I should take you away for a romantic weekend when you're back

That would be nice. Somewhere in mind?

Yep but don't want to spoil the surprise Wow.

Maybe I should go away more often!

Don't you dare. I may not survive

Haha. OK gotta go as I promised to go shopping with my Mom. Catch you later hot stuff

Speak later pretty lady

I had some research to do. I didn't for one minute think that Anna would view a football match in Grimsby as fulfilling her criteria for a romantic weekend away. I had two choices; the first was to plan a separate weekend for the two of us, though that created problems for me with football of course. The second was to make sure that the Grimsby game was only part of the weekend, which sounded like the best option. I looked at the map again. Ages ago, Anna had mentioned she had a good pal of hers from uni who lived in York and she wanted to visit her one day. That could work. It was about another ninety minutes from Grimsby to York, but if I could persuade her to take the Monday off work, then we could spend a nice day in York. Plus meet up with her friend potentially too. By the time I'd finished, I'd found a nice hotel in the centre of the city and several places we could visit.

Anna eventually rang me at just after 2am UK time. She was full of apologies for calling so late. She was thoroughly enjoying being home and spending time with her parents. They'd only just finished dinner which was why she was calling so late. I told her I couldn't care less what time she called. We chatted for about thirty minutes, before Anna said she had better go back downstairs to see her parents. But before we said our goodbyes, she suddenly remembered about the weekend away.

"Gosh! I nearly forgot! So, tell me, where is this weekend going to be?"

"Well, you know you mentioned you had a friend in York and how you wanted to visit her?"

"Yes! Christy! We roomed together in my year at Durham. She was excited when she heard I was back working in the UK and we've talked about getting together for ages. She says it's a beautiful place."

"Yep, I've heard the same. We could go when you get back and see the city."

"OK, so what's the catch?" asked Anna, suspiciously.

"What do you mean what's the catch?" I said innocently.

"You are planning to go at a time which you'd already told me was a real busy time of year for soccer. There's more to this than you're letting on, pal!"

I spilled the beans and told her the full story. By the time I'd finished there was a deathly silence on the other end. Then she spoke.

"Oh my God! You crack me up," she said, laughing as she spoke. "This is going to make such an awesome story to tell my folks and all my girlfriends!" She was having trouble getting the words out now, she was laughing so much. "My boyfriend offers to take me away for a romantic weekend, just so long as I go to some football game in the middle of nowhere first! You are hilarious! Stop! My ribs are hurting," she said, gasping for air.

I had to admit that I was relieved she was seeing the funny side of it, and, looking at it from her perspective, it wasn't perhaps the most romantic proposition. Once she'd stopped laughing, I then played the ace card.

"Actually, the real weekend away is in May. I've booked us flights to Prague."

"What?! You're kidding, right?"

"Nope. Always wanted to go. Thought you might want to tag along," I said, smiling.

"Matt, it's supposed to be beautiful. Aww...maybe you have got a romantic streak after all! Thank you!" She paused. "But you're not off the hook for that first weekend away! This is gonna make such a great story. I need to do some digging and find out about Grimsby! Love the name!"

We were both laughing when we said our goodbyes. I knew I'd hear a lot more about our romantic weekend in the coming weeks!

14

Ten days later, at close to 2.30pm, I was manoeuvring my car into a tight space in Fuller Street, one of the many side streets close to Blundell Park. Anna was looking a little pensively at the leaden sky. It had stopped raining for now, but there was the promise of more to come in the dark clouds overhead.

Like quite a number of football clubs, Grimsby Town's ground isn't actually in Grimsby itself. It is in the town of Cleethorpes, which is a couple of miles down the coast. Judging from what we'd both read about the place, it is probably very nice in the summer, with its pier and sandy beach, but as the wind whistled in from the North Sea, which was only a few hundred yards away, it wasn't too welcoming on a December afternoon.

Anna pulled on her hat, gloves and scarf and raised her eyebrows at me as if to say, "I must be mad." I grinned at her and put my arm around her waist, and we walked quickly towards the ground. There were others in black and white scarves and hats doing the same. The pavements were wet from the earlier rain and the wind was gusting. Not a nice afternoon for the goalkeepers I was thinking.

We followed everyone else, although it was easy to see the ground as the floodlights towered over the adjacent houses. I'd read up a little on the club and there had been talk of Grimsby building a new ground a few years earlier, but like so many of these projects, the proposed site had issues with it and eventually the club gave up.

We'd been told to go to the main entrance, and we'd get our passes from the receptionist. It was all very straightforward. A lovely grey-haired lady, who you just imagine had been working at the club for the last thirty years, handed us an envelope with two tickets and a match programme, and told us where we needed to go. She told us to feel free to go into the boardroom at half-time or at the end of the match, just in case we needed a cuppa to warm us up.

As it was a little over ten minutes to go until kick-off, we decided to take our seats. As Harry had said, we were in the area reserved for the press. I got my pad and pen out, together with the team sheet that had been tucked into the programme. Grimsby were playing Exeter City. I could only imagine how long the journey from Exeter had taken. There was an intrepid band of visiting spectators clad in red and white, huddled together, but the ground, which had a capacity of over 9,000, looked decidedly empty. The Mariners, as they were known, were having a poor time of it and were one place off the bottom of division two. Exeter were comfortably mid-table, but not looking in any danger of going up, so it wasn't hard to see why the delights of being indoors or even early Christmas shopping was preferable to a raw late-November afternoon for the locals.

By the time the referee blew his whistle for half-time, I could see why Grimsby were struggling. Exeter were a goal up and could easily have been two or three ahead. There was some booing from the home supporters, though even that felt a little half-hearted. But I'd found plenty to write about. Harry was quite specific in what he wanted me to look at. First and foremost, playing formation and who played where. Next, it was set pieces, both for and against; corners, free kicks, goal kicks and who did what. That was where Anna came in. I asked her to help me by calling out the shirt number of Grimsby players and if they were left-footed or right-footed, while I wrote my notes. I think she quite enjoyed being involved and asked more and more questions about what I was doing as I explained the formation and the jobs different players were doing. Harry's other ask was to identify strengths and weaknesses of individual players. Were they quick or slow? Good in the air? Tracked back? There was a lot to cover, but Anna was increasingly helpful, and two pairs of eyes were definitely better than one.

We were both ready for a cup of something hot at half-time. I felt it would have been a bit odd to go into their boardroom and I wasn't exactly dressed smartly, so we asked one of the stewards in the corridor if there were any refreshments for the press. He was very friendly and actually walked us to the room. There were Thermos flasks of tea and coffee and plates of biscuits. There were three or four people in the room and, unsurprisingly, they all seemed to know one another. They nodded to us as we walked in, but I could see they were curious. We clearly weren't press or they would have known who we were. Anna had popped to the ladies. One of the men broke away from the group and came across to where I was standing.

"Hi there," he said, offering his hand. "Trevor Green from the *Grimsby Telegraph*. Haven't seen you here before?"

"Matt," I said, shaking his hand. "No, first time here."

I hadn't planned on a conversation with a local journalist and was wondering how I could make an escape. Just then, Anna walked back in and introductions were made.

"Ah, I detect an American accent. What brings you to Blundell Park of all places? Not normally on anyone's list of British tourist attractions!"

"Oh, Matt's doing some scouting for his team, so I was asked to tag along."

I could have killed her! But the cat was well and truly out of the bag. So, I told Green what I was doing at Grimsby and like any good journalist, he scented a story that might be better than reporting on Grimsby losing at home again. As the second half was just about to start, we agreed to chat after the final whistle.

"Good job you didn't get a job with the CIA!" I said to Anna as we settled back in our seats.

Anna didn't know what I was talking about, so I had to explain that I really didn't want to be interviewed by the local press and I was hoping to remain incognito.

"Whoops! Oh well, it's all good PR for the club, isn't it?" She countered, smiling brightly.

I grudgingly conceded that it probably was and at least I had the second half to compose my thoughts and work out what I might say.

I saw that the home side had made a change at the break, and as the second half got underway, I noted that they'd changed from a 4-4-1-1, to playing three at the back and lining up 3-5-2. Quite a shift, but they did look better for it. They equalised with fifteen minutes and the game ended 1–1. The home supporters also woke up and started singing. One song in particular made us both smile once we worked it out: "We only sing when we're fishing." Checking with a steward standing nearby, apparently it had been sung for generations and was reference to the heritage of Grimsby being one of the biggest fishing ports in the country for several decades.

I had plenty of notes and covered everything that Harry had asked me to look at. We were both chilled to the bone and when we got back to the press room, we were very happy to see there was hot soup and bread rolls, in addition to the coffee and biscuits. The *Telegraph* reporter gave us time to thaw out with the soup and hot drinks before he came over for a chat, which we appreciated. When he saw we'd finished, he wandered over, cup of tea in one hand and his phone in the other.

"OK to chat now?" he asked politely. "You don't mind if I record it? Saves trying to take notes!"

"Yeah, that's fine."

"So, what did you make of The Mariners then?"

"I thought they looked better when they switched formation after the break. Made them more solid at the back and having two up front made them more of a threat going forward. But if Exeter had taken their chances in the first half…" I left the rest unsaid as I didn't want to sound too negative about Grimsby.

"Fancy your chances then, having seen that?" Green asked, raising an eyebrow.

"If you go into a game thinking that you can't win, you've lost before a ball's been kicked. Any team can be beaten. We will come up here with belief that we can get a result. We know it will be extremely hard though. We'll need to play well, take our chances and maybe need a little luck too. You don't get to play professional football unless you're a good player. Grimsby have plenty of good players from what I've seen today. We'll have our work cut out."

"How many supporters do you normally get for your home games?"

"About 200 to 250, depending upon how many the opposition bring."

"And how many do you think you might bring to Blundell Park?"

"Hard to say. I think there's two or three coaches coming. I hope we'll have a few hundred here."

"Would you mind if I asked your young lady a question?" Green asked, looking at Anna.

"Err, no, of course not," I probably looked as surprised as Anna did.

"So, Anna, how did you come to be on a scouting mission for Reigate and what do you make of Grimsby?"

Anna laughed. I was keeping my fingers crossed she'd be diplomatic.

"Well, this was Matt's idea of a romantic weekend away. I guess that's what happens when you date a guy into his sport! I thought your goalie was awesome and I was happy when Grimsby got that great goal. It was different though, watching football analytically and emotionally detached for once."

"You get emotionally involved in Matt's games normally then?"

"Absolutely! I was never into soccer before I met this guy, but the first game I went to watch was like, wow! I could see why folks get caught up in it."

"Anna thinks that all our games will be like FA Cup ties." I interjected. "I haven't yet taken her to Harrow on a freezing Tuesday night in January, when there's about eighty people there!"

I smiled as I said it, and Anna rolled her eyes but smiled too. But there was probably some truth in it. Anna had only watched our big FA Cup games to date.

"You said analytically?"

"Oh, right. Well, I was helping Matt by calling out jersey

numbers, which foot they preferred using and their places on the field."

"I see," said Green. "And what do you think of Grimsby and Lincolnshire?"

"I just love seeing England. Everywhere has so much history and what I'd love to do is come back up here when football's not on the agenda and the weather is a little warmer to check out the beaches and villages and, of course, a few pubs!"

Green smiled and nodded. Anna was charm personified. She sounded like she meant it too, and it wouldn't have surprised me if she was planning a return visit.

"I'm sure you both have better things to do than talk to me, and I'd better go down and see what the Grimsby manager made of it today. But thank you both for your time and maybe I could grab you for a few words after the cup tie, Matt?"

"It's been a pleasure, and yes, of course. I'd be happy to do that."

"Enjoy the rest of your romantic weekend, Anna," said Green with a smile and walked off to re-join his colleagues.

"What a lovely man. That was fun!" Anna had a big beaming smile and squeezed my hand with hers.

"I told you we'd have a fun weekend!" I was pleased she was having a good time so far. "Shall we say our goodbyes and hit the road?"

By the time we had thanked our hosts and made our way back to the car, most of the crowds had dispersed. The rain was falling steadily now and with the fresh sea breeze, it was coming in almost horizontally, so the umbrella Anna was carrying was fairly useless. But it was a relatively short walk. Once back in the shelter of the car, I suggested a short detour to the pier and specifically to a fish and chip shop called Papas. According to visiting fans, they served some of the best fish and chips in the country. I told Anna she couldn't possibly visit the English seaside without a walk along a pier and a bag of fish and chips. She looked at me as though I was a little bit mad, but she told me to go for it.

Twenty minutes later, we were sitting in the car, looking out to the dark sea as the rain lashed against the windscreen. But we were demolishing the one portion of fish and chips that we'd decided to share. Anna declared it was the best fast food she'd ever eaten. I had to agree. It was well worth the windswept walk from the car to the chippie and back again. While we ate our improvised dinner, I checked the Reigate result on the league website. We'd drawn 1–1. Not a bad result as Worthing is a tough place to go. They usually get crowds of around 2,000, plus they have a plastic pitch, so the element of home advantage is certainly there. I saw I had a couple of messages in the players' WhatsApp group. I took a quick look while I wolfed down more chips. As expected, the messages were all along the lines of how brilliant Smithy had been and how I hadn't been missed at all. I smiled. Anna saw me smiling and so I showed her the messages. She just rolled her eyes.

We arrived in York around 8pm and found Christy's house quite easily. The weather hadn't improved much and when she suggested we open a bottle of wine and stay in for the evening, no one objected. Anna and Christy barely seemed to pause for breath as they did their level best to catch up in the shortest time possible. Christy's boyfriend, a guy called Michael, dropped in a little later and was a die-hard Leeds United fan, so the conversation soon switched to football.

It was a really nice weekend. Anna thoroughly enjoyed being with Christy (and me) and loved walking around York. I gave them some time to themselves on Sunday afternoon, so Michael and I found a pub which was showing Leeds against Huddersfield Town, which is a real local derby. All too soon it was Monday afternoon and we were on our way back to London. Out of interest, Anna googled the *Grimsby Telegraph* as we were driving home.

"Oh my GOD!" She exclaimed suddenly.

"What's the matter?" I quickly looked across to see Anna with a hand over her mouth, eyes wide.

"You are not gonna believe this! That journalist did write a piece about us! And get this! The headline is 'Reigate send American spy to run the rule over Mariners!' Can you believe that?!" She said laughing.

"Oh Lord!"

"It reads: 'The Grimsby Town press box isn't usually where you'd expect to find glamourous ladies from the eastern seaboard of the United States. Still less would you be expecting them to be there on a spying mission on behalf of the Mariners' FA Cup Second Round opponents, non-league Reigate Athletic. But Anna Fitzgerald and her partner, who just happens to be Reigate's keeper Matt Dempsey, were there to check out the Mariners. Ms Fitzgerald was particularly impressed with Town's keeper Sam Russell, who it must be said had a fine first half, making a series of spectacular saves to keep Exeter at bay.'"

"Is that it?"

"No, but the article goes on more about the chairman and his financial affairs. Although it does end with one more reference to 'the glamourous spy!'"

I groaned. "What does it say?"

"Whatever the outcome of the FA Cup Second Round encounter, Reigate's own Mata Hari will have played her part."

"Haha! That's a nice finish."

"Mata Hari? Wasn't she some sort of spy?"

"Yes. In the First World War. Spied for the Germans and used her feminine charms to gather information apparently."

"Jeez! So, I'm now being compared to a promiscuous spy?!"

"Well, you can see how good you are at getting information out of me later if you like!"

That got me a whack on my leg. But she was enjoying her fifteen minutes of fame and was already busy sending a link to the article to her folks, to Christy and several more of her friends. It was quite an end to a busy, but enjoyable weekend.

15

The initial excitement had subsided some while ago and several of the lads were now dozing or listening to their own music. There was a card school going at the back of the coach. The rain was coming down heavily, and the traffic on the A1 was slow as a result. But we'd left the ground at 8am, making sure we had plenty of time. There were five coaches behind us, somewhere in the murk, full of Athletic supporters. Our coach was players and officials only, so Anna was on another bus with the other girlfriends and wives. She thought it was a much better option, as she knew I wouldn't be much fun to talk to.

We had about another hour to go according to the driver, traffic permitting. He estimated that we'd reach the ground at around 1pm so long as the traffic didn't get any worse. There were TV monitors in the coach, which we naturally tuned to Sky Sports. I think we all got a thrill when we saw our name on the ticker on the screen which was listing all the Second-Round games. The club had really pushed the boat out for this game and thanks to the chairman, we were using a coach that

Crystal Palace's first team usually hired for their away games. To say it was plush was an understatement. Anna had taken one look inside and demanded to know why she was travelling in economy while I was in first class!

Since getting thumped at East Thurrock, we'd been in a decent run of form. I had managed to play in the clash against top of the table Leatherhead. It was a case of sweet revenge. We won 1–0 and I got voted Man of the Match. I found out when I opened my copy of *Non-League News* on Sunday morning. It is always the home side that writes the match reports for the paper and gets to select the MoM award, so it made it all the more special to have been given the accolade by the Leatherhead match reporter. We'd deserved it and although I made six or seven decent saves, only one was in the category of "a bit special", when I turned a point-blank header over the bar. I'd then missed the next two games as agreed with Harry. We won a home game on the Tuesday night against second from bottom Corinthian Casuals 2–0 and then got a 1–1 draw away to Worthing, when I was in Grimsby, which was a good result. I returned for a home game against Bognor Regis Town that we narrowly won 2–1 and then earlier in the week, on Tuesday night, we had demolished Cheshunt 5–0, though it helped that they'd been down to ten men for almost all the second half. Still, we were playing well, feeling confident and looking forward to the game against Grimsby. We'd climbed to seventh in the table and still had two or three games in hand on most of the teams above us.

There had already been plenty of distractions in the days leading up to the game. It had really started midweek. Jess called my mobile while I was at work. I had assumed she wanted to speak to me about the game. She did, but not in a way that I had imagined.

She said that a source had told her the Grimsby players were going on strike, as they hadn't been paid since October. We'd read a few of those stories about players not getting paid, but the Grimsby chairman had always maintained that new funding was coming into the club and everything would be resolved shortly. Jess told me that the new funding had not materialised, and the players had called in the Professional Footballers' Association to fight their corner. It had been a small story, though one we were all aware of naturally. But neither was it that unusual for lower league clubs to have cash-flow problems from time to time, so we really didn't think too much about it.

Jess, however, was adamant that a full-blown strike was on the cards as the players had lost patience. They were doing it on FA Cup Second Round weekend to get the greatest possible coverage in the media and highlight their plight. I took it all with a pinch of salt and I think Jess was a little miffed that I wasn't all that excited by her news. But on the Friday morning, my phone pinged with a dozen messages in a very short space of time, as friends and teammates were asking me if I'd heard the news that the Grimsby first team squad were officially on strike and would not be playing in the club's cup tie with Reigate Athletic!

Naturally, I checked various online news channels before I really believed it. One of the first things I did was to send a slightly apologetic text to Jess saying she had been right. I didn't get a reply, which suggested she was a little annoyed with me.

None of us had any idea what sort of team Grimsby would be fielding. A lot of the lads thought that the first teamers would climb down and play the game. They'd made their point and their strike had received a lot of media coverage was the theory. I wasn't so sure. If you go that far out on the ledge to go on strike in the first place, it seemed unlikely to me that they would back down immediately unless the club paid them.

I was still lost in my thoughts when the coach turned into Imperial Avenue. We could see the floodlight pylons through the misty rain. A yellow-jacketed attendant waved us into the car park and another steward was pointing to where we should park the coach. The lads were all buzzing with excitement as they looked at the stadium on our left. It was 1.10pm, so it was still relatively quiet.

But not that quiet. As soon as the driver had parked and we started to disembark, a reporter and camera crew wearing Sky Sports jackets emerged from a huge Sky Sports trailer that was taking up a large part of the car park. The little group came hurrying towards us, splashing their way through puddles. Harry was one of the first off the coach and the reporter was ready and waiting with her microphone and cameraman.

"Harry, Charlotte Jaquart from Sky Sports. Could we have a quick word?"

She asked politely enough, but she stood right in front of Harry and didn't look as though she was going to take no for an answer. Harry wasn't a great fan of speaking to the press as a rule, but realised this was a big day for the club and we needed all the publicity we could get.

"OK, but it will need to be quick as I need to get the lads ready for the game."

"Brilliant! Just a few questions. Dan," she said turning to the guy without the camera, "tell the studio we're ready to go live."

Dan was already on his phone, holding an umbrella over the reporter, while she got herself ready. The players were all getting their kit out of the coach luggage storage but doing it slowly enough so they could watch what was going on. Dan gave Charlotte the thumbs up and the cameraman lifted the camera onto his shoulder. Dan was still on the phone and began counting down from five. He then pointed at Charlotte, who was pressing her earpiece into her ear.

"Yes, Jim, I'm here with the manager of Reigate Athletic, Harry Thackery, whose side are due to be facing a Grimsby Town team in just under two hours. But because of the strike by the Grimsby players, who maintain that they haven't been paid for several weeks, no one knows what Grimsby side will contest this FA Cup tie. Harry, what sort of team are you expecting Grimsby to put out today. We're hearing it might be their under-23 side?"

"To be honest, it doesn't make much difference. Whoever they have in their line-up, they will be professional players and we will treat them with the same respect."

"But surely you must fancy your chances now, if none of the Grimsby first team are playing?"

"We don't know that. Until I see their team sheet, I'll assume we're facing the side we've prepared for all week."

"I just spoke to John Steadman, the Grimsby manager, and all he said was that he'll be putting out the strongest side possible. But you must have a great chance of getting through to Round Three now?"

She had asked the same question in three different ways, but Harry was refusing to bite.

"It will be a very tough game whoever lines up for Grimsby and my players know that."

Dan drew his finger across his throat to indicate that was time up.

"And there you have it, Jim. An air of uncertainty and mystery hangs over this cup tie, with non-league Reigate Athletic still not sure who they'll be lining up against at 3pm. This is Charlotte Jaquart reporting live from Blundell Park, Grimsby."

"And, we're out," said Dan, indicating the interview was over.

"Thanks, Harry," said Charlotte, handing her mic to the cameraman. "Is it OK if I grab you straight after the game if you win?"

"Err, I guess so."

"Thanks. Good luck."

She gave us all a big smile, revealing perfect white teeth. She turned smartly on her heels and headed back the way she'd come with film crew in tow. About fifteen pairs of eyes were watching her go.

"Right, let's go!" yelled Harry, making sure he got everyone's attention.

Ten minutes later we were sitting in the away dressing room. It didn't look very different to our own. It was about the same size, with wooden benches and a clothes rail with hooks. Harry got everyone settled down and once we were quiet, he gave his customary short, pre-match speech. This one was a little different and for once, we were all listening intently.

"You need to remember three things today, which I know is a lot for one or two of you!"

That got a few smiles and chuckles. Everyone assuming that it was aimed at someone else and not them!

"First. They are a professional club, with full-time professional players and coaches. IT DOES NOT MATTER who lines up opposite you. First teamers, reserves or youth team. They will be good players and if you go into this match thinking anything else, you will be out of the Cup before you know what's hit you. Respect them, but don't fear them. We've proved when we're on our game, we can live with anyone." Harry looked around as he said it, making eye contact with every one of us.

"Second. Play our game. Don't worry about theirs. You all

know your assignments on their corners and free kicks, but I want us to get the ball down and play. Do NOT play the occasion. Yeah, this is the Second Round of the FA Cup. But it is also just a football match. Get out there and enjoy it. Play with your heads as well as your hearts. As long as we play our football, I don't care about the result.

"Third and last. We've got about 500 supporters out there. They are proud of you. I am proud of you. Make sure they are still proud of you at the final whistle."

Harry paused, looking at each one of us in turn. We were all looking intently back at him, soaking in every word. He then went round and shook every player's hand in turn, wishing them good luck. Then he walked out. Cue the music. It was not my choice, but it was loud and got some of the lads going.

At ten past two, Jez told us to go out and get warmed up. We'd need it. As we walked out onto the pitch, it was still raining and there was a biting wind, but at least it wasn't that strong. I looked up into the stand to see if Anna was there, but I couldn't see her. I didn't really expect to. If she had any sense, she'd stay in the warm until the last possible minute. But I did see a lot of yellow and blue away to my left. I ran towards the Osmond Stand, hands clapping as I did so. I got a big cheer back as I did. As I got closer, I saw that Harry had been right. We had brought a LOT of people with us. There must have been several hundred. It was a special moment.

I went through my usual warm-up routine with Smithy and felt good. The pitch was very wet, but at least there was no standing water on it and the ball was moving normally over the surface. It was a typically dismal winter's afternoon, and the floodlights were already on. I could hear the occasional screech of a seagull above the general noise, just to remind me how close to the sea we were. At twenty to three, Harry shouted for us to come in. I was soaking wet, but at least it was my warm-up gear that was wet. My match wear was still nice and dry. Not that it would stay that way for long once I got out there, but it was better than sitting in wet clothes for the twenty minutes before kick-off.

Once back in the dry, we all went through our normal last-minute routines. The air in the room was heavy with a smell of wet clothes and bodies, mixed with Deep Heat and Vick, which a lot of players put around their nostrils or on their chest to help their breathing, or so the theory went.

The referee's buzzer sounded and with the normal handshakes and back-slaps, we were on our way out through the door and into the tunnel. It was narrow and not wide enough for both teams to line up alongside each other. The ref and his two assistants were leading us out. I looked at some of their players. I didn't recognise any of them. They were all very young. The rumour about them playing their U23 side must have been true! I got a huge boost, but I didn't say anything to my teammates, as Harry's words resonated through my head. They may be young, but they were professionals, U23s or not.

As we came out of the tunnel, the noise hit us. The stadium held about 10,000 and although it wasn't full, there was a decent-sized crowd. We lined up in the middle to do the traditional pre-match handshakes. Their players all had a mascot with them. Young boys and girls in Grimsby shirts looking either excited or bemused by the whole experience. Final handshake done, I jogged to the goal at the visiting supporters' end. Our crowd seemed to have grown even more, and there was a real roar this time to welcome the team as we did our final loosening up. I looked up at the main stand to see if I could spot Anna, but there was a solid mass of people seated there now and it was hard to pick out individuals. I knew she was there though, and that was all that mattered.

The ref, dressed in a fluorescent lime green shirt, blew his whistle to start the game and finally all the waiting was over.

The Grimsby players started with great energy, trying to close us down and win the ball. But we started confidently, and Harry would have been delighted how we were passing the ball around and retaining possession. Although we like to keep the ball on the floor, we will also go the aerial route if the option presents itself. In the eighth minute, that's what we did. Harry had been bold and started Addi, largely because my scouting report said that if they played three at the back, there would be plenty of space on the flanks. Although Grimsby had different personnel, the system they started looked to be the same 3-5-1-1. Stevie fed the ball out wide to Addi and our young winger wasted no time in whipping a head-height ball into the Town box, where Antonio met it with a glancing header at the near post. The ball flew into the top corner of the net. Our supporters behind me erupted and I was punching the air in delight as my teammates were mobbing Antonio at the far end of the ground. It was a dream start.

One quarter of the ground was a mass of yellow and blue flags, scarves and banners waving wildly. The rest of the ground watched in stony silence. If they hadn't known before the game, the Grimsby fans now knew their team faced a real battle.

Right from the restart, Grimsby strung several passes together before one of their wing-backs floated a high, hanging ball into our area. A few weeks ago, with my dodgy ankle, I'd have left it for my defenders to deal with. But I was feeling much more confident now and with a loud call, I came all the way to our penalty spot to pluck the ball out of the air, despite a challenge from their big striker. As soon as I landed, I looked at any options to throw the ball out. I saw Addi waving his arms on the right touchline, close to half-way. The wing-back was out of position. I have a decent throw, so without hesitation, I hurled the ball Addi's way. He took the ball on his chest and motored down the line.

The Grimsby lad who was on the left of the back three had to come over to try and stop Addi. That left a big gap between him and the lad in the centre of the three who was marking Antonio. Beno saw the gap and sprinted into it. Sometimes Addi is inclined to run with the ball too much, but not this time. He spotted Beno's run and played the ball into the space vacated by the defender. Beno took a touch and was into their penalty area, but wide of the goal. As the central defender came across to cut him off, Beno fired a low ball across the six-yard box. Antonio got there just ahead of the covering centre-back and with the deftest of touches, guided the ball into the far corner, past the keeper's despairing dive. 2–0! We'd only been playing ten minutes according to the electronic scoreboard. Our crowd were going mad behind me and Stan and Simo ran over to celebrate with me as they knew it was my throw that led to the goal.

The young Grimsby players looked stunned. There was some pointing and gesticulating, but three or four had their heads down, unable to believe it. Harry was on the edge of his technical area with one finger pointing to his temple. The message was obvious. We needed to play with our heads now and not get carried away. If we let Grimsby back into the game by conceding a silly goal, we'd give them confidence. We needed to be professional now and manage the game.

For the next twenty minutes, we did just that. Keeping possession, we played the ball around crisply and neatly, while the Grimsby youngsters chased shadows. We had a couple of good situations, but failed to make the most of them. At my end, they put three or four high balls into our box, which was just giving me catching practice. With about ten minutes of the half left, I made another routine catch from another cross. I was surprised they were persisting with it. This time, instead of rolling it out, I kicked it long towards Antonio. Harry tells me to do that every so often, just to keep their defenders on their toes.

I made good contact and the ball, wind-assisted, travelled deep into their half. Antonio went up for the ball with two of their defenders. No one won it cleanly and the ball dropped about a yard away from the three of them. Any striker with two goals to their name in a game is always going to fancy their chances of adding a third and Antonio was no different. He was first to react and from at least twenty-five yards, tried his luck. He didn't make great contact though and the ball bounced a couple of times as their keeper dived to gather his rather weak effort in. I had already turned away as I was a few yards outside my area to needed to get back in position. As I did, I saw our fans suddenly go wild. I turned to see the ball nestling in the back of the Grimsby net. Somehow it had squirmed through their keeper and we were 3–0 up! Antonio was off, his arms waving wildly as he began celebrating his hat-trick, with the rest of the lads in hot pursuit.

But my attention was drawn to the Grimsby keeper, who was laying on his back in his six-yard box, with his gloves covering his face, unable to believe what he'd done. I felt a pang of sympathy for him. We'd all been there as keepers. When we make a bad mistake, ninety-nine times out of a hundred it results in a goal and everyone knows it is our fault. One of his players went over to him and hauled him to his feet. That's when you need your teammates.

If the Grimsby players had been stunned after the second goal, they were shell-shocked now. A couple were down on their haunches. In a normal game, you'd have expected the home crowd to be booing and jeering their players by now, but the Town supporters knew they were young and inexperienced, and the last thing they needed was abuse from their own fans.

The ref's whistle blew for half-time and we walked off, hardly able to believe we were three nothing up. The dressing room was loud and raucous as we were all talking at once, excited with our first half display.

Harry walked in and didn't look overly pleased, as he called for quiet.

"This ain't over lads. You go out thinking you're already in the next round, and you'll get a nasty shock. I don't want to be trying to explain to that Sky Sports lady how we lost a three-goal lead after the game."

He paused to let that thought sink in. We all knew he was right. He'd wiped the smiles off our faces with just a few well-chosen words. That was the magic of Harry. He didn't rant very often. Nor did he like the sound of his own voice and go on and on. When he said something, it was worth listening to. He went over a few things that we had done well, and some that we could have done better in the first half. Jez added a couple of things and then we were getting ourselves ready to go again.

As we lined up ready for the second half, the Grimsby boss was making two substitutions. It looked to me as if he was doing what he'd done in the game I'd watched with Anna and was going to 4-4-2. Certainly, they were lining up with a back four now.

Sometimes when you go in with a healthy lead, subconsciously you relax a little and instead of giving 100%, you're only giving 90% because you think the game's won. But we started off the second half the same way that we'd ended the first. We were totally in control. We didn't look especially threatening going forward, but then neither did they and of the two teams, we were far happier with a midfield stalemate.

It looked to all the world as though we were cruising to victory. But football has a nasty way of surprising you. With about twenty minutes left, Stevie was playing "keep ball" with a series of short passes to his defenders. Not really going anywhere. Just retaining possession. One of the young Grimsby lads, purely out of frustration, took exception and went flying in with a full-blooded challenge. It was late and it was high, and it caught Stevie half-way up his shin. Luckily, Stevie had seen it coming and was already jumping out of the way, but still got caught. Furious, he jumped back up to confront the Grimsby player, his head pushing into his opponent's face. The Grimsby lad went down and that's when it all kicked off. A twenty-man melee erupted, as our lads rushed in to pull Stevie away and their players rushed in to defend their teammate. Even I got involved trying to separate our players. It must have taken three or four minutes for the ref to restore order.

He called Stevie and the Grimsby lad over to him. He pulled his yellow card out and booked their player. I fully expected Stevie to get the same. Then to my horror, I saw him reach into his back pocket and show Stevie a straight red card. Stevie was aghast and several of our players, including John, ran over to protest. But naturally it changed nothing. Stevie slowly trudged off, as I saw the ref also brandish a yellow card at Beno, who'd obviously said too much.

I looked up at the scoreboard. It said we were in the seventy-second minute. The rain was getting heavier if anything and the wind that was with us in the first half was now blowing strongly in our faces. Although we were down to ten men, we had a three-goal lead and around twenty minutes to play, so I don't think a single Reigate player or fan was unduly worried. That was until Grimsby scored.

It came out of the blue. They had looked pretty toothless

to that point and we had coped comfortably with their attacks. But as so often happens in football, you can't legislate for individual mistakes. Simo had played the ball across the back to Stan. He took a touch, but just as he was about to launch it up-field, his standing foot slid from underneath him on the increasingly treacherous surface and he went down on his backside. The only player anywhere close to him was one of the Grimsby forwards, who'd been half-heartedly trying to close Stan down. Hardly able to believe his luck, the forward took possession and charged towards goal, with just me to beat. I advanced to narrow the angle. I wasn't going to commit myself. He was going to have to make the decision.

The forward elected to try and slide it past me rather than go around me. But by the way he shaped his body, in that split second I knew what he was going to do and was already diving that way as he shot. I got a solid hand to the ball and it ran away to my left. But as I started to get up, I saw that another Town forward was winning the race with Jamie to the rebound.

As keepers, one drill we all do in training is to dive and save the first shot and then get up to dive again for a second. This was the same as the drill. I got to my feet then launched myself, sliding on the wet surface, as the Grimsby player got to the ball. He was barely five yards away, and his shot cannoned into my right knee and rebounded away. The momentum of my dive and the wet surface meant I was still sliding. I twisted my head to see the ball had looped up into the air off my leg and was falling perfectly for the Town forward who had the original chance. This time he had the simple task of nodding it into an empty net.

I was furious. I'd saved two shots and yet they'd still scored. I thumped the muddy ground in disgust as I knelt there yelling at my defenders. Suddenly it was the home crowd that were noisy. One of the Grimsby lads rushed into our goal and picked the ball out of the net to get the game restarted. We were in no hurry though, despite the ref telling us to get a move on and pointing at his watch to indicate he'd add the time on. I looked up at the clock. We were in the eighty-second minute.

I looked at my teammates as we prepared to kick off. John had both hands out and was giving the calm down gesture. Beno and Charlie were clapping their hands and trying to rev everyone up. Tommy was pointing up at the clock to remind everyone there was only eight minutes of normal time left. It summed it up perfectly. We weren't sure whether to twist or stick. That became obvious with two minutes left. Tommy knocked a great ball down the line for Addi. If Addi was a little more experienced, he would have headed straight for the corner flag and tried to keep possession or win a throw or a corner. Instead, he feinted and tried to take his man on. And lost possession. Even worse, I saw most of our midfield had gone forward in support of Addi, expecting him to try and take it to the corner flag and keep them penned in. But suddenly they had a counter-attack on and there were gaping holes in our midfield.

The Grimsby defender who'd nicked the ball off Addi looked up and hit a perfect cross-field ball to their wide-right player. He took the ball down superbly in stride and ran at our left-back. Jamie was back-peddling, trying not to commit and let the player go past. But the Grimsby lad dipped a shoulder, making Jamie think he was going outside. Jamie bought the dummy allowing the pacey forward to cut inside. He was outside the box but decided to let fly. Stan was closing him down and blocked the first effort. But the ball dropped perfectly for the guy who got their first goal. He didn't hesitate and caught the bouncing ball sweetly. Luckily for us, he hit it too well and it was more or less straight at me and, arching backwards, I tipped it over the bar. There was a collective groan from the home supporters. It looked a spectacular save, but it was a save I would expect to make. But at that stage of the cup tie, my defenders were rushing over to high five me. I was pushing them away and yelling at them to mark up.

We thought our opponents would wait until their big defenders came up and they probably should have done. But sometimes inexperience can work for you. Instead of waiting to get the set piece set up, they took a quick, short corner. We weren't ready and were all over the place with our marking. The ball was fired in by their wing-back. Somebody got a touch with a header at the near post and I stuck out a hand to make a reflex save. But the ball dropped into the six-yard box. There followed the mother of all goal-mouth scrambles as bodies dived in to try and score or to block shots. One, twice, three times, they got a shot on target and each time one of our lads got something in the way to block it. The last shot ricocheted off someone and all I could do was watch as the ball hit the inside of the post. I dived backwards and scooped the ball away. The Grimsby lads all had their hands in the air in celebration. Simo booted the ball out for a throw-in.

The Grimsby players were imploring the ref to go and consult his assistant. This had a strange feeling of déjà vu. I had no idea if I had got to the ball before it had crossed the line. I knew it was desperately close. I watched as the ref spoke to his assistant. I didn't see how he could tell from his side of the field, as my body would have been blocking him. He couldn't give it.

The ref nodded. He turned and pointed – for a goal! The stadium erupted in delight. We were stunned. A couple of the lads chased the ref as he ran back. I ran over with Simo to speak to the assistant. I didn't swear as the last thing we needed was another player dismissed for foul and abusive language. But I was direct and to the point.

"How can you give that? You couldn't see if it had crossed the line! You were guessing!"

The assistant was telling us to go away and adopting the thousand-yard stare, looking at some spot over our shoulders but not making eye contact. Simo was yelling at him and the Grimsby supporters were yelling back at us, suggesting we go away, or words to that effect.

I saw Harry waving us away. I knew he was right, so I pulled Simo away. Nothing we said was going to change the decision now. We had to focus on seeing out these last five or six minutes. All the drama of the goal/no goal decision had taken us past the ninety minutes. The board came up to indicate there would be six minutes of added time!

Grimsby were suddenly a yard quicker than us as we desperately clung to our lead. None of our players wanted to make another mistake, so we ended up just knocking the ball long and quite aimlessly up the pitch. That meant it just kept coming straight back. We tried to push up, but we were sinking deeper and deeper, which just invited Grimsby on. A shot from twenty-five yards went narrowly wide, although I had it covered. Stan and John both got towering headers in to clear the danger temporarily. Our supporters behind me were whistling furiously and pointing to their watches. Time had to be almost up. Another ball was launched into our box. I made my mind up early that it was my ball. As I advanced out of goal, I quickly realised it wasn't coming as deep into the box as I'd first thought. Too late now. I had to go for it. I went up with a couple of their players and a couple of ours. No one had heard me yell for the ball in the bedlam and my defenders were doing their level best to clear it. I got the ball in my fingertips, plucking it almost off the head of one of their centre-backs who'd been thrown forward. I fell to the muddy ground on the penalty spot, clinging to the ball. The catch was greeted with an enormous cheer from our mob behind me. I was patted, none too gently, on the head by several of our lads as I very slowly picked myself up off the ground and prepared to launch the ball up-field. As soon I did, the ref blew for full time.

My main emotion was one of relief rather than joy. It would have been horrendous if we'd blown a three-goal lead. We hugged one another and commiserated with the losers. We went over to our fans and thanked them as we celebrated together. I don't think any of our supporters cared that we'd only won 3–2. They were just happy that we'd won.

There was a strange mood in the dressing room afterwards. We were, of course, pleased that we'd won, but we were also annoyed with ourselves for letting the young Grimsby side back into the game. The sending off hadn't helped, but we should have been able to control the game better once we were down to ten men. Stevie apologised to us all, but we all told him he had nothing to apologise for. It was just one of those things that happen in football. Refs are human and will sometimes get it wrong. Players make mistakes and so do the officials. Of course, it was a lot easier to be philosophical when you'd won. We were certainly a little subdued, and it took Harry to put things into perspective when he came in a few minutes later.

"Forget the last fifteen minutes. For seventy-five minutes, we controlled the game, played some great football and scored three goals against a Football League side AWAY FROM HOME. I am proud of each and every one of you. Yeah, you gave me a few extra grey hairs towards the end, but at the end of the day, we did what we came here to do. We won! And gentlemen, we are now in the THIRD ROUND OF THE FA CUP! You've done the club proud, the supporters proud and the town proud. Now stop moping around and start bloody well celebrating!"

With that, he revealed a bottle of champagne that he'd been holding behind his back. He'd already removed the foil and probably given it a good shake, because as soon as the cork popped, he was spraying it everywhere. The mood changed almost instantly, and Jez came in with a couple more bottles. Harry had let the Sky camera crew in briefly to capture some of those traditional shots of half-naked players jumping up and down and singing badly out of tune.

"Matt!" yelled Harry. "A reporter wants a quick word with you."

Luckily, I still had all my kit on, though arguably I was wetter now than I had been standing out in the driving rain. I went out into the corridor outside the changing room, where the reporter was waiting. It was Trevor Green from the *Grimsby Telegraph*.

"Hi Matt. First of all, congratulations. It was a thrilling game of football.

"A bit too thrilling for my liking! But thanks."

"Thanks for agreeing to talk to me. I've just spoken to the Grimsby Town manager. He's very unhappy about the second goal and accused you of cheating. What do you say to that?"

I was dumbstruck. I had no idea if the ball had crossed the line or not. But to be accused of cheating is not something any sportsperson likes to hear. I could feel myself getting angry but tried to control it.

"Cheating? I have no idea if the whole of the ball crossed the line or not. I knew it was close, but I just did my best to keep the ball out. But cheating? No way."

"He was angry you went over to the lineman to protest too."

"Yeah, because I honestly don't see how the assistant could give it as he couldn't have had a clear view to make a decision from his position."

"So, you genuinely had no idea if it was a goal or not?"

"Absolutely not."

"OK, thanks, Matt. I guess we'll have to wait until later when we see the Sky coverage of the game."

We shook hands and I went back into the dressing room. Harry saw the look on my face and asked what had happened. I told him. He was furious. He was all set to go and have it out with the Grimsby boss, but Jez and I talked him out of it. It wouldn't help. Emotions always run high after a game, and sometimes the smart thing was just to let things cool down.

I was still a bit miffed by the time I reached the bar. In fairness, the Grimsby staff were brilliant. They were all congratulating us and wishing us all the best in the next round. Lovely, genuine and very down to earth people. Anna knew something was wrong as soon as she saw my face. I told her what the Grimsby boss had said.

"Jesus Christ! How the hell can he say that? No one around me in the stand seemed to be sure either way. It all happened so fast. It's crap that he's taken the shine off things for you."

Just then Jess appeared from the scrum around the bar. She saw me and walked over. I was a little on edge as she and Anna said hello. But they smiled and were actually quite pleasant to each other, much to my relief. Jess had already spoken to Harry and knew what the Grimsby boss had said.

"Listen, Matt, I know Charlotte, the Sky reporter who's here with their broadcast team. I might be able to get us into their trailer and take a look at that goal if you want?"

Sky were showing highlights of the game later that

evening, along with several other Second-Round matches. The old days of the BBC having the monopoly on the FA Cup were long gone and all the football broadcasters were showing the games.

"If you can, that'd be great. I'd like to know one way or the other."

"Leave it with me," she said, heading for the door.

Ten minutes later, she was back at the door, beckoning to us. I pushed my way through to Jess, with Anna following in my wake.

"She says it's fine. We'll have to be quick though as they're starting to pack up their gear."

We hurried after her, out through the main doors into the car park where the Sky Sports trailer sat. It was a huge beast. Probably the size of two regular trucks mashed together. Charlotte greeted us at the stairs into the trailer. Quick introductions were made and then we followed her inside. There was a mass of equipment. Lots of monitors and things that looked like mixing desks, plus a number of things I had no idea what they were used for. Charlotte waved us over to a monitor.

"This is Jorge. He's a wizard with this stuff."

Jorge smiled and we gathered round the monitor. He had already got the recording lined up.

"Charlotte said you wanted to have a look at their second goal?"

"Yes, please," replied Jess quickly.

It occurred to me, rather belatedly, that she might have a story here too. The clock in the top corner of the screen showed we were watching the eighty-sixth minute of the game. He fast-forwarded to the key moment, as the ball struck the post. He slowed the speed down and we all watched closely as I dived to scoop the ball out. I realised I was holding my breath.

The main camera was on the same side as the lineman and it was really hard to tell, even though Jorge was able to zoom in.

"No way to tell," I said quietly.

"Hang on. We have a camera on the other side of the ground. Let me grab that footage."

He played around with his console while we made small talk. Well, Anna, Charlotte and Jess did. I just wanted to see the other camera's footage. After a few minutes, Jorge announced he was ready. He fast-forwarded the recording to the same moment in the game. We all watched intently, as he slowed it down as I dived and then stopped it as my hand started to scoop the ball back.

"No way!" said Anna.

"It doesn't look like it," Charlotte agreed.

"Anna's absolutely right. Definitely not. It's not the whole of the ball." Jess was adamant.

She was right. We had a good line of sight from the camera on the far side of the ground. It was close, but as Jorge zoomed in further using his gizmos. It looked clear that I'd hooked it back in time.

"Use the graphics, Jorge, just so we can be sure. We can use them in the highlight later."

Although it wasn't the goal line technology that was in use in the Premier League, modern technology using different cameras could create a 3D image in a graphic to show where the ball was in relation to the goal. As Jorge explained as he fiddled with dials, there was a small margin for error, but it was 95% accurate. We waited expectantly. The graphic came up on the screen. It clearly showed that only half of the ball had crossed the line but certainly not the whole ball. Anna now looked less certain, until we explained the rule to her.

"That guy owes you an apology!" Anna said angrily, once the rules had been clarified to her.

"It doesn't matter. He'll soon see the footage himself and realise he was wrong and made himself look stupid. People say things in the heat of the moment. The main thing is that people can't say I'm a cheat."

"Very magnanimous of you, Matt," said Jess, "but I completely agree with Anna. He does owe you an apology."

Anna held out her hand and she and Jess bumped fists, smiling as they did so. It was almost funny that they'd gone from mortal enemies to besties in the space of an afternoon. I never would understand girls! Charlotte had a thoughtful look. Maybe she was already planning a quick news piece: "Cheat Row Overshadows Shock Win".

For me, it was enough that my name was cleared. "Nope. Leave it. We'll be leaving here shortly. It's no big deal."

We thanked Charlotte and Jorge and stepped out of the trailer into a dark and very wet November evening. I went ahead as the two girls were walking together, huddled under a Sky Sports golf umbrella that Charlotte had given to Jess, with lots of hugs and promises to stay in touch. I reminded myself to ask Jess how she knew Charlotte.

We headed back into the bar, just in time to hear Harry announce above the din that the coach would be departing in twenty minutes. I hadn't had time for a drink up to that point, so I fought my way through to the bar. I turned around to ask Anna what she wanted, but she was no longer behind me. I decided to get her a glass of white wine anyway. I'd just been served when I saw Jess waving at me from near the door. She had Trevor Green with her. I managed to make my way through the scrum, spilling drink as I went.

"Matt, would you mind if we stepped outside again for a quick word?" asked Green.

I assumed that Jess had told Trevor about the video footage of the goal.

"To be honest, Trevor, I'd just like to forget about what was said."

"Matt, it will only take a minute," said Jess. "Please."

I reluctantly agreed and quickly gave the two glasses in my hand to Jamie, with instructions to find Anna and hand them over. I followed Jess and Green through the door and down a corridor and into a small room. In the room was the Grimsby Town manager. He held out his hand.

"Neil McGoldrick," he said in a gruff Glaswegian accent.

I shook his hand and waited.

"This young lady told me that she'd seen the footage of the second goal from Sky and that the ball never crossed the line. I just wanted to apologise to you face to face for saying what I did. It was bang out of order. I was frustrated with everything that's going on here and said something in the heat of the moment that I very much regret."

"Jess and I have agreed we're not going to mention it in our reports of the game, as long as you're happy, Matt?" Green said quickly, before I could respond.

"I've messaged Charlotte and she's agreed too, as the bigger story is the player's strike for Sky, so she won't say anything," added Jess.

"That's all fine by me. I appreciate the apology, Neil."

"Thanks. Good luck in the next round, son. You're a good side and you'd have given our first team a real test if they'd been out there today."

"Good luck to you too. I hope that everything gets sorted out," I replied.

We all shook hands and Jess and I left Trevor with the Grimsby boss to finish the post-match interview.

"Was that your idea?" I asked Jess, as we walked back along the corridor.

"Sort of. Actually, Anna and I came up with it together.

We both thought it was wrong to leave it up in the air and it made sense to get it sorted before anything appeared in the news. I spoke to Trevor Green and he agreed that it was pointless making the Grimsby boss look bad. He's got enough on his plate."

"I'm glad you did. Thanks for doing that. It was nice to get the apology and good that it's not going to become a story."

"No problem. But now you owe me," she said, smiling as we stopped in the main entrance.

"I somehow thought there might be a price tag attached!"

"Well, now we know the second goal wasn't actually a goal, what do you think about the decision?" Jess had pulled out her phone and was holding it up in front of me to record the conversation. The consummate professional, I thought, smiling to myself.

"You don't waste any time, do you? OK, so I wasn't sure myself whether or not the ball had crossed the line. It was a marginal decision. The reason I was upset at the time was that I couldn't understand how the lineman could give it, because my body was blocking his view. I understand we all get things wrong, but it felt to me like it was a guess, and you have to be sure to award a goal. But in the end, it didn't matter, although it could have done if they'd grabbed a third. I'm not sure if he felt pressured by the crowd, but it was a really poor decision by the officials."

"Wow! Not your normal diplomatic self. Is it OK if I use that?"

"Yep. Right, time to hit the road I reckon. Thanks for all your help, Jess."

I bent down and gave her a quick peck on the cheek. She looked flustered and was blushing furiously. She turned hurriedly away.

"Need to go and get a few words from Harry before he

disappears onto the coach," she said quickly, as she disappeared back into the bar.

At the time, I thought nothing of it. It didn't mean anything to either of us. Or so I thought.

16

Two days after the Grimsby game, Anna and I, plus a couple of hundred others, were packed like sardines into our clubhouse. We could barely move, and the atmosphere was electric. Even Anna had wanted to come this time, after I'd explained to her that in the Third Round, all the biggest clubs in the land came into the competition. At first, she thought I was pulling her leg when I said we might get Chelsea or Man United. I don't think she quite believed me until I was watching Sky Sports News the next day. Anna was sitting next to me on the couch, showing very little interest until they started doing a feature on the "minnows" left in the competition and of course, we were one of those. They talked about our win at Grimsby and showed the goals again, including the now infamous "ghost" second goal. Anna got a kick out of that because it showed the anger on my face as I ran to confront the assistant and always teased me about it. The feature also covered the two other clubs from the "lower leagues" that had battled through to the Third Round, in addition to us. Lancaster City from the Northern Premier and Wimborne Town from the Southern

Premier. I knew the scenes in our clubhouse that evening were probably being repeated in Dorset and Lancashire.

The previous day, Anna had asked me, once she realised that I hadn't been pulling her leg (as I was inclined to do), what my dream draw would be. Obviously, I had thought about it, but, being a footballer, I was a bit superstitious and was worried if I said a big club, we would end up drawn away to Mansfield or Scunthorpe. No disrespect to either of those clubs, but obviously we all wanted a Premier League club. But Anna had a way of not letting me off the hook when she wanted an answer, so eventually I succumbed and said either Chelsea, as the club I'd supported since I was a boy, or Liverpool, as the current champions.

The draw was once again live on the BBC. The room hushed slightly as the presenter gave some of the numbers of the balls that would go into the velvet bags. In addition to some of the big guns, the presenter then made special mention of the three lowest-ranked teams left in the competition. Lancaster City were number twenty-nine.

"Reigate Athletic will be ball number forty-seven," the BBC presenter announced, to a huge cheer in the clubhouse. "And Wimborne Town are number fifty-four."

An ex-professional and a current international from England's women's team were drawing the home and away sides respectively. All the balls went into the two bags and we all waited nervously. The first half dozen ties were nothing to get excited about and then came the first big tie, as Arsenal were drawn against their bitter rivals, Tottenham Hotspur. That got the room buzzing. Then number fifty-four was drawn out – Wimborne.

"Wimborne Town will play...number twenty-three, Liverpool!"

An excited buzz went around the room. Good for them,

and just the sort of draw we wanted for ourselves. More ties were drawn out. Lancaster were drawn away to Brentford. Not a bad tie for them, but obviously not as good as Wimborne's. There weren't many balls left now and we were still in one of the bags. So were a couple of big clubs, including both the Manchester clubs.

"Number thirty-one, Manchester United will play..."

You could hear a pin drop in the room.

"Number twenty-nine, Manchester City!" The presenter chuckled as we all groaned.

Two more big clubs gone. There was only Burnley and West Ham left in the draw from the Premier League now. Three ties later and both of those had gone too.

Then the hand plucked out the magic ball.

"Number forty-seven, Reigate Athletic, from the Isthmian Premier and conquerors of Grimsby in the previous round."

A home draw!

"Will play..."

We watched as the manicured hand delved into the bag once more.

"Number sixty-one, Sunderland."

That got a cheer. Sunderland were in the Championship and we all knew they were comparable with Premier League clubs when it came to the history and size of the club, as well as the fan base up in the North East.

"Is that a good draw?" asked Anna, trying to make herself heard above the noise.

"Yep. It is a good draw. They're a huge club. And we're at home too."

There was plenty of excitement in the clubhouse and everyone was smiling. The game was to be played in the first week of January. We still had to get through December's fixtures, but it would be a great way to start the new year.

We didn't have a game on the Tuesday evening for once, so we stayed a long time in the bar, as did everyone else, talking about the draw and the game against Sunderland.

Three days later, I was at work, when my phone rang. It was Jess. I hadn't seen her on the Monday night, so it was the first time we'd spoken since Grimsby. After we'd exchanged pleasantries, she got down to business.

"I've just spoken to your chairman, and he tells me that it's now 99% certain that the game will be switched to the Stadium of Light for health and safety reasons. What do the players think of that?"

The Stadium of Light was Sunderland's ground. I was surprised, because I'd heard nothing about it, but then there was no reason for me to know about it before it was announced. It made sense commercially though. The Stadium of Light held something like 50,000. Because of my financial background, I was always interested to see how the money side of things worked in the FA Cup and had done a little research once we'd got to the first round. In the first and second rounds, the home club paid 5% of gate receipts to the FA for their "pool", which was essentially how they funded the prize money for the competition. The clubs share the remainder of the gate money equally. So, 47.5% to each team. Rumour had it that we'd made roughly £75,000 from the Grimsby game from our share of the gate. In the Third Round, the FA's cut rose to 10% of the gate. But if they had a crowd of say 25,000, that would be a huge amount for us, plus any TV money too.

"We'd obviously prefer to play at home in front of our own fans, but I can understand it makes more sense commercially to switch the game to their place. There will be a lot of people who want to see the game."

"And giving up home advantage?" Jess asked.

"Speaking personally, I think it will be brilliant to play at somewhere like the Stadium of Light. None of us have ever experienced that before, playing in front of a big crowd in a huge stadium."

"OK, thanks, Matt. Bye."

It was an unusually abrupt end to one of our chats. I didn't think too much about it. I just assumed she had other people to speak to. I sent a message to our players' WhatsApp group to see if anyone else had heard anything, and a text to Harry, asking the same thing. The answers came back pretty quickly and all negative. Everyone was asking where I'd got the information. I didn't reply as I didn't want to land Jess in it in any way.

It got quite a debate going on our WhatsApp group, with some of the players saying that they wanted to play the game at home, while others were looking forward to playing in such a great stadium. I suppose it just proved that whatever the decision taken by our board, some people would agree, while others would object. But the commercial reality for the club made it something of a no-brainer for me. The income for any small club was just too much to turn down. I went back to work, but an hour later, Harry called me.

"I suppose you got that story from your journalist friend?"

"Err, yes boss. But I hope she won't get into any trouble for leaking it."

"No, she actually spoke to the chairman and he tried to get hold of me. He was just waiting for the FA to sanction it as both clubs were happy with the switch. It's just come up on the Sky Sports website and apparently it's all been approved. That journalist we met at Grimsby posted the story. There's also a story online in the *Surrey Herald*, with a quote from you in there. Just thought I'd let you know. Looks like we're off to Wearside!"

"Thanks for telling me. I'll have a look."

With that we said our goodbyes and I quickly pulled up Google to have a read of both stories. They were remarkably similar. I assumed that the two journalists were still in touch. The Sky Sports story didn't carry my quote, but instead had quotes from both chairmen, essentially saying both clubs were happy to work together and were looking forward to the game.

The next couple of weeks flew by. We were still playing catch up with our league programme. The Saturday after our FA Cup victory, we had to play in the other big competition for non-league sides – the FA Trophy. It is basically the FA Cup for all non-league sides and the final is played at Wembley, which is the big attraction. The prize money and glamour is nothing like the FA Cup, but then no non-league side is going to get to the final of the FA Cup and play at Wembley. The FA Trophy gives you that chance.

We'd been drawn away to Salisbury. It was another long coach trip, though more like three hours and not the best part of six as it had been to Grimsby. We were by no means at full-strength either. Stevie was serving the first game of his suspension. Antonio had a calf strain, Beno had a hamstring strain and Simo's wife was due to give birth in a few days, so the boss had decided he'd be too far away in Salisbury if the baby arrived early. Anna had decided that she'd done her football duty recently and would give this one a miss.

The Salisbury ground was a little bit in the middle of nowhere. There was a light dusting of snow on the pitch and it was bitterly cold. Despite that, there was a reasonable crowd in the ground. I wondered if it was because the locals wanted to see the non-league "giant killers" beaten. Possibly.

Unfortunately, the game turned out to be as bad as the weather. It was very scrappy to put it mildly. As one of our travelling supporters remarked after the game, the highlight of the first half was the ref blowing his whistle for the interval.

The second half wasn't any better. I hardly had to make a save worthy of the name, and nor did my counterpart at the other end. I was more in danger of getting hypothermia from inactivity. The goal that ended up settling the tie was in keeping with the rest of the game. With about ten minutes left, Salisbury put together a decent passing move and they got the ball out wide to their left-winger, who'd just come on as a sub. He was quick and went easily past Kieran, our right-back, who was one of the U23 lads, filling in for Simo. He'd done well up to that point, but he was tiring.

The winger cut in and let fly from just outside the box. But he got it all wrong and sliced the ball horribly. Unfortunately for us, his miscue went straight to one of their players in the box who hit it first time. John got his body in the way, but it bounced off him and dropped perfectly for their centre-forward, who stabbed it home from ten yards to win it for Salisbury. It was a rubbish goal to concede, but totally in keeping with the overall quality of the game. We tried to salvage a draw, but we lacked creativity in midfield with both Beno and Stevie missing. Rosey had also limped off just after half-time following a heavy tackle, and we really didn't look like scoring.

Harry wasn't too unhappy after the game. He said we'd put the effort in, but just lacked quality on the day. But he couldn't fault our desire or work rate. Just our quality in possession. To be honest, he knew, as did we, that if we'd won another cup game, we'd just fall further behind in our league programme. None of us wanted to lose, but I don't think too many of the players or coaching staff were especially upset.

My ankle had held up well since the Grimsby game and the combination of a little rest, more treatment and no further knocks to it helped speed up recovery. We played three more games in the run-up to Christmas, beating Haringey 1–0 at home and Eastbourne away 2–1. I was rested for the next round of the Surrey Cup, as were all the first team squad this time. Our U23s played and ended up losing to Whyteleafe 2–0, but it was good experience for them, and to be honest, it was a cup we didn't need to be in with our league fixtures piling up.

Anna and I spent a very nice Christmas Eve and Christmas Day together, basically doing very little, which suited us both as we'd had a hectic run-up to Christmas. We'd barely seen each other due to events and office parties. It made the time we spent together over the festive period even more special. I didn't overindulge though, as we had a tough game on Boxing Day away at Dorking.

Dorking had been relegated the previous season back into our division from the National League South. They were just down the road from us, so it was a local derby, ideal for Boxing Day and likely to draw a decent crowd. There was always a little bit of feeling between the two clubs, which pre-dated my arrival at Reigate.

It was a clear, crisp December day, and it looked as though half of Dorking had decided to get some fresh air into their lungs and turn out for the game. The official attendance gave it as 838, but it certainly felt and sounded like many more than that. Dorking were in fourth place and looking to bounce straight back after relegation. We were three points behind, but we had three games in hand. So even though we were only half-way through the season, it felt like an important game for both sides.

We started off really poorly. If you didn't know better, you'd say half our side had enjoyed Christmas Day a little too much. It was a portent of things to come when in the third minute, John let a routine pass go under his foot, straight to Dorking's number nine. Instead of trying to go round me, he tried to dink the ball over me as I went down. But I had one arm straight up in the air as I went to ground and the ball struck my arm, allowing John to belt the rebound into touch. We were giving the ball away far too easily and Dorking were swarming all over us. I pushed away a shot from twenty-five yards and then tipped a header over the bar from a corner. I had to be quick off my line moments later to hack away a defence-splitting through ball just before a Dorking midfielder got there. Someone hit a piledriver from almost thirty yards, but I saw it all the way and managed to hold it, rather than parry it away. I then made a reflex stop after the ball ran loose from a corner. That was probably my best save, as it was low and close to my body, which are sometimes the hardest to reach. Somehow, we made it to the break at 0–0.

Harry's half-time talk was short and to the point.

"If I had ten substitutes and was allowed to sub EVERY outfield player, I would! You don't deserve a break. You didn't work hard enough to need to sit down in here. Get back onto the pitch NOW and sort it OUT!"

We looked at each other in surprise. But Harry wasn't joking. He held the dressing room door open. John got up and led the way and the rest of us followed him. There was a buzz around the ground as the spectators saw us coming back onto the pitch and couldn't work out why.

Forming a small circle on the half-way line, we thrashed it out. Everyone had their say and some harsh words were said, but we all took it, and no one was exempt. We accepted that we'd been rubbish and we needed to make a vast improvement in the second half. Just as our opponents were taking the field again, Stevie made everyone smile as we broke from our huddle by telling us we couldn't play that badly again, even if we wanted to. He was right. We couldn't.

Anyone who watches football knows how pivotal half-time can be. A team that was dominant in the first half can lose their way and a team that couldn't string two passes together can suddenly play like world-beaters. It's strange what a fifteen-minute break can do to a game.

It was as though someone had flicked a switch. Suddenly we started to find our touch and our range of passing. For the first twenty minutes of the second half, Dorking were chasing shadows and barely got a kick. Beno scored direct from a free kick just outside the box on the hour, and from that point there was only going to be one winner. We added a second ten minutes later when Antonio rose highest to nod home a corner and it was all over bar the shouting. I was called into action with ten minutes left, when one of the Dorking players hit a dipping volley from the edge of the box after the ball was half cleared. I just managed to get fingertips to it, which was enough to deflect the ball onto the top of the crossbar and over.

We were a happy bunch in the bar after the game. Another win and another clean sheet, but more importantly, we'd come together as a team and sorted it out for ourselves after the first half horror show. I was at the bar trying to get drinks for myself and Anna when I got a tap on the shoulder. I turned around to find a man holding out his hand to me.

"Matt, we haven't met before. Let me introduce myself. I'm Bryan Morgan. I'm with Crystal Palace. I was wondering if we could have a quick chat?"

I looked at him, not quite knowing what to make of it.

"Yeah, of course. Just let me grab my drinks and tell my girlfriend."

I eventually worked my way back to Anna with drink in hand. She was sitting at a table, deep in conversation with Harry's wife, who was making a rare appearance at a game. She barely reacted when I told her I was going to have a chat with some bloke from Palace.

Morgan had found a quiet spot by the pool table and was waiting patiently. After a brief exchange of pleasantries, he got to the point.

"Matt, I'm a scout for Palace. We've been watching you for most of the season. Aaron Smith recommended you to me. He and I used to play together at Brighton, and we've stayed in touch over the years. I've watched you a few times and so has our goalkeeping coach. We've both been impressed. We'd like to invite you to a trial."

For a moment, I was genuinely speechless. Half of me was wondering if this was some elaborate wind-up. But Morgan seemed genuine and the business card he'd placed on the table in front of me looked real enough.

"I'm really flattered, Mr Morgan. When would it be?"

"Well, not until after the Sunderland game of course, as we know you'll want to focus on that first. So sometime towards the middle of January? We'd like you with us for a week."

"A week? I'll have to get the time off work in that case. It may need to be nearer the end of the month as I'll need to give them a little notice."

"Of course. Give me your number and I'll text a couple of suggested weeks to you and then you can let me know which one works best. You don't have an agent, do you?"

"No."

"Good. Agents usually end up complicating things and slowing everything down. Anyway, I need to get going. I'll be in touch shortly. Thanks for your time." Morgan got up to go and we shook hands as he did.

"Does my manager know?"

"Well, you're not under contract according to Aaron and so strictly speaking you're a free agent. But it's up to you if you want to say anything. Obviously, if we decide to offer you a playing contract, we'll speak to the club, but until you've been for the trial, it's probably a bit premature. But if you want to tell him, go ahead."

"OK, thanks, Mr Morgan."

Morgan departed, giving a quick wave in the direction of Smithy as he went out. Smithy looked at me and grinned, giving me a thumbs up. I returned the gesture, but my head was all over the place. I sat there on my own for a few minutes, staring into space, hardly able to believe what had just happened. I didn't even notice Anna approach until she plonked herself down in front of me.

"Penny for your thoughts, Mr Goalie," she said, taking my hands in hers.

I told her who I'd just been speaking to. At first, I think she thought I was messing around. But then I showed her Morgan's card and she quickly realised I was telling her the truth. Her eyes were wide as I recounted the conversation. Although she wasn't an expert by any stretch of the imagination, I'd done a pretty good job with her football education, and she knew enough to know that Palace were a Premier League outfit.

"Jeepers! That's awesome. What are you gonna do? I assume you'll go for the trial?"

"Of course. It's one of those 'once in a lifetime' opportunities. I'll have to sort it out with work, but I've got plenty of holiday I haven't taken yet."

"You gonna tell Harry?" She was looking intently at me.

"What do you think I should do?" I really wanted to hear what she had to say.

"He's helped you a lot, especially when you got hurt and sorted out all that treatment for you. I think you owe him. But this is not my world, and I don't know if this is the 'right' thing to do in this situation." She paused. "Why don't you ask Smithy?"

That made perfect sense. It was even possible that Smithy

had already mentioned it to Harry, as they were quite good mates. I reached across and took Anna's hands in mine and leaned forward to kiss her gently on the lips.

"You know, you're pretty smart sometimes. For a Yank."

"And you're pretty romantic. For a Brit."

Together we got up from the table and I went to speak to Smithy. It turned out I had nothing to worry about as far as the boss was concerned. He'd given Smithy the green light to contact Palace in the first place.

17

Unless you plan to fly, Sunderland is quite a road trip. You certainly wouldn't want to have to spend five or six hours on a coach and then play a game. Thankfully, our board decided to spend some of the money they were making from the cup run on the team. We ended up travelling to the North East on the Thursday. It was a long and tedious journey and took all of six hours, thanks to the rain and sleet that followed us all the way from Reigate. Despite the long journey and the bad weather, we were in excellent spirits. The club was putting us up in a hotel in the city centre, but we were more excited by the news that we had been invited to use Newcastle United's training ground on the Friday.

Newcastle and Sunderland are not many miles apart and are bitter rivals, even though they'd been playing in different divisions for a number of years. Apparently, after the draw was made, the Newcastle chairman had called our chairman and offered us the use of their training ground. They were away to Charlton in the Third Round and would be down in London the day before the game, so wouldn't be using their training facilities. Of course, it was a great PR coup for Newcastle, and they got some nice coverage from the press. Especially when Brian was quoted in the media when the news become public.

"Just make sure you beat them!" was Brian's recollection of the Newcastle chairman's parting words.

That quote certainly got some media coverage! All good fun for us, but best of all was that we had the use of a Premier League training facility on the Friday.

We were booked into a Travelodge in the centre of the city and eventually arrived there around 5pm, after battling through the city's rush-hour traffic, which added another half hour to the journey. It was a fairly standard Travelodge. Clean and tidy, but no frills. Most of us were sharing rooms to keep costs down. Anna was horrified that we had to share and even offered to pay extra so I could have a room of my own. I had to explain it was all part of the bonding that goes on and besides, I was sharing with Smithy, so hardly someone I didn't know.

Anna and the rest of our supporters would be leaving from the ground at around 8am on the Saturday morning. Rumour had it that we had almost 3,000 supporters coming. If that were true, Reigate would be a ghost town that day. Mind you, I knew that supporters from other local clubs were coming to support us too. While that wouldn't happen in the professional game, where rivalry is bitter and deep-rooted, in the non-league game, other non-league clubs were delighted when one of their brethren gets to play the big boys in the Third Round. It's the dream of every non-league club to get that far, so seeing someone else do it means everyone can dream about it happening to them one day too. Plus, everyone loves a cup upset.

Smithy and I got our room keys from reception, found our room and dumped our bags, before heading back downstairs. There was no bar or anywhere to eat in the Travelodge, so

Harry had arranged for us to go and eat at a local sports bar called Sloanes, which was only a short walk away. In addition to plenty of TVs showing Sky and BT Sports, there were also pool tables too, so we were happy enough to spend a few hours there.

Being competitive people, there was soon money riding on each game of pool. Nothing too much, just a fiver or a tenner to make it interesting. Because we had arrived early and there were several tables, most of the lads played. I think I won two and lost two games before Harry decided it was time to eat, so I broke even. None of us were drinking even though Harry had said nothing about a drink ban. That's what we all liked about the gaffer. He treated us as adults and expected as to act accordingly. It was the standard burger and chips sort of food you'd expect in a sports bar. Not exactly the food of athletes, but once in a while it doesn't hurt. We were split into small groups of four or six to eat. The place was starting to fill up and by the time we'd eaten, most of the pool tables were in use.

The plan was to eat early and then get a good night's sleep. It was a good plan, until a group of local lads found out who we were. They had started talking to Stan and Simo who'd been waiting for a vacant pool table. Pretty soon, most of Sloanes knew who we were. Far from it being a problem, we become minor celebrities for the evening. Sunderland people love their football and love AFC Sunderland. They were genuinely pleased, and I think really surprised to see us in one of their local haunts. Not something that the average visiting team would do, that's for sure! But we enjoyed it as much as they did. None of us were used to being the centre of attention and pretty soon we were signing all sorts of things for them. For the next couple of hours, groups of us were chatting with the locals or playing pool with them. I lost track of the number of offers of drinks I received. We turned most of them down, but

I think a couple of lads had a bottle of beer or two. Of course, the local lads kept telling us how we were going to get a good spanking when we played their beloved Black Cats. Some of them knew we were training at Newcastle the next day and made their feelings very plain about their near neighbours. But it was a fun evening and we all got a taste of what it's like being a celebrity, for a couple of hours at least. Harry eventually called time on us at 10pm, otherwise we'd probably have been there until closing time.

I didn't have the best night's sleep, in part down to my roomie doing a passable impression of a cement mixer, which he called "a little snoring". We were also in the city centre, so it wasn't exactly quiet outside either. I was up bright and early the next day. Well, early at least. We had a team meeting at 10.30am and then we'd leave for training around midday. So we had the first couple of hours to ourselves to either sleep in or go and explore. It wasn't an option for me to go without breakfast, so I had to go and find something, although it looked less than inviting as I peeked out from behind the curtains at the ominous clouds.

Leaving my noisy roommate to his dreams, I strolled out of the Travelodge. It was a raw, overcast morning in Sunderland and the sky promised rain before much longer. I zipped my coat up and pulled on some gloves. The first order of the day was to go and find some breakfast. The high street looked a little sad with quite a few vacant shops, mixed in with charity shops and a few coffee bars. The North East had never really recovered from the loss of the shipping industry.

With a bitter wind blowing, I wasn't inclined to explore too much and found a Starbucks after a few minutes' walk and settled for that. I ordered a large cappuccino with plenty of chocolate and a couple of chocolate croissants too. Not exactly healthy, but I needed food, and there wasn't a lot open at seven forty-five in the morning. I found myself a table and sat down with my coffee and pastry.

I was tempted to call Anna, but she'd be on her way to work and it would probably be a crappy call with the signal cutting as the train she was on went through tunnels and cuttings. I settled instead for looking at various sports pages on my phone as I ate. It was funny seeing a number of mentions of Sunderland v.s Reigate Athletic. It somehow didn't feel real. The BBC sports page was giving more prominence to the Wimborne v. Liverpool tie, which I could understand, especially as Wimborne had resisted the temptation (and the money) of switching the tie to Anfield. It made for a much better story than ours. In fairness to our board though, they had looked after the players, with the hotel stay and the luxury coach. The gaffer had also told us on the journey up to Sunderland that he'd been speaking to the chairman on our behalf and all the squad were getting a bonus of £500 each for getting to the Third Round. It wasn't a fortune, but it was a nice gesture and we hadn't had to ask for, or even suggest, it. It had just been offered to us. A few of the lads suggested it should be more, given how much the club was making, but Harry told us that most of the money was being reinvested in improvements to the ground and they were looking at the possibility of installing a 3G pitch. Personally, I always preferred a grass pitch, but I understood the commercial reality of a plastic pitch for clubs like us. I could easily see a time when almost all non-league clubs would have 3G pitches.

I also looked at the *Surrey Herald* website. There was a long article by Jess looking ahead to the game. As I wasn't in any great rush, I ordered a second coffee and settled down to read it. Jess and I hadn't spoken much since the Grimsby game. I assumed it was simply because we both led busy lives. The feature, as she'd promised, was an entertaining insight into a number of the players and the management team. I was struck by how well she painted a picture of each individual with her words. Not everyone can write like that. On the spur of the moment, I decided to message her.

Hiya! Sitting in Starbucks in Sunderland with a coffee reading your article.

She responded almost immediately.

Wow! You must be bored. What time's training?

12.30. Not bored at all. Great article. You write so well

Thank you. I enjoyed writing it. Nice club and nice people

True. But you should be writing in the national press

Haha. I've got a way to go before that. But sweet of you

I mean it. I think you're really talented

Wow! So many compliments. Is this someone else with Matt's phone?

Lol. I can be nice sometimes

Sometimes! OK gotta go do some work. Enjoy training

I ended the exchange with a smiling emoji. It was probably time I headed back. Although we weren't leaving for training until midday, Harry had told us we'd have a team meeting at 10.30am to go through some things. Because the Travelodge was pretty basic, someone at the club had managed to book us a room at the nearby university. It was still the winter holiday break for the students, so I suppose we'd got a good deal.

I walked quickly. Not because I was late, but simply to stay warm. The wind was biting, and the rain had just started falling as I made my way back to the hotel. A number of the lads were milling around in the reception area. Most were on their phones, and several had cups of coffee in their hands. The local area certainly wasn't short of coffee shops. We'd been told we were leaving at 10am. I think most of us thought we were getting on the coach again, but when Harry arrived, he announced we'd be walking and it would be good to stretch our legs. Anyone would have thought he'd just said we'd be walking in bare feet such was the level of grumbling and moaning as the squad looked outside at the steady drizzle. Harry led the way and told us it was only a fifteen-minute walk.

It is often said that dealing with footballers is very similar to dealing with kids. As we followed Harry down the high street, in pairs of groups of three or four, I couldn't help but be reminded of some of the school trips I'd been on in my youth. Hoodies up, heads down, with hands stuffed in pockets to keep warm, we probably looked more like a street gang than a group of footballers and we got a few odd looks from shoppers as we slouched along.

Harry was right though, and it only took us just over a quarter of an hour to reach the campus. In the summer, it might have looked different as there were trees and grassy areas, but on a January morning it looked pretty bleak. The buildings were modern and not very attractive, but we were just happy to get out of the drizzle and the cutting wind. In fairness, the inside was better than the outside and looked quite new. It was certainly bright and open. There was an electronic board welcoming the players and officials of Reigate Athletic, which was a nice touch. While we milled around, Harry talked to the receptionists and one of them got up and led the way. We didn't have to go far. As we approached a set of double doors, we saw tables piled high with fresh fruit, Danish pasties and flasks of tea and coffee. Harry told us to grab some food and then come into the auditorium. It was funny how quickly the mood changed as we all piled our plates high.

It was one of those lecture theatres where the seating is raked upwards so you're looking down on the person on stage. In this case, Harry and Jez. Jez hadn't been with us on the walk, so I assumed he'd been here setting things up. Suddenly, the lights dimmed, and a wave of noise filled the auditorium. The sounds of fans singing "We love you Sunderland, we do" was then drowned out by loud rock music. The big screen then burst into life with a video of the Stadium of Light as the home side walked out. It gave me goosebumps I have to admit! After a couple of minutes, the music and the video stopped, and the lights came back on.

"That gentlemen, is what it will be like a few minutes before 3pm on Saturday," Jez announced, letting it sink in. "We wanted to prepare you for it, so you'll know what to expect when you're lined up in the tunnel at five to three," he paused for effect. "The music is crap though, isn't it?"

That broke the tension and there were a lot of laughs and smiles. I quite liked the music, but I knew we'd all remember Jez's comment when we heard it on Saturday afternoon, and I had no doubt that a few of us would laugh and smile as we remembered his comment. Nice psychology, I thought.

For the next forty minutes, we were shown video clips of how Sunderland set up to attack and defend set pieces, their shape and formation and their general pattern of play. Somebody had gone to a lot of time and effort to prepare all this and I was suitably impressed. It was only later that I discovered that Harry had leveraged his old pals' relationship with the AFC Wimbledon manager to get hold of this dossier. Not that we cared. We were living the dream of being professional footballers. The overnight stay and now the video analysis. It was giving us a real taste of pro football.

At the end of the briefing, we all trooped back out through the reception area and found the coach waiting for us. Before we'd set off from Reigate, we'd all been told to bring a separate bag with our training kit in it and leave it on the coach. Now I understood why. Going straight from the university to the training ground made perfect sense. We'd been fed and watered, so we were all set.

We climbed on board, excited by what we'd just seen and eager to get to training. Quite a stark contrast with the group of sulky schoolkids that had followed "teacher" from the Travelodge this morning. Once again, I couldn't help but be impressed at how Harry had put all this together. I was sat next to Stan. He looked his normal, serious self.

"That'll be quite an experience walking out to that on Saturday," I said, smiling. But the big Serb just stared straight ahead.

"Pah. Red Star Belgrade much louder," he grumbled.

I couldn't help but laugh. Stan could be impressively dour and miserable when he put his mind to it. But he did like the video analysis, and was impressed by how professionally we were taking the game. I messaged Anna and told her what we'd just sat through. She wanted to know what the music was so she could listen to it. I had no idea but told her she'd probably find it on YouTube.

It took us about half an hour to get to Newcastle United's training ground. We drove up to the big wrought-iron gates with the Newcastle badge. Once we'd been cleared by a security guard, we drove into the car park and found a spot. We were a bit like tourists. Every one of us had our phones out, taking pictures of the place and each other as we got out and grabbed our training gear from the storage hold. The interior was everything you'd expect from a Premier League club. One of the Newcastle staff was there to meet us, and she escorted us to the changing area, which was massive and almost palatial. She told us it had been refurbished a year or so earlier by the new owners and it certainly looked impressive. But once we were in the changing room, Harry quickly reminded us we were here to work. We weren't the only ones at the training facility as we soon discovered. As we walked out onto the training area, we were directed to the pitch that had been set aside for us. There were several full-size pitches and we could see others in use, which the helpful Newcastle lady told us were their academy side and U18s preparing for matches.

The pitch was in pristine condition considering it was early January, and you could tell just how excited everyone was to be there. Because we were playing the next day, it would be a very light session, physically. The emphasis was on our formation and how we would set ourselves up when they had the ball. By necessity, there was a fair bit of stop/start and standing around while we went through it time and again. We ran through set pieces, both for and against. Harry and Jez were constantly yelling instructions and occasionally swearing as a player got something wrong. We spent probably an hour on our tactics before Harry and Jez allowed us to do some ball work. Smithy and I did our own session, which was intense, but very welcome after being cooped up on a coach for several hours the previous day. The outfield players practised playing "keep ball" in small grids, with one and then two players trying to win back possession from four or five others. As the session began to wind down, the defenders went off to do an "attacking the ball" drill, which consisted of the coaching staff launching long balls towards our back three or, to vary things, back four, with one player attacking the ball while the others dropped off to cover. Not very exciting, but like most things in team sport, it is built upon repetition. Doing things again and again until they become instinctive.

Our forwards and midfield usually end most training sessions with a shooting practice. Smithy and I took turns in goal. It was a drill that most clubs seemed to run. Play the ball into a man on the edge of the box, who'd lay it off left or right, and the player then had to shoot first time. Easy when the ball is laid off onto a player's naturally stronger foot. More entertaining when players were forced to shoot with their weaker foot, which was obviously one of the points of the drill. Smithy and I made it a point of pride not to be beaten at all if possible, and certainly not when a player was shooting with his weaker foot. Naturally enough, the banter and general abuse increases whenever a shot is miscued. But if Smithy or I failed to stop one, we got it in the neck too.

When we trained at the club, most of the sessions lasted about ninety minutes, so the players didn't get home too late on a midweek night. But we had no real restrictions that afternoon. I think everyone, including the coaching staff, were just enjoying using such high-quality facilities. After around two hours, Harry and Jez decided we'd done enough. But some of the lads thought we ought to end with a penalty shoot-out. Each player took a penalty against Smithy or me. If you scored you carried on and took another, but if you missed you were out. Stevie decided to add a little to the event by insisting every one of the lads and coaching staff that wanted to take part put a tenner in and winner take all. That added to the pressure nicely and pretty soon the number of players still in the competition had been whittled down to Antonio, Beno, Simo and, surprisingly, Harry. Harry didn't really talk about his playing days, but we all knew he'd been at Wimbledon and also played at Charlton and Leyton Orient, so he'd obviously been a decent player.

With some players, you can read where they're most likely to place a penalty by the angle of their run-up, or how they shape to hit the ball. With Harry, I really couldn't get any clues, so it became pure guesswork. Of course, every time I dived the wrong way, I was accused by the rest of the lads of letting the boss score to keep my place in the team! That made me all the more determined to stop one, but he kept firing them past me and Smithy, who wasn't faring any better. Pretty soon it was down to Beno and Harry. You'd have hoped Beno would be there as he was the team's designated penalty-taker, but no one had expected the gaffer to be in the "final". The final was five pens each, with the best score winning. They took the penalties in turn as you would in any shoot-out. After four penalties each, it was 3–3, with both having missed one. It was Harry's last kick. I still hadn't saved one of his. This time I elected just to stand still and react, rather than make my mind up in advance. Harry had seen me dive to a corner each time, so elected to do a cheeky chip known as the "Panenka", named after the Czech player who cheekily chipped the ball into the middle of the goal to settle the shoot-out at the end of the 1976 European Championships final. I remember watching that kick on YouTube once. Talk about nerves of steel! The last penalty, to win the final against the then world champions, West Germany, and he chooses to chip the ball down the middle of the goal. It's brilliant – unless the keeper doesn't dive! I ended up catching Harry's delicate chip with both hands, standing still. The rest of the lads fell about laughing.

Harry was laughing too, but as ever had a response.

"Smithy, you'd better save Beno's last pen or I'll be looking for a new goalkeeping coach. And after smart-arse saved my kick, if you do, you'll get to play against Sunderland tomorrow! No pressure."

Beno sent Smithy the wrong way with the final kick to win the shoot-out and then spent most of the coach ride home trying to extract the promised tenner from each player who'd taken part in the contest. I'm not sure how much success he had. But it was a happy group of players (with the possible exception of Beno) as we left the Newcastle training ground. We were all talking about the facilities and how impressive everything was. We all knew we were in a unique position of seeing how top-flight footballers went about their work on a day-to-day basis.

Harry had one more surprise up his sleeve for us. We were back in Sunderland when one of the lads up the front of the coach shouted out that he could see Sunderland's ground off to the right. Sure enough, we could all see the distinctive shape of the stadium. We began to get nearer and there was a buzz of excited chatter. Then Harry stood up at the front with microphone in hand.

"Lads, I've arranged for us to pop into the ground to have a look round." The buzz of excited chatter went up tenfold. "I wanted you to get a feel for the place before tomorrow. Sunderland didn't have to do this, so let's make sure we're on our best behaviour. OK?"

We were like a bunch of excited schoolboys. Phones were already being pulled out to take photos as we approached the stadium. As it was a Friday afternoon, we were able to pull up in the car park just outside the main entrance. The Sunderland badge with "Stadium of Light", welcomed us as we got out and walked towards the main entrance. Players were taking selfies and pictures of each other. It again reminded me of a school outing, as Harry and Jez tried to keep us all together and heading in the right direction.

At the front door there was a lady in a smart outfit, who introduced herself as Jean, and said she would be showing us around in a very broad Geordie accent. We went through into the reception area. Everything was red and white.

"I'm assuming you lads would like to go out and see the pitch first?" she asked, already moving towards the tunnel area.

I was already thinking about making this same walk tomorrow and how different it would be. Now, it was silent. The chatter had stopped for a moment. I think we were all doing the same thing. Visualising the next day. We walked through the red folding tunnel. I could already see the red seats on the opposite side of the ground. We all stopped by the side of the pitch, cameras out, as if we were on a stadium tour like any other group of supporters. The pitch was being watered, so we weren't able to go onto the playing surface, but that didn't matter. I looked around me at the huge stands, imaging them full tomorrow afternoon and very, very noisy. Butterflies were milling around in the pit of my stomach and for the first time, I felt really nervous about the game. Looking around, I doubted I was the only one.

"Drink it all in now, lads," said Harry quietly. "By tomorrow afternoon, this will all feel very familiar."

Up until then, I hadn't really thought much about why we were here. Now it dawned on me that Harry was cleverly trying to take away some of the nerves and some of the awe that we all felt by visiting what was, by any standards, a magnificent stadium. Gradually, we relaxed, and the laughter and the banter started up again.

Jean took us to the dressing rooms (well, the away one anyway), and then to the players post-match area, where we would meet friends and family. She also showed us the press room, where Harry would probably have to go after the game. We spent about an hour there in total, as we kept stopping to take photos and occasionally chat with a member of the Sunderland staff, who were ever so friendly, but probably as curious about us as we were about them.

I sent Anna a couple of pics of me pitch side and in the dressing room. I didn't expect a reply from her as she was at work. I then sent Jess a picture of the interview room and immediately got a thumbs up emoji from her, and then a message:

Slightly better than standing in a crowded bar with people spilling drinks on you!

You might have to wait your turn for an interview with me tomorrow

Haha. I might even find some real footballers to interview!

Nasty girl. I might just start saying no comment to you from now on

You wouldn't turn down your favourite reporter

No, but I might turn down you

Lol

We're off again. See you tomorrow I hope

I'll be there. Good luck tomorrow Matt

I put the phone back in my pocket, smiling, and went to catch up with the others.

18

It was 12.30pm on Saturday. We were getting back on the coach, but today there was very little chat and no messing around. It was a very different mood to the last time we'd boarded the coach. Kick-off was two and a half hours away. Finally, after all the weeks of anticipation since the Third-Round draw had been made, it was match day.

Whereas yesterday we'd all been happy to sit next to a mate, today most of us preferred to sit on our own and just get into our own little bubble. I'd had a nice chat with Anna an hour earlier. They were making good progress and were expecting to get to the ground shortly after we did. She told me that she couldn't believe how many people were on the coaches. We had eight coaches booked and they were all full to capacity. Such had been the demand for places that the club could probably have filled several more. I knew others were driving or taking the train. Anna said she'd seen quite a few cars go past them with Reigate scarves or flags fluttering from windows. The chairman had told us a couple of days earlier that the club had asked Sunderland for 5,000 tickets initially and within days of going on sale, we'd sold out and had to ask our hosts for another 3,000. In theory, Sunderland were supposed to allocate 15% of their capacity to us, so we were actually getting more than our allocation. But I suppose the Sunderland ticket office doubted that a visit of a semi-professional team would sell out the ground, so they were probably happy to sell us a few more.

The traffic was relatively light as we drove through the city. But what we did notice was a lot of people in Sunderland shirts. Everyone had told me that football was more like a religion than a pastime in this city. I was now starting to believe that. Because we had our team name on a board at the front of the coach, people soon realised who we were. Some of them waved at us, while some of the younger lads used some more interesting sign language. But most of it was good-natured, as obviously no one locally saw us as anything more than cannon fodder. Reading some of the papers that morning that we had shared around, most were predicting a comfortable home win for the Black Cats. In terms of footballing ability, fitness and technique, that was a fair prediction. Nine times out of ten, they would probably beat us by three or four goals. But we were all hoping this would be that tenth time. That one game, where they play badly, or are complacent and go through the motions a bit. On the flip side, we'd need to play at 110%. Everyone would have to play to the very best of their ability and make no mistakes. Most of all, if we did conjure up a chance, we'd have to take it. We were under no illusions. But at the same time, we weren't expecting to get beaten. If we went in with that mind-set, we probably would get a good hiding.

As we got nearer to the stadium, we passed a couple of pubs that had plenty of people in red and white shirts drinking outside. It was a bitterly cold January afternoon, but there were blokes in short-sleeved replica shirts standing around with pints in hand. They breed them tough in the North-East. It was close to 1pm, so still a little too early for the match-day crowd to be arriving. As we drove the last half mile or so, the Stadium of Light loomed large on our right. For some reason, it looked different. Yesterday it was just a football stadium. Today it was our very own "theatre of dreams". By 5pm, we could be on the back page of every newspaper, or just a small footnote in this year's competition.

The coach pulled up outside the main entrance to drop us off. No walk across the car park today. There were crash barriers erected as a path for us. To our surprise and delight, there were several dozen Reigate Athletic fans there to greet us. As we disembarked, they were clapping and calling out the names of individual players to wish us luck. There was also a BBC camera crew filming our arrival, as our game would be part of the highlights package that we'd all watched many times before on a Saturday night. We stopped to shake hands and, rather strangely, a few of the lads even signed autographs. That wasn't something we were used to doing, but if that's what people wanted, we felt duty-bound to oblige. Even more bizarrely, there were some Sunderland fans there also asking us to sign stuff. Mainly mums and dads with young children. It must have taken us a good ten minutes to get from the coach to the main entrance. I have to admit I didn't get asked to sign anything, as four or five of the lads seemed more than happy to grab the limelight, so I loitered near the back of the group. It all felt a bit surreal for me that anyone could want my signature!

Walking in was a very different experience to the one the previous day. It was a hive of activity, with yellow-jacketed security men and women walking around with purpose engaged on some match-day duty. There was no friendly welcome from Jean this time. It was all business as we were led to our dressing room. But one thing that had worked was Harry's mind-games. It all felt quite familiar now. We knew what to expect as we walked into the dressing room. Ian, our kit-man, had driven to the ground ahead of us, so when we walked in, our kit was neatly laid out and our game shirts were on hangers in the individual cubicles. We were all carrying our boots and wash bags, although in my case I had three pairs of goalkeeping gloves too. Why three? One I used in the warm-up, which tended to be a slightly older pair. One for the match itself, which I'd used for probably a dozen games already and a spare pair just in case the match gloves got damaged or fell apart in any way.

Harry told us to dump our stuff and follow him out onto the pitch. The folding tunnel hadn't yet been extended, so we just walked through it and out into the stadium. The gates had only just been opened so there were very few fans in the ground as yet. But there was a lot of activity. There were groundsmen putting the finishing touches to the pitch; camera crews setting up; security people being briefed in some seats away to our right, plus a lot of other people just going about their duties. In a way, it was interesting seeing behind the scenes and appreciating how many people were involved to put on a match at a stadium like this.

Today, we were allowed on the pitch. The grass was wet, as presumably it had been watered earlier. Most top-level pitches were watered frequently before a game (assuming it wasn't raining), simply because the modern game was built upon a possession-based, short passing style and a slick surface ensured the ball zipped across the surface. It was grey overhead, with a forecast of showers later in the afternoon, but thankfully from my perspective, there was little or no wind. The pitch was superb. We'd all seen old TV footage of how the old pitches in the 70s and 80s often used to be nothing but thick mud by this stage of the season. But not anymore. Sunderland's pitch was just a green carpet. If you couldn't play football on this surface, you were in the wrong sport.

I walked down to the goal at the right-hand end of the ground. As I often did before a game, I went and stood on the goal line and touched the bar, and then went to the left-hand post and touched that, before repeating the process on the right post. No idea why I did it. It was just a habit. I stood in the goal and just looked around the ground, imagining how it would look in a just over an hour and a half. Most of the rest of the lads were milling around in small groups, chatting, or just looking around, probably doing what I was doing.

Harry decided it was time and called us in. We arrived back in our changing room in dribs and drabs but finally we were all inside and Jez closed the door.

"There is no pressure on us today. None. The pressure is all on that lot next door," Harry said, pointing to the door. "They are EXPECTED to beat us. They are expected to win by three or four at least. I can guarantee that their manager is right now telling them to be professional and respect us. Telling them that we have nothing to lose. Trying to get his players into the right frame of mind. He will fail. I know that. There will be a few of their lads, and possibly more than a few, who'll be thinking this will be a stroll in the park. They'll think we're not fit to lace their boots and today will be nothing much more than a training game or a 90-minute shooting practice. Our job today, quite simply, is to earn their respect. This is about playing for pride. Playing for each other. Playing for our friends and family. Playing for all of our supporters and for the club. What I want at the end of the game is for them to know they've been in a contest. I don't care about the result. I do care about them and their fans respecting us," he paused and looked around, making eye contact with each of us.

"None of us will probably get another day like this in our footballing careers. Enjoy it. Make the most of every second. But remember one thing. It's eleven blokes out there. They are good players, but don't be afraid of them. If they were any good, they'd be playing in the Premier League!" That got a few smiles and laughs.

"You all know your jobs," added Jez. "Let's just go out and play our normal game. If we do, we'll be fine. Right. Let's get changed and get out there and warm-up."

Fifteen minutes later, we jogged back out onto the pitch, ready to start our warm-up. It was just after 2pm according to the scoreboard. In the time we'd been in the dressing room, the stadium had begun to fill up. That was especially true of the Strongbow Stand to our left as we came out. It was a mass of yellow and blue. Our fans were there in force. As soon as they saw us some out, a massive roar went up and a chant of 'We love you Reigate, we do' started. It was pretty amazing, and all the players walked towards the stand with their hands above their heads, applauding. There were quite a few Sunderland fans in the stadium too, and much to our surprise they were clapping us too. When I'd done a bit of reading up about the club before the match, most write-ups concluded that the Mackems were some of the friendliest fans in the country and the Stadium of Light had one of the best atmospheres. Well, their fans were certainly living up to their billing.

We got back to business and began our warm-ups. I joined in with the rest of the players as we did some stretching and then short, sharp running and stuff designed to get your muscles warmed up and nice and loose. We did that for about ten minutes and then Smithy and I went off to do our normal warm-up. Normally we warm up in near silence, except for the occasional self-appointed comedian. But there was already a lot of noise in the stadium. There was a hum of excitement and energy. You could feel it. It certainly got the adrenaline pumping. I wondered what it would be like when we walked out at kick-off. Although I knew I had to focus, I wondered whether Anna was here yet. The players' wives and partners had all been invited into a special area before the match where they would be wined and dined, so I knew she was being well looked after. I also found myself thinking briefly about Jess too. Assuming she was here by now, she was probably in the press box, studying the team line-ups and getting herself ready for the game. When we'd had the tour of the stadium the previous day, we'd been shown the press box area and the dedicated seating outside, complete with computer ports and desks for laptops. A far cry from our ground where the only Wi-Fi was in the bar. I pushed all that out of my mind and concentrated on my warm-up. I was enjoying every second of it. I was in a great stadium, about to play in front of thousands of people, in the oldest and most famous football cup competition in the world. I had one of the best warm-ups of my life and Smithy could barely get a shot past me.

In no time at all, Jez was on the side-lines signalling us back in. As we started to walk back towards the dressing rooms, there was thunderous applause from our supporters, which we acknowledged as we walked in. For the first time, I noticed the Sunderland players warming up. Several of them looked up as we walked in. They'd probably watched some video of our previous cup tie and almost certainly they'd sent a scout to watch one of our league games. But even so, I bet several of them were thinking "Who the hell are this lot?"

The dressing room door was shut and we each began our normal ritual of stripping off the sweaty training stuff and putting on the match gear. We all immediately noticed we had a brand-new strip, with a new sponsor's name on it. I found out later that a company had offered the club ten grand as a one-off deal to have their names on the shirts for just this single game. The power of TV and the FA Cup. By the time we had got ourselves ready, you could really feel the tension in the room. None of us had come close to playing in a game like this before and probably never would again. It was the stuff of dreams.

We looked expectantly at Harry, waiting for his usual words of wisdom. Instead, he walked around the entire first team squad, shaking hands with each of us and having a quick word as he did. When he came to shake my hand he simply said:

"Go out there and prove you're one of the best young keepers around, son."

Once he'd finished his round of hand-shaking, he stood half-leaning against the door, arms folded, looking so laid-back and casual.

"Be brave in possession. Work your socks off in the opening half hour. The longer we keep them scoreless, the more their crowd will start getting twitchy and that will build the pressure on them to score. If we concede, we shake it off and start again. You have earned the right to be here today. Now go out there and enjoy it!"

Everyone began shouting and clapping at once. Pumping ourselves and one another up. Giving each other high fives, hugs or fist bumps. We were ready. The buzzer sounded and ten seconds later, we heard one of the assistant referees banging on the door and asking us to come out. We walked out of the dressing room. I was in my normal position, second in line behind John. The Sunderland players were starting to line up in the tunnel. They didn't look at us. We didn't look at them. Everyone stared straight ahead. A group of children were led down the tunnel between us, dressed in Sunderland shirts. We were each given a child's hand to hold. I looked at the little girl whose hand I was holding. I doubted she was more than eight or nine. She looked scared.

"Hi, my name's Matt. What's your name?"

"Jasmine," she whispered.

I must have looked big and scary towering over her, but there wasn't really room to crouch down.

"Don't be scared. I'll look after you," I said, smiling. She smiled back and said something. I didn't quite catch it, so I asked her to repeat it.

"My dad says you're going to get smashed eight nil!" she said more loudly, with a cheeky grin.

My counterpart, Rutger Reinwald, the Sunderland keeper, was opposite me and laughed out loud. I did too.

"Kids!" he said, with a strong German accent.

"Yeah! Have a good one, mate," I said to him, as he looked at me.

"Thank you. And also you."

At that moment, the referee got the signal to walk out and we were on the move. As we came out into the daylight, a wall of sound hit us from all sides. The intro music was blaring from the speakers and both sets of supporters were cheering and clapping. I felt Jasmine's hand tighten in mine as the noise enveloped us. I'd been at big football games before, and heard the noise, but it feels very different when it's all being directed at you. The PA announcer was adding to the din as he welcomed us onto the pitch. We lined up in front of the main stand for the ritual handshakes. I tried to spot Anna, but it was impossible with so many people. Most of the handshakes were pretty perfunctory. The exception was when I came to shake hands with Reinwald. We did make eye contact and once again wished each other all the best. The shared bond between goalkeepers. It certainly does exist and I for one enjoy being part of that unique band of footballers.

Handshakes complete, I quickly said goodbye to Jasmine, as Jean arrived to escort the youngsters off. We all broke away and headed towards the end where our supporters were massed. It was a memorable sight. A mass of yellow and blue everywhere. There were probably a sizeable percentage who'd never seen us play before. But none of that mattered. All that mattered was they were here and making quite a racket. The PA announcer ran through our line-up and each player got a cheer from our supporters and some half-hearted boos from the home crowd. I got goosebumps when my name was read out. The cheers were even louder as the Black Cats' starting eleven was announced.

Smithy went through a final and very quick warm-up routine with me as John went to toss up with their skipper. The ref blew his whistle and indicated we were to stay where we were. We were ready for the kickoff. Everyone else cleared the pitch. The referee checked that I was ready and checked with both his assistants. Then he looked across to the touchline to the fourth official, who gave him the thumbs up. He blew his whistle and Antonio got the game started as he played the ball back to Stevie. We were finally underway!

We strung together half a dozen passes quite comfortably, as Sunderland weren't overly committed to shutting us down in our own half. Tommy then played a ball down the line for Addi. They say the young have no fear. There were no signs of nerves as he took the ball down beautifully and turned to face his man. In most high-level football, the instruction is not to give the ball away. Most players would have turned and laid it off safely to a teammate. Not Addi. He simply knocked the ball past his man and effectively said to him, "Let's see who's quicker." It wasn't a contest, Addi flew past the defender and got to the ball first. He didn't look up but crossed it immediately into their box. Addi and Antonio had developed a good understanding and as soon as Addi set off, Antonio was on the move too. As the ball was crossed in, Antonio had arrived at the near post ahead of his marker and got a powerful header on target. I thought it was in, but Reinwald produced a brilliant save and flicked it over the bar. You could hear the "OOOHHHH" all around the ground before both sets of spectators burst into applause. Either for the save if you were a Sunderland fan, or the great bit of play by us if you were an Athletic fan. I was applauding both. It was a top-drawer save.

Our resulting corner wasn't the best, as Stevie's low ball failed to beat the man stationed just outside the six-yard box and was headed clear. The ball went as far as Tommy, who was stationed there to pick up any clearances on the right side. He got the ball under control, but as he went to play it back to Simo, who was on the half-way line, and build an attack, he slipped slightly on the wet surface. As a result, the ball went straight to one of the Sunderland forwards who'd been left up for the corner. No real danger, I thought, as we had two defenders back and he was on his own. The sensible thing to do was to hold the ball and wait for support. But he didn't do that. Instead, he started running at us. Simo was backing off, just trying to slow him down, while Jamie was covering. The forward was going route one. He was quick and for a moment it looked as though he'd pushed the ball too far ahead of him. Simo thought so too and went diving it for a tackle. But he didn't make it and the Sunderland lad nicked it past him. Players from both sides were sprinting out of the Sunderland box to try and catch up with play, but they'd never make it in time. Jamie was trying desperately not to commit, but the forward was feinting one way and then the other and Jamie was being twisted inside out. The Black Cats' forward breezed past Jamie too, as our left-back made a last-ditch effort to get a challenge in. I could hear the roar of the crowd. I came out fast and the Sunderland lad hesitated momentarily before going to my right to take the ball past me. I scrambled as he went past me. He was shaping to knock it into the empty net, so I just hurled myself and slid along the wet turf. I didn't save it so much as the ball hit an outstretched arm and off for a corner. The Reigate fans behind me erupted and I could almost hear the groan that went around the rest of the Stadium of Light.

The crowd was still buzzing from the dramatic start. We had everyone back and marked up for the corner. We'd watched the video highlights of their games the previous day at the university. Not that it did us any good at all. The ball was played to the back post where Sorenson, their big Swedish centre-back had peeled off and lost his marker. He headed it back across goal and Stevens, his defensive partner, met it with a bullet header which flew past me into the net from a couple of yards. The roar that greeted the goal was deafening. Four minutes played and we were 1–0 down already. When we watched the goal later, we saw that two of their lads had screened off Stan and Antonio, who were marking the two central defenders. As our lads went to follow their players, they each "ran into" another Sunderland player, freeing the two attackers. It was clearly a foul, but cleverly done, so it just looked like an accidental collision.

The Black Cats scented blood and their crowd, no doubt, saw us as lambs to the slaughter. We were very much on the back foot. The Sunderland players were several steps up from Grimsby in the previous round. They looked bigger, quicker, stronger and with more technical ability than us. We tried to play, but we were pressured instantly and began giving the ball away cheaply as we rushed passes. Sunderland were playing some super football, it had to be said. In the next fifteen minutes, it was a siege and they could have gone two or three goals up. Stan and John were immense and threw themselves into challenges and headers they had no right to win. With eleven minutes gone, I turned over a shot from all of thirty yards. It wasn't that difficult a save, though the ball was moving around a little. From the corner, Sunderland ran a variation of their first corner with another man screening off one of our defenders. This time the header cannoned against our bar and we scrambled the rebound away. I barely moved it was such a powerful effort. I decided there and then I needed to start coming for these corners, or we were going to concede again. Sunderland forced yet another corner moments later, as Jamie got in a last-ditch tackle to prevent a Sunderland player going past him. The corner was swung in and I called loudly, but I doubt any of my defenders heard a thing in the din. I went up in a crowd and managed to pluck the ball from the air. That brought a round of applause from the Reigate faithful behind me. But still Sunderland pressed. A quick one-two on the edge of the box put their skipper through, but he chose power rather than finesse and fired the ball straight at me. It cannoned off my clenched fists and away for Sunderland's fifth corner. We'd only played eighteen minutes I noted on the stadium scoreboard. Another floated ball in and again I went for it. This time I managed to get a solid right fist to the ball and punched it clear.

We were camped in our own half and defending desperately. Anna told me later she could barely watch, as she was sure Sunderland were going to thrash us. We gave away a free kick wide on the left, deep in our half. Another ball was floated into our box. Again, I made my mind up early and decided to come for it. As I started to jump to claim the ball, I felt my legs get taken out from underneath me. I got nowhere near it. The Sunderland skipper got his head to the ball and nodded it into an empty net. The Stadium of Light went wild. Eighteen minutes gone and we were 2–0 down. I knew I'd been fouled and looked for the ref. He was pointing to the centre circle, indicating the goal was good. I started to chase after him to register my protest, but as I did, I spotted the assistant on the left touchline standing with her flag in the air. A couple of the lads spotted the flag too and pursued the ref, imploring him to go and consult his assistant. I'd sprinted to the ref too.

"Ref! Ref! I was fouled! Go ask her! Go ask her!" I was yelling at the top of my voice. For a moment I thought he was going to ignore the flag, but he stopped and then went running over. Now he was being pursued by their players too, telling him it was a good goal. He stopped and began to talk to his assistant, waving both sets of players away. We stood and waited anxiously. The crowd had stopped their celebrations and were waiting too. There were some boos, but the majority were waiting for the verdict. The ref listened as the assistant explained why she'd flagged. We couldn't hear a word. After maybe twenty seconds, which seemed to last a lifetime, the ref pointed again. But this time he was pointing towards our area to indicate a free kick. I breathed a sigh of relief, but the Sunderland players went mad and so did the home crowd. Three or four of their lads got a little too animated and the ref showed a yellow card to one of their players to try and restore order.

Like so many other sports, football is a game of momentum. That decision to disallow the goal certainly gave us a lift. It also knocked them a little. No reason why it should, but psychologically, in their heads, the goal had been given, they were 2–0 up and already well on course for the next round. Now it was back to a single goal lead and nothing was guaranteed. We began to get a foothold in the game. Not that we threatened their goal at all, but we began to break up their attacks and get some possession of our own. They still looked dangerous and we were having to work hard to keep them at bay. The game clock in the stadium said twenty-eight minutes gone. Half-time was still an age away.

Stan turned as a ball was played over his head. He was running back towards me and I was running out in case he didn't manage to reach it. But as the ball bounced, he stretched and volleyed it back towards me. I was already out of my area, as I wasn't sure Stan would get there. But Stan had caught it well. Arguably too well because I quickly realised the ball was in danger of sailing over my head and into the net. One of the Sunderland forwards was chasing the back pass, knowing I couldn't use my hands. I back-peddled quickly and then jumped as the ball arced towards me. I managed to take the ball on my chest. As it dropped, the Sunderland player was only a couple of yards away. I couldn't wait so I threw myself into a scissors kick and managed to volley the ball away for a throw. To this day, I don't know how I did it. But I made good contact and cleared the danger. I was on my back, just outside the box. The Sunderland player, a lad from the Ivory Coast called Yohan Koffi, loomed over me. He shook his head in amazement and then his face lit up in a big grin. He extended his hand to help me up. I gratefully took it and Koffi pulled me to my feet. Applause rang around the Stadium of Light. I'd like to think it was for my acrobatics, but I suspected it was more for the sporting gesture. Jess wrote in her report later that it was a wonderful moment of sportsmanship in a game where it is now all too rare. I had to agree with her. It was a nice moment. It didn't stop me glaring at Stan for putting me in trouble though. The big Serb glared back. Stan wasn't big on apologies.

We dug deep and the work rate in front of me was incredible, but I had no idea how we were going to do this for another forty-five minutes after the break. We kept Sunderland at arm's length for the next ten minutes and the stadium clock was showing forty-two minutes played. It was at that moment that we put our mark on the cup tie and showed everyone at the Stadium of Light that we could play too.

I came out to collect an over-hit pass and spotting Simo free, deftly chipped it over a Sunderland forward out to my right-back. I watched that pass in the highlights later that night and winced. It only just cleared their player and wasn't the wisest pass in the world, three minutes before half-time. Nevertheless, it made it to Simo. He played it first time with the deftest of touches inside to Beno. Beno dipped his shoulder, and lost his marker, before spraying a beautiful cross-field ball out to Jamie on the left, close to half-way. Jamie chested it down and found Stevie with a short pass. Stevie took it past one of their midfielders and played a superb ball to Rosey, who was making a run through the Sunderland lines. He didn't have to break stride. Rosey looked up and saw Addi out wide and fired a pass out to the youngster. The Sunderland full-back had learned to respect Addi's raw pace and stood off him a little, which allowed our winger to whip a low cross into the box. Rosey had continued his run and flicked the cross on to the far post where Beno was steaming in. He met it perfectly on the laces as it dropped. Reinwald, in the Sunderland goal, had no chance. The ball flew past him. I heard a roar from the supporters behind me. And then a groan as the ball smacked against the far post and flew away. I saw a couple of our lads with hands on their heads, particularly Beno. The Reigate fans behind me were applauding the football, while bemoaning our bad luck. I noticed that their fans were applauding us too. They know their football in the North East and it had been a superb move.

A couple of minutes later and the ref's whistle blew for the interval. I turned and clapped our fans as I walked away and towards the tunnel. There was applause all around the

ground. It had been an enthralling cup tie so far and both sets
of supporters were getting their money's worth today.

We walked into our dressing room and grabbed drinks
and in some cases grabbed Mel to sort out some little niggle or
cut. Harry just strolled around, with his arms folded, looking
calm and relaxed. Jez was patting everyone on the head, back
or shoulder as he walked around the room, telling us how well
we'd done in the first half. Once we were all settled, Harry
began.

"I've seen us play a lot better than that, lads. Shit goal to
give away so early on. But we now know what their game is
on corners, yeah? So, if he doesn't come and get it"– he was
pointing at me – "then the nearest bloke must attack the ball,
just in case someone's been blocked off. And if you do get
blocked, fight through it AND scream blue murder to the ref
and assistant after. John, I want you to talk to the ref when we
go back out and make them aware of it." He paused. "It took us
almost twenty-five minutes to start playing. We MUST have
the courage to get the ball down and play. All of us. They're
good players, but they are not supermen. We can play around
them. We can play through them. We proved it just before the
break." Harry paused again and went over to the whiteboard
and grabbed a marker pen.

"Right, we're going 3-5-2 this half. Stan, John and Simo,
you're the three. Jamie you go wide left in the 5. Stevie, you're
playing the holding role in front of the three. Beno, Tom,
Addi, you're the four across with Jamie. Rosey, you play in the
hole behind Antonio and link play. Everyone know their jobs?"
Nods and "yes, boss" were Harry's answer. "Addi, that full-back
is scared to death of you. Take him on every time and the rest
of you get him the bloody ball!" Harry said it with meaning
but was smiling as he said it. He knew we were working hard
to do just that.

It was a brave move to go three at the back, but we'd lost the midfield battle in the first period, so maybe the change would help us. Or it could backfire, and we'd be too open at the back. But that's why Harry was the manager. To make these calls.

A few minutes later the buzzer sounded, and we were on our way back out. I was jogging towards the goal where all the home fans were packed. Here goes nothing I thought. I started applauding them as I ran towards them. To my surprise, quite a few applauded back. Don't get me wrong, there was a fair share of good-natured abuse too, but I wasn't being treated like the enemy.

We didn't make it too obvious from the kick-off that we'd changed formation. Harry had instructed the lads to line up in the same 4-4-2 before the second half got underway and then shift. After a few minutes, I noticed two or three people standing in the Sunderland technical area, holding up hands with fingers raised and gesturing animatedly as they tried to get their players the message. For the first ten or so minutes, the new formation seemed to be working. We were getting more of the ball and closing down their midfielders much quicker. I heard the first mutterings of frustration in the massed ranks of the Sunderland faithful behind me. Their only shot was from range and flew well wide.

On the hour mark, Sunderland made a sub. The PA announced that Julio Alvarez was coming on. I remembered from the briefing that he was a midfielder. They took one of their two forwards off and let me tell you, that was not a popular move. I heard enough from the voices behind me to know that the Black Cats supporters were not impressed. It was our bench's turn to wave and gesticulate. Harry and Jez were both indicating that they'd gone to 4-5-1, presumably to match us in midfield. Pretty soon, it was clear it was working.

Having fresh legs in midfield lifted them and we were starting to look tired, even though there were still twenty-five minutes left. We'd put a lot into that first half, and it was showing. Alvarez was their focal point, and the Spaniard was soon running the game.

The home side was looking much more threatening. Alvarez himself tested me from twenty-five yards with a skimmer that I managed to hold at full stretch. John made a great sliding tackle to stop Ritchie getting through on goal. Stan stuck his head in the way of a goal-bound effort to deflect it over the bar for a corner. Obviously, they'd decided at the break to play their corners further away from goal to stop me coming for them. Pierson had got free again and headed towards goal. I was moving for it when Koffi nipped in front of me and got a flick with his head. It was pure reflex on my part because Koffi was only a yard away, but I thrust out a hand and managed to palm it over the bar. Koffi wasn't smiling now. He had a look of anguish on his face as he'd thought he'd scored. It wasn't until I watched it on the highlights later that I realised what a good save it was. We managed to deal with the subsequent corner, and now there were nineteen minutes remaining.

Jez was holding up the board to indicate that Tommy had to depart. Luke McDonald, who'd lost his place in the starting line to Addi in recent weeks, entered the fray. Luke was a quiet bloke, but boy did he have an engine and loved a tackle. He'd probably only been on three of four minutes before he clattered into Alvarez and earned himself a yellow card. Unfortunately, he'd clattered into him a few yards outside the box and quite centrally, giving them a free kick in a very dangerous position. I called for a five-man wall and lined it up to guard the left side of my goal. They had three players on the ball, and I knew they could go with either a left- or right-footer. In these situations, it is a bit like a penalty. You can stay still and hope the ball is in reach, or you can go early and hope you've made the right choice. If the ball was curled up and over the wall and you waited, you'd get nowhere near it. However, if you went early and anticipated it, you could look a real mug if they fired it into the side of the goal you were supposed to be guarding. I decided to gamble that he would curl it up and over the wall and was already moving that way as he hit it. It was destined for the top left corner, but it's hard to get real pace on the ball too, so it gave me just enough time to get across and tip it over the bar with my right hand. The commentator on the TV highlights that night called it a "spectacular save". It was, although the reflex stop a few minutes earlier had been a much better save.

The scoreboard indicated eighty-six minutes had been played. We were still hanging in there by the skin of our teeth. I was thinking a 1–0 defeat was a pretty good result for us and we certainly hadn't been humiliated. That was when Beno picked out Addi on the right wing, with a sumptuous pass. Addi had been quiet because we hadn't had much of the ball in the second half. In fact, Jez told me after the game that Harry had told him to take Addi off, seconds before Beno's pass found him. For once, Addi didn't try and go past his man. We later joked it was because he was knackered from all the chasing back he'd had to do. Whatever the reason, he took a touch, looked up and hit a long deep cross into the box. The Sunderland player went up to head it clear, but misjudged it and the ball went over him, straight to Charlie Rose, just on the edge of the box. Rosey brought it down on his thigh and volleyed it as the ball dropped. It flew past Reinwald into the back of the net. For a split second, there was a stunned silence in the stadium as if no one could quite believe what they had seen. Then there was a huge roar from the far end where the

Reigate fans were massed. We all went crazy. I sprinted the length of the pitch to join in the celebrations as we chased Rosey, who had whipped his shirt off and was running around madly front of our fans. By the time I arrived, he was on the ground and buried beneath the rest of the team who'd piled on top of him. I jumped on top of the pile. Rosey was eventually booked by the ref for taking his shirt off, but by the time we were back in place for the restart, the clock was showing eighty-nine minutes. One minute plus injury time to hang on! We were going to get a replay.

The fourth official held up his board to indicate there would be four minutes of added time. The scoreboard was showing ninety minutes now. The Sunderland fans behind me were now quite angry and starting to berate their own players. I could see others leaving. It wasn't how they'd imagined the afternoon turning out, especially after their early goal.

We had everyone back behind the goal and we were booting the ball anywhere now. It didn't matter. Just burn more time. Sunderland had also given up passing the ball. They'd sent their big Swedish centre-back, Sorensen, up to play as a makeshift centre-forward. Another long ball was lofted into our area, too far out for me to try and claim it. Sorensen and Stan went up for the header. But they put each other off and neither made contact. The ball cleared both of them. Luke was standing right behind them and was surprised that both missed the ball. He had one arm slightly away from his side and the ball struck it. Immediately 20,000 Sunderland fans yelled for a penalty. The ref agreed and immediately pointed to the spot. We were aghast. Luke had had no chance to get out of the way. Almost to a man, we surrounded the referee to protest. But he just backed off and waved us away. I have to admit it didn't look that great on TV later, but we were angry and emotions were running high. Common sense tells you that the referee is never going to change his mind, but common sense goes out of the window at moments like that.

Eventually order was restored, and I walked slowly back towards my goal, looking at several thousand Sunderland fans who were grinning and cheering and probably giving me some stick, though I couldn't hear anything above the general noise. Their penalty-taker was a left midfield player called McPherson. In the scouting report, I remember it said he usually went to his left and as I looked to our bench, both Jez and Harry were pointing to my left side. McPherson placed the ball on the spot. We made eye contact and I just grinned at him. Penalty-taking is a psychological game between keeper and penalty-taker. I tried to show him I was confident, though it was all for show. The stadium hushed. He took a short run up. I decided at the last moment to go to my right, guessing he'd go his normal way at this late stage in the game. He didn't. He fired it straight down the middle. But as I always do on a penalty, I left a leg trailing behind as I dived. The ball hit my trailing leg. It flew up off my foot, but straight into the roof of the net. The roar was deafening, as their players and fans celebrated. I lay on my back on the goal line, hands over my eyes in frustration and disappointment. I saw later on the TV highlights, virtually every one of our players was on the ground, absolutely distraught at having the draw so cruelly snatched away.

We kicked off again, but were really just going through the motions as we knew the final whistle was only moments away. It sounded a minute later. Several of us slumped to the ground. It was heartbreaking to have been so close to an incredible result, only to have it so cruelly taken away from us in the dying moments of the game. I was sitting on the ground in my penalty area when I saw Reinwald approaching me. He crouched down beside me and patted me on the back.

"You played excellent game. Head up. Be proud," he practically shouted into my ear above the noise.

His words meant a lot. He grabbed my forearm and pulled me up to my feet. The Sunderland fans behind my goal were applauding and so I clapped them back and waved as I walked slowly away with Reinwald walking beside me. Several of the Sunderland players shook my hand and said the normal stuff you say at the end of any game, and I mumbled stuff back. It was all a bit surreal that it was over, and we'd lost. We were all gutted and just wanted to get into the sanctuary of the dressing room. But Harry quite rightly turned us back and insisted we go and applaud our own fans. As we walked towards them the noise was amazing and I was told by Anna later that everyone in the ground, not just our fans, was applauding. She said she had tears in her eyes at that moment. It was a great moment as our fans kept up the applause, chanting "Reigate, Reigate". But eventually, one by one, we turned away and trudged slowly back to our dressing room. I picked out Anna standing with the other Reigate girls in the thinning crowd and waved briefly as I headed down the tunnel. I was one of the last into the dressing room. Everyone had their heads down and no one said a word. We were all lost in our own thoughts and our own private misery. Even Jez was quiet. Losing is never a nice feeling and losing in the last minute of any game is always a real sickener, but especially a game of this magnitude.

There was a knock on the door and Jez opened it. The Sunderland manager, Gunter Kaltz, stuck his head around the door and simply said, "I just speak to your manager and tell him you should all be proud. You make us work very hard and have our respect for the way you play today. Very good." Jez closed the door again.

It was only a few words, but like Reinwald's words to me

on the pitch earlier, it meant a lot to us. It also broke the ice and we gradually got the dressing-room chat going. There were a lot of complaints about the penalty, but I have to admit, once we saw the replays on TV, we could understand why it had been given, under the current laws. None of us blamed Luke for one moment. It was just one of those things that happen in a game.

Then Harry walked in, oddly enough with Jess in tow. No one had really done much more than take shirts or boots off, so we were all fairly decent, but I doubt it would have phased Jess anyway.

"Boys, I cannot tell you just how proud I am of each and every one of you. You gave them a real fright today. But like their manager said, you earned their respect and that counts for a lot. I invited Jess in here, as she's a friend of the club, and to give her the chance to ask you a few questions in private before you go out there and get pounced upon by the rest of the press and hangers-on. So, keep your kit on for ten minutes as we don't want to shock the young lady with those spotty white arses! BUT, when you leave this room, you go out there with your heads held high. You have every right to feel gutted. We all do. But don't forget for a second how close we were to getting a draw against one of the best sides in the Championship. Let's celebrate that."

As he normally did, Harry then turned and walked out, to leave us to unwind gradually. His words about not getting changed fell on deaf ears though. Footballers are not a shy lot by nature and didn't really care that Jess was in the room. Most of us did at least wrap towels around us as we headed for the showers. I saw Jess talking at length to Rosey, presumably about his goal, and to Luke, who still looked distraught. I spent a while in the shower and as I walked out, I was surprised to see that Jess was sitting by my stuff, drinking one of our

Lucozade Sports. I sat down next to her, dripping wet, but, as I assured Anna later, who was stunned that Jess was in our dressing room at all, with towel firmly wrapped around me.

"Hey," she said, smiling.

"Hey yourself. Funny seeing you in here." I made an effort to smile, but it was a real effort.

"Yeah, Harry offered as he said it was big enough in here not to get in the way and gives me a chance to post a match report with quotes while I travel back on the bus. It was really nice of him."

"He's a decent bloke. And we know you're always fair and objective in the stuff you write about us."

Beno hurled a wet sock at me. "Hey Jess, please don't write that this clown saved us from a hammering. He should have saved the bloody penalty!" He was grinning as he said it.

"Can I quote you on that?" Jess asked mischievously.

"Bloody right you can!" Beno was enjoying baiting me.

"Sorry, Jess, you were saying something before my brain-dead teammate interrupted you so rudely," I said, throwing the sock back at him.

Jess held her phone out in front of her in a now familiar way, switching on the record function.

"Do you mind if I ask you a couple of questions?"

"And if I said yes, I do mind?" I asked, smiling.

"Obviously, I'd ignore you and carry on regardless."

"I thought you might say that."

"So, what were you thinking when you fell behind so quickly?"

"To be honest, I was a little worried that we were going to get a good thumping, just like that little girl had predicted!"

"Sorry? What little girl?"

I proceeded to tell Jess about my exchange with the Sunderland mascot just before kick-off. She laughed out loud when I got to the punch-line, causing a few of the lads to look around.

"Did Matt let his towel slip, Jess?" suggested Stevie. Jess just ignored him. Her journalistic antennae had picked up something.

"Oh, that's priceless! I wonder if she's still here. This is such a great story! Thanks, Matt! I'm going to speak to the Sunderland people and see if they can track her down!"

With that, she got up and headed out of the dressing room, leaving me rather perplexed. A few more lewd suggestions followed from my subtle teammates, but I chose to ignore them. That was the shortest interview ever. But I understood that when a journalist gets a whiff of a good story, they're like a bloodhound. I finished dressing and headed up to the players' lounge where the wives and girlfriends were waiting. I'd barely got through the door when Anna flung her arms around my neck and gave me a big kiss.

"Oh my God. That was just such an amazing experience. Such a fantastic game. You were just awesome!"

"Would have been better if we'd hung on for the draw."

"But just to get that close to those guys is incredible. You should be so proud. I am. We all are."

"Maybe later we will be, but I just feel gutted right now."

"Everyone around me, even their fans, were saying how good you were. If you don't feel proud, I sure as hell do!"

She took my face in her hands and looked me in the eyes as she said it. I realised I needed to be a little more gracious. A bad loser is never much fun to be around and, as she had often said to me, live in the moment. I couldn't change the result, but I could try and take the positives out of it. I tried to pick myself up and went to help myself to a big bowl of chilli and rice that was in two steaming urns on a table laden with food.

We'd just settled down to eat with John and Simi when Jess came rushing in. After a quick hello to everyone at the table, she said very nicely to Anna, "I'm really sorry, Anna, but can I borrow Matt for five minutes? I have a brilliant story and I promise this won't take long."

Much to my surprise, Anna was sweetness and light in her reply. What I didn't know was that the two girls had accidently found themselves in adjacent seats on the coach up to Sunderland and once they'd started chatting, they didn't stop for most of the journey. They discovered they had a lot in common. I was certainly pleased to hear that when Anna told me later. With Anna's blessing, I stood up and followed Jess.

"So, what's the big hurry?"

"That little girl. Jasmine. She was up in the lounge where the mascots and parents go after the game for tea and cake. The Sunderland PR lady was ever so helpful and let me into the area. I told her parents what had happened and asked if I could talk to Jasmine. She was very cute and hilarious too. She said she was scared of you at first, because you looked like a giant, but then you were really kind. But she loves Sunderland, so she wanted them to win. Her parents listened to it all and were somewhere between embarrassed and laughing out loud!" She paused for breath as I looked at her, smiling at her enthusiasm. "Anyway, I just rang a journalist friend of mine who writes for the *Daily Mail*, and she said it was such a nice story and she'd run the story *with my name on it*! But they want a photo of you and Jasmine for the piece. Please, please, please, Matt!"

I laughed. "Of course. Let's go."

"Oh, thank you, thank you! Hurry! We need to go upstairs before they leave." She grabbed my arm and almost dragged me into the lift. I was smiling, and probably smirking too.

"Don't laugh! This is huge for me!"

"OK, OK! I'm here. Do you want a quote from me too?"

"Oh yes, that would be great!"

"How about: 'I was trying to work out who was the more nervous as we walked out. Her or me! But as soon as Jasmine said she hoped we'd get smashed, I just laughed and relaxed.' That OK?"

"Perfect! She said the Sunderland keeper laughed too?"

"Yeah, he just said, 'Kids!'"

"Brilliant! I can add that in too. Two opposition players brought together by an eight-year-old!"

The lift arrived at the floor and Jess grabbed my hand and dragged me out and along the corridor with her, at somewhere between a fast walk and a jog. There was a middle-aged woman in a smart navy uniform with a red and white scarf, standing outside the door.

"Oh, Emma, thanks so much for waiting. This is Matt, the Reigate goalkeeper."

"Yes, I recognised you. You gave us a bit of a fright out there today," she said as we shook hands. "The photographer is in there already. Shall we?"

We walked in and I immediately spotted Jasmine, who was standing with a young couple. The man, who I assumed was her dad, had a Sunderland shirt on and Mum was wearing a red dress. Real supporters.

"Hi Jasmine," I said, waving at her. She waved back.

I shook hands with both parents. Her mum apologised for her cheeky daughter, and her dad told me he hadn't meant any disrespect when talking about us getting smashed, but I assured them both that I had found the whole thing funny. The photographer quickly got us into line, and we did a few shots with her and the family and then several with just me crouching down with Jasmine. It was a nice moment. The photographer seemed happy and walked off. We all shook hands again. As I turned to leave, Jasmine asked quietly, "Can you autograph my shirt, please?"

It was the first time I'd ever been asked for my autograph. I saw Jess smiling too. When Anna got to hear about it, she teased me for days afterwards by constantly asking me to sign things. A few days after the game, while we were out shopping together in the local supermarket, she really got me. We'd split up to get separate items and I was busy selecting some fruit when she sneaked up behind me, thrust her baseball cap at me that she'd been wearing and said very loudly, "Oooh! It's the famous Reigate Athletic goalie! Can I have your autograph, please!" Several people looked round, wondering what was going on. Two small boys then came over asked for my autograph too! I could have killed her.

But now Jasmine looked as though butter wouldn't melt in her mouth, so I was more than happy to oblige. We said our goodbyes to the family and headed back towards the lift. Jess was looking excited. She said she needed to go and speak to her journalist pal and see what they needed. She turned to walk away, and I headed for the lift. Next thing I know she'd given me a big hug and a peck on the cheek.

"Thank you so much for doing that. I owe you big time!" With that, she turned and hurried off.

I re-joined Anna and the rest of the guys downstairs, and an hour later, Harry announced it was time to hit the road. He also said that wives and girlfriends were welcome to travel back on the players' coach as there was plenty of room, which was a nice touch and I think made it a livelier journey, with a lot a banter and a few songs. But as we boarded the bus, most of us were a little subdued. We knew that the dream was over. Each of us knowing that it may never happen again in our careers. This was our moment in the spotlight. To briefly live the dream of playing in the big league and everything that went with it. This season's FA Cup run had been an amazing journey, but it had finally come to an end and we knew we had to come back down to earth. What none of us knew was that we wouldn't come down to earth with a bump. It was more like a crash.

19

On Saturday, we had played against a Championship side in front of 26,873 people. On Tuesday night, we played Potters Bar Town away in front of ninety-seven people. They were third from bottom. We were fifth. We lost 3–1. I think it's fair to say that Harry was not best pleased after the game. But we were all flat, right from the pre-match warm-up. It was so hard not to compare and contrast. I think we all knew it might happen and tried to make sure it didn't, but it was so very hard to get ourselves up for the game. We were pretty awful and got exactly what we deserved from the game. Nothing. Funnily enough, Harry didn't really tear into us after the game. He walked in and stood there for a moment looking at us. Then he said, "I knew this would happen." And that was it. He turned and walked out. With five words, he managed to make each and every one of us feel guilty. I think we'd all have much preferred to have him scream and swear at us.

Of course, I had other things on my mind too. On the Monday after the Sunderland game, I'd phoned Bryan Morgan to try and sort out a date for my trial with Palace. I also had to speak to my boss about taking some time off. Not for the first time, I thanked my lucky stars Sarah was a football fan, which made things so much easier. Eventually, we agreed on the last week in January. I was still finding it very hard to believe and to be truthful, I was full of self-doubt that I was good enough to be playing at that level. Eventually, Anna got tired of hearing me say it and gave a real dressing down. Her point, which was made quite forcefully, and with her finger in my chest at one point, was that if I didn't believe in myself, how were others supposed to? She was right, though I did try and defend myself by reminding her what a huge step up it was. But Anna was having none of it. She was great. She pointed out that Palace wouldn't have wasted time scouting me and inviting me if they didn't think I was good enough. As usual, she was spot on. I knew I had to adopt a much more positive approach.

While my head was slowly getting into the right frame of mind for the trial, the team were struggling to do the same after the Sunderland game. After the disappointing result at Potters Bar, we had Horsham at home. It was our first game back since the epic game at Sunderland. I think we all wondered how many of those 5,000 plus supporters who went to the Stadium of Light would turn up on a frosty and bitterly cold mid-January afternoon. The answer was not many. We certainly had a decent gate. I heard it announced as 317, which was up on our normal gate, but still pretty disappointing considering how many we'd taken to the North East just seven days earlier.

I think we were all suffering a huge emotional let-down and it was hard to shake off the feelings and the memories of the previous Saturday. We'd all lived the dream, if only for a few days. Being treated like professional footballers, playing in front of that huge crowd in a wonderful stadium and coming so close to pulling off a shock result. That would live with us all forever. We arrived in dribs and drabs for the game. No coach today. I couldn't help but reflect how our ground seemed tiny. Our dressing room felt like a broom cupboard. I knew it wasn't a fair or realistic comparison, but with the Sunderland game so fresh in our minds, it was perfectly understandable that we all felt that way. Understandable, but unhelpful and probably unhealthy too. Living in the past wasn't going to help us in the matches we had still to play. Our opponents now saw us both as a big scalp, and also a team they wanted to put in their place. Every non-league player would be jealous of what we achieved. Except perhaps the players of Wimborne Town, who'd hosted Liverpool, and Lancaster, who'd played at Cardiff. Lancaster had been beaten 5–0 and Liverpool had stuck seven goals past Wimborne, so arguably our result had been the best of the three non-league teams.

Harry and Jez understood what was happening. I think everyone associated with the club understood it. Doing something about it though was another thing altogether. It was noticeable how quiet the dressing room was as we gathered for the game. It's not as though we weren't talking and having a bit of a laugh. But if you were to compare it to how we were before the Sunderland game, I'd say it was only about half of the normal level of noise and banter. Harry and Jez did their best to motivate and encourage us, but the usual bounce and energy just wasn't there. It wasn't as though we didn't care. We still wanted to win and play well. But we were all just a bit flat.

That's probably why we walked back into the dressing room at half-time 2–0 down. We were a pale shadow of the side that had pushed Sunderland all the way the previous weekend. We'd been one down after seven minutes and then two down in twenty minutes. If I'm honest, I'd probably blame myself for the second goal. It was a shot from the edge of the box. I got both hands to it, but as it was wet and muddy, I'd elected to parry it, rather than try and hold it. Unfortunately, I parried it straight to one of their players, who slotted home the rebound. I just hoped that there was no one from Palace watching me.

We sat on the wooden benches, looking how we all felt: cold, wet, and dejected. We completely deserved a rollicking from Harry. We fully expected it. He walked in and shut the door behind him, which was a relief in itself, as we could hear the excited chatter coming from the opposition dressing room, delighted to be two up.

"Boys, you have two choices here. Either you accept that our FA Cup run was brilliant while it lasted but now it's over, and life, and football, goes on. Or you continue feeling sorry for yourselves that this is not the Stadium of Light and there aren't 25,000 people watching you play. If you do, then you'd better get used to this feeling of losing, because it will happen again. And again. And again. It's your choice."

With that, he and Jez walked out and closed the door quietly behind them. For a minute or two, no one said a word, as we all sat staring at our boots, letting Harry's words and the truth of what he'd said, wash over us. I'd half expected John to say something, as skipper, but to everyone's surprise, it was our youngest player who spoke first.

"This is shit, bro. The man is right. This ain't the FA Cup and we ain't playing Sunderland. We gotta deal with it. I don't wanna feel like this every game," Addi said quietly.

"Yeah, nor do I," said Stevie.

"We much better than this. We must fight," growled Stan.

You could almost feel the hurt and anger amongst the players as we agreed that this was not us. We'd been embarrassed in the first half. Horsham had played well, but we'd made them look like world-beaters. The good thing was that we'd proved several times already during the season that we could put a poor first half behind us and turn things around in the second half.

Teams and manager talk a lot about "setting the tone". It's really to do with setting a standard for the team or giving an example of what's required. Beno is probably five feet eight and lean as a whippet. He's not anyone's idea of a midfield enforcer. Yet thirty seconds into the second half, he put in an absolute cruncher of a tackle on their number eight, who was also their skipper. The ball went out for a throw and I saw a few of our lads applaud and grin. I don't think anyone had ever seen Beno tackle like that. But I knew what they were thinking: "That's the standard, and if Beno can do it, so can I."

To say it was one-way traffic in the second half is a bit of an understatement. I don't think I touched the ball more than three times and I was more concerned about keeping warm than I was about their strikers. Stan pulled a goal back in the fifty-third minute with a thumping header from a corner. We had learned a little something from Sunderland screening people on corners and adopted it for our own use. In the fifty-ninth minute, another header from a corner, using the same off the ball blocking, freed up the skipper, who put us level at 2–2. As soon as that goal went in, I knew there was only going to be one winner. In the sixty-fifth minute, we took the lead, when Luke's through ball sent Addi clear, and he slotted it past their keeper. The Horsham players looked a bit shell-shocked. Antonio made it 4–2 in the seventy-second minute with a close-range finish after some dazzling wing-play from Addi. Five minutes from time, it seemed somehow fitting that Beno added a fifth from the spot. It was certainly one of those games that people would talk about years later. We walked off the field to huge applause from our supporters. It was just a shame that a few more that had followed us to Sunderland hadn't been at the game. If they'd watched that second-half performance, I could guarantee they'd want to come back.

I laughed when I saw Anna's WhatsApp message after the game. She'd decided she'd done her bit as a WAG in recent weeks and devoted enough time to following me around the country. It was also a miserable January afternoon, so when she said she wouldn't be coming to the game, I was naturally a little disappointed, but hardly surprised. But her message did at least show that I'd been on her mind:

> *I looked at the half-time score and I was scared to look again! I thought I'd have a grouch of a boyfriend this evening!*

> *Oh ye of little faith! We were just toying with them*

> *Yeah, right! BS mister!*

> *Lol. OK, so we had to turn it up a notch*

> *I was in a clothes shop, trying on some stuff. I didn't want to look but just had to know the final score. When I saw it I think I just said, Oh thank God! Must have been loud as some people turned and looked at me!*

> *Haha. A real Reigate fan now. We're always on your mind lol*

> *You ain't kidding pal! What the hell have you done to me??!*

> *That's why they call it The Beautiful Game, beautiful!*

> *So smooth. See you later, star*

When I was in the bar, I saw I had another message. This one was from Jess, asking if I could call her about a story she was running. I found a relatively quiet corner of the bar and rang her number.

"Hey. Thanks for calling. Pretty impressive result today."

"Yeah. If you want to call it 'a game of two halves' in your write up, you'd not be wrong," I said, laughing.

"Actually, I wasn't there today. Stuart was covering the game. I was covering the Woking game."

"Ah, so now the glamour of covering Reigate's Cup run has gone, we're no longer worthy of your time?"

"Very funny. I go where they tell me. But listen, Matt, I am really grateful for what you did for me at the Sunderland game. It meant a lot and I got a story in the national press, which is huge for me."

"Hey, it was my pleasure and it was a fun thing to do. It was a lovely story you wrote. Apart from one thing you got wrong."

"Oh?" she said curiously. "What was that?"

"You made me sound like a nice bloke. We both know I only did it to get in the papers!"

"Oohh, you complete tosser! I thought I'd got something wrong for a moment," she said, laughing. "But that wasn't what I was calling about." Now it was my turn to be curious.

"OK, not the game, not the Jasmine story. So, what is it?"

"Someone told me that Crystal Palace have been scouting you and you're going for a trial at the end of the month."

I was surprised to say the least. We'd deliberately kept it quiet as we didn't want my teammates to find out. Harry said it could be a distraction, especially if the team thought I could be leaving in the middle of the season. I quickly weighed up my options. I couldn't just lie and say no, because Jess would find out sooner or later, and if she knew I'd lied to her, she'd be royally pissed off with me, and rightly so. On the other hand, I didn't want to confirm it and get everyone at the club distracted by it.

"Matt? You still there?"

There was only one way to handle this. I was going to have to trust her.

"OK. Yeah, it's true, Jess. I know there's no point asking you how you found out as you won't tell me. But here's the thing. We're trying to keep a lid on it, so we don't distract everyone during our promotion push."

"Yeah, I get that. But it's still a good story."

"Understood. So, I'm going to ask a big favour. You keep it under your hat until after I've had the trial and I promise you'll be the first to know if they offer me anything. If they don't, it's not much of a story anyway, is it?"

"But, Matt, if someone else finds out and runs with it, I lose the story."

"I appreciate that, but if someone else runs it, I promise you can speak to me and Harry and we'll give you more detail and quotes."

Now it was Jess's turn to go quiet while she mulled it over. I knew I was asking a big favour. There was a deep sigh on the other end of the line.

"OK," she said resignedly. "I guess I owe you for last weekend."

"Thanks, Jess. I promise that you'll be the first to know after the trial's over."

We said our goodbyes, and I breathed a sigh of relief. Not for the first time, I wondered how good an idea it was to have a journalist as a friend, as that's how I saw her now. On the other hand, if we hadn't been friends, she'd probably have run the story without my agreement. A real double-edged sword. My phone pinged again, and I assumed it was

Anna arranging timings for later. Instead it was a message from Morgan.

Really sorry to do this Matt. We're going to need to change the date. The boss and his assistant are now going to be in Germany for a chunk of that week to discuss a new kit deal and watch a couple of players. They want to see you for more than a day. Can we shift it to mid Feb? Mon 15th looks good here.

Aside from having to sort it out with Sarah at work, it wasn't too much of a problem. As Anna pointed out later, it was flattering that the Palace manager wanted to see me train and make his own mind up, rather than leave it to the rest of his staff. Besides, what else could I say but yes?

Shouldn't be a problem. Just need to clear it with work on Monday. I'll confirm then if that's OK?

Perfect. Thanks.

It had been quite an afternoon one way and another I reflected, as I got into my car a little later. It was bitterly cold, and there were now some flurries of snow in the air, as I slowly pulled out of the car park, avoiding the pot-hole that seemed to be getting bigger and deeper with each passing week. It suddenly struck me that *if* (and it was a big if) Palace did offer me a contract, I'd have some big decisions to make. Up until Anna's pep talk earlier in the week, I'd really been thinking of it more as a great experience rather than something that could change my life. But it had been difficult today, readjusting to the small and cramped facilities, especially compared to the relative luxury at Sunderland. However, it was also a great little football club, full of people I liked and respected. It would be very hard leaving this place.

There was my job to consider too. I had to admit I'd not given it much thought. But if I did start playing full-time with Palace, I'd have to resign. That would be a huge step. I enjoyed my job and the people I worked with. On the other hand, I knew that I wanted to play or at least try to play professional football, so I had to give this a shot. I decided I was overthinking it, or at least thinking too far ahead. First the trial. Then see what they said and then there might be a decision to make. Or not.

Luckily, Anna had arranged dinner for us with two other couples that evening. It would take my mind off football for a while.

Two hours later, I was sitting in an Italian restaurant called the Spaghetti Tree, with Jen and Seb, a couple that I'd met before and liked, and another couple who were new to me, Ella and Ian. What neither Anna nor I knew was that Ella was a Palace season-ticket holder. It came up in passing when we were talking about what we'd all been doing that afternoon. I hadn't volunteered anything yet, as I knew not everyone was interested in football and didn't like to draw too much attention to myself. Anna and Jen had been discussing their respective clothes shopping expeditions when Anna asked Ella what she'd been up to.

"We were at Selhurst Park, watching that useless lot lose at home to bloody Norwich!"

Anna and Jen looked quite shocked, while I burst out laughing. Suddenly the conversation switched to football as Anna proudly started describing her life as a Reigate Athletic WAG and going to exotic places like Grimsby and Sunderland.

"Wait, so you play for Reigate, Matt?" asked Ella.

"Yep. I'm their goalkeeper," I admitted with a smile.

"Whoa! I didn't know that! Anna, why didn't you tell us?! I'd much rather have gone to watch you guys at Sunderland then watch us lose at Arsenal last weekend!

Ella and Ian wanted to know all about the Sunderland game. I tried to change the subject at one point, but even Jen and Seb, who weren't really into football, sounded interested, especially when Anna told the story about Jasmine and showed people the pictures of me with her and the article in the *Daily Mail*. Then Anna just happened to mention I had a trial coming up at Palace and that was it! Ella and Harry were like dogs with a bone and wanted to know everything. The conversation was all about me, which I was a little uncomfortable with, and I suggested more than once we talk about something other than me and football. It didn't work and actually it turned into quite a helpful conversation, as Seb asked me what I'd do about my job. We kicked that one around over our fourth bottle of Chianti and everyone chimed in with their thoughts. The consensus was that I had to go for it and in the worst case I could always resume my career at a later date, assuming I wasn't a millionaire by then, which made me laugh. But Seb advised me to talk to my boss, Sarah, and see how flexible she might be about taking me back if things didn't work out at Palace, assuming they wanted me beyond the week's trial. Nothing to lose by asking, Seb reasoned. Good advice, I thought.

We were the last people in the restaurant and talking loudly, no doubt thanks to the red wine. Like a lot of Italian restaurants, there were football pictures up on the wall. I noticed there were team pictures of Roma dotted around when I walked in. We asked the young waitress for the bill; she looked a little relieved that we were finally about to leave. But then the owner came over. He was a heavy-set man, who looked like he enjoyed his food and wine. I was wondering if we'd been a bit too raucous.

"I listen to your conversation," he said in heavily accented English. "I am a big Roma fan as you see. Best team in Italy! But I go to watch you at Sunderland last week with my son Fabio. Splendido! You gave them a big surprise!"

I was only now beginning to realise how much of an impact that the Sunderland game had had on the town.

"Thank you. We really were blown away by all the support we got up there."

"I get you all some Limoncello. On the house. We celebrate your great game!"

He went behind the bar and poured out seven glasses full of the bright yellow liquid, bringing them to our table on a silver tray. He handed each of us a glass and said, "Saluti!"

"Saluti," we echoed and downed the fiery liquid. He refilled our glasses and then proceeded to tell everyone about my saves and how much I reminded him of the legendary Italian keeper Gianluigi Buffon. Anna googled Buffon while the restaurant owner was talking. She shared a photo of the Italian keeper with the girls. There was lots of giggling and it was unanimous that Buffon was a hunk. I said that all keepers are hunks, which made the girls laugh. But Anna declared that some were "far hunkier" than others pointing at the picture of Buffon. She had a used napkin flung at her head after that comment. But it was a fun way to end the evening.

An hour later, we were laying in the wreckage of Anna's bed. She was wrapped in my arms in that warm afterglow following a passionate and very steamy session. I was half asleep, but Anna seemed wide awake.

"So, what are you going to do if Crystal Palace offer you a contract?"

"Cross that bridge when I come to it," I said with eyes closed, rather hoping to get some sleep.

"C'mon, Matt. You must know by now." Anna wasn't going to leave it alone.

"I guess it depends what the offer is. If it's something like a month-to-month deal, it's a huge risk for me to take. But if it's for a year or longer, then that's a lot more attractive. But I've no idea what they might put on the table, and obviously I've got my rent and bills to pay."

"I get that. But you could always move in with me if things went sideways," she said quietly.

That got my attention and I looked at her, no longer sleepy. We'd never discussed living together, partly because I always thought of Anna as a very independent woman. Anna mistook my silence for a less than enthusiastic response.

"Of course, it was only an idea," she said quickly, with a hint of hurt in her voice.

"Hey! It's a wonderful idea. You just surprised me that's all. I thought you preferred your independence. I would love to be with you, day and night." I pulled her closer as I said it.

"Only for my body!" Anna said, looking me in the eyes, but now smiling. Sometimes I say the right things.

"Of course! What other reason could there possibly be?" That got me a fairly hard punch in my upper arm.

"Oh Jeez! I must be nuts to even think you want me for anything else!"

"Well, maybe one other thing."

"You are on real thin ice right now, pal, just so you know! Don't even dream of mentioning my cooking!"

I paused, debating whether to be my normal flippant self, or tell her what I knew she wanted to hear. In the end, a combination of emotional intelligence and self-preservation tipped the balance.

"The other reason is that I love you and want to be with you. Whenever we're apart, I feel like a part of me is missing."

Anna sighed and snuggled closer into my body.

"For an English guy, you can be pretty romantic sometimes. I love you too and feel just the same."

"So, is your suggestion of moving in together conditional upon me being unable to afford my rent any longer when Palace cut me loose after I pack in my job?" I asked her, smiling.

"Well, I guess we better try it out for size before that happens, just in case I can't handle having your sweaty and muddy gear all around my tidy flat."

"That sounds a lot like a 'yes.'"

"Let's discuss it properly when we're both sober and awake. But yeah, you can say it was a yes."

One of the final things that went through my mind before I fell asleep that night was just how much my life might be changing in the months ahead. It was an exciting thought.

20

After blitzing Horsham, we rediscovered our mojo. The FA Cup run and the Sunderland game felt increasingly like a distant memory as we focused on the league. We still had plenty of games to play and four or five games in hand on most of the teams above us in the table. Our real concern was the weather. If we had a few weeks with heavy rain or frozen pitches, we faced the prospect of playing three games a week as the season drew to a close. Most sports scientists will tell you it takes the body about seventy-two hours to recover from a game of football. Having less than forty-eight hours between games made impossible demands upon the human body. Even the pros struggle when forced to play that often, as occasionally happens to top sides competing on all fronts. For us, there was no way we'd be able to maintain a decent level of performance. All we could do was to keep playing and pray that the weather gods would smile upon us.

The Tuesday after the Horsham game, we were at home again, this time to Lewes, who had to travel up from the south coast. They were in the lower half of the table, but in our league, you couldn't take anything for granted. Despite some heavy rain, which at one stage threatened to curtail the game, we cruised to a 2–0 win. I was pretty much unemployed as a brace from Antonio saw us home. However, it wasn't all plain sailing. Addi limped off after a heavy challenge and Beno tweaked a hamstring. We'd been remarkably lucky with injuries in the season to date (myself excepted), but as the number of games piled up, it was almost inevitable we'd lose players to injury.

With Addi ruled out, Harry decided to gamble on youth again and promoted the lad from the U23s who'd been banging in goals all season. We all knew it was quite a step up to go from U23 to men's football. The difference in strength and experience made it a tough transition for some. It also changed how we played, as we no longer had Addi's pace to stretch opponents. Beno was also missing with his hamstring and Luke McDonald came back into the side.

We were away to Hornchurch on Saturday, who were just behind us in the table. Hornchurch is a funny place, as the pitch has an athletics track around it, so the crowd – which is always a relative term in non-league football – is a long way from the action. But neither side gave the 192 spectators much to get excited about. The football was as dull as the grey sky overhead, which threatened far more than either team did. The result was a 0–0 draw, which didn't really suit either team. We looked a bit toothless with Addi and Beno missing. To make matters worse, Antonio went off just after the interval with a twisted ankle. We didn't play badly. We just couldn't carve out any clear-cut opportunities. We kept the Hornchurch forwards at bay reasonably comfortably and by half-time, I think most people would have put money on a 0–0 result. It just had that feel.

With another game on Tuesday, we knew we were getting down to the bare bones with the squad. We had

Beno, Addi, Antonio and Simo all missing. The first three were injured, while Simo was away with work. Luckily, we were playing Potters Bar. Although they'd beaten us a couple of days after the Sunderland game, that had been their only win in twelve games and they'd been beaten 6–1 at Dulwich on Saturday. Even with an injury-hit squad, we fancied that we were too good for them. We also had a good U23 side to call upon. Although they were lads still learning their trade, they had energy and enthusiasm and did a lot of hard running in midfield. Potters Bar found they were harried and pressurised constantly, and we kept winning the ball back in their half. What we lacked in quality, we made up for in work rate. It wasn't pretty, but it was effective. Rosey scored twice. Once in each half and I only had one real save to make when I pushed a low, skimming drive away for a corner at full stretch. The final 2–0 score line was more emphatic than it looked.

On the Saturday, we were at home again, this time to Enfield and wanted some payback for the 2–1 defeat just before Christmas. Fortunately, they were another side out of form and had only one win and taken four points out of the last eighteen. Although we had Simo back, the other three lads were still out. We'd got away with it on Tuesday, but I wasn't convinced we could repeat the trick. It wasn't until we got to the ground that we found out that Harry had pulled another rabbit out of the hat by signing two players on loan for a month. There was Leon Mitchell, a young midfielder from Colchester's academy and Des McCutcheon, a forward from Charlton who was coming back from injury and needed game time. Unlike the pro game, we didn't have a January transfer window and could continue to sign players until April. Of course, neither player knew the team or our style of play. We had to hope they were quick learners.

An hour into the game, McCutcheon had scored the first and third goals, and two of our three goals had come from defence-splitting passes from Mitchell. As usual, Harry had come up trumps with his signings. We gained ample revenge for our earlier defeat with a thumping 4–0 victory. McCutcheon could certainly play. Big, strong and quick with it. But there were a few things I noticed that I didn't like. Notably when he "left his foot in" as it's known in the trade on their centre-back late in the game. Usually after a player hits a pass or clears a ball everyone's eyes, including the ref's, follow the ball. That's when certain players make sure they leave their calling card on shins and ankles. McCutcheon also made a few comments about the "shitty facilities" and "how easy it was to play at this level" in the dressing room after the game, that did little to endear himself to his new teammates. Mitchell was the total opposite. Quiet, respectful of his surroundings and of his new teammates.

As I was walking into the bar, I noticed our skipper and Harry in an animated discussion in the corner of the room. Harry looked angry and went to talk to McCutcheon. It was a short conversation and McCutcheon walked out looking none too pleased. John began walking around the room talking to each player in turn. As he did, each one of the lads headed out of the bar. When he came to me, he simply said, "The boss wants to speak to us in the dressing room."

I raised my eyebrows but headed back to the dressing room. It hadn't been cleaned yet and there was mud, discarded kit, plastic bottles and all sorts of rubbish lying around. We picked our way through the debris and sat in our usual places. Harry walked in, looking pissed off.

"Boys, I just wanted you to know that I've told McCutcheon we're terminating his loan with immediate effect. I'll phone Charlton later, but I wanted you to know why. It may not help us on the field, but I won't have players that are disrespectful towards this club, disrupt our dressing room and don't play the game the way I want it played. Have a good evening."

With that, he turned and walked out. There were a lot of open mouths and surprised expressions on the faces around the room. But I admired him for taking such a quick decision and one that I felt was exactly the right thing to do. He may have scored goals for us, but he might also have damaged the team spirit, and once that goes, it's very hard to repair. It was a thoughtful bunch of players that slowly drifted back to the bar. There was no sign of McCutcheon. Getting such a damning verdict from Harry certainly wouldn't help his career at Charlton.

None of us knew how soon our injured lads would return. But looking on the bright side, Leon Mitchell looked quality and would almost certainly help us out over the next few weeks. My phone pinged with a message. It was from Jess.

Shortest loan spell ever! What happened!?

That girl was remarkably well-informed. I realised there and then that I wasn't the only player that spoke to her. Only the players in that dressing room knew what had happened.

Yeah, not the right character for us. Good call by the boss

Scores twice and is sent packing. Interesting call!

Yep, but that's why he's the gaffer

You going to tell me what happened?

McCutcheon did some things and said some things that were out of order

Such as?

Sorry. Can you ask H? What's said in the dressing room should stay there unless he decides to tell you

You can be very annoying!

So I've been told!

OK. Sigh. Will try H

Sorry!

I didn't get a reply. I very much doubted Harry would say much. But then she had at least one other player that was keeping her informed, so I wondered why she was asking me. I gave up trying to work it out and went to talk to John.

"Hey skipper. Mind if I join you?"

John was sitting at a table on his own, using his phone.

"Grab a seat, mate," said John, waving at the empty chairs.

"I assume it was you that told the gaffer about the stuff that McCutcheon said?"

"Yeah. I thought he could have been a bad apple. I was really angry when he started talking shit about the facilities and the standard of football. And that was after we won, and he scored. I was thinking what he'd be like when we lost, or he didn't score."

"Mate, it was absolutely the right thing to do as skipper. And for what it's worth, I totally agree with what you did and what the gaffer did. He could have been really bad for us." I held out my fist and we bumped fists.

"Cheers, Matt. I'm not sure everyone agrees, but I think it was best for the team."

"Agreed. Hopefully, we'll get the injured lads back soon. Anyway, gotta go collect Anna, but just wanted you to know that I think you were spot on, skipper." I drained my glass and stood up.

"Cheers, mate. Appreciate it."

We were almost at the end of January, which I doubt is anyone's favourite month. It was pitch black driving down the country back roads that I always favoured. In the spring and summer months, it was delightful, but this time of year, it was full of mud and fallen branches. Anna asked me why I drove that way in the winter months when the main road was just as quick. It was a good question. I think after games I sometimes felt the need to be on my own for a little while. Just to get the game out of my system and work through what I did well and where I could have done things better. It was a little post-match routine I'd got into.

I was home in twenty minutes. I wasn't sure if Anna had anything planned for the evening. But I dressed as though we were going out. Just in case. It took another twenty-five minutes to get to Anna's place, but I was feeling good as she buzzed me in.

The moment she opened the door, I knew something was wrong. She looked as though she'd been crying. She didn't say a word when I walked in. She just rushed into my arms and held me tightly. I stroked her hair and hugged her back.

"Hey. What's wrong, love?"

She took a few moments to answer. I didn't rush her.

"It's my dad. He's not very well. Really not well." I felt my heart sink. They were a very close-knit family.

"Oh no. I'm so sorry to hear that. Do you feel ready to talk about it?" Anna just nodded. I steered Anna to the sofa and sat her down before going to the kitchen area and grabbing a bottle of wine from the fridge and a couple of glasses.

"OK, take your time. I'm listening."

She took a big gulp of wine and, in a voice thick with emotion she told me how she'd been Skyping with her folks as normal, but she knew something was up just by the way they were talking. Almost as though they were acting out a part. They didn't say anything at first, but Anna had persisted because she knew something was wrong. I knew full-well how persistent she could be. Eventually, her mum broke and told her. Her dad had been diagnosed with cancer. He'd been for his regular annual check-up as part of his medical insurance two weeks earlier. His doctor had called him with the results a few days ago. Prostate cancer had been diagnosed. They were beginning treatment immediately. She paused and took another gulp of wine.

I knew very little about cancer, though the word on its own was enough to give me a chill. But in my mind at least, the medical profession was getting better all the time at detecting and treating it. I said as much, trying to be positive.

Anna nodded and told me it was one of the most common forms of cancer among men, especially middle-aged and older men.

"But that's a good thing, right? They know how to treat it." I tried to sound optimistic.

"Yes, they know how to try and treat it, but it's still the second biggest killer of men after lung cancer," Anna said quietly. "I've been researching it online since I spoke to them an hour ago."

That took the wind out of my sails very quickly. It was hard to know what to say. The likely repercussions of this news were also starting to dawn on me. I knew there was only one course of action.

"You need to go home luv. You need to be with your dad and your mum. They need you." It felt as though something was squeezing my heart as I said it. I knew it was absolutely the right thing to say and the right thing for her to do. But that didn't make it any easier.

"Oh, babe! I know. You're right. But I don't want to leave you. I don't want to be apart from you." She was crying. "I want to be with my dad. But I don't want to be without you!"

"Hey, we won't be apart. Not really. We'll message, we'll speak every day. But most important of all, our hearts will always be together. It may be 3,000 miles, but that means nothing to us. Our love will get us through this."

Her big blue eyes were looking deeply into mine, as tears trickled down her cheeks. I squeezed her hands.

"It may only be for a short time. Your dad's tough. He'll fight this and you'll give him the strength to beat this thing."

"How did I get so lucky to find you?" She was crying and smiling at the same time. "You're so understanding and always know the right thing to say." She looked so vulnerable. "I was dreading telling you that I had to go."

"I'm not going anywhere, lady. I'll be here waiting for you when you return. However long you're gone. You can't get rid of me that easily!" I smiled as I said it, though it was false bravado. I wasn't feeling like smiling one bit.

But I knew that feeling sorry for myself would be selfish and I needed to focus all my attention on Anna and trying to keep her spirits up as much as I could.

"OK, let's get a plan of action together, babe. There are several things you need to do. First things first. Text your boss and tell her what's happened. I'm sure from what you've told me about her, she'll be understanding and supportive. You might have to ask for some paid and unpaid leave."

"I was thinking about that when you came in. I still have

two weeks holiday, but we were planning to go to Prague. I don't want to mess all that up. I was so looking forward to that." She gulped and sobbed.

"Whoa! Hang on. This is much more important than the two of us going off and having fun. There will be plenty of time for that in the future. Stop thinking about that and let's focus on the here and now."

I was amazed how calm and reassuring I sounded. Almost as though I was playing a part in a movie. I suppose in a way I was. My role was to act the part of the strong and stoic boyfriend, whose heart was breaking inside, but wasn't going to show it. I felt I was playing the part pretty well so far.

"You're amazing. You know that?"

"Yep, I do know that," I said, smiling, and was rewarded with the hint of a smile on Anna's face too. "Now, get on the phone to your boss."

"Maybe I should wait until tomorrow. I don't like to bother her on a Saturday evening," Anna said, hesitantly.

"Well, either you ring her now or I will," I reached for her phone.

"OK, OK! I'll do it. Jeez, you can be a pain in the ass!" We both smiled at that.

I'd met Anna's boss, a lady by the name of Nancy, who hailed from San Francisco, and seemed to epitomise the laid-back west coast when I chatted to her at their company Christmas party, though Anna said she was as hard as nails when she needed to be. Luckily, she answered on the second ring, and I sat next to Anna, listening to her half of the conversation. But it seemed to be pretty positive and the words "thank you" said several times, together with a few more tears as she talked. The call didn't last long. Anna hung up and let out a big sigh and reached for her wine.

"Everything OK?"

"Nancy was just wonderful. She told me that there's nothing more important than family and I needed to prioritise that for now. She's given me two weeks off immediately starting Monday and said if I need more time, then I can work from the New York office a couple of days a week and then from home in Boston the rest of the week. It will mean a bit of messing around on planes or trains, but I'm sure I can make it work if I have to. At least I'll be with my folks for most of the week. She was so kind and so understanding that I kept wanting to cry."

I pulled her close to me. Anna wrapped her arms around my waist and buried her face in my chest. She was crying softly.

"Hey! This is my best shirt! If you make it wet or get mascara on it, you'll be in real trouble!"

That made Anna laugh, and she was somewhere between laughing and crying as she untangled herself from me. "If I didn't know better, I'd think you're on a mission to keep my spirits up, mister."

"Me? Nah. Just worried about my pristine pink shirt!" I looked at her and we were both smiling. "OK, next job. You need to book yourself a flight for tomorrow. Grab your laptop."

"Tomorrow? But I was thinking of going Monday so we can spend a little more time together."

"You need to get your cute butt out there ASAP. You will only be thinking about everything and worrying if you stay here. Flights will also be harder to find on a Monday. Let's see what they have and go from there."

After checking various airlines, it turned out I was right and there was greater choice and cheaper fares for flights on the Sunday afternoon. After a short debate, I persuaded her to go for the British Airways flight leaving London Heathrow at 4pm. I knew her mind would be on her Dad and the best thing for Anna was to get home as soon as possible. She reluctantly agreed I was right. Fifteen minutes later she was booked on the 4pm flight.

"I'm taking you to the airport tomorrow. No arguments."

"I was hoping you would. I'll try not to dissolve in floods of tears when we say goodbye."

"I'll make sure I wear an old shirt in that case."

"Just when I was sitting here thinking I have the most wonderful boyfriend in the whole world, you go and spoil it all," said Anna, slowly shaking her head in mock disappointment.

I smiled. "Too much of a cross for me to bear. OK, this is going to be our last night together for a little while. Where do you want to go?"

Anna was silent for a moment and then said, "Nowhere. I just want to be alone with you."

We ended up getting a Chinese and we went through two bottles of wine as we just sat and talked long into the night. The conversation was a typical one by our standards, ranging from deep and meaningful, to light and funny, then very romantic, all without skipping a beat. We always covered such a range of topics. But even we found it hard to know how we managed to jump from a conversation about healthcare and politics in the United States, to my inadequacies as a chef and then to the relative merits of Crystal Palace Football Club! That was one of the things I loved about the girl. Apart from being drop-dead gorgeous, she was also bright, funny and had a perspective on almost everything. One that was considered, well-thought-out and hard to argue against, although I did try from time to time!

We lay cuddled up on her comfortable sofa as we talked about anything and everything. Except us. We both didn't want to go there; there wasn't a whole lot we could say. Neither of us wanted to think about the possibility that Anna might not be back for months. I tried very hard to quell a feeling of panic that was bubbling up inside me. The thought had already seeded in my head that she might not come back at all. I tried to push it away and concentrate on the here and now, not on the future. But it was very hard. I don't know if she had the same thought or not, but there wasn't a great deal of point talking about it, as neither of us knew how things might turn out.

Half of me wanted to fly out with her. But my trial with Palace was in ten days' time and whatever I may have thought of doing, I knew Anna would never forgive herself if I missed the trial for her. I decided to get through that and then see how things stood. Both for her and for me. I was fully prepared to tell Harry I was going to have to miss some games if Anna wanted me in Boston for a couple of weeks. I knew it wouldn't go down well with him or my teammates, as this was a critical part of the season, with games coming thick and fast. But for probably the first time in my life, football was suddenly a lot less important. I told Anna that I could come out to Boston to be with her. It started her crying all over again.

"I wouldn't dream of asking that of you, Matt. I know how important football is to you, and in the past few months, I've also realised how important it is to so many other people too. Your matches in the FA Cup and seeing all those people supporting the team at Sunderland was just awesome. And that night in the Spaghetti Tree with my pals. Just hilarious. But I now get just how much football means to people over here. It's had a big impact on me too. I'm so proud of you."

"You're not asking me. I'm offering. That's the difference. Sure, football means a lot to me, but you mean more. A lot more." I meant it too.

"I don't know what I did to deserve you. But I'm so glad you're in my life right now. I really don't know what I'd do without you," Anna said quietly, her head resting on my shoulder.

We didn't end up going to bed until around 2am. I don't think either of us wanted to waste our last few hours together sleeping. Just before I switched off the light, I set the alarm on my phone for 8am, as Anna still had to pack and we needed to leave around midday to get to Heathrow in good time, assuming there were no hold-ups on the notoriously unreliable M25.

We made love slowly and tenderly, taking our time and savouring every moment of it. Neither of us knowing how long it might be before we would have the chance to be physically together again. Afterwards, I lay awake in the darkness. Anna was wrapped in my arms and her steady breathing told me she was asleep. But I didn't want to sleep. I wanted to make the most of every moment of being with her. There would be plenty of time to sleep when she was gone.

But eventually my eyes grew heavy and the next thing I knew, the phone was buzzing on the bedside table. Anna was already awake and propped up on one elbow, looking at me.

"Good morning, luvvie," she said softly.

"Good morning, beautiful. How is it you look more gorgeous with each passing day?"

"Get outta here. I must look a mess. My eyes will be red and puffy from all that crying yesterday."

"OK, you look a mess. I have no idea what I ever saw in you! Better?"

She laughed, which was lovely to hear. "Much better! You know I'm crap at dealing with compliments. OK, I need to get cracking and get my act together. I'm going to take a shower first. Care to join me?"

Needless to say, it wasn't exactly a quick shower, but we could certainly verify that we were both spotlessly clean by the time we both got out of the shower cubicle.

The rest of the morning went by in a flash. Anna had a

hard time working out what to take, as she didn't know how long she'd be staying. The east coast would be cold, so it was all the bulky winter clothing she had to try and squeeze in. There was a brief panic when she couldn't find her passport. It wasn't in its normal place. Puzzlement was slowly replaced by rising panic as she searched all the places she might have put it, with no success. She said she'd already checked her handbag. I'd often joked that rooting around in her cavernous handbag was a little like going back in time. While Anna was looking in her bedroom, I decided to have a proper look in her bag and tipped the contents onto the carpet in the lounge. There was a huge pile of stuff, but no passport. Just before I started to put it all back, I had a thought. I lifted up the plastic liner at the bottom of the handbag. There it was! Tucked under the plastic.

I was her hero – for at least two minutes before Anna surveyed the contents of her handbag piled on the carpet in front of her. In addition to money and make-up, there were loads of receipts and even match tickets from Bromley, Grimsby and Sunderland.

"Wow. I guess I ought to go through this."

"Only if you have several hours to kill! Shove it all back in. You can sort it out when you're home. Just have an archaeologist on hand, in case there are some important historical artefacts in amongst this junk."

"Oh, how I'm going to miss that sparkling wit and English sarcasm!" Anna's voice was heavy with irony.

Panic over, Anna finished packing and messaged her parents to tell them she was coming. It was still early on the east coast, but she got a message back almost instantly, saying how thrilled they were and that they'd meet her at the airport. She sent her flight details and ETA. I was glad she was being met. It would be emotional for sure, but way better than having to find a cab and standing in line in the freezing cold.

All too soon we were on the road and heading for the airport. It was one of those sunny, but very cold January days. Maybe that was why for once the M25 was behaving itself, and the traffic was moving freely. We arrived at Terminal 5 in good time, three hours before the flight. I found a spot in the car park easily enough and made a careful note of the floor and row. Once before I'd parked in the same car park and hadn't bothered to check where I was. It took me a long time to find my car. Lesson learned.

We took the lift to departures. As ever, the airport was full of people either in a hurry or wandering around looking bemused and lost. We located the British Airways check-in. Anna had already checked in online before we'd left her flat, so it was a simple matter of finding a self-service terminal and printing off her boarding pass.

Up until that moment, we'd both been focusing on all the things we needed to do to get Anna ready for her flight. As the machine spat out her boarding pass, there was nothing else to do. All that remained was for Anna to walk through the departure gate.

"Well, I guess there's no point in dragging this out," she said, smiling. In the time I'd known her, I'd quickly learned that she really didn't like saying goodbye.

I was about to say something witty and light-hearted, when she suddenly threw her arms around my neck and gave me a long and passionate kiss. The world around us just ceased to exist. It was just the two of us. That moment was to live long in my memory.

"This isn't goodbye. OK? This is just see ya later." She smiled as she looked up at me.

Although her tone was light, I could see the tears weren't far away. I could feel my eyes welling up too and there was a big lump in my throat and a lead weight where my heart was. But I had to play my role and be strong and brave, and not make it even harder for her. It felt like an out-of-body experience. I could hear myself saying things and my face was smiling and trying to keep things light, but the voice in my head was screaming "Don't let her go!"

"You take care of yourself and message me when you land, OK?"

"I promise. Please drive safely. I know your head will be all over the place too."

"I'll be OK. Don't worry about me."

Anna had stepped back and had both her hands in mine. There was nothing to say that was going to make this any easier.

"I love you," I said softly.

"I love you too, with all my heart."

She smiled, let go of my hands, and turned, wheeling her small silver suitcase towards the departure gate. I stood there, watching her as she walked away. She turned, smiled and waved one final time, before disappearing through the gate.

I stood there, rooted to the spot. It was a surreal moment. I couldn't get my head around the fact that she'd gone, even though my eyes had seen it. Finally, my brain got the message through to my feet and I slowly turned and walked away. I just felt in a complete daze. The optimistic part of me was trying to tell me it was only temporary. But it was competing for attention with the more dominant, pessimistic thought that it might be the last time I ever saw her. I know I bumped into at least two people as I walked slowly back to the car park. I was grateful I'd written the floor and row number on the car park ticket, as my head was in a spin. I was on full autopilot as I got in the car and drove home. We'd agreed not to message each other while she was waiting to get on the plane, as she was worried she'd change her mind and not go. I wasn't sure I believed her. My reading of it was that she needed to keep herself strong for supporting her parents and she was compartmentalising, as she admitted she did from time to time. Focusing on one thing and putting everything else to one side.

I wouldn't hear from her until around 11.30pm UK time, assuming the flight was on time. It was going to be a very long afternoon and evening ahead of me. I managed to drive home safely, but I couldn't begin to tell you anything about the drive. I didn't particularly want to be home on my own, but nor did I want any company. I pulled up outside my flat and switched the engine off. I sat there for ten, fifteen, twenty minutes. The bright, sunny weather of earlier had given way to low, black clouds, which was certainly more in keeping with my mood. Eventually, I got out of the car and went inside. I sat in my favourite chair and stared out of the window. The first spots of rain appeared on the glass and a few minutes later it was raining steadily. I just sat there, staring out into the gathering gloom, all sorts of thoughts jumbled together in my head. The daylight gradually gave way to twilight, but I barely moved.

It was almost 4pm. Anna's flight would be taking off any moment. Just then I heard my phone ping. I was going to ignore it, but I thought maybe, just maybe, it was Anna. I got up and picked up the phone from the kitchen table. There was a WhatsApp message. It was Anna.

Just getting ready for take-off. Miss you like crazy already

I quickly typed back:

Miss you more. Safe travels luv

Awww I should have said miss you like crazy and love you to bits

I was smiling as I typed:

Love you too babe. Message me when you land will you?

You got it. And don't you dare mope around missing me!

As if I would!!! Have a good flight. Keep your chin up

You too. I need you to stay strong for me. Oops! Being told off for being on my phone! Later hon

See ya beautiful

It was almost as if she knew how I was feeling. Anna was right. It wouldn't do me any good to mope around and feel sorry for myself. I was already in a much more positive frame of mind. I knew it wasn't going to be easy, but I had to get on with life. I made myself a cup of tea, grabbed a packet of Jaffa Cakes as I suddenly felt hungry and switched on the TV to watch the Liverpool v. Spurs game. It was a distraction if nothing else.

Two hours later, having sat through a fairly uninspiring 2–0 win for the Merseysiders, I'd made up my mind how I was going to spend the evening. Anna had given me her keys as I'd offered to sort out her fridge and also to change the bed, as she'd not had time to do either. I wasn't planning to do any chores this evening though. I just wanted to be at her place. I sorted out my work clothes and gathered the other bits and pieces I needed and chucked them into an overnight bag. Now I'd made my decision, I was in a hurry to get there. The weather had deteriorated, and it was chucking it down with rain, mixed in with a little sleet as I stepped outside. I was cursing under my breath that I'd parked the car a couple of hundred yards down the road. By the time I'd slammed the car door shut, I was soaked.

Fifteen minutes later, I walked into Anna's flat. It was still in a state of organised chaos from earlier and I promised myself that I'd tidy up in the next few days. But for now, I wanted to leave things exactly as they were. I knew I'd made the right decision as soon as I'd stepped across the threshold. Just being there was comforting, surrounded by her things and the memories of so many happy days and nights spent there. I put some of her music on while I unpacked my bag and hung up my suit and work shirts on the back of her bedroom door. I'd brought more than one shirt just in case I stayed a little longer.

I was half asleep on the sofa when I heard my phone ping. I'd put it on loud, just in case I did nod off. I glanced at the clock on the shelves and saw it was 11.40pm. I picked up my phone expectantly and my heart skipped a beat when I saw it was a message from Anna.

Hey stranger! Just wanted to let you know I landed safe and sound a few moments ago. My folks have already messaged me to say they're waiting at the gate for me. Hope you had a good chilled evening

I typed back:

Hey sexy! Thanks for letting me know. Hope you have a nice reunion and give my best to your folks, especially your dad

Awww. I will. Need to get my ass in gear and get off this crate. I'll call you tomorrow if that's OK? Miss you xx

*Can't wait to hear your voice. Seems like ages already. Spk
tomorrow. Miss u2xxx*

I realised I was smiling as I put the phone down. It was all
a little surreal and I still felt like I was playing the lead in
some romantic chick flick. I don't think either of us doubted
our feelings for one another, but being torn apart like this
just underlined how we both felt. Twenty minutes later, I
climbed into her bed and pulled the duvet over me. It was
hard to imagine that it was only last night that we'd been
there together. It felt like days already. I sighed heavily and
turned off the light. I thought I might have trouble sleeping,
but the lack of sleep the previous night caught up with me and
I drifted off almost immediately, though as I did, my head was
still replaying our final scene together at the airport departure
gate.

21

The week went past in something of a blur. I was almost glad to head into work every day as it gave me something else to think about. I started staying later at work as I didn't relish the thought of going back to my empty flat. Anna and I messaged each other several times each day. As usual, we covered a wide range of topics and emotions.

On one level, she was happy to be there, as she felt it had given both her parents a boost to have her around. But she was sad about her dad, and sad to be without me. But I did my best to keep her spirits up and more than once I'd explained all the obvious benefits of not having me around. As I pointed out, she didn't have to endure romantic days out to the seaside in December with me. Or fourteen-hour round-trip coach journeys to the North East.

One night when we were on Zoom, I made her laugh so much that her mum came into the room to find out what was so funny. I had been re-telling (and embellishing a little) the story about the first night we'd slept together in her bed. I'd managed to get a fairly large graze on my thigh from the rock-hard pitch during the game that afternoon, which in all the excitement of our date, I'd rather forgotten to sort out properly. I will never forget the expression on her face when I got up the next morning with her sheet still semi-attached to a weeping mess on my thigh. I distinctly remember Anna taking one look at it and then pointing out, without any humour in her voice, that the sheets were expensive Egyptian cotton that she had bought only last month. In a suitable state of embarrassment and panicking that I'd ruined the relationship, the first thing I ever bought Anna was not flowers or champagne, but new cotton bedsheets from M&S!

I heard Anna explaining the story to her mum. Even funnier for me was that she started getting told off by her mum for making me feel bad about a sheet! Anna couldn't believe her mum was siding with me and for a few hilarious moments we had a three-way chat going, with Anna trying to defend herself from her mum, and me playing the hard-done-by, long-suffering boyfriend. In the end, Anna was shooing her mother out of the room and it was me cracking up with laughter.

But although the calls and the messaging were good fun and kept us connected, it wasn't even close to having her with me.

Football, of course, was a welcome distraction. Our good form was continuing which helped. The Tuesday after Anna left, we travelled to Bognor Regis, which is always a tough place to play. Beno was back, but Addi and Antonio were still out. I had "one of those games". They happen every so often when everything you do turns to gold. Even if you make some sort of mistake, the football gods are smiling on you and you get away with it. We were definitely second best that night, but whatever the Bognor lads tried, they couldn't find a way past me. Some of the saves were routine, but a couple were special. We didn't find the net, but we didn't concede either and afterwards, we looked on it as a point gained, rather than two dropped, as for once we'd been largely outplayed. But the point took us up to third in the table, a point behind Leatherhead and three behind Dulwich, who were the new leaders.

January had given way to February, though the weather hadn't improved very much. The dark days continued, and it seemed to be constantly raining. The miserable weather pretty much matched my mood. I wasn't exactly the life and soul of the party and seldom went out except for work and football. I had told Anna (sort of confessed actually) that I was spending more of my time at her place than I was at mine. She declared me completely insane, but admitted she was also very moved by it too. She did, of course, ask me not to ruin any more bed sheets, which made both of us laugh.

I was also getting used to phone calls at all hours of the night. I had told her to call me whenever she needed to talk. Initially, she'd been reluctant to wake me, but after doing it once or twice, we started developing a routine where she'd often call me late into her evening, which was very early in my morning. My phone would ring anytime from midnight to 5am. I quickly got used to it and although Anna spent the first few minutes apologising and saying she felt guilty about waking me, it didn't stop her calling, as we both needed to hear each other's voice.

Her dad's condition was deteriorating slowly but surely. She'd been there ten days already, and there was no real thought in her head of coming back to the UK in the immediate future. I understood her position and though I desperately wanted to hear her say she was coming back, I kept telling her she was right to stay. I knew I had to do my best to keep her strong and not think selfishly. Her boss was also being really understanding, which was a weight off her shoulders, though at some point soon she would have to return to work.

There wasn't much I could do. I just made sure I was always there for her and tried to be upbeat and positive whenever she called, even though I was feeling pretty lonely without her. Work, football and increasingly frequent visits to the gym became my social life.

But I still had the Palace trial to look forward to. Anna kept reminding me to turn my attention to that and not spend it all on her. I knew she was right. The trial was only a week and a bit away. But first there was the small matter of our home game on Saturday. First v. third, as Dulwich Hamlet were the visitors. If it was anything like our first game at their place, it would be a cracker. There would be a great atmosphere too, as they always brought a lot of fans. We'd tried to counter that by giving away a couple of hundred free tickets to local schools and the local NHS Trust. Plus, we'd offered half-price entry to anyone who'd travelled on the coaches to the cup tie at Sunderland. We were certainly hoping for a big and partisan home crowd.

Training on the Thursday night was largely spent looking at the film of the previous game against them and learning from our mistakes. They were plenty of those. But we also looked at how we'd exploited some of their shortcomings in midfield and at the back. Although they were top of the table and deserved our respect, we certainly weren't afraid of them. It was a very light session physically because we'd played so many games in a short space of time. We were quietly confident, and our confidence was boosted still further with the news that both Addi and Antonio had passed fitness tests and were fit for the Dulwich game.

I was getting dressed after training on Thursday when I saw I had a message from Bryan Morgan. I clicked on it, half expecting him to say the trial was being put back again or something. But instead it was confirmation of timings, the address of their training ground and where to go on arrival. Suddenly it felt very real. With everything else happening, it hadn't really been at the front of my mind. But now it most certainly was. I quickly replied and confirmed receipt of all the info and said I was looking forward to it.

I had to report at 10am on the Monday morning, though that would mainly be for a medical check-up and a few physical tests. On Tuesday there was training from 10.30am until 3pm, which included lunch. On Wednesday, I was playing for their U23s in a game against West Ham, which kicked off at 2pm and had to report at midday. Then Thursday was training from 12 until 4pm and Friday was 10am until noon. I let it sink in. It was still quite hard to believe it was all happening. I hadn't expected to be playing in a match either, and against another Premier League side too. This was going to be quite an experience.

I forwarded the message to Anna as I knew she'd want to know the details. No doubt we'd talk about it later. I hoped by giving her something else to think about, it might help distract her a little.

I didn't feel like being sociable, so I jumped in my car as soon as I was showered and changed and headed back to my own flat for once. Although it had been a relatively light session, I'd still had a good work-out with Smithy, so I had some wet and muddy training gear to chuck into my washing machine at home.

I woke early for some reason on Saturday. I'd had a decent night's sleep for once as Anna had said I needed a good rest before such an important game and she'd not be calling me until Saturday night. I tried to convince her I'd be fine, but she was as stubborn as a mule when she wanted to be and once her mind was made up, that was that. It was only 7am. I debated going back to sleep, but I was completely awake and knew there was no point. It was raining outside as the weather forecast had predicted. It was set in for most of the day. Only one thing for it. I changed into my gym clothes, grabbed a banana and a glass of orange juice, and headed out into the cold and wet. I would only do weights and flexibility work this morning. No need for cardiovascular as I didn't want to make my legs heavy for the game later. It was something I always used to do before I'd met Anna, but oddly enough the contest between the gym or staying in bed with my girlfriend had never been that close.

The gym was unsurprisingly empty when I arrived, but by the time I left about forty minutes later, it was getting busy. I had that slightly smug air as I walked to the gym car park, passing bleary-eyed men and women who were heading into the torture chamber with that look of grim determination. I treated myself to a Caffè Nero on the way home and made myself a large breakfast. Fruit, cereal, toast and coffee. It would have to keep me going until after the game, as I never liked eating much beyond midday when I was playing, so a hearty breakfast was always the preferred option. I remembered with a smile the first time Anna had seen one of my pre-match breakfasts. She couldn't believe I could eat that much.

I wondered what she was doing while I ate my breakfast. It was around 9am, so with the five-hour difference it was only 4am on the east coast. No doubt tucked up in bed, hopefully dreaming about me. I smiled at the thought.

I spent the rest of the morning doing a few chores. Living between two different flats basically meant I was always tidying or cleaning one or the other. Once the chores were done, I sat down with the laptop and wrote a long email to Anna. It was about nothing in particular, but it was very easy to write to her. She always said how nicely I wrote, and how she loved getting my emails. This morning's email might test that statement, I thought, smiling as I typed. I certainly had written a fair bit about the big game that afternoon, plus my thoughts about the trial the following week. But then again, if she wasn't able to cope by now with my love of football, I doubted we'd still be together.

The morning went quickly and before I knew it, my phone was telling me it was midday and I needed to get myself ready to go. My kit bag was packed, but that didn't stop me taking everything out to re-check it and make sure it was all there. I'd once forgotten my boots when I was fifteen or sixteen and playing in an evening game for a men's team a couple of leagues below Reigate. My dad, bless him, who always came to watch me, had rushed back home and collected my boots. But I'd had to borrow a spare pair from one of the other lads in order to start the game. The boots I borrowed were size nine. My feet were size eleven! I have never been so pleased to hear the half-time whistle go, allowing me to take off the size nines and massage some feeling back into my feet. Oddly enough, I'd had a really good game in the first half. The superstitious part of me was thinking that maybe I ought to keep the nines on for the second half. But in the end, my feet made the more persuasive argument and I changed into my normal boots for the second half. We still won.

Bag checked, I was on the road earlier than I really needed to be, but I hated hanging around killing time, so I decided that getting to the ground a bit early wouldn't be the worst thing. I arrived at 12.50pm. Harry had told us to get there by 1.15pm, so unsurprisingly I was the first player there. But I certainly wasn't the first person there. The ground was a hive of activity. The tea bar was being opened, as was the club shop. The match programmes had just been delivered, so I helped myself to one to read later. I popped my head into the boardroom and saw that both club secretaries were filling out the team sheets. It always surprised me that it was still done manually, rather than electronically. Some traditions die hard. Doreen was busy making teas and coffees for the directors, but she always offered me a cup as an early arrival and I usually accepted. It had become something of a pre-game ritual. As I helped myself to some sugar, the ref and his two assistants walked in. I recognised the referee. I couldn't remember from where though. We exchanged pleasantries. I was just about to walk out when Simon, one of our directors, walked in. He took one look at the ref and said to me:

"Better be careful that you don't get yourself sent off again, Matt. Still, we all make mistakes!"

It suddenly dawned on me. It was the same ref that had sent me off at Folkestone earlier in the season! No wonder I recognised him. There was a nervous chuckle from the ref and Simon grinned at him and then me. I wasn't too sure if that barb was especially helpful, but it did make me smirk, although I tried hard not to show it. I decided to head for the relative safety of the changing room and leave Simon and the ref to reminisce about the Folkestone game.

I sat on one of the benches in the dressing room, reading the programme. One by one, the rest of the lads strolled in, together with our coaching staff. Mel was always one of the first to arrive, as she liked to get all of her stuff set out in the small physio's room before the players started demanding her attention.

Beno was an early arrival and set up the music box. We tended to take it in turns to avoid us getting fed up listening to one person's choice all the time. Much to my surprise, he had some Nickelback booming out before long, followed by Aerosmith. Not the sort of music I'd have associated him with, but that was part of the fun of everyone getting their go at being dressing room DJ.

For once, no one was late. We all sat quietly as both Jez and then Harry reminded us how they wanted us to play, but also about some of the things we knew the opposition wanted to do, especially at set pieces. It was only for ten minutes as it was really just a case of reminding us of the things we'd discussed on Thursday at training. Once that was done, Harry and Jez left us to change and go through the normal pre-match routine.

By the time we finished our warm-up and were walking back to the dressing room, I noticed just how much the ground was filling up. There was a lot of pink and blue Dulwich colours in the crowd milling around the entrance, but there was a good amount of our yellow and blue too, which was good to see.

We sat down and fiddled with our usual last-minute bits and pieces. Harry waited for us to settle before he spoke. It was short and very much to the point.

"Last time, you gave these bastards a three-goal start, and they still couldn't beat us! Let's not do that again. Last time you showed them too much respect. Last time, half of you didn't start playing until the second half. I don't want a repeat of last time. Get on the front foot right from the start. Don't let them settle. Get amongst them. Press them high up the pitch. Make them worry about us this time." He turned and walked out.

The ref's buzzer sounded, and we were on our feet, yelling encouragement at each other. There were lots of hugs and handshakes as we got ready to go out. Non-league crowds are rarely noisy before a game and arguably our supporters weren't very noisy during a game either. But this time we could hear the buzz around the ground as we waited in the tunnel to go out.

We walked out into the grey and slightly misty February afternoon. For once it wasn't raining, but it was gloomy enough for the floodlights to be on already. There was a really good crowd in. It was rare indeed to see both grandstands and the covered standing area full, but full they were. They gave the crowd out later as 900 something, but it felt as though there were more in the ground than that. However many were there, they certainly got their money's worth. I saw Jess talking to Mark Francis, the Dulwich boss, as he walked out of the tunnel. She gave me a little smile and nod. I smiled back, but she'd already turned back to Francis.

Just as in the first game, there was an early goal. But this time it was us who found the net in the first five minutes. Stan passed the ball back to me. I looked up quickly and saw that Leon Mitchell was in acres of space in the centre circle. I fired a low pass into his feet from more or less the penalty spot. It was one of those passes that looks great when it finds its man. But if I'd miscued it very slightly, it would probably have ended up at the feet of one of the Dulwich forwards. Luckily for me it didn't. Leon brought the bullet of a pass instantly under control, turned and chipped a delightful ball up towards Antonio, who had the Dulwich centre-back pinned behind him. Antonio took one touch and then laid it off to Stevie. For some reason, Stevie decided to hit it from all of thirty yards. Long-range shooting is certainly not one of his strengths as a player. In fairness it wasn't a bad strike, but it became a great strike when the Dulwich skipper on the edge of the box stuck out a foot. The ball caught his heel and deflected it wickedly. Their keeper had been going one way, but suddenly the ball was going the other way. He stood flat-footed as the ball rolled into the net to put us one up.

The muffled announcement from the PA system gave the time of the goal as the fourth minute. It was the perfect start.

But it didn't last. One of the many clichés in football is that you're never more vulnerable than when you've just scored. Like most clichés, there is a certain amount of truth in it. It was certainly true today, as just two minutes later, Dulwich equalised. It was a goal that we should never have conceded. Leon tried to beat his man half-way inside our half, instead of just playing a simple pass back. He lost possession and with half of our team already moving forward, we were caught in transition. The Dulwich man quickly played the ball wide and their left-winger curled in a beautiful cross. John was still desperately trying to get back into position, and was behind their centre-forward who got to the cross first. His firm header flew past me into the far corner.

Leon hung his head, knowing he was largely to blame. It would have been easy enough for a few of the lads to have a go at Leon. Certainly, if it had been Stevie or Tommy who'd done that, we would have let them know in no uncertain terms. But Leon was a young lad, still learning the game and bawling at him wouldn't have done his confidence much good.

Even though I hate conceding goals, I walked up to the edge of the box and yelled, "Leon, head up son. Forget about it. Keep playing."

Stevie went to him and had a few words. Antonio went past him and ruffled his hair. We needed him playing well. We all knew we had to lift him. But it didn't work. For the rest of the half, Leon was tentative, and twice got caught in possession as he dithered. The first goal was obviously still on his mind. In the twentieth minute, he tried to play a cross-field ball out to Jamie, who was doing what the boss had told him to do and try and exploit their lack of pace on the right. But the pass was woefully underhit and picked off. We were all over the place at the back as there was a big hole on the left where Jamie had gone forward. John moved across to close down the

Dulwich lad, but it left only Stan to cover the middle. The Dulwich player chipped a ball into the space and suddenly it was a foot race between Stan, their centre-forward and me to get to the ball first. It was just inside the box as the three of us converged. I just got there first, stretching out a foot and just managing to deflect the ball away from their man for a corner. Naturally, the Dulwich player went over my leg and made a drama performance out of it, as most forwards do these days. I said something to him to that effect as I ran back towards the goal to set up for the corner. But then I saw the Dulwich fans behind my goal cheering and clapping. I turned around and saw to my horror that the referee was pointing to the spot! NO! Not again surely!

I sprinted towards the man in black to remonstrate. Three or four of our lads were already around him, arms outstretched or head in hands in disbelief, explaining how wrong he was. That was when I saw him reaching for his pocket. This was déjà vu. This same idiot was going to send me off again! Stevie actually grabbed his hand to stop him pulling the card out and we were imploring him to talk to his lino. By now he had virtually all of our team around him. I think in hindsight, he bottled it a bit. He eventually did trot across to his assistant. After what felt like minutes of discussion, while the home crowd booed, and the visiting supporters chanted "Off! Off!", he finally made up his mind. He pointed to the spot and pulled out a yellow card which he showed to me and also waved it at Stevie, presumably for grabbing his hand. We were still incensed. But now so too were the Dulwich players. They were saying I had to go as it was a clear goal-scoring opportunity. I heard the ref telling them that there was a defender back covering the goal. Now it was their turn to look gobsmacked. I knew there was no one who could have got back in time. It was one dreadful decision, compounded by another dreadful decision. If he really thought I had fouled the Dulwich forward, I deserved a red card. Both sets of fans were booing now, and it was chaos.

After several minutes, both sets of players realised that no further pleading would make any difference and trudged away, muttering as they did and none of it very complimentary about the match official. I was furious and as the Dulwich player I'd supposedly brought down stepped up to take the spot kick, I couldn't help myself.

"You're a cheat," I hissed at him as I walked past him.

No one likes being called a cheat. He certainly didn't and pushed me in the chest. We angrily squared up to each other, our faces inches apart. He was goading me, I knew that, hoping I'd get sent off. It was stupid on my part as I'd just been booked, but the blood was pumping, and common sense was out of the window. John rushed in to pull us apart as the ref again reached for his pocket, which caused me momentary heart failure. But this time he waved it at the Dulwich player for the push. There was more jostling as other players got involved to push each other or try and play peacemaker. To say that the referee had lost control was an understatement.

It took another minute or two before order was restored. I grudgingly retreated to my line. Judging by the language coming from the away supporters behind me, I was fast becoming public enemy number one. As their man placed the ball on the spot, I jumped and tugged down on the crossbar, causing it to vibrate. The Dulwich player complained to the ref, who walked up to me and told me to stop, unless I wanted a second yellow. I stared past his shoulder as if he wasn't there, but wisely kept my mouth shut this time.

Finally, the kick was ready to be taken. I had the feeling he was just going to blast it by the angle of his run-up, so rather than dive, I elected to stay put. He did blast it. It was almost straight at me. I got both hands to it and deflected it over the bar. My teammates were mobbing me, and it gave me a lot of satisfaction to see their penalty-taker on his knees in disbelief. But we hadn't counted on the man in black getting involved again. The Dulwich fans went from stunned silence to a loud cheer. He was pointing at the spot and saying the penalty had to be re-taken. He was telling everyone that I'd moved off the line before the kick. This time all I could do was to just laugh out loud. All keepers move. It's incredibly rare to see a kick re-taken for that. I was beginning to think this was personal. I've never seen John so furious. He was towering over the ref, pointing a finger in his face while yelling at him. He wasn't alone. All of our team were. I just stood there shaking my head in disbelief. The yellow card was brandished again. Definitely at John and possibly at Addi too.

Our crowd isn't always the most vocal, but they were furious. I heard plenty of our fans yelling "Cheat!", together with "How much have they paid you?", with plenty of adjectives added to the mix. Thankfully, cooler heads on our side, like Simo and Rosey, started to pull John and the others away. They knew that we could recover from a goal down, but if we went down to ten men as well, it was probably game over.

This time it was the Dulwich skipper who picked up the ball and placed it carefully on the spot. It wasn't my finest moment, but I couldn't help myself. I walked off my line towards him and said, "I'll save this one too, mate. Unless your ref helps you out again."

The referee wisely ignored me, as did the Dulwich captain. He took a short run-up and side-footed it calmly into the bottom left. I'd gone the other way. He looked at me and put his finger to his lip, telling me to shut up, as he turned away. We'd probably have a laugh about it after the game in the bar. During the game, all sorts of stuff gets said and done. I didn't blame them for any of it. I knew our forwards would have tried to win a penalty too had roles been reversed. Was it right trying to con the ref? Of course not, but we all did it and laughed about it when decisions went in our favour, but were suitably outraged when they went against us. Double standards? Absolutely!

There was still a football match to be played and although we were 2–1 down, we were very much in the match. Oddly, we were the team more energised by the penalty and for the next ten minutes, we went steaming into 50:50 challenges and won most of them. Antonio went close with a header from a free kick and then their keeper did well to push away a pile-driver from Beno. We penned the visitors in with some slick, incisive football. But Dulwich defended well and kept us honest at the back with a couple of quick counter-attacks. As the half drew to a close, I saw the board for added time being readied. By anyone's estimation, there was probably between five and seven minutes to be added due to all the time taken up by the penalty. The board went up. It showed two minutes! Cue more boos around the ground and some laughter too at the complete incompetence of the match officials. I saw Jez go ballistic at the hapless linesman who was running the line near the home dugout.

The referee blew his whistle to end the half. As soon as the whistle sounded, I saw a couple of our ground staff and two of our directors in yellow steward jackets walk quickly out on the pitch towards the officials to escort them off. A number of our lads were keen to have a conversation with the officials, but Jez and Harry pulled them away, and Harry was ordering us to get into the dressing room. I was still seething and wanted my say. I felt someone pulling my arm. Hard. It was Mel.

"Please, Matt, please just shut up and go inside. You'll only make things worse," she said determinedly.

I looked down at our petite physio, doing her best to drag me with her and my anger just vanished in a heartbeat. Seeing Mel trying to restrain me made me more than a little embarrassed that she was having to do so.

"OK! OK! I'm good!" I said, starting to jog off the pitch and away from any possibility of a confrontation.

I'm not certain that Mel believed me, because she jogged alongside me and made sure I didn't change my mind. By the time I walked into the dressing room, there were a lot of angry voices. The anger was all directed at the match officials, which I had no doubt they heard as they walked past and into their dressing room.

"Shut up and sit DOWN!" Harry was in no mood for a conversation. We quietened down.

"Forget that tosser in black, boys. If you start focusing on him and not focusing on doing your jobs then we will lose this match. Yeah, dreadful decisions by the ref, BUT we made some dreadful decisions too. Leon, you've got ten minutes this half to stop feeling sorry for yourself and start playing like I know you can. If you don't, you're coming off. Clear?"

"Yes, boss."

"Matt, if you get yourself sent off for mouthing off at the officials, I will fine you a month's wages. Clear?"

"Yes, gaffer."

"Stevie, if you run around like a headless chicken again like you did in the last fifteen minutes looking for a scrap, you'll be on the bench beside me. Got it?"

"Sorry, boss."

Harry carried on calling out individual players and highlighting what they'd done wrong and what they needed to do to put it right. By the time Harry had finished, none of us were thinking about the ref and the injustices of the first half.

We were thinking about what we needed to do as individuals in the second period.

By almost any measure, the first half had been a cracking game of football. Most people in the ground were eagerly awaiting the second half, assuming it would be as good as the first. It's one of those oddities of football that a really good first half is almost invariably followed by a poor second half. Partly because the players will have put a lot into an end-to-end first half, and partly because the managers will have made changes that invariably tighten up the game and reduce the space that had been there earlier. Our second half was no exception to that unwritten rule. The two sides began to cancel each other out. All I had to do was collect a couple of crosses and punch away a corner. My opposite number was no busier than I was.

With just under twenty minutes left, we were still a goal down and having more of the ball, but without creating any real chances. But for now, the action was at our end, as a long-range effort had nicked one of our players and gone for a corner. The corner was swung in and I went up for it among a crowd of players. I went to punch it clear and made good contact. As I came down, my right foot landed on someone else's foot and I turned the whole ankle right over. I felt something pop. I tried to get up but found I couldn't put any weight on my right foot. Luckily, the ball had gone out and I went down again, yelling to tell my teammates and the ref I needed treatment.

Mel came sprinting on and crouched down beside me. My ankle was on fire and I knew it wasn't good. An impact injury hurts like hell initially, but the pain usually subsides quite quickly. Muscle and ligament injuries were a different matter.

"What happened, Matt?"

"Landed on a foot, Mel. My ankle went right over. I felt something go."

She moved my right ankle a little and I yelped with pain.

She tried moving the foot up and down a little and waves of pain radiated through the outside of the ankle.

"It's not good, Matt. I think there might be a break or a torn ligament. You need to come off," she said, shaking her head.

"Help me to stand, Mel. Let me try to put some weight on it," I pleaded. "There can't be long left."

Mel opened her mouth to say something but then rolled her eyes and did what I asked. She pulled me up. I gingerly took a step. The pain shot from my ankle all the way up my leg. It was excruciating. Mel took one look and didn't ask me this time. She made the substitution gesture to the bench. To make matters worse, Smithy wasn't on the bench today. He rarely was now I was fit again.

"Mel, let me try it for a few minutes before we make the change. It might wear off," I said in desperation.

"No!" said Mel firmly. "You can't even put weight on it, let alone run or kick."

Deep down, I knew she was right. My heart was telling me to give it a go, but my brain had already reached the same conclusion that I couldn't carry on. Jez came running on when the bench realised it was serious. Simo was going to have to go in goal, so I peeled off my shirt and gloves and handed them to him. Luke was getting ready on the touchline to replace me. Mel suggested we get the stretcher for me, but I refused, and, in the end, I put my arms on the shoulders of Jez and Mel and hobbled off, using them for support. After they had got me seated in the dressing room, they both went back out, leaving me alone. To say I was devastated was an understatement. Not only was I missing the rest of this crucial game, I knew deep down that it was a bad injury and I was going to be out for a while. That would mean my trial at Crystal Palace wouldn't happen unless there was some sort of miraculous recovery. I felt devastated.

A couple of minutes later I heard a roar outside. Someone had scored. Maybe we'd grabbed an equaliser. A point was better than nothing and would stop Dulwich taking all three. I stopped feeling sorry for myself and hobbled to the door, which was ajar. I saw Bob at the end of the tunnel, microphone in hand, announcing the goal.

"The scorer of Dulwich's third goal in the eighty-fourth minute is number eight, Damarie Douglas."

Game over, I thought. No way will we come back from 3–1 down. I limped back into the room, every step an ordeal. I slumped back onto the bench, put my head in my hands and closed my eyes, trying unsuccessfully to block out the pain.

"Hey Matt, are you OK?"

I looked up and saw it was Jess, looking anxious. She quickly added, "Sorry. That's a stupid thing to say. I know you're not OK."

"Probably not the best time to ask me for a quote, Jess."

"That wasn't why I came in," she said, hurt on her face, which of course made me feel even worse, if that were possible.

"Sorry. That was a shitty thing to say. I'm just gutted."

"I know. Tonight, and the Palace trial. That's why I wanted to check on you."

"Look on the bright side. At least you don't have to worry about whether to write the story about my Palace trial now!" It wasn't much of a joke, but at least it brought a half-smile to her face.

"There's no chance you'll be OK?"

In answer, I gingerly pulled off first my boot and then my sock. The ankle was already swelling up.

"Ooohhh. That doesn't look good," said Jess. "Oh God, I'm saying all the wrong things! Do you need to go and get it checked at the hospital? I can drive you if you want?"

"Thanks, but I'll see how it is tomorrow. Harry will probably get me to see the Wimbledon club doctor again."

"OK, but if I can help just ask. You might need a chauffeur as it's your right foot."

"Thanks, Jess. That's very nice of you, but I think I'll be alright. I'd better go and get showered before everyone else comes in, so you might want to leave to avoid any more unpleasant sights," I managed half a smile at my feeble attempt at humour.

"Oh. Sure. Sorry! Take care, Matt," she said, looking a little embarrassed.

Ten minutes later, when most of the rest of the team had trooped in, looking as glum as I felt, I still hadn't moved, let alone showered and changed. As soon as Mel walked in, she immediately came over and knelt down in front of me, looking closely at the ankle. She asked me to move the ankle in several different directions. A couple of the movements were agony.

"The good news is that I don't think there's a break, although without an X-ray, it's an educated guess. But the bad news is that I think there's ligament damage on the outside of the ankle. But I could be wrong; it might just be a sprain," she said, trying to sound positive, but not really convincing me.

"If it is ligament damage, how long will I be out?" I wasn't sure I wanted to hear the answer, but I needed to know.

"It really depends upon the extent of the damage. But probably six to eight weeks," she said quietly.

Six weeks would mean being out until early April. The season finished at the end of April. It dawned on me that this injury could end my season. The dream of a professional trial and a glorious end to the season had just gone up in smoke. Mel saw my face.

"Hey Matt. I could just as easily be wrong about all this. Let's just wait and see before we jump to conclusions. OK?"

I nodded. A few of the lads asked me how I was, but no one was really in the mood for talking. The defeat was a real blow to our promotion prospects. My injury did nothing to help the mood in the dressing room. Harry came in and did his best to try and lift the spirits. He told us we'd been the better side for most of the game, but sometimes it just wasn't your day. He was right. That was certainly the case tonight. He came over to check on me and said he'd ring the Wimbledon club doctor shortly to see if he I could go and see him again. This was all horribly familiar now.

I managed to hobble in and out of the shower and get changed. I wasn't in the mood to go into the bar, and as far as I was concerned, the less I had to walk, the better. I got into my car and went to switch the engine on. As I started to press down on the accelerator pedal, a bolt of pain shot through my ankle and I realised that driving wasn't really an option. I hated to rely on someone else, but she had offered. I dialled her number.

"Hello?"

"Hey Jess, it's Matt. Are you still in the clubhouse?"

"Yes, I've just finished interviewing Harry. Why?"

"Can I take you up on your offer of a lift home? I don't think I can drive."

"Of course! Where are you?"

"Sitting in my car in the car park."

"Hang on! I'll be there in a couple of minutes. My car's the black Nissan Juke in the far corner."

"Thanks, Jess. I know your car. I'll see you over there."

I hung up, grabbed my kit from the boot and hobbled over to Jess's car. She arrived moments later. She unlocked it and I eased myself slowly and carefully into the passenger seat.

"Thanks for doing this. I'm not very good at accepting offers of help," I said apologetically.

"Typical guy!" said Jess, pulling a face.

"Guilty as charged!" We both smiled as she pulled out of the car park.

She started talking and I knew she was doing it to take my mind off things. We chatted about nothing in particular, but despite my black mood, the conversation flowed easily enough. I realised as we were talking that I knew almost nothing about her, apart from her job. She'd never offered anything, but then again, I'd never asked. Time to remedy that, I thought.

"So, what do you do when not interviewing grumpy footballers?"

She laughed. "They're not all grumpy. Only the goalkeepers!"

"I hope you aren't implying that I'm grumpy, Ms Gallaway!"

"Would I do that?" she asked innocently.

"C'mon, you haven't answered the question. Boyfriend?"

At that exact moment Jess turned into my road and the female voice on her phone told us we had arrived. I let out a sigh of exasperation.

"Saved by the bell," she said, smiling. "Are you going to be OK hobbling inside?"

"Probably. It would be rude of me not to offer you a coffee at least. But I'm sure you have plans for this evening."

"Well, my plans revolved around writing the match report for the paper and ordering in a Chinese and a bottle of wine, so not hugely exciting."

I didn't really stop to think about it and the words were out of my mouth before I did.

"Well, my evening is even less exciting as it involves a bag of ice and watching TV. But if you want to share a Chinese and a bottle, I'd welcome the company."

Jess glanced over at me. It quickly dawned on me that it might have sounded more like a date than I'd intended. I was about to try and explain that I hadn't meant it like that, when, to my surprise, she said, "Sure, why not?"

It turned into an unexpectedly nice evening, despite my ankle. Jess insisted on waiting on me and ordered the Chinese and some Tiger beers, rather than the wine. The only real pause in the conversation came when the food arrived and we started to eat, but that was only temporary. I finally got to know a little more about her.

It was an interesting story. She was born in Tunbridge Wells in Kent and lived there until she went to university in Nottingham to study journalism. After university, she'd decided to travel and spent six months doing a tour of South America. During her travels, she'd fallen in love with Brazil and especially Rio de Janeiro. She also met a young Brazilian, who played football for one of the Rio clubs called Fluminense. He invited her to watch him play at the iconic Maracanã, and she said that's where she fell in love with football and, of course, with this young Brazilian too. She ended up staying another six months and thought she'd met the love of her life. But in something of a cliché about footballers and football romances, she eventually found out he had another girl in tow, so she came home, heartbroken, jobless and penniless. But the football bug had well and truly bitten her, and she realised it was sports journalism that was her calling.

"And the rest is history," she concluded. "Been doing this for six years now, but I'm still hoping to make my way to the national press one day."

"I can also understand why you keep yourself at arm's length from footballers too."

"It's part of it, I guess. But it would also be very unprofessional of me to strike up a relationship with a player when I'm supposed to be an objective reporter."

Just then my phone pinged. It was a message from Bryan Morgan asking me to call him. I showed Jess the message.

"Good news travels fast," she said, with heavy irony.

"So it seems. Do you mind if I call him now?"

"Of course not. I'll clear the stuff away," she said, getting up from the table. I sighed and dialled Bryan's number. This wasn't a call I was looking forward to.

"Hi Matt. Thanks for calling back. How's the ankle?"

"Hi Bryan. Yeah, it's sore right now and a bit swollen. I think I'll know more tomorrow."

"We had one of our scouts at the game watching you. That's how I knew. Listen, even if the injury isn't too bad, I don't think it makes sense to come for the trial next week. You obviously won't be a hundred per cent."

Even though I knew he was right, and I would probably have told him the same, it still felt like a punch in the guts. Jess was looking at me sympathetically.

"Yeah," I said reluctantly, "you're probably right."

"Listen, son, we're still interested, but obviously things move quickly in football. The best bet is for you to get yourself fit again and then let me know when you are, and we can take it from there."

I couldn't help but get the feeling that I might have missed my chance.

"Understood, Bryan. Is it worth just trying to set a date now?" I realised I sounded a little desperate, but I wanted to know that I still had a shot.

"Probably best to leave any decisions for now, son. You need to work out how long you're going to be out for. We're not that far away from the end of the season anyway, so let's just play it by ear. OK?"

"OK, Bryan. I'll give you a call when I'm fit and playing again."

"Yep. Good luck and I hope it's nothing too serious. Cheers, Matt."

I put the phone down and slumped back in my chair. Jess asked me what he'd said so I gave her a quick download of the conversation. She did her best to sound positive.

"He's right, Matt. Until you know how long you're out for, there's not much point setting any dates. You need to get fit and start playing again first."

"Yeah, I guess so. It just feels like my chance may have gone."

"Hey! That's not what he said. You need to stay positive. It will give you something to aim for."

I looked at Jess, suddenly very glad she was here. I managed half a smile.

"I'm trying to feel sorry for myself here. You're spoiling the moment!"

She laughed. "You're not the type to feel sorry for yourself. But if I see it happening, I'll soon snap you out of it."

"Thanks, Jess. I'm really glad you're here. You've turned what would have been a really crappy evening into a nice one."

"I'm glad I stopped by too."

We were both looking at one another. No words were said, but Jess walked to the sofa and sat down next to me. I could feel the electricity between us. She turned to face me. Her large, brown eyes looking deeply into mine. Time seemed to stop. We both knew we were about to cross a line in the sand. Jess leaned forward. Our faces inches apart. But instead of kissing me she gave me a big hug. I hugged her back, surprised but maybe a little relieved too.

After a moment or two, Jess let go of me and said, "I think I'd better go, Matt, before we do something we both end up regretting."

I just looked at her. I wasn't sure what to say or what to

do. My head was all over the place. I will admit that part of me wanted Jess to stay. But I couldn't do that to Anna, and it wouldn't be fair to Jess either. So, I didn't say a word. I just watched Jess as she picked up her handbag and walked towards the door. As she stepped across the threshold, she turned and smiled and then closed the door softly behind her. I closed my eyes and sighed deeply. I picked up my phone from the table and scrolled through my contacts until I found Jess's number. My finger hovered above the call button. Suddenly the phone rang, making me jump. It was Harry.

He was ringing to see how I was and to tell me he'd arranged for me to see the Wimbledon doctor on Monday evening. We spoke for a few minutes. By the time we'd finished the call, the moment to call Jess and ask her to come back had passed. I knew she was right. We would probably both have regretted it and now I was feeling horribly guilty for even thinking about it. There was my girlfriend, 3,000 miles away, dealing with a sick parent, and I was thinking about another woman. I suddenly felt awful. I really didn't deserve a girl like Anna. Thank God Jess was more strong-willed than I was.

I messaged Anna, hoping she'd be around to talk. She replied almost instantly.

Hey matey. How did the game go?

Not so good. We lost 3–1 and I got injured again

Oh no!! How bad!?

Bad enough to miss my trial

Oh God. I am SO sorry luv. That's awful. I feel so so bad for you

Can I call you on Zoom?

I'd love to talk, but we're at the hospital now having some more tests done. Shall I call you when we get home?

Of course. I hope everything goes OK

Thank you. Keep your chin up babe

Thanks, beautiful. Speak later

I felt even guiltier than I had done earlier. I really didn't deserve a woman like Anna. I settled down to watch some TV and hopefully take my mind off both football and women. The problem was that I couldn't forget that moment when Jess and I were inches away from kissing and digging a great big hole for ourselves. There was certainly a spark when we were alone together. That couldn't be denied. The solution, of course, was obvious. I had to make sure we weren't in the future. Of course, Jess was probably thinking the same thing and had made it pretty clear that she didn't want to date any more footballers.

I dozed off on the sofa and woke two hours later, feeling stiff, sore and guilty. My ankle was looking more swollen despite the ice. I saw there was a WhatsApp message from Anna. She said they'd had a long and quite wearing day at the hospital and she felt emotionally drained. She hoped I didn't mind if she took a rain check on the call this evening. She promised to call the next day when she would be more with it.

I messaged back and said of course I didn't mind. In point of fact, I really did want to speak to her. But what else could I say? A fitting end to an awful day. I limped off to bed, feeling suitably sorry for myself.

22

My Uber pulled into the car park at Parkside Hospital just off Wimbledon Common. My ankle was still too sore to be able to drive safely, so I was spending a fortune on taxis.

My meeting with the Wimbledon doctor on Monday had been a relatively short one. Because of the swelling he wasn't able to offer much more than an opinion on the extent of the injury. But he did agree that it needed further investigation. Once he knew I had private health cover through my firm, he called a colleague at Parkside and booked me for an MRI scan on Thursday afternoon.

I hobbled into reception and was immediately given numerous forms to complete. I didn't have to wait long before my name was called. I got up and hobbled after a young male technician to the MRI scanning room. I had to admit I was quite curious about what was going to happen, as I'd not had an MRI before. The technician briefly explained the procedure and told me the scan would take about twenty minutes. He told me I didn't need to undress. All I had to do was roll up the leg of my tracksuit bottoms. Briefing over, I followed the technician into the MRI room, and he told me to lay down on the narrow "bed". He checked for about the third time that it was my right ankle and then told me to place it between two blue pads, so it was a bit like the meat in a sandwich. He straightened my ankle and tightened the pads and reminded me how important it was that I remained as still as possible during the scan.

Suitably positioned, he gave me headphones to put on and asked me what music I'd prefer to listen to, giving me half a dozen choices. It wasn't a question that I'd been expecting, so for some reason I blurted out "rock", which meant there was now little chance of me having a doze.

As the technician switched both the machine and the music on, I was quite grateful that it was only my leg that was actually in the MRI machine itself. Having your full body in the machine looked a little claustrophobic to me. The scanner was also bloody noisy and the soft rock ballads in my headphones were almost drowned out by the drone of the machine. It was an exceedingly long twenty minutes and I was glad when the technician removed my headphones to tell me it was all over.

Normally, it takes a few days before you get the results, but it pays to have friends in high places, or in my case, Harry, and the Wimbledon club doctor who worked at the same private hospital. I was told I could wait in the patients' waiting area or go into the canteen and get something to eat. I chose the latter, even though it was mid-afternoon. One thing I could always do was to eat. I got myself a tuna sandwich and a latte and found myself a table in the corner. I'd been told it would probably be the best part of two hours before the doctor could see me with the results, so I settled down with my food and my phone to kill some time.

There was a message from Jess wishing me good luck.

Neither of us had mentioned what had happened on Saturday. Although the smart thing would have been to keep our distance from one another, it hadn't happened. It felt to me as though we'd become closer, but more as friends rather than anything else. She asked to be kept up to date about my injury, but as a friend, she'd said, not a journalist.

There was another message from Anna, asking me to call her when I had some news. It was probably a good thing that we hadn't spoken on the Saturday in the end. By Sunday, I'd got my head in a better place and was feeling less guilty and less sorry for myself. Less guilty because I knew Anna was the girl for me. I convinced myself that it had just been a passing moment between Jess and I and that nothing had happened. I knew deep down that I wasn't being totally truthful with myself, but it felt better putting that spin on it, even if it was just for my benefit. By the time I'd eaten and had a bit of a back and forth with both girls about MRI machines and musical choices, an hour had flown by. Harry had also told me to keep him in the loop. All three of them had been great in different ways. Jess kept telling me not to feel sorry for myself and get myself back in the shop window. Anna was more sympathetic, but told me I'd get another shot and to keep dreaming. Harry said none of the stuff with Palace mattered for now. My only focus should be to get myself fully fit. Everything else would have to wait. All three were right in different ways.

While the first hour had gone quickly, time was beginning to drag now. I was on my third latte and so bored that I'd even started looking at work emails, even though I'd told the office I was at the hospital for the afternoon. Eventually a nurse popped her head around the door and called my name. Standing up after sitting for all that time was a bit of a struggle, but I managed to follow her out of the door and down a long corridor. We went all the way to the end. I wondered why everything is always further away when you're injured.

Eventually we arrived at a door which just said "Consulting" on it. The nurse knocked, but opened it almost before the answer came.

"Good afternoon, Matt," said Alan, waving me in. "This is becoming something of a habit."

"It's not been my best few months in football, that's for sure," I said, smiling ruefully.

"Indeed. Take a seat, please. I expect you want to find out what the MRI showed us," he said, turning his laptop towards me and getting straight to the point. "There's good news and bad news. The good news is that there's nothing broken. A break down there can take quite a while to heal. But the bad news is that there is a tear, just here," he said, pointing to a spot on the screen with his pen. "See there? Your calcaneofibular ligament is torn."

I wasn't absolutely sure what I was looking at, but I was prepared to take the doctor's word for it. "So, what am I looking at in terms of rehab?"

"Did you feel or hear a pop when it happened?"

"Yes. I presume that's not good?"

"It's what I would have expected. To answer your question, this is a Grade 3 injury to the ligament. It's going to take time to heal unfortunately. How long it takes is rather down to you. But for this sort of injury it's a minimum of six weeks, and judging by the MRI, I'd say you're looking at eight to ten weeks. And that is provided you do what you need to do in terms of rehabilitation and don't try to start playing again too soon."

My heart sank. Eight to ten weeks meant that I was out for the rest of the season. It was the news I'd been dreading. I had hoped it might only be a sprain and I'd be back in four to six weeks, although having done a little online research, I'd been preparing myself for the news I'd just been given.

"You'll need to wear a protective boot for four weeks, twenty-four hours a day. Even in bed. We'll get one for you before you leave. That will allow you to walk around without doing any more damage to it. We'll give you a walking stick too, as it takes a little getting used to walking in one of those things."

I was still absorbing the time scale for the injury and was probably only half-listening as the doctor explained what I needed to do. He gave me a leaflet with a rehabilitation programme and timeline, but was at pains to point out that every ankle and every person is different and that the programme was only a guideline. He stressed the importance of regular consultation with a physio to ensure that the ankle was being monitored and the programme adjusted according to how it responded to the exercises I would be doing. I made a mental note to ask Harry if he could get me in to see the Wimbledon physio a few times. It wasn't that I didn't have confidence in Mel. It was simply that the Wimbledon guy was a lot more experienced, and had access to a lot of equipment that Mel could only dream about.

Alan stood and held out his hand to indicate that the consultation was over. Still slightly in a daze, I shook hands, and thanked him for his time. There were several people who'd told me to let them know as soon as I had the results of the scan, but I wanted a little time to myself first, just to get my head around the news, before speaking to anyone.

I booked an Uber to take me home. Fortunately, there are a lot of them around Wimbledon, so I only had to wait ten minutes. By now, I'd had enough of the hospital and just wanted to get out of the place. The Uber driver turned out to be one that didn't particularly want a conversation, which suited me fine, as neither did I. As we drove back, I messaged Harry with the bad news. He responded almost immediately and told me to keep my chin up. He also said he'd arrange some sessions with the Dons' physio, even before I asked, which was good of him. I messaged a few of the lads too. John, Stan and Stevie had all asked me to let them know. I knew they'd tell the others. I kept the messages short and to the point. All three responded slightly differently. John said pretty much the same as Harry, telling me to stay strong. Stan told me he expected me back in four weeks and not to be a pussy, which made me smile. Stevie's response almost made me laugh out loud. It was laden with expletives, but the gist of it was that ordinary league matches were a bit beneath me now.

The traffic was light, so by the time I'd finished messaging Harry and the lads, I was almost home. I sent a slightly longer message to Anna and gave her a bit more detail, but I didn't hear anything back from her. No doubt she was at the hospital or perhaps working. I sent a similar message to Jess. She rang me back almost immediately.

"Hi Jess. How are you?"

"Oh, Matt," she said, her voice full of sympathy. "I am so sorry. That's such bad luck. You must be gutted."

"Yeah. It certainly wasn't the diagnosis I was hoping for. But I had a feeling it would be bad news, having read up on that sort of injury. Still, I have to look on the bright side. No surgery required and the ankle should be fine again. Just needs time to heal." I was trying to sound positive, as much for myself as for Jess.

I don't think she was buying it though. "That's true, but still a crappy time of the season for it to happen. Both for you and for the team."

"Part and parcel of football. It happens. Nothing I can do about it now, except to focus on the rehab."

"I've got to head out in a minute, but I want you to know that if you ever need someone to talk to, I'm here."

"Is that on or off the record though?!" I asked, trying to lighten the mood a little.

"Very funny." Jess's voice was dripping with sarcasm. "You know what I mean."

"I do and I appreciate it, Jess. You're a star."

"You take care of yourself OK?"

"Yes, boss!"

"See you, Matt."

It was the first time we'd spoken since the evening we'd spent together. It felt like we'd both avoided the issue. Maybe that was for the best. Pretend it never happened. After all, what could we say? We both knew there was something there, but we also knew that it couldn't go anywhere, so being friends was definitely safer ground. Besides, I had no idea if Jess even wanted it to go anywhere, given her history with dating footballers. Probably not.

Still nothing from Anna. Oh well. We'd probably speak that night, as we often did when she had a bit more time.

Just then my phone rang again. I didn't recognise the number. It was one of those, do I/don't I moments. I almost let it go through to voicemail, but in the end, I decided to answer it.

"Hello?"

"Hi, is that Matt?" The caller had a slight accent, which I was trying to place.

"Yes, who's this?"

"Matt, this is Frankie de Jost. I'm the assistant manager at Sunderland Football Club. I hope you don't mind me calling. Your manager gave me your number."

For a moment, I was almost lost for words. Why on earth were Sunderland calling me? "Err, not at all," I said, rather lamely.

"Great. I know you are injured and possibly out for the season your manager said. But hopefully this will make you feel better." My mouth was a little dry suddenly. He paused, perhaps expecting me to say something. When I didn't, he carried on. "We've been watching you since your cup game against Grimsby. We had someone at the game to watch both teams, but our scout came back and said we should keep an eye on you. Then, of course, we had the chance to watch you first-hand when you played against us. I was impressed, as was the boss."

"Umm, cheers. But we all played well that day."

"True. But we very much liked what we saw. We had someone at most of your league games after the cup tie. Of course, we spoke to your manager and he told us about the Palace trial, so we had to put our interest a little on the back-burner, as we thought you'd probably choose Palace over us if the trial went well."

"Not something I have to worry about now, I guess."

"Yes, we were a little surprised that Palace didn't arrange another date, but they probably have other options they are looking at. Maybe their loss is our gain." Now I could feel my heart pounding. "We'd like to invite you up to Sunderland, Matt. Pre-season training starts on July 3rd and we'd like you there. We think you've got what it takes, so we'd like you with us for a month. If everyone is happy at the end of that period, then we can discuss how we move forward. What do you say, Matt?"

I was hearing every word but finding it very hard to take in. My head was spinning. Five minutes ago, I had been feeling sorry for myself. Now, I was being given the chance of a lifetime! People often talk about being speechless. This was one of those occasions.

"I know it's a lot to take in, Matt," continued Frankie, "but we're hoping you'll say yes. If you need time to think about it, you can call me back."

"God no! Sorry! I'm just a bit stunned! I don't need time to think about it. Yes. Absolutely! I'd be delighted."

"Excellent. We'll be in touch in the next few weeks to sort out your travel and accommodation. It will be a lady called Tania Winters, who's our player liaison manager. She'll work all that out with you. Your manager said you're going to see the Wimbledon physio?"

"Yes, for a couple of sessions, I think.

"Great. We've got a doctor that we use in London to do medicals for players down there, so once you get a clean bill of health from the physio, let me know and we'll get him to give you the once over." My palms felt sweaty and my legs felt weak. I couldn't believe this was happening.

"Thanks, I will." I realised that I was sounding like someone with a very limited vocabulary, but my brain and my mouth were badly out of sync.

"OK, perfect. Thanks, Matt. I look forward to welcoming you to the Stadium of Light. Again!" He laughed. "Cheers."

"Thank you, Frankie. Bye."

I hit the end call button and slowly put the phone down. I sat back in a daze, still trying to get my head around it. My whole world had been turned upside down in the space of five minutes. As I started to think about it, it slowly dawned on me that I had just made several hugely significant decisions by saying yes to the month's trial. While Sarah, my boss, had been great about allowing me time off for football, was she going to give me a month off? Especially as there was a chance I might be resigning at the end of that month if the trial went well. Then there was Harry and the boys. If I went to the trial, he'd have to find a new keeper, just in case I signed for Sunderland. But if Sunderland didn't make me an offer, I might not have a place at Reigate either. I'd hate to have to go and find a new club if that happened. But perhaps the biggest dilemma of all was Anna. If I was playing and living in the North East, how on earth could I manage to keep my relationship with Anna going, with her living and working in London? I couldn't imagine Anna giving up her career to come and play WAG full-time.

There was so much to think about. People often talk about their head spinning. Mine was on a roller coaster. I started to go through the various permutations of what might/could/ would happen in a few months.

My phone rang again. It was Anna.

"Hey handsome. I saw your message. What a bummer. I know you were hoping it wouldn't be so bad."

"Hi beautiful. Yeah, it was a bit depressing, but that's yesterday's news," I said, smiling.

"Huh? What's up?"

I quickly filled her in about the call from Sunderland. She listened intently until I was finished. "I'm still getting my head around it to be honest."

"Oh Matt, that is awesome! I am so so proud of you. It's your dream come true."

"Yes," I said hesitantly, "but I'm wondering how it's going to work between us now." There was silence for a few moments. Anna sighed.

"The news about my dad wasn't good today. They reckon he's got a year to fourteen months. Maybe more, but maybe less. It's too advanced to do much about it." Her voice was catching as she tried to stop herself from crying. I felt like someone had punched me in the gut.

"Oh God. I am so sorry. That's dreadful. I feel so sad for you. I don't know what to say."

"There's not much you can say, love. I know how much

you care." She paused again. "I hate to do this when you've just had such great news." She sighed again, deeply. "There's no easy way to say this." She paused, as though gathering herself. Now it was my turn to listen intently, with a growing feeling of dread. "I'm not coming back to London, Matt. I want to spend this time with my dad and be there for my mom too."

There was a long silence. My mouth was dry, and my heart was pounding. While this scenario had crossed my mind, I'd always pushed it away and believed that Anna would come back at some point. I really didn't know what to say.

"I feel so awful telling you like this. But it's something I just have to do. I hope you understand." She was crying gently now. That just made me feel even worse. I knew she needed my support now more than ever.

"Hey, you're doing exactly the right thing, babe. This time with your dad is precious and your mum needs you. I understand." I was hearing the words coming out of my mouth, and I knew they were exactly the right words, but my heart was breaking as I was saying them.

"You are amazing. How did I get so lucky in finding you?" Her voice was thick with emotion.

"You're pretty amazing yourself. It was me that was lucky to have had that time with you." I could hear a catch in my voice too as I tried to keep myself from welling up.

"I love you with all my heart. I don't want this to be goodbye." She was sobbing now.

"I love you too." I didn't want it to be goodbye, but I couldn't think of a way we could make this work.

"This is so very selfish of me and it's probably very unfair to ask, but I was hoping you might be able to come out to spend some time here and meet my folks." That landed like a bombshell. I was thinking she was saying goodbye and now this. I was all over the place emotionally. Anna took the silence as a no. "You can say no. I totally get it if you want to end things."

I wasn't sure it was a good idea for either of us, but I also knew she needed my support right now. "Hey, I don't want to end anything and it's not selfish of you at all. If you want me there, of course I'll come," I tried to sound more certain than I felt.

"I also want to sit down and talk about us, face to face, and not do this over the phone while we're 3,000 miles apart." Anna hesitated before continuing. I knew she was trying to find the right words. "I don't know what our future looks like right now, but I do know I want to keep you in my life, even if we decide we can only be friends."

The thought of being just friends was something I didn't want to think about. Although a part of me desperately wanted to see her and hold her, I also knew that this was only going to make it harder for both of us.

"You need to follow your dream and go to Sunderland. I need to stay here in Boston. I guess most people would say we haven't got a prayer of staying together. But I just can't shake this feeling that we were meant to be together, and I'm not prepared to give up on us yet." She paused. "But I totally understand if you want to move on," she offered in a quiet voice.

She was right. On all counts. I did need to go and give Sunderland my best shot. It was what I had always dreamed of doing. Anna needed to be with her parents. And yet, I also felt we were meant to be together. As Anna was talking, I was also thinking to myself there were still so many unknowns. Anna's dad. My Sunderland trial. My job. Her job. This could still go in a lot of different directions in the next few months.

If we had to say goodbye, then I knew I'd rather spend a little more time with her, even though I also knew it could end up being heartbreaking for both of us. There were no guarantees about anything in life. But one thing I did know – I wasn't going to give this girl up without a fight.

"Move on? You're not getting rid of me that easy, woman! When do you want me out there?"

23

Ten days later, I was sitting in the departure lounge at Heathrow Terminal 5, waiting to board my flight to Boston. The previous few days had been manic. I'd had a long conversation with Sarah about my job. She had been incredibly understanding. In the end we had agreed that I would take unpaid leave from the company at the end of June, but she would use temps to fill my role until the end of August. If it didn't work out for me at Sunderland, she said she'd have me back if I wanted to come back. In return, I had to promise to get her and her daughter tickets anytime Sunderland were playing in London. I knew it was a tongue-in-cheek comment, but if everything did work out, I made a mental note to honour that promise.

The player liaison officer from Sunderland had also been in touch. She'd been lovely on the phone and told me accommodation had been arranged for me in a complex where a few of the other single players chose to stay. There was nothing to pay for the room during the trial period, which I hadn't been expecting and was good to hear as I would be technically unemployed. I would get £150 per week, which was to cover food and petrol, but she said that most of the players ate at the club after training, so I wouldn't need to spend much at all. Given that I'd decided to keep my flat in Reigate, and I still had to pay my rent and bills, I needed to keep costs down, so it was something of a relief that I wasn't incurring any additional outgoings.

It felt good to have all of that sorted. Now all I needed to do was to sort out my love life. In truth, I had very mixed emotions about going to Boston. On one hand, I was really excited about seeing Anna again. Spending time with her and seeing where she grew up would be brilliant. I'd never been to Boston and by all accounts it was a lovely city, so that would be good too, especially having Anna as my tour guide. On the other hand, I knew the three weeks would go by in a flash, and at the end of that time, I'd still have to get on a plane, and we'd be 3,000 miles apart. Again. For a long time potentially.

Anna had a "live in the moment" approach to life, which I'd always found refreshing and I'd decided to adopt her philosophy for the next few weeks in particular, and the next few months in general. It was hard to plan anything right now and that included our relationship.

In the back of my mind, there was a half-formed plan about going to live with Anna in the US if my trial at Sunderland didn't work out. It had slowly crept into my head in the past few days. It was really no more than an idea, and I knew that like all plans, the devil was in the detail. It would also mean making a real commitment to each other. I also knew I needed to be thinking positively about the trial, or there was no point even going.

The flight was being called. I picked my rucksack up and headed for the gate. Although I was also heading for a very uncertain future, I smiled to myself as I recalled Anna's words to me the previous evening.

"Live in the moment, luv. The future will take care of itself."

That it would.